Even the Breath

Valentine Leonard

Lavender Ink

New Orleans

Printed in the U.S.A.
First Printing
10 9 8 7 6 5 4 3 2 1   17 18 19 20 21 22

Book design: Bill Lavender

Library of Congress Control Number: 2017944232
Leonard, Valentine
Even the Breath / Valentine Leonard
p. cm.

ISBN: 978-1-944884-24-6 (pbk.)
978-1-944884-25-3 (ebook)

Lavender Ink
New Orleans
lavenderink.org

Acknowledgements

I am ardently thankful to my MeWE community of daring writers who have tirelessly listened, read, and responded to the morsels that eventually became this book. Connie Cruthirds, Robin Casey, Jarad Bingham, Bob Klyce, Paulette Regan, Joe Casey, Julie Shankle, Cay White, Carolyn Taylor—your trust in me pulses through the veins of each of these characters.

I am deeply grateful to Bill Lewin, first enthusiastic reader and numinous shaman who pointed the way toward the publisher I needed; to Bill Lavender for "getting it;" to my sister Cécile, who asked the difficult questions; to Andy Robinson for his keen editorial insight; to Anna Esquivel, partner in the worthy crime of creative unfolding and inspiring editor.

Also, respectfully grateful for Olivia Lomax, who introduced me to the miracle of Kundalini yoga and showed me how to walk the edge of grace; for Ana Brett and Ravi Singh, wondrous and empowering teacher-yogis-poets—the best yoga quotes in this book are most likely theirs. For the golden chain of saints and sages of the ages who have evolved this technology to let us fulfill our highest human potential by expressing our gifts unapologetically.

Much gratitude for my fellow Sibella band members, Sarah Dietsche and Tamar Love. Making music with these two preposterously gifted women has taught me the most about the creative process and the joy that happens when you ditch perfectionism.

Thank you to my talented mother-in-law, Marianne Leonard. Our provoking conversations about our craft have sustained me in seeing this project through more than she knows.

Most tender gratitude for my parents, Henri and Mic Moulard. Their rebel spirit, keen intelligence and generosity have granted me the ability to make a life arched upon healing and creation.

Finally, sweet sweet gratitude for the man of my life, David Julian Leonard. Even in my darkest of days, he makes sure I am held in the arms of the force that transcends and binds us, like Love.

Even the Breath

À Mic, ma mère adorée, inoubliable
Amazone en talons hauts.

The poet/saint Kabir was asked, "Where is God?"
His answer: "God is the breath inside the breath."

I

You Cannot Breathe

Good caretakers are harder to come by than children's bodies.

When Prune got to the Ward, Carla was in a bad way, hair in need of a wash and dark circles eating at her cheekbones. As far as Prune could tell, her sister hadn't moved in three days, since the man-nurse with the yellow eyes held her against his breast and hummed. *There are too many of us now,* Prune thought. *They can't afford these lullaby luxuries. It will affect our productivity, but what can you do?*

The kids were at evening's sorry excuse for Satsang and there was no noise other than the harvesting machines' shrill beeps. It kept Prune on edge, but when Carla's cracked lips moved, she knew not to touch her and pulled up a chair.

"What is it, Carlota? What do you need? *Dis quelque chose!*" Carla's irises rolled up under her cigarette-paper eyelids, as God-intoxicated yogis' do. *So this isn't an episode,* Prune sighed.

Carla gave a half-smile and her hands flopped on either side of her chest. The beeps got louder, their tempo more sustained, from weighty polka to andante samba. Prune leered at the imaginary flash this prompted of President Hetherington and her minions caught in a swirl of feather-clad trannies at the carnival in Rio. Prune imagined the shareholders panicked and turned on, their very fear their most potent source of pleasure.

Water sounds to the cadence of an Afro beat waded in from the shower room. *Probably one of the kids sneaked out of meditation to use the loo,* Prune thought. She tidied up Carla's bed, sprinkled chamomile water on a moist towel, and wiped her little sister's forehead, the corners of her mouth. Frail like a lizard, her chest ebbed and flowed consistently. She was in a good place for now.

After Carla finished feeding Attila the remains of their charbroiled bratwurst dinner and the dishes were set to rinse in the brook, Anastasia launched into her bedtime story.

"During a time that once was, is now gone forever, and will come back again soon, there was a broad man, commander of a four-mast ship whose red sails could be seen slicing through the horizon stretched like a laundry line between foreign lands. His crew had turned haggard and sallow-complected like an old onion, the sun and saltine air having, month after month, flaked melanin off their surfaces. In all of nine years, neither eager wives nor curious babes, neither filet of sirloin nor giggly whore had they nibbled on. For nine years, only cruel jokes invoking much body secretions and other unmentionables, bland fish, and a remarkably vast array of gym locker smells, had filled their ghastly routines. For nine years the commander, once gentle as a Serbian potato baroness, had forbidden any and all of his men to set foot on land so long as they hadn't captured the greatest fish that ever swam those seas."

"Please Anastasia, not *Moby Dick*! Can't you think of anything better than ego-bruised, unwashed men to help me go to sleep?" Carla held her palms over her ears.

"It's not what you think." Anastasia was stung.

"No? Some tortured officer whose grandeur built on looting in the service of Empire has long ago wilted, sucking dry his crew for the sake of eliminating what dwarfs and awes him? Sounds a bit cliché to me."

"It's not a cliché, darling. It's an archetype. And for goddess' sake, when the heck did you, all of ten little yearlings, get to read *Moby Dick*?"

"Dad gave me his copy of the first French edition for my seventh birthday. It came with its own set of original watercolors. The one showing Ahab in rags with his flying-saucer eyes haunted my dreams for ev-er. I had to beg Prune to let me into her bed. I even put up with her farts. But I didn't get to read it in the original until I was around eight-and-a-quarter. My English has never been that good."

"Just like my Karl. The man lived in America for forty years but he never bothered to learn prepositions, so he'd tell his buddies to knock themselves up with the goulash and ale, which always drew merriment out of the most taciturn."

Each lost in her own reminiscence, the old gal and the girl fell silent. Carla got up from her moss pallet, squatted down by the swimming hole, and started to pile up flat rocks into a rickety tower of Pisa. Watching the wisp of her back palpitate as the girl reached for a stick to stabilize her structure, Anastasia felt a knot in her throat. *Such a babe she still is,* she thought. *Always stretching gravity, testing resistance as if it were a game of no consequence. Ah, the blessings of childhood.*

"Or coma," Carla retorted. Her tower crumbled, splashing frigid water onto the old woman's leathery arm. They both watched the goose bumps pop up, each bump crowned with one strand of translucent hair, then recoil slowly.

"Did I say that out loud, or can you read my thoughts? No more old gal sentimentality for me, I guess. Not with a cynical brat like you around."

Carla put her small hand on top of Anastasia's wiry one. "I'm going to need that sentimentality, Stasia. I know what's up. Prune's getting drained. Her love won't forever make up for what they're sucking out of me. Someone needs to help her with the hard work of feeling. Better you than me."

"I know, monkey. So be it then. I'll be your Hallmark

Godmother nervously dabbing a perfumed chiffon under my nostrils every time you're not looking. Now let me get some sleep before I have to swoon." Anastasia grabbed Carla's wrists and pretended to wrestle her into her lichen nest, then threw the Mexican blanket on top of her head. Carla neatly spread the blanket over her legs, tucked one fringed end under her chin, and reached for Attila's behind. The wolf groaned, shifting a little to accommodate her touch. The base of the spine, where tail meets butt, was his soft spot. Carla began the scratching ritual that would soothe them both to sleep and Attila yawned. With his head resting on his front paw, he kept his attention trained on Anastasia. The crone tossed, turned, and swore in Czech as her silver dreadlocks got tangled in the fishnet hammock. Then all of a sudden, she was snoring like a cicada sawing August.

Attila stretched out his hind legs to offer ample *derrière* availability. Carla was using her free hand to hold one eye open. She'd always found sleep to be a waste of time, with all the tadpoles to harass and all the books lonesomely waiting on their shelf for her to bring them to life. But lately, with this gross matter-body of hers having fully given in to The Center's life-force leeches, sleep had peculiarly unpredictable ways to pull her back and forth between—what shall she call these? Worlds? Planes? Life and death? Which was which?

In any case, sleep now held more secrets than Carla wanted to know.

Undetected behind his mop, Ruben had assessed a detailed database of Ward Q's staff. In two-and-a-half days of janitorial invisibility here, he had found that the evening-shift nurse with the pink hair and squeaky shoes was a tucker. She smiled when the children's proud toes had to be, under her authoritative tucking, flattened. The man-nurse with the frothy hair was a squeezer. His was the early morning shift, before prayer and meditation, when the horizon turned green and the kids still lay draped around each other like wet laundry. Squeezer's jaw trembled a lot and his corn-colored eyes were constantly on the verge of tears. And his thing was squeezing: a frail clutch on the kids' shoulders that left it undecided whether he was offering comfort or jostling for balance. Ruben found this nurturing tendency noteworthy given that at The Center, staff and crew were discouraged from affectionate contact with the children.

"Ss... sss... ssself rr... rre... rre... reliance," said the freckled monk in a saffron robe who'd hired Ruben. "That's what we here at Chinergy stand for. How else are you going to build a strong society? Ss... sss... sss self-reliance and c-c-c-ccc..." Ruben was clicking his tongue mimetically. He ran a mental list of C-words to help Swami John finish his thought. "C... ccommunity!" John finally cried, eyebrows raised in victory.

Ruben wanted to know how, exactly, The Center envisioned the connection between self-reliance and community but the perspective of a drawn-out discussion with a stuttering Swami convinced him to hold his tongue. Also, Ruben reminded himself, *Mexican janitors don't think.*

Upon first alighting in America, during his brief stay in Miami with unsmiling cousins, Ruben had found that every Latino there was considered Cuban regardless of the variety of corrupted regimes or Cold War-manufactured crises they were fleeing. But here in New Mexico, Cubans, Hondurans, Salvadorans, Guatemalans, and Nicaraguans were indiscriminately regarded by gringos as Mexican. North America's historical coma had gobbled up discernment of facial features along with all tonalities other than English's nose-bled iambs. But Ruben's virtual non-existence in the eyes of his employers afforded him almost unlimited access to private information. He was determined to guard this diplomatic immunity of sorts like a catholic mother her daughter's virginity.

With bamboo smothering the bay windows, Ward Q remained dim most of the day. Only right before the sun splattered on the blue mountain did a few snide rays alchemize everything into gold. Ruben held his broom close to his chest. In this light, the neat rows of white-sheeted cots looked like the waves of cotton candy pinned to the roof of his *tía* Aurora's shop in the barrio of his childhood. After school, little Ruben would bundle himself in the hammock with Negrito the one-eyed cat and they rocked themselves to sleep gazing up at the sweet clouds.

From the east, where stood a gaudy temple, echoes of a mantra wafted in. Jarring bells ripped the children's unison and the hair on Ruben's forearms raised at attention. *Such a pingero for togetherness, I am.* In the empty room he could feel his own breath in his chest, so familiar yet always so momentous a revelation: how alive he felt, and how effortlessly his pulse fell in a call and response with the translucent voices.

The mop went dry. Streaked with hair and dust, the bottom of the bucket looked like forgotten Ben and Jerry's. Ruben took off his flip-flops and, with the bucket dangling at his side, he tip-toed across the length of the ward toward the shower room. He emptied the bucket, watched the dirty water whirl down the drain, and in the cold puddle from the faucet he tapped his foot to the beat that latticed the mantra. He wiped his feet on one of the terry-cloth robes lined up outside the stalls. Then a new sound—a swishing sound, like waves nipping at the shore—beckoned him toward a beige curtain.

Prune said, "Alright, gotta go. There, I'll leave you with a toot to remember me by. *Salut mon chou!*" She scrutinized her sister's face for a reaction. A smile would have been grand, but a sigh or a whimper would have done the job. Carla showed nothing.

When Prune stood up there was a strange man staring at her from behind the curtain. A grin sliced his face in half as he said, "*Hola.*"

"Who the fuck are you?"

He drew open the curtain, pointed to a bucket and mop behind him, and with a thick singing accent he said, "I am the new super. *Me llamo* Ruben." He stepped forward, nodding toward Carla. "What wrong with *la muñeca*?"

Pedro was holding his fork like a pen, struggling to reach into an oversized platter. "Prune! There she is guys! I told you she'd make it."

"Yo, Pedro. *Que tal?*"

"Not much." He scrunched up his nose and his Elvis Costello glasses rode up the bridge of his nose, then slid right back down.

"*Frijoles* and greens, surprise!" Prune scrunched up her nose too and pulled up a chair next to him. She took in the assembly, recognizing most faces but not sure of the names. Aside from Pedro these kids were all newbies. *God, the turnover is getting shorter by the week,* she thought.

"So, *hermano.* Tell me who everyone is. Stories are precious. I never share them with strangers." Before Pedro could say anything, a girl stood from the opposite end of the table and offered the handshake you'd expect from a Navy Seal.

"Me, I'm Alia," she said without a smile, black eyes locked in with Prune's.

"Please to meet you, Alia. I'm Prune."

"I know," the girl shot back and reverted to her eating.

Pedro's neighbor pinched his arm. The boy shoved him away.

"This here is Luther. He's a chicken and he has frog breath."
Luther seemed not to notice when Prune said hi.

Next to Luther was Hakim, badly defaced by a harelip but with endless eyelashes and yellow ringlets bouncing off his forehead. Prune nodded and he nodded back.

With her pointy chin barely reaching up to the edge of the table, teeny Lou was waving her arm as if from afar. A white handkerchief could have fluttered there, like with a relative leaving on a ship. Was it Lou's bare skull, or the bruises on her bony arm that set off a rumbling behind Prune's navel?

At the other tables, children were beginning to pick up their trays and file toward the bank of gray containers, each labeled with crayoned inscriptions featuring jungle animals. A zebra-skin lion for plastic. A fierce-looking giraffe for compost. A hippopotamus in a tutu for paper and cardboard. Prune couldn't get used to the orderliness of these gatherings. She longed for the clatter that filled the *cantine* of her elementary school in Paris and echoed all the way down the cavernous hallways where they set up their mattresses for giggly nap time. And yet, how she'd dreaded it all then—the mushy food, the forced naps, the other children's promises of eviscerating revenge or perennial friendship.

"Ok, *compañeros,* we better get started. Here we go. There was once a people, very far away from here in an itsy-bitsy country that once ruled the whole known world. These people lived in a dark cave, with their necks so tied that they could neither turn to the right, nor to the left."

"Sounds pretty boring," Alia said under her breath.

"Quite indeed." Prune smiled. "So those folks, they can only stare straight ahead at the cave's back wall, which stays held in darkness. Behind them, at the mouth of the cave, burns a big bonfire. And between the people and the fire there is a parapet."

"A what?" Luther wanted to know.

"A little wall," said Hakim, bringing his index finger in front of his deformed mouth.

"Right," Prune nodded. "And atop this wall runs a road. Now on this road, merchants, passersby, donkeys even, are carrying all sorts of things—vases, burlap sacks of salt, fine embroidered silk—"

"And camels? Do they have camels on the road?" Lou squeaked.

"Sure, camels, and goats," said Prune.

"And dromedaries? Do they have dromedaries?" Pedro pleaded.

"Shut up. Let her tell the damn story," Alia spat. Pedro and Luther rolled their eyes but their focus was right back on Prune.

"Of course, all those animals and the people on the road are making noise and chatting about the big storm approaching, the seamstress who made out behind the barn with the strange boy from the next town, the fast-dropping price of salt. But the folks in the cave, they only ever hear the bits and pieces of conversation that happen right in front of the cave. They never get to hear whole stories. And what's worse, all those noises and words echo against the walls of the cave, you know, like they do in the canyon up by Tesuque. And all they ever see are the shadows of the people and animals and all the things they carry projected against the back wall of that cave like Chinese puppets."

"-nese -nese -nese… -pets-pets-pets," Pedro chimed in. Luther chuckled.

Alia was shaking her head. "Pedro, give us a break, will you?" To Prune she said, "Please go on."

"So, for those who are held prisoners in the cave since they were little, all the distorted shadows they see and the echoes they hear—"

"I get it!" cried Hakim. "They think it's the real thing!"

"Exactly," said Prune. "Because that's all they've ever known. So, what do you think would happen if, say, one of them could break her shackles and move her head, turn around, maybe even walk out?"

Pedro was biting his lip.

"She'd get to look at the actual turquoise vases and the yellow dromedaries?" offered Hakim.

"Maybe, er, maybe she'd see all the pretty drawings on the walls and the little animals that creep in an out of the cave. Or maybe she'd think she's dreaming," said Lou.

The children glanced at each other, then like one they turned to Alia. She said, "I guess she'd be real confused, for sure."

"Or she'd think she's off her rocker," added Luther. Everyone nodded. A few more children had gathered around their table, standing there like pink flamingoes.

"Now, what if she were to look directly into the bonfire? Or the sun, even?" Prune asked. The children's faces were glowing as if they were standing around that bonfire.

"It would burn?" Pedro risked with a glance toward Alia.

Barely audible, Hakim added, "She'd be blinded."

"Yep. And no one wants that, do they? To be blinded by the burning bush, everyone they know thinking they're crazy?" The booming voice broke the spell and the flamingo children scattered in a cackle.

"Tony, what a surprise." Prune made no effort to hide her exasperation.

"Hi, kids! Prune, honey, don't you think they're a little young for Plato?"

"Well, until you got here we were all into it," Alia managed through clenched teeth.

Lou slid down her chair and noiselessly headed for the bay window that the first wave of escapees had left ajar. If Anthony noticed, he did not point it out.

"Come on, ankle-biters!" Prune clapped her hands. "Time to bundle the meat in the towel, as they say where I come from."

Luther, with Hakim on his heels, skittered behind Lou. Alia took her time to tuck her chair neatly under the table, pick up the dirty dishes, and pile them up on her tray. Pedro fell in step behind her to wipe crumbs with his sleeve, all the while staring square at Anthony's brow.

"Night, Prune," said the boy.

"*Bonne nuit, hermano!*" She gave him the thumbs up as he reluctantly followed Alia out.

"Boo!" Anthony said flabbily at their backs. "So, *mademoiselle* Prune. Attempting to corrupt the youth yet again. You know where it led that old fool Socrates."

"I know, Tony." Prune got up to leave the CEO's Secretary and the darkened dining hall behind. "Immortality."

If, as the poet claimed, Havana's *San Cristóbal* cathedral is "music set in stone," then The Center's temple was a methamphetamined DJ's very late night spin. Blinding in the cloudless sky, the gold cupola smothered the squatty adobe structure meant to support it. It was probably a reference to the Moors' conquest of Iberia, but Ruben found that it conjured associations with a hot-dog stand rather than the greatness of Allah. The worst dissonance played out on the main portal, each door a medley of wood, turquoise, and mother-of-pearl featuring a tall Buddha complete with curved unibrow, large hair curls, and hands in *gyan mudra* with pointer finger touching the thumb. Fervor and peacefulness expected within. But what was with the bored gargoyles squatting on a ledger held by marble demons? And the mosaic figure captured in a *balancé* step across bits of multicolored glass? The face was familiar. It swelled the flanks of each flower pot around The Center's plaza, towered over Ward Q's patio in imposing bronze, and was frescoed in a conversation between Confucius, Margaret Thatcher and Donald Trump on the *cantina's* wall.

The temple's door was surprisingly heavy. Vapors of sage and sandalwood lingered in the foyer. After the bang of the door died off behind Ruben, silence stayed. When his eyes adjusted to the darkness, he blinked at the smoky sunbeams that dashed in through small holes at the top. He stood there for a moment, alert to the dark puddle of yuck eddying about his kidneys. Then he went for the openings at the top of another set of flapping doors, making sure to avoid the dozens of small flip-flops that lay scattered about on the tile. That's when he heard it again—the swoosh.

In the center of the vast room stood a column much like those that Napoleon stole from the Egyptians to memorialize his hegemony. Ruben had never been to Paris, but his great uncle Félix had played there several times to suave crowds who squirmed about earnestly as the brass stampede caught up with Tito Puente's timbales. Even after he'd stopped remembering the words for black beans and urinal, Félix would launch into long tirades speckled with carefully enunciated *Champs-Elysées* and *la Concorde*, where said obelisk resides. In fact, didn't another such column somehow end up in D.C.?

Here, again, the toga-clad figure bulged from the obelisk in the heart of The Center's temple. Around the base floated chrysanthemum blossoms scattered amid votive flames. At least thirty kids of all ages sat in neat centripetal rows, cross-legged, chin to chest, eyes low. The same gallows-like machines as the ones behind Ward Q's curtain lined the circumference of the room. From their steel mouths descended thin tubes, which sipped like straws from baby cribs. One plump sock jerked out of a woven crib and a blue current scurried up the tube, first in spurts, then in a continuous glow-stick flow. Soon, all the tubes were throbbing like the Christmas light-ropes that snaked along the edges of *tia* Aurora's *tienda*. Ruben recalled the grown-up looks on the boys who hovered late at night, waiting for dried up corn ears to be tossed. Aurora would turn her back and cuss at Negrito the cat, but little Ruben saw how the blue shadows carved the boys' faces. He saw how *la Revolucíon* had forgotten to tend to the hollows in their cheeks. It struck him that here at The Center, it was that same "I've got no time for play" usually chiseling at busy adults that coated the kids' energy fields. Like this girl, who was pulling on her toes methodically, one after another, hoping to screw them off. When Ruben squinted enough to perceive her aura, all he could grasp were tangled ribbons of fire snaking in and out of her belly. Alia felt his gaze upon her and jerked her head around to search the darkness that shielded him. Ruben ducked, but couldn't avoid the prickling burn of her glare.

From somewhere inside the building grew the ripple of a gong. Ruben leaned further in for a better peek. The children stirred and stretched, rubbing their eyes. The startling clip-clop of high heels on wood smothered the gong's last shudder, announcing the arrival of President Dawn Hetherington.

She cleared her throat and began, "Triumph to Ch'i!" Ruben assumed she was referring to the Chinese concept of life force, the vital impulse that informs all living things.

"Triumph to Ch'i," the kids shot back with one, vacant voice.

II

With All the Lost Things

*W*ith all the lost things and vacated bug armors gathering there in the dust, corners were always for Ruben a source of exceptional satisfaction, worthy of his appalling crooning. "*Pom pom pom... Y lloro sin que tu sepas... Tiene lagrimas negraaaas...*" This is why he insisted on using a broom rather than a vacuum cleaner. Vacuums make too much noise, and they simply take away the poetry of floor cleaning. "*Tiene lagrimas neeegraaas como miiii viida... pam pam pam pom.*" Vacuums are ravenous. They swallow everything they can get their mouths on. No courting, no savoring, no discovery. Vacuums are like recession-Americans at an all-you-can eat buffet. "*Que yo no quiero sufrir...*" Brooms, on the other hand, especially the ones with the long straw strands, can display the elegance of fingertips. They brush and stroke, either tentative or assertive, but always discerning. "*Contigo me voy mi santa aunqe me cueste...*"

Hmmm, there's something soft, cushiony. No, too small to be a pillow. Let's see. A sock? No, too firm. With the angled end of his broom Ruben pulled the unidentified object from under a cot. It slid right out on the shiny tile.

"Man, leave that alone." Out of nowhere, Prune was stomping toward him. She grabbed the neat little white square and tucked it in her shirt pocket.

"*Hola chica.*" Ruben went back to his sweeping. "I know what is this. I grew with many aunts. No shame in being a woman."

"No shame taken. But no one needs to know."

"I don't talk to no one," he said, wanting to sound casual.

"Good," Prune said. She started toward the bay window.

"*Hasta Lluego,*" Ruben said cheerfully.

She stopped, turned around, and asked, "*De donde eres?*"

"*Cuba. Y tú?*

"France, mostly. *Mi madre es de* Guatemala."

"*Verdad?*"

Prune made sure no one else was there. Lowering her voice she added, "*Diga me,* Ruben. Do you know how to dispose of this discreetly?"

"Sure. I'm in charge of all the garbage. Except for that raccoon family, no one loiters by the trash cans."

"Can you *promise* no one will find this?" Prune reached into her pocket.

"Sure, I can. I keep the kitchen scraps separate for composting so the critters won't go dig in there."

Prune took out her bundle and placed it carefully inside the bin next to Ruben's cleaning supplies. She made sure to conceal it under a giant dust bunny. "There's going to be more," she said. "Where can I find you?"

"Everywhere that needs cleaning." Her look told him this wasn't enough.

"Here," he added. "I clean here every other day, six to seven, while *los chicos* are at supper."

Prune reached into her back pocket and handed him a crumpled five dollar bill. "Can you buy more? I'll meet you here on Thursday."

"What kind? Normal? Super? Wings, no wings? Always, Kotex?"

Prune stared, apparently confused. "Normal, I guess. Just don't let anyone know. Please." There were tears in her eyes. Ruben itched with questions, but two babbling kids walked in.

Prune mouthed, "Thursday" and swiveled around to hi-five the boys.

Wedged into Center CEO Dawn Hetherington's plush sofa with his Dr. Pepper on ice and his feet cozying up to the fire, Anthony said, "You know, Dawn, I'm afraid that little French girl will soon become a liability."

Hetherington took a swig from her Miller High Life, and from the bowels of her executive chair she answered, "What, the froggie with the comatose sister? What's her name, Peach?"

"Prune. Prune Tum Michaux. Her father, Marc Michaux, was a big deal in postmodern philosophy circles a few years ago. I think he had his own radio show in France."

"Philosophy on the radio! What do they do? Sit around with their thumb up their arses to figure out the sound of a tree falling in the forest when no one's there to hear it?"

"He was a bit more political than that. I read him at Cornell. Hospitality, resistance, sustainability. Something to do with Life as a creative solution to the problem of power differentials. Metaphysics as ethics. France's answer to Nietzsche, if you will."

Dawn said nothing. Anthony knew that part of his boss's genius consisted in surrounding herself with exceptional intellects. He also knew that her rare discernment in matters of others' aptitudes or the potential long-term yield of any endeavor couldn't make up for her plain lack of intellectual curiosity. He never tired of watching her waddle like a swan on dry ground whenever philosophical concepts were mentioned. He tracked the forming of the crinkle between her eyebrows when she sensed that the conversation might reveal a fissure in her mightiness.

Finally Dawn offered, "Wasn't her mother the trouble-maker? Some leftie from Honduras?"

"Guatemala. Nobel Prize nominee. Yes, you could call Rosa Tum a leftist, if raising hell against über-armed militia that slaughter the Indians who grow our broccoli for slave wages is what leftists do. Her detractors used her asylum-seeking move to Paris and playing house with Michaux to cast doubt on the sincerity of her fight. Who knows where those two ended up. For all I know, they could have killed each other over some bourgeois marriage that people like them are totally unfit for. But rumor has it she was kidnapped. And Michaux hasn't been heard of in a while. His own mother was the one who signed her grand-daughters over to us. So, the older one…"

"Peach?"

"Prune."

"What about her?" Dawn mumbled through a Virginia Slim, patting the inside of her purse for a light. She gave up, sighed, and rolled her chair over to the fireplace. Anthony grasped a glowing stick of embers before she did and held it up to the tip of her cigarette. There was a faint hissing sound as she sucked in a long hit. Her cheeks caved in. She took her time to blow out the smoke and said, "How old is she anyway? Isn't it time she buggered off to the F Ward?"

"The night nurse has been monitoring her refuse. It appears that *mademoiselle* Prune has yet to start bleeding."

"The girl must be at least sixteen! Isn't she growing tits?"

"I don't know. It's hard to tell with the potato sacks you have them wear." Anthony blushed a little as he said this. Mechanically, Dawn checked her décolletage for any misplaceage. She pulled on the exposed skin above the nipples to perk them up a bit and raised her voice to a flirty pitch.

"Don't you worry, sweetheart. I know you don't have much of a taste for little girls. Mature birds have so much more to offer to real lads like you." She was glaring at his biceps. He managed to refrain from rolling his eyes.

"My concern is that the kids don't just like her. They respect her."

"They respect me."

"They fear you, Dawn. That's not the same, don't kid yourself."

"You respect what you fear, don't you, Tony?"

"No. I respect what I love, what I want to get close to. Those kids love Prune, Dawn. You and me, they despise."

"So what, you jealous?"

"Maybe." Anthony was visibly pinched. "But my point is that if they respect her, she could—how should I put this—galvanize them."

"Galvanize them?" Dawn flicked the butt of her cigarette into the withering fire. "Have you seriously looked at those kids, Anthony? Aren't we doing a fantastic job? What exactly is a bunch of pre-pubescent living-dead going to do to you, Mr. Clean?"

"She's teaching them some questionable material. She made it look like a bedtime story, but it was straight out of Plato's *Republic*."

Dawn let out a forced cackle that trailed into a cough. "Plato's *Republic*? Hooo, now *that* sounds terrifying! Let me get on the line with the Commander-in-Chief and have him send in the Special Forces! I hear they've brought a few tanks back from Fallujah. We're going to need them to protect us from a long-dead Greek philosopher and his army of ten-year old zombies! How postmodern of you, dear. Now, tell me again, since you're so bright. When was the last time Plato's *Republic* was used to galvanize a revolution?"

"I'll see if we can get data on the girl's hormonal fluctuations." Anthony got up from his chair. "I'd feel better if she were tied down with a pregnancy and away from impressionable children who have time to spare and not much to lose."

"You do that, my dear," Dawn said to his back as he carefully closed her office door behind him.

From inside his tiny oven of a booth, the sleepy guard waved at Ruben and the gate slid open. Ruben's truck hurtled on through with a smoker's cough. His breath eased as the guard's booth vanished in a cloud of dust in his rearview mirror. Ruben recognized this feeling. The same loosening of the back ribs and lifting of the heart happened every time he walked away from the peeling walls of *La Academia*, the military training school he'd been drafted into as a freshly mustached fifteen-year-old in Havana. On the recently renamed *Calle del Popolo*, only the bright *flamboyanes* and a gnarly old man or two would hang around, on account of being rooted to that soil. All other *Havaneros* instinctively knew to clear out the area where their boys were being moulded into weapons.

Ruben took in the expanse of the no-man's land around The Center. This was desert country. He drove by a boarded up gas station with its corrugated patch of roof banging in the wind and recalled the article he'd read about the string of store close-outs in the area. In quick succession, Maria Esquivel's wooden angels factory—a local institution that drew sweat-stunned tourists in their shiny rentals—and three gas stations had shut down, forcing the scattered Honduran and Anasazi population to drive twelve miles to Española for beef jerky and shaving cream. That was about four years ago, shortly after Dawn bought the run-down Spanish Mission hacienda she turned into the glowing Center.

Algo está muy mal ahí, Ruben thought. He was drumming his fingers on the steering wheel and turned down to a whisper Bono's goat-in-heat wail on the radio. *That girl is terrified.* Heat vapors rose above the asphalt as he turned into the sparse CVS parking lot. The taste of melting tar stuck to the back of his tongue when he pulled up to park, his tires squishy under him.

On his way to the gym, Anthony's hands were nearly convulsing. To release the tension, he shook them a little and sipped in a laboring breath. His chest fanned out of the vortex at the base of his throat. That felt nice.

Swami John was huffing and puffing on the treadmill, holding his robe like a bride leaving church and revealing sinuous calves covered in orange fuzz. He greeted Anthony with a grin but kept his eyes riveted on the television screen and its loud bands of closed captioning. As part of his recent promotion, John had been assigned "Citizenship From Sparta to The Center," one of the classes Anthony designed, test-drove, and taught for its first two semesters. Yet Anthony could not help but feel something like sympathy for the young monk. The pathological nervousness; the pathetic speech impediment; the ghastly whiteness, which turned fuchsia with any exposure to New Mexico's outdoors; the nauseating kindness toward children and staff; and most notably, the idiotic obsequiousness. With Dawn it reached almost sublime doormatitude. Somehow, it all combined to convince Anthony that John was quite certainly a con artist and a skilled strategist—perhaps a corporate spy, or some kind of government plant masquerading as a cretinous Buddhist scholar?

Presently, the Swami's face verged on purple as he attempted a Himalayan climb on the treadmill. Anthony tasted bile at the back of his throat as he imagined having to mouth-to-mouth the monk in case he passed out. "John, I suggest you either find yourself a sturdy llama, or start heading downhill. This here run up to the top will kill you and I would hate having to pick up the pieces."

"Uh… uh… I'm almost d… dddd-there," the Swami huffed, his knuckles pallid on the treadmill's handle bar.

"Alright, then. Just holler if I need to call nine-one-one." Anthony walked over to the weights wall and regarded them for a moment. The monk was clearly smart, you had to hand him that. At twenty-six, he had under his rope belt a Ph.D. in Anthropology from some German university, and a Max Planck fellowship had brought him to The Center to gather up data about Chinergy's groundbreaking activities. Within a few months, the Swami had completed an enthusiastic report concluding that The Center was indeed spearheading the most inventive clean-energy technology to date, with the potential to revolutionize global economics. *Time Magazine* had picked up on it, glossily asking on its cover if this could be "The End Of Our Oil Addiction?" The *New York Times* wanted to know if Chinergy would allow us to quit financing the Mid-East's war against us.

Anthony was struggling to tune out the Swami's all-too-intimate panting. He settled on forty-pound weights for warm-ups, lay down on the bench, spit in his palms, rubbed them together, then grabbed the weight bar and held back a gasp as he pushed.

John's report had earned their little project sizable funding from diverse transnational corporations and a handful of foreign government agencies. This in turn had earned the monk the position of *Dean of Guidance and Vitality*—which basically meant that he taught a couple of classes, ran the children's daily *Satsang* (seated prayer and meditation), and was also The Center's bursar. *That* meant access to a broad and overall uncontrollable spectrum of qualitative and quantitative data—*lots* of power.

With a sigh, Anthony carefully rested the weights back in their saddle. He got up from the bench and glanced at the Swami who was now attempting lunges. John's newborn air dredged up alarmed awe in Anthony. Perfect innocence, abysmal need, and infinite potential form a dangerous combination in a competitor.

Anthony rummaged about for the boxing gloves, but couldn't find them. He took to the punching bag with high kicks instead.

On the other hand, the monk's current status meant that Anthony's time could be devoted almost entirely to the P.R. and lobbying he'd been living for since he'd discovered, back in an eighth grade public speaking tournament, that winning his peers' approval required only telling them what they wanted to hear, and that what they wanted to hear was not necessarily the truth. They just needed to know that the privileges they'd been handed down by their genes (whiteness, health), their parents (whiteness, money), or their culture (whiteness, power) remained as unassailable by time or circumstance as a Twinkie. Of course, the essential irony that came with the job had not escaped Anthony—that in order to fit in socially, he had to break the most basic societal norm: truth-telling. Aren't all language, scientific knowledge, contracts, and economic interactions predicated upon the assumption that most people, most of the time, tell the truth?

Like every evening, a chirpy garland of toddlers filed toward the temple, each child chained to another by a colorful plastic loop. Ruben was watching the procession from the compost station when a sudden shooting pain in his shin made him buckle.

"Watch where you loiter!"

Ruben had to crane his neck up to take in the stranger's height. From below and backlit against the throbbing sun, her shaved head was an eclipse.

"Oh, come on," she offered, glancing at her wheelbarrow. "It can't hurt that bad; there's nothing in it. Here, give me a hand, will you?" Startled, Ruben took the shovel she was handing him, and she kicked up an interminable leg to knock the lid off the compost can with the tip of her boot. "Fill it up. The prickly pears are fixing to croak. Have you noticed it's always those that look the strongest that give in first? You'd think that with them being indigenous, they'd make it, no problem. But look at that!" She pointed at a flattened clump across the gravel path. "All those thorns, and for what? Not an ounce of living flesh left to protect."

Ruben tapped the top of the compost pile he was packing into her wheelbarrow. A green melon rind stuck out like the lone sail of a ship on Cuba's horizon. "Maybe this will save them," he said, handing her back the shovel. "Rotten fruit is good gasoline. Like rum. Life-force likes a little pick-up-me sometimes."

"Shoot, you tell me!" she said, pointing at the temple's doors.

"I wish I could shovel this mess on top of those kids instead of the crap they're shoving down their ears right as we speak." Grenadine tossed the shovel on top of the compost pile, which spit a few coffee grinds to the ground. Ruben watched the melon rind sink.

"What God do they pray to there?"

She looked him up and down. "You're the new cleaning guy, aren't you?" She picked up the handles of the wheelbarrow and turned to face north, where a bright dot was just appearing above the tabletop mountain. "Depends on who you listen to. They come up with so many names. Yahwe, America, Buddha, Allah. They'll even throw in a gal's name to appease us once in a while— Mary, Venus, Liberty. I guess you, like everyone else, are going to have to find out for yourself. But seeing as you're asking me, I'll tell you what. They've got one thing right: God is One. Whichever one you turn to, it's all the same, talking about who can kick whose ass so the victors can suck the living soul out of the victims. Who cares what the victory is about?"

Grenadine dropped the handles. The wheelbarrow wobbled a bit before coming to stillness. One hand was planted on her hip, the other rubbing her low back. "You thought Greenspan was clever, with his plan for a Global Third World? You thought the twenty-first century was going to be Chinese? Nope. I'm telling you. Mao is dead. The dollar is dead. Oil is dead. Sex is dead. Obviously, Jesus is dead. Hell, even Marx is dead, but the old fool got something right: exploitation. The only thing that's still alive and well? Scavenging! Now, there's sustainability! We're just like those damn prickly pears, man." She pointed at a deflated cactus across the trail. "Composting, recycling, saving, my eye! I just do what I can to survive here and now. And sometimes, what I can isn't all that much." Grenadine dabbed at her temples with a red bandana and the sunset sparkled against the silver shotguns that dangled from her ears. "Sometimes all I can do is crumple up like a brown paper bag on the inside, bristle up on the outside, and then hope for the best. But the one thing that's for sure is, we're each gonna try to get just a little bit more than what we really need." She winked at Ruben through the tiny frame she'd made with her almost-touching thumb and pointer finger.

"Just in case, you know? I mean, look at you. I can tell you're a good guy, as far as guys go. Heck, you've got to be a pretty good dude to keep a straight face when buying pads for your girlfriend at CVS. Oh, don't look so shocked. I saw you. Had to get me some minty gel this afternoon. I don't mind all this organic mess they fork over to us here, but I draw the line at toothpaste. I just don't do fennel in my toothpaste, you know? Still, though, good guy and all, you couldn't help but act like my empty wheelbarrow had hurt you just a tad more than it really did."

Ruben started to respond but she cut him off. "Don't tell me you didn't. Your face was wrung up like an Afro braid but your lips shone with drool. You might not want to call it looting, but it is. In this case, you were only going for a bit of comfort, a little IOU from the hot black chick." Her tongue darted at the droplets of sweat that had been slowly skirting her cheekbone to ride her upper lip.

Ruben waited. Grenadine turned to face him.

"So you want to know what God they pray to in there? I'll tell you. He's as old as the world and his real name is Loot." Ruben nodded, lifted his hat to mop his forehead with the towel he wore like a scarf. She consented to regard this as a gesture of respect. "Grenadine, Master Gardener," she said, seizing the handles of her wheelbarrow. "Good to meet you, good man." She kicked a large rock out of her path and started toward the North Star without waiting for his response.

"Is that a mustache?" Alia's fingers grazed the rim of Pedro's upper lip. Her hand felt cold, but it slipped an electrical current as

34

it rubbed the brand new down against the grain.

"Leave that alone!" A flush of sweat coursed from Pedro's neck to the inside of his palms, making it impossible to touch her for fear he'd eek her out with his clamminess. He gazed at her face. Mesmerized, she continued to rub his upper lip with her whole finger's knuckle.

"When did this happen?" She studied the eiderdown like the caterpillars she kept in jars.

"I don't know. It's been happening." He felt a sneeze form at the back of his eyes but blinked it back.

"Well, it wasn't there yesterday."

"How would you know?"

"I know."

But how could she, a girl, know better than him what was going on with *his* body?

"That must mean you've got hair in other places too." Alia turned away and became absorbed in proper folding of the Ward's laundry. Her father was a high-ranking officer in the Egyptian army, and for her laundry folding was a matter of the highest precision. Pedro could feel the thumping at his temples.

"None of your damn business," he said.

"Do you have armpit hair?" She raised her own arm up high to reveal secret, lightly shaded skin. Then, oblivious to his twitchiness, she carefully set aside a perfect rectangle of fabric.

Something in the ease of her gesture brought back the smell of soap that used to make him queasy at his Mama's laundry shop. Pedro would have given two limbs to go back to Yelapa. Back to the colorful laundry out on the balconies, the mules' clip-clop on the pavement, the roosters' call and response from their trees. In the thumping at his temples, he ached for the bougainvillea leaning, heavy, out of his mother's hair. He ached for the yodeling army of washing machines and the smell of soap nestled all the way into his Corn Flakes. He wanted the Rainy Dawn that emitted from his Mama's blouse when she took off his shorts to throw them in with a client's load. Wanted to stand before her in his sparkly white underpants, showing off his big boy muscles and demanding that she punch his abs to see how strong he was. Wanted her to laugh and tickle his tummy and tell him that he was her man, that he would always be. And more than anything, Pedro wanted to be man enough to stand before those dogs the *federales* threw at her, and to let the dogs tear him apart instead of her. He wanted to be covered in blood and to turn those dogs back onto the men who trained them, the men who trained the men who trained the dogs, the men who paid for the training and then went home to kiss their children good night in their comfy little beds.

Pedro placed the palm of his hand on his belly, hoping to pat the nausea away. Alia was making a pile of punctiliously folded underpants.

He said, "You fold your panties?"

"Do you have hair elsewhere?" Rows of orphaned socks were lying side by side and she surveyed them intently. He was flailing for a retort and she delivered the final blow. "Probably not. You're such a baby. Me, I have Pubic Hair." It felt like a punch in the gut.

On her way back from breakfast, Prune had to wade through a solemn thicket of children gathered around Carla's bed. Her sister's body lay limp as usual, but with neon blue garlands visibly pulsing at her wrists and temples, where the skin is thinnest. At Carla's side, sitting cross-legged on the floor was Ruben. His eyes twitched behind closed eyelids, and one could see the ebb and flow of his stomach as he breathed. In the vacuum left by the harvesting machine's unusual silence, Prune felt as if this breath were all she could hear, all she would ever hear—an ocean of breath, like conch shells held over both ears.

"How is she?" Prune asked no one in particular, containing her anxiety to a whisper.

"We don't know," said Alia. "But I think he's there with her. Look." A blue glow similar to what pulsed inside Carla's body crawled like vines out from under Ruben's polo shirt, climbed up the sides of his neck, and got lost in the bocage on his head.

At first, what Ruben saw looked very much like the hillside viewed from the road up near Tesuque, where the dusty blanket polka-dotted with saltbush shrubs spreads as far as the eye can see. The silence was complete but for the tic-a-tac-a-tic of some lone bird calling out to the vastness. Then there was the chanting. Foreign sounds. A woman's voice, gravelly, like the desert dust had settled inside it. Ruben started toward it, and as he got close, the contours became more defined.

"*Adi Shakti, Adi Shakti, namo namoooo.*"

Ruben knew those sounds. Shakti, the primal cosmic power that moves through the universe. Shakti, the great feminine force, Lord Shiva's mistress, seductress, co-creator. Shakti. Of course.

He'd been putting away his Greenox in the janitorial closet when he remembered he'd left his bathroom-cleaning wand in Ward Q. It was getting late but he decided he'd better go get it. Pedro greeted him at the curtain with a wheezing supplication, so Ruben followed him to Carla's bedside. Several children stood, their heads bobbing back and forth between the girl and the harvesting machine she was hooked to. The usual flickering lights and beeps were gone, and Carla looked spectral. The blanket she kept tucked under her chin was completely, abnormally still.

"*No respire,*" Pedro labored. "*Haz algo!*"

Ruben nodded and did the only thing he could think of. He sat down on the squeaky clean floor next to the girl, raised his right arm up to a sixty degree angle, hand clamped into a heavenward tiger claw, and set the palm of his left hand flat on Carla's inert chest. Then he closed his eyes, began to vigorously pump his navel to stoke his inner fire, and prayed.

Finding Carla's breath took some searching. It had, indeed, left her body. It had found a swing in the middle of a wildflower field and sat, swinging higher and higher, back and forth, back and forth, oblivious to Ruben and his plea.

"Give it another try. She's so young. You can't go so soon."

The breath kept wheezing by him, faster, higher. It seemed ready to take off and bob away like a helium balloon.

"I serve life," the breath finally said, the word sounding like "lie" as it flitted away. "I'm done serving necrophilia." And Carla's breath let go of the swing's ropes.

Ruben filled his chest with as much air as he could muster and held it in. He pulled up his lower muscles, lengthened the back of his neck like a soldier at attention, shut his eyes tight, and contained all the six-plus liters of breath that it was humanly possible for him to contain. He hoped this would maintain the thread of a connection to Carla's Prana, her life-force. When he could no longer hold, he sipped in just another milliliter and felt the smallest blood vessels in his brain cry for the oxygen his blood could no longer supply. That's when he heard it. The song.

An old woman with a helmet of silver dreadlocks sat crossed-legged with her bare buttocks on a boulder. Her arms flailed about her head in the empty sky. She heard his step but didn't skip a beat.

"*Kundalini, Mata Shakti, Mata Shakti namo namooooo.*"

"I bow to you, too," Ruben said, nodding his chin to his heart.

When he looked up, the dust was rising into a swirl of lustrous amber. Dark green vines crept out of the scraggy creosote bush that grazed his shin. In seconds, leaves lush like large-breasted women softened the bedrock with rainforest fuzz. Still sitting on her boulder, the old woman laughed an open-mouthed laugh, unrestricted.

"You took your jolly time," she said, "but I am glad to see you, Ruben. Let's get to work; the girl is waiting." She took hold of the back of her knees and rocked and rolled on her spine, using the momentum to bring herself all the way up to standing. There were bolts gushing out of her eyes. Her bare breasts dangled like chimes as she bent over to pick up her skirt, which lay crumpled on the ground. She slipped it on like a sweater, pouring from the top down to her hips. Her skirt was threaded with gold and embroidered hibiscus flowers reminiscent of the traditional Siboney dress that Ruben's aunts wore for special *fiestas*. It danced from side to side as the crone swiveled around and started briskly, barefoot and topless, along the mossy trail that was forming before her. Following the tinkling cadence of her anklet, Ruben fell in step after her.

Questions adumbrated in his mind like nocturnal animals, but they dissolved with each of the moss's kisses upon the arch of his feet, each footstep a certainty—or a leap of faith (which amounts to the same)—toward the impossible world that breathed itself open before them.

Carla was squatting down in the middle of an ancient bridge. A large dog looked on drowsily as she threw pebbles into the creek underneath and hummed lalala's to the pulse of the rushing water. The girl didn't hear them coming, but the dog rose up for a half-hearted bark. A cobblestone wobbled when Carla got up and turned to face them. Ruben saw her standing for the first time. He saw her eyes for the first time. She smiled a child's smile, with holes in it but full to the brim of who she was, no more, no less.

"*Hola Ruben,*" she said as to an old friend. "What's cooking?"

The crone gestured for him to walk over to the girl, and Ruben was grateful to see the dog plop back down.

"You look a bit constipated. What's wrong, you scared of wolves?" Carla offered.

"Well, wolves I don't know. Dogs, I can't say I'm terribly comfortable with."

"Don't mind Attila," the woman said. "He has good taste in men. Got it from me. He won't bother you."

"It's good to see you, *muñeca*. You look well. Your friends have been worried."

"Oh, I know. Pedro can be such a Jewish mother sometimes. He gets all worked up. He always imagines the worst."

"Well, you did stop breathing."

"Look." Her arm fanned the stunning surroundings.

Ruben noticed a swimming hole peeking through the greenery a few steps away. The metallic blue of the water called up the boy in him—the thirsty, sweaty boy who had to slow down his step to wait for his grandmother as they came into hearing distance of the rushing waterfall. Invariably, there came a time when *abuela* would stop, deliberately lean on her walking stick, look up at him, and knock a perfect two-three *clave* rhythm against the earth with the end of her staff—bang, bang… bang bang bang! This was their signal and, unleashed, he'd gallop up the last of the trail to dive head first in the freezing water. Each time brand new, the heart-stopping shock woke him to the blood in his brain, his calves, his boy parts. Everything quickened. Algebra homework, the precise dates of José Marti's achievements, *abuela*'s sleep apnea, and cousin Miranda's bruises all meshed into a supernova that scrubbed the inside of his skull clear.

"I'll race you there!" Carla took off toward the swimming hole with the wolf on her heels. Right behind them, the old woman stuck out her tongue as she passed him in a peppy sprint. Ruben chuckled and started after them. Attila hit the water first. Then Carla, making as big a splash as her size allowed. Then Anastasia and Ruben, like one. The people howled and the wolf squealed, all trying to catch their breath as they splashed about.

When they finally settled, floating on their backs and gazing up at the glistening air above, Carla said, "See? I have all I need here."

"You can't stay here," said Anastasia, casually spitting a geyser out of puffed cheeks.

"Why not? You and Attila get to stay!"

"Attila and I are old. I mean, *old*, Carla. You still have a few things to figure out, and you can't figure them out here."

"You can teach me. I'm pretty quick."

"You sure are, squirt. But it's not anything anyone can teach you. Even if I wanted to." Carla rolled her eyes at Ruben and swam past him to climb out of the water. She took off her dripping t-shirt, spread it out on the hot rock, and lay down on top of it.

"Welcome to Anastasia's vapid palavering, *señor* Ruben," she snorted. "Good luck fishing for a straight answer out of her."

"This is as straight an answer as I can give you, peanut. It's not the one you want, and I'm sorry I can't change that," Anastasia shouted from her perch by the water cataract.

Struggling against the rumbling current, Ruben swam toward the crone. "Nice to meet you, Anastasia." He grabbed onto of a slippery rock to steady himself. "I'm glad we agree: I need to take her back with me."

"I know," said Anastasia.

"Can you tell me how to get back?"

"You found your way here. Just trace your steps back." And she disappeared behind the curtain of heavy downpour.

Ruben looked inquisitively at Carla, who was sprawled like a starfish in the sun with her head on the wolf's ebbing flank. Without looking up the girl said, "I'll show you the way. You haven't come all this way for nothing, now, have you?"

Ruben opened his eyes to the same scene he'd closed them to: a ring of children regarding him with liquid eyes. The harvesting machine hiccuped, then started beeping again. There was a pause during which all eyes were on Carla. When the girl's eyelids twitched and she let out an almost imperceptible sigh, a quiet cheer rippled through the children.

III

But You Can Dream

$\mathcal{A}$t one A.M., Prune lolled about, staring at the black void above her bed. *I wasn't cut to be a mother,* she thought. Maimed stuffed animals, blue-eyed dolls, even a live hamster or two, yes. For a few years, she'd raised a Sunday orphanage in the lanky hallway of their Paris apartment. The pilgrimage started right after Father Dubois' droning threats of eternal limbo, especially for sinners like herself who never visited his confessional. At seven, she reasoned, she had little to confess. She didn't think God cared much about her stealing candy from the corner *Tabac*. She'd read Robin Hood and seen the Errol Flynn version twice, so she knew that all she was doing was redistributing the wealth. Mr. and Mrs. Tabac had an infinite supply of candy; she didn't. Her weekly allowance barely covered her *pain au chocolat*. Besides, she was sharing with her friend Roberto, who had no allowance at all, so it was really an act of charity. Also, the confessional smelled like armpit and garlic.

Thankfully, Prune's father Marc insisted that she'd be free to skip on those confessional calls. Catholic school was as much as he'd indulge his wife's "internalized colonizer and naïve loyalty to the missionary nuns who'd taught her to read," he said. He granted Rosa this much only because said nuns had sided with her people when no one else gave a fuck that her people were being massacred.

Little Prune liked to suck on the Body of Christ because it stuck to her palate and gave her a lisp she found very chic. She may not have been terribly devout, but she made sure never to bite into the mushy wafer for fear it would hurt Him, or His son, or whoever He was, and then who knows what disaster might befall her hamster and her family?

The pilgrimage would launch after lunch. Prune bundled up in her pink Liberty comforter Leo-the-headless-lion, Juliette-the-uppity-doll whose eyelids she had smeared with black Khôl from Tunis, and a green blob of acrylic fur whose name or species remained undetermined. They would start on the long journey that was to take them, by dinnertime if the winds and wild beasts allowed, to the opposite pole of the apartment. For there lay the Promised Land.

Everyone knows that promised lands are always beaches with soft warm sand that sparkles between toes and welcomingly blue waters that leave salt crisps on the chin. With its beige velour bedcover and indigo shag carpet, Marc and Rosa's bedroom provided quite the beach. Cars roared like the surf outside the window, and the furious honking of those who honk passed for great yachts entering the harbor. There, the placidity was even more relishable on account of the immeasurable challenges it took to reach, not the least of which was the great blizzard (a word Prune had garnered from Jack London) that continuously howled through the hallway. This blizzard caused her and her orphanage to advance slowly as meditators on a mindfulness retreat and between the winds, the pit stops, and the story-telling sessions tucked between two bookshelves underneath the framed Mallard ducks, crossing the hallway itself could take a few hours.

In her narrow Ward Q cot, Prune tossed about some more. The beeps of the harvesting machines were the cold drip of Chinese torture. Arguing that the noise made it hard for the children to get the rest they needed to sustain proper productivity, Squeaky-the-nurse had obtained that the harvesting be tapered off during the night. But in the dead of the night, Prune could now isolate individual machines' signature sound. Tonight it was Lou and Hakim's Prana that was being vandalized.

At seventeen, Prune had never hoped to have to sponge-bathe anyone. But she couldn't stand to watch the nurse herd and hose down these bony ones like Jews. She'd read somewhere that every child needs someone who would die for them. *I don't know that I would. But if I love them well, will they live long enough for us to blow this place up?*

The Center's playground was state-of-the-art and featured centerfold in the brochure that parents, guardians, corporate visitors, and placement organizations were handed upon touring the grounds.

Before resuming classes for the afternoon, Swami John liked to sit Zazen in the thin shade of a Pinyon pine. This was the time when, in warm and non-Protestant climates, people closed the shades and stretched down on a straw mat to reboot. Today was a treat because, in addition to the buzz of bees, John could hear the shrieks of children playing in the sunlight. No one had thought about including playtime in their tight daily configuration of meditation-studies-harvesting. *They knew that the children could be trusted to come up with their own,* John told himself. But the truth was, they rarely did.

"Hakim, no tagging!" Prune's tender admonition made the Swami smile. Peeking through one half-open eye, he caught sight of little Lou on the swing, with her standard Center hemp-gown flying over her head as she squealed, "Higher! higher! higher!" Behind her, Pedro dutifully redoubled his pushing efforts.

Next to the crowded jungle gym stood Alia, directing two opposing teams of clumsy monkeys. A boy with a germ-mask and cornrow braids moved at a sloth pace. Just as the kid was about to let go of the monkey bar, Hakim came bouncing out of nowhere to bend over under him so the boy could rest his feet on his back before moving on. *Good kids,* thought John. *Even the tough ones.*

In the sand box, three boys were building a castle when three girls came tearing through it with sticks, screeching like parakeets. One of the boys jumped to his feet to chase after them while the other two looked on, too weak to react. John closed his eyes and brought his attention back to his breath. He was reminding himself of the solid earth under him when a kid came crashing into him. It knocked the Swami right off and they both landed with their teeth in the dust.

Luther spat out the sand, then started to whine when Prune came running. "Is everyone alright?"

His whining abated as a council of children surrounded the brouhaha. John sat up, flicked the soil off of his cheek and sleeves, then turned to do the same to the boy.

"Hands off, lowly mongrel!" Luther labored to stand and had to call out to his friends. "Helpers!" Three pairs of arms helped him to his feet. Half of his face was still soiled and on wobbly knees, he opened his arms wide, stretched the hem of his gown behind him, and took off skipping. Piercing sounds rose from the school of kids as they followed suit, their gowns gleaming like fins.

Puzzled, John glanced over at Prune. "They're talking Dolphin," she shrugged. John raised an eyebrow so she added, "It's a superpower thing. You'd have to be in the Dolphin Knights Social and Pleasure Club." John smiled daftly. "You wouldn't understand," Prune concluded as she walked over to sit on a bench next to four girls who were confabulating with their arms wrapped around their knees.

Almost time for class. The Swami felt very very tired. He thought about skipping class. Maybe go on a field trip. It was such a gorgeous day, with clouds fluffy as sheep grazing infinity. John took in the *mesa,* those flat-top mountains that rimmed the badlands around The Center. He remembered squatting in the clover on a Bozeman playground as a kid, and catching bees with his cupped hands, trusting that if he was swift enough, they wouldn't sting him. Because "if they can't see you, they can't bite you," his mother would always say. And she was right.

Between the playground and the *mesa* stood a glistening chainlink fence. Ten-foot high but so tense that it almost blended with the clouds. One might have not even noticed it if it hadn't been for the *hornos*, those adobe mole-hills modeled after the Taos Indians' ovens. A thousand feet apart from each other, the beehive-shaped huts rimmed the fence that penned The Center. Inside each one, John knew, armed guards took turns keeping watch. Anthony had made no secret of the fact that they had unequivocal instructions to shoot on sight.

"The trick was a hit in the nineteen-hundreds when Jeremy Bentham came up with it." John jumped when Prune suddenly materialized to say this close to his ear.

He nodded. His social philosophy courses were coming back to him. "The pan... pan... pannnnnnnopticon, right?"

"Yup. Panopticon: the all-seeing eye. I have no idea how many guards are watching us at any given time, or even if anyone is. But just in case they are—"

"—It is wisest to bbbbbb... be...be...behave as if dddd... dddd... they were," John declared, relieved that the matter seemed settled. Then he pulled a bell out of the pleats of his tunic and, zealously starting straight into the heart of the playground, he thrashed the bell about to broadcast the end of recess.

Marc Michaux and Rosa Tum met in the shadow of the Pantheon Palace, where the rue Descartes crosses several medieval alleys. In the precocious five o'clock night, café patios fill up with soon-to-be engineers from the École Polytechnique. Stubbly young men huddle around gas heaters in the chronic brine of Paris' December.

Rosa, goat-footed girl from the high plateaus of Atitlán, hadn't lost a breath on the climb, but she skipped one when she saw Marc's face sticking out like a poppy from the bouquet of students gathered around him. Wine drops splattered on his hand as he clanked his glass with a boy in a Tartan scarf. Marc was laughing loudly and licking his fingers when he noticed her. Who wouldn't have? Rosa was about twice as broad and half as tall as any average Parisian. A cube woman with a round face peeking out of a knitted hat with ear flaps.

She sat at the only available seat on Le Bizut's terrace, not minding that the chair was wet. The myriad lights that leaked from boutiques and restaurants glittered on the pavement. In the glow of the gas heater, Rosa's brown skin was bright pink. Marc's, like everyone else's there, was the dirty yellow of Santa Cruz' stray dogs. She tried to concentrate on the menu that the humidity had glued to the table, but her brain was a lazy eye irresistibly reaching toward him. His eyes were so pale that, had he not stared at her with such intent, she would have thought him blind. She dug into her burlap bag and pulled out a thick cigar. She was rummaging for matches when the Tartan-wrapped boy brought a flame to the end of her cigar. Later on, she followed them to a dark apartment on the *Rive Droite* and Marc's students drew them into a drinking game, the rules of which she didn't quite catch. The graduating lad poured cataracts of champagne into their slim glasses. The boys had never met anyone from Guatemala, at least not anyone who neither cleaned their house nor expected spare change for serenades in a subway hallway. Their interest in the stocky revolutionary, a woman and a political refugee at that, was real.

At two A.M., an extraordinarily pimply-faced boy snickered, "So, do you have any modern toilets in your village, or do you have to shit in a hole, like us?" It was time to go.

Marc pointed down the wide Haussmanian street that climaxed in the old Opera house, a glimmering beauty crowned with gold. "Come on, it'll only take a minute. It's sheer magic! You must see the Galeries Lafayettes' Christmas vitrines, Rosa! "It is high art!" He slurred a little, pulling at her coat's sleeve.

Rosa told herself she was yielding to the appeal of historical architecture. She'd salivated like a Carmelite before cheesecake when, cuddling with sister Elisabeth's tattered Encyclopedia Britannica, she'd stumbled upon pictures of Napoleon the Third's opulence, the Chagall ceiling coming back to haunt her at night with its flying lovers. She started after Marc, struggling to keep pace with his long Parisian stride. He slowed down imperceptibly until her elbow lined up with his wrist, and he coiled his cashmere warmth around her. It smelled of English thyme and skin.

The first store window discombobulated a long, uncannily white woman—a Barbie doll magnified in her pink-padded fish tank, but Parisianized for the occasion with an A-cup and a Marie-Antoinette wig. She hung sideways and weightless like a formaldehyde fetus. Rosa held back a cross sign but couldn't avoid a slight genuflection, a reflex acquired from watching her grandmother, who never failed to wave her finger at the oddity behind the pharmacist tiller in Santa Cruz to remind girls like her of the hazards of sex.

"Isn't it astonishing?" Marc turned excitedly to face Rosa. The cold drew red circles on his cheeks and he looked like the boy-and-his-sled from the only children's book in the Sisters' library.

"Mmmh, mmh," she said, tucking her truth in his cashmere scarf. He led her by the hand to the next window. It was blue-lit and featured numerous rabbits in some designer's version of Christmas clothes—Rosa had gathered from her strolls through the city that frilly undergarments provided this year's main inspiration for high fashion. She found herself longing for her Nanna's rough cough by the wood fire, with all the maize cobs painted green, red, and purple piled up around the chipped statue of *el Cristo negro*. But her hand felt contained in Marc's. If she told him how ludicrous she found those displays, would he let go of it? She squeezed his hand and told herself she didn't want to let it go.

Anthony said, "I love the sound of thunder and rain. It puts me to sleep." He rolled away from Grenadine and yawned. "Nighty night, baby." Another spear of lightning split the sky and the crash came seconds later, an afterthought. Grenadine pushed off the cover and headed for the bathroom. The sky cracked open again and Anthony whimpered in his pillow.

In the mirror above the sink, Grenadine made a face that said, *What the fuck?* Hadn't she sworn on her sister's cremation urn that she would never have sex with Anthony again? Another strike of thunder, very close, and the lights went off. Anthony whimpered again. Exasperated, she pulled the bathroom door shut all the way.

He'd said the baby was fine, that Gaia was in good, professionally caring hands and wasn't being harvested. Grenadine made herself believe him; it was easier that way. She felt her way through the dark toward the commode. The icy porcelain bit her ass and she sprung right up. "Can't even fucking pull the toilet seat down." She slammed it down and sat on top of it.

"What is it, honeybun? You Ok?" Anthony's voice came in muffled.

"Fuck you!" Grenadine hissed through clenched teeth. What she meant was, *I'm so pissed off that I don't know what to say to you and that makes me mad at myself. I don't know what to do with any of these feelings, I can't stand feeling them, they make me feel way too alive, and being alive means remembering, and I want it all to go away. Fuck you, fuck my father, fuck the abused fragments of me, fuck The Center, fuck my impotence, my lust for you whom I despise, my cowardice, my un-fucking-believable power—to kill, love, forgive, save—and my reluctance to claim it, use it, be it!*

As Grenadine got up to wash her hands, the lights came back on, blasting their fluorescence on the thin scars inside her wrists,. She rubbed the soft soap foam over the lines and watched them disappear under the froth. A knock on the door made her jump.

"Grenadine, you good?" That voice, right there, too close. It made her eardrums gag.

"Fine," she managed.

"You ok?" His tone more irritated than concerned now.

"Fine!" She barked at the door. What surprised Grenadine, as she stood there in front of the bathroom mirror, not knowing whether to try to compose herself or beat the door down, was the fear she saw. She'd thought she might find anger, contempt, hate, self-hate even. But this was sure enough fear, and it was bottomless, as if it tethered her to other times, other relationships. Like it was much bigger than Anthony, bigger than the scars on her wrists, bigger even than the child she'd birthed and never mothered.

Anthony had gone very quiet. Maybe he'd picked up his socks and left. Grenadine glanced at the razor that lay in the shower, felt the magnetic pull of it, relished for an instant the thought of her raw flesh, the slow pulse of freed blood. But no.

Anthony launched into his most thespian voice just as she opened the bathroom door. "Inside the parted casing of my wrist I see the blood that runs through my daughter's veins, I see the love my mother wasted on my father, I see the longing and hatred, the hatred because of the longing, of pale men like him for my mother's people." Standing butt-naked in the semi-darkness he paused, whistled, and switched off the flashlight that he was shining on Grenadine's open notebook. "I had no idea you were a poet. A *tortured* poet. Girl, what else are you hiding from me?"

"Give me that!" she roared, lurching. He leapt up on the bed, switched the flashlight back on, and read, "In the copper stains on my sleeves, I see the gold that grew in our rivers but was never ours, I see the diamonds that sparkled in the sweat of our backs to tumble like cotton bales inside others' mansions, others' immaculate boredom, others' victories."

Grenadine grabbed a corner of the comforter on which he stood and pulled with all her might. Anthony stumbled but managed to land firm. He tossed her notebook on the bed and recited, *grandioso*, the last line of her poem. "Yes, today's was a good cutting for in it, I could once again find me."

The storm had moved on and in the moonlight that fell on a naked, towering Grenadine, Anthony caught a flash of the blade she held in her hand.

"Oh come on." He searched her face but found only the white of her eyes. His spine caught a ray of light as he passed the window to creep toward the exit door. Grenadine was almost on him. Mentally he scanned his options and found that they all required finding and putting on his clothes. He needed a little time. "I'm sorry you're so mad," he ventured. The blade flared. He jumped back. Hunched like a wrestler, Grenadine exuded raw menace, flawless power. He searched the ground for his pants as images of the sublime Indian Goddess Kali flooded him, with her necklace of skulls and skirt made of enemies' severed arms. Aroused, he was abjectly exposed. He spied a pillow on the floor and snatched it, holding it pleadingly in front of his crotch.

"Get out. Put it back in your pants and get the fuck out of my room."

Anthony found his pants and scrambled into them. Then he foraged for his shirt and shoes but Grenadine opened the door and, gesturing with her knife she said, "Now." Her nipples hardened in the cool from the hallway. Anthony stared at them as he carefully walked by with one shoe in his hand and his crumpled shirt over his arm.

"See you, bitch." He stepped out into the Technicians Hall hallway and winced as she slammed the door behind him.

The loud bang woke up Ruben. He could remember waking up this way often, sweaty from dreams filled with motorboats racing away from Cuba's shore amidst the din of revolutionary triumph. Men singing of freedom and women feeling each other's arm, testing the neighborhood's waters for a safe place to send their children when *El Che*'s dream would again demand sacrifices immeasurable. His grandmother's pans buzzed against the wall like the shiny blue flies that hovered around the fish gut that fishermen tossed by the *Malecón*. Outside, the night's residue of merengue slacked down to a bolero heavy with rum and lust, while *abuela's* snore wove itself in and out of the fan's clank clank. Smiling at the racket, little Ruben told himself that as long as his Nanna breathed near him, he'd be fine. *It's the big boys they're drafting,* he reasoned. *They don't want me.*

Scrawny and timid, Ruben had seen enough girls like his cousin Miranda stumble on the arm of fat Gringos in sunglasses to know that Cuba did need a change—another change. Many of his uncle Arnolfo's friends still spoke nostalgically of "the great hope from Argentina," but Arnolfo fell silent whenever they told tales of taking up arms again, and *abuela* shook her head at the cigar-filled air, mumbling spells that made them gaze at each other and vacate her living room pronto.

Ruben's grandmother had started training him as soon as he could hold the spoon to stir her decoctions. At six, he knew by heart ten incantations and the name, allopathic, and alchemical function of one hundred herbs, seeds, and roots. For example, when properly burned, oregano leaves prove efficient in keeping the law away—a useful spell to anyone living in a military dictatorship. When rubbed on the skin along with black soap, it also helps keep troublesome in-laws away.

Folks called on *la Vieja* with all sorts of ailments, from arthritis to zoophilia. "*Mira, cariño mío!*" she'd say. "With a little investigation, you'll find that all suffering can be traced to one root only: a broken heart. Always, it is the heart you must heal. Always, in the end, it is Oshun, the orisha of love, you must call upon. *Siempre el corazón!*" she'd shout, beating on her chest like Tarzan.

"Fuck me, brother John! Don't you know it's a sin to drag your fat boots in my dandelion when you've got all these kids with nowhere to go?" Swami John went even redder in the face than his rosacea usually kept him. This, of course, egged on Grenadine. "All they've got left is their damn wishes. And here you are, big old brother John with his yellow toga—what is it they call this color, Colicky baby?—and size fourteen-and-a-half boots, rooting around my dandelion like it's a line-dancing saloon!"

The monk began to cough so hard that Pedro sprung up from his study circle by the lotus pond and ran over to where John was doubling over.

"*Buena Madre de Dios!*" Pedro muttered, smacking John's back with the flat of his hand. It didn't help and John staggered, hacking like a tuberculose. Dandelion fairies fluttered everywhere. A buzz rose from the pods of studious children. Lou came to stand by Pedro to watch. One by one, like dust motes, the kids began to cloud around the commotion. When John fell to his knees with little Pedro saying his Hail Mary's over him, Prune could no longer pretend to ignore the situation. Jean-Jacques Rousseau's noble savage, whom she'd just introduced to her study group, would likely not have minded the interruption, she reasoned.

Prune distrusted Swami John, but she respected his efforts to introduce philosophy into the children's curriculum. Besides, today's lesson called for an exemplar of feeling-based ethics. She agreed with Rousseau that the ground of moral behavior has to be compassion, a natural repugnance to see our fellow sentient beings suffer—rather than rational calculation or a disinterested sense of duty.

"Call me naïve, but I much prefer to explain evil-doing as learned behavior introduced by societal norms, and posit a humanity naturally benevolent at heart. The implication is that if we change the norms, if we make better laws, it is possible to correct our evil ways and bring about a fair and just world for all." Pedro lit up at that. Lou stuck two fingers in her mouth and settled down in Hakim's lap. Luther had the tip of his tongue sticking out as he scribbled, stealing anxious glances at Alia's notes. Alia hunched over her notebook, pen held up in one hand, fingers twirling her hair with the other, waiting for what was to come.

Now here they all were, clearly showing interest in John's predicament. Hakim and Luther stood a few feet away from Pedro, ready to back him up if asked but unwilling to take the lead. They were clearly more concerned for their friend than for the aggrieved monk. Lou now lay in the grass, dozing. As for Alia, she simply refused to acknowledge the incident and had scooted over to pour over Prune's copy of *The Discourse on the Origin of Inequality* to scribble down more notes in her notebook. The other kids looked on the swaggering Swami as if he were a chemical experiment. Granted, he had done little to arouse their sympathy. Mostly, he shadowed Dawn like a well-groomed poodle and did his best to avoid exposing his crippling stutter to the children's hankering for scapegoats. Still, Prune shuddered. What had happened to the kids' "natural repugnance to see other sentient beings suffer?"

The Swami squatted down in his puddle of "Colicky baby" and dry heaves. Towering over him, Grenadine glittered with scorn, ready to squash him under the heel of her boot. *My, you don't want to get on the wrong side of her*, Prune thought. How superbly Grenadine wore this scorn, though! The dandelion fairies had congregated around her and the air shimmered. It brought to mind the ancient paintings of Kali, fierce Hindu goddess of time, death, and creation that Marc had taken his daughters to see at the *Musée des Arts et Métiers*. Carla had been the first to point out the painting, thrilled that the Goddess was shown with her tongue sticking out and blue skin. Prune had keyed in on Kali's necklace, made of human skulls strung together. "How can she be at once a creator goddess and a killer?" Marc explained that all creation requires destruction, and that, as the origin of all creation, Kali precedes even time, even light, even life and death.

If Pedro hadn't snatched the water bottle and handkerchief Prune was clutching, she might have forgotten to offer them to the Swami.

John gulped down a big swig of water and sat, spent, on a bald patch of grass. "Thank-k-k... Thank you, boy."

"Great. Now you can go back to harvesting the crap out of that kid who might well just have saved your life," Grenadine spat. She mimicked a military salute with a glance at Prune as she walked away.

Show over. The children wandered back toward their study pods. John stretched out his legs and lay all the way down on the ground, one arm over his face, big belly rising and falling with his breath.

Pedro sat down next to him. "You good, now? Want me to call a nurse?" John shook his head no.

Pedro looked inquisitively at Prune, who said, "Alright, John. We'll be over there. Holler if you need us." John kept his arm over his face, mouthing, "Ok." Prune gestured for Pedro to stand up. As they walked back toward their little gang, she draped her arm over the boy's shoulders.

When they were all settled in, Prune said, "Now, the alternative to Rousseau's compassionate savage is Hobbes' view that outside of societal norms, humanity would be in a constant state of war of all against all, and our lives would be solitary, poor, nasty, brutish, and short."

After a pause, Alia said, "Does it have to be an either/or?"

Back in her room, Grenadine had to step over the mess on the floor to pull the blinds open. The fall chill gushed in when she yanked up the sash. She kicked Anthony's sock under the bed, then picked up a corner of the crumpled comforter. As she hauled it up onto the bed, her notebook tumbled open on the floor. She picked it up, closed it carefully, and set it down on the nightstand next to the bottle of Patrón. It was eleven A.M. and she needed another shower.

When she stepped out of the bathroom, steam rose from her skin. She closed the window and sat down on her bed, took a swig of tequila, picked up her notebook and pen, and wrote:

Dear Gaia,

I picture you, fidgety seedling lodged in the pit of a harvesting coffin.

I, your lotus mother who gurgles on mud thick as sorrow.

I water and weed and scratch at the red sands of this place, hoping to grow a hope.

I have read that goji berries, fountains of vitality, thrive in parts such as these. There is a small bush back behind the compost area. I have designated it as your stand-in. I hold its nettlesome branches to my breast.

I sing to the bush. I sing the songs that my mother sang, and her mother.

A-louette, gentille alouette, a-louette, je te plumerai, je te plumerai la tête, je te plumerai la tête…

No berries have formed yet, but I dare promises out of its blossoms, tight like your fists after they cut the lifeline that anchored me to you, to joy, to meaning.

I met someone today, dear Gaia. A girl. A woman. She too, holds her fist tight. I read in that fist another promise: that the bud you are will blossom. That the life that left me when they took you is pummeling, still. That you will grow to read this, to read me, to teach me what I have taught my mother, and she her mother: To survive.

Her name? Prune. A berry name, like mine.

IV

Your Hands Are Not Tied

"What did you say her name was?"

"Pereira. Celeste."

"Mexico?"

"Portugal, I think."

"And you trust her?" Dawn set her lit cigarette down in the oversized ashtray on her desk and blew her nose.

By Anthony's quick estimation, fifty to sixty butts lay in that thing—probably a day and half's worth of his boss's anxiety. He shrugged. "As much as I trust anyone."

They heard a loud knock on the door and Dawn shouted, "You're late!"

Anthony got up to open. "Come in, Ms. Pereira. Glad to see you again. Have you met our CEO, Dawn Hetherington?"

"Hello, Doctor Anthony. Hello, director."

"Have a seat," Dawn said without getting up to greet the nurse. Celeste chose the high-back cathedral chair over the club armchair. She sat with her feet and knees together, taking a moment to adjust her skirt before locking eyes with Dawn. With her furrowed and slow dignity, Celeste reminded Dawn of the matron who surveyed her dorm at St. Hilda's. Dawn couldn't decide right away if that meant she hated, feared, or admired the nurse.

"I think Celeste has some things to tell us, Dawn. What have you found out, Ms. Pereira?" Anthony said as he walked over to the window. "May, I?" he added with a little cough when Dawn lit another cigarette. He didn't wait for an answer to open the window and stand in the crisp air. The first snow was still weeks away, but he could smell the iron smell of frost melting off hedges. He wondered if the distant chafing sound he was hearing was Grenadine snipping at ancillary sprigs.

"She's not woman yet," said Celeste.

Anthony's stomach made a fist. *Or she's more of a woman than I can handle.*

"Bollocks. Tony, didn't you say Peach was almost eighteen? Have you her lab results?" Dawn wanted to know.

"No," said Celeste. "But Prune has no blood."

"I'm sure she has *some* blood," said Anthony.

"She has no *woman* blood." Celeste didn't bother hiding to check her watch.

"Whose bloody time do you think you're wasting, you pair of plonkers?" Dawn stomped her half-smoked cigarette into the pile of ash. "Celeste, you're a nurse, right? We're *paying* you to be a nurse, right—not some damn nanny, or midwife, or whatever witchy blood-divinator they have in your country? In this country, nurses use *scientific* methods. I don't know how you figured out that Plum didn't have any 'woman blood,' but I hardly see how that would constitute reliable information-gathering. What the hell is this, Tony?"

"Prune. The girl's name is Prune."

"I don't give a flying fuck what her name is! All I want to know is, is she ready to be transferred to the F Ward and finally bring the bacon home, instead of eating our grub and arse-wiping the little rascals?"

"The lab results are on their way. And while I agree that Prune spends too much time caring for the brats, we have found that her presence in the harvesting room coincides with spikes in their Ch'i productivity. We're trying to understand—"

A timid knock on the door, and Dawn shouted, "Come in!" Swami John's crimson face peeked out from the crack in the door.

"I said, come the fuck in," Dawn said without looking at him.

"Hello, President Heth… Heth…"

"Give me that," she said, pointing at the large clasp envelope he was clutching like a life buoy.

John shot a desperate glance at Anthony. "The… the… that?"

"Give the lab results on Prune's blood work to Dawn, John," Anthony said.

"This is my article on the Sssss… Sssss… Spartan Transvaluation of Ed… ed… edd-tt-dd-tt-ducational Values." Celeste chuckled.

Dawn glared at Anthony. "What's he doing here? Look at that, even the bearded lady is laughing at me."

Celeste crossed her arms in front of her chest and leaned back into her chair.

Anthony said, "John has some fresh ideas about how to interpret the data we've been collecting, and I thought—"

"Stop thinking, Anthony darling. Can you do that for me? Can you stop wanking your teeny weeny brain and get me those bloody lab results?"

"No," Anthony said flatly. John stopped breathing. Celeste couldn't remember having had this much fun since she'd caught a five-dollar matinée showing of Miss Congeniality at the old Paradiso Theater.

"Fine," said Dawn, as if no war declaration had just been made. She lit another cigarette, took a hit, let it out. "John, why don't you tell us about your fresh ideas, son?"

Coming up for air, John blurted, "It appears as if supportive words and loving care foster greater Prana productivity. We've suspected this for a long time—after all, isn't Love the source of all life? And I'm sure you've heard about plants doing better when subjected to kind touch and harmonious music. But lately, a cross team of researchers at Johns Hopkins and Osaka University has proven that the same applies to water, and *a fortiori* all living beings, in particular mammals—meaning, humans." Celeste crossed herself. She was the only one to notice that John had, for the first time, uttered a whole smooth sentence.

"As far as we can tell, the kids' harvestable life-force output is higher when Prune is around, and we think that it has to do with her caring behavior toward them," Anthony explained.

"Are you telling me that if we love the brats, we'll get richer?"

John was nodding his head vigorously. "Isn't it uuh… uuuh… amazing?"

"Shit, fuck me!" The ash on Dawn's cigarette was growing to the length of her French manicure.

"Certainly," said Anthony. "Quite amazing indeed. Of course, that complicates matters. On more than one front."

"The girl stay?" offered Celeste.

"Perhaps," said Dawn, pensive. "I guess we're going to need to figure out if she's a better asset loving on those punks or making more baby bodies. Is that something we can do?"

"I'll talk to Doctor Jarvinsky," Anthony said.

"If I may—" All heads turned to John. "Ee… eee… eeeee it's really a question of quality versus quantity."

"He's right. It may be worth maintaining the capital we have rather than producing more low-quality products. This is solid American industry vs. Chinese consumer economy," said Anthony.

Dawn shook her head. "Well, look where the American industrial model has left us. China owns half of this country, a third of the rest of the world, and counting. Your models are outdated, sweetie. Think."

"I thought I should stop thinking."

"What I do with the girl?" Celeste wanted to know.

"First you get me the bloody lab results," barked Dawn. "We figure out if she's fertile. Then we find out if she's a better asset doting on the kids or knocked up," she added in John's general direction. Then, as if to herself, "Shit, our shareholders are going to kill me. How the hell are we supposed to like the little buggers?"

Anthony was reeling. *Don't you 'sweetie' me, you cunt!* Even the nurse must be laughing at him now. John had seemed a little distraught, but then he always did, and by now he must be gloating in the glow of his new Pet Numero Uno status. *Well, you can have it*, Anthony thought, crunching down the gravel path.

Ward F sat nestled in a depression about a mile away from Welcome Central—far enough away from visitors' sight and the children's nosy forays to avoid raising too many awkward questions. Anthony generally steered clear of the oppressive prefab. He'd spent enough time inside similarly clinical structures when changing the messed-up sheets of incontinent fruities at Door of Hope in order to pay for his tenth-grade textbooks.

As he approached the squat building, he slowed down but decided to ignore the slab of concrete in his stomach that urged him to turn around. The buzz of the intercom seemed ridiculously loud. The annoyed face of a young guard appeared on the screen.

"Hi, I'm here to see my… Gaia Johnston."

"Good afternoon, sir." The voice was breaking up like a country radio. "Place your ind… and…dle fing… in…"

Anthony pulled out his pass and held it before the blinking spot above the buzzer. "I'm Anthony Johnston, President's Hetherington's Office Manager."

"I need your… in the…, Mr. Johnston," said the guard, going back to his Sudoku. Anthony contemplated punching the smug white face on the screen. Instead, he stuck his fingers in the box. His own face, mug-shot style, stared at him from the screen and he felt a surge of hatred. The flimsy door clicked open. Anthony stepped in the airlock. "Close the door, sir," came the disembodied voice. Anthony closed the door behind him, and the thick glass door before him soundlessly disappeared inside the wall. "Toddler Ward," he heard the guard grunt in his walkie-talkie. "Johnston."

Anthony started down the windowless hallway. An overhead

light quivered. He couldn't tell whether the buzzing in his ear was coming from within or without. He passed one door with a hand-painted sign above it that read, "Primary." Through the wavy plexiglass he made out the unmistakable silhouette of the harvesting machines lined up like Nicaraguan rebels awaiting execution. Noticeably, the familiar ocean sound of the machines wasn't there. *They must turn them off to give the brats a break,* he reasoned.

"Mr. Johnston!" Anthony swiveled toward the booming voice. There stood an inordinately tall Indian man. Astride on his forearm was a grinning, curly-headed babe. "This is your daughter, Gaia." A large bubble formed on Gaia's lips when she squeaked her delight at the flickering overhead light, her chubby legs kicking at the void.

Ward Q felt defeated with all its empty, unmade beds—except Carla's. The girl's body lay, almost imperceptible under a neatly squared blanket. The only sign of the spunk Ruben had witnessed in the Dreamscape was the mess of bangs on her forehead.

"Carla has always seen things." Ruben hadn't noticed Prune there, leaning against a pillow on a nearby cot.

"Must you always frighten your friends?" He asked with a hand on his heart.

"Only you. Consider we're even now."

"Phew." Ruben pretended to wipe the sweat off his forehead.

Prune closed the book in her lap and continued. "On dark December afternoons, Mom would set our dinner plates on the ledge of the gigantic fireplace, the siren call of the TV back in the den impotent next to the dancing flames and candles galore to melt. Candle deformation absorbed all my energies, but Carla liked to stare into the fire. She would squat on her milking stool next to mine, crane her neck and gape. Once in a while she'd point at a spark and ask if I'd seen the yak there, or the seahorse carrying a marmoset. I only saw orange waves of awe fanning over her forehead but I'd say I'd seen it." Ruben parked his cleaning supplies cart next to Prune, sat on the cot across from hers, and waited.

"The chestnuts had to be placed in an antique iron pot with holes in the bottom. They popped open when ready, but we weren't allowed to peel them ourselves—not since I grabbed one and lost all sensation in my thumb. There. Yes, there. Right near the tip. I don't feel a thing. Go ahead, try to pinch it."

"Let me see." Ruben began to knead the broad flat of his thumbs into the mound of flesh at the base of hers.

"Peeling the chestnuts was Dad's job. He was also in charge of warming up the milk. He knew to serve mine tepid and to leave Carla's on until right before the milk's skin grafted permanently to the pan's. He sprinkled a little sugar, one spoon for me, three and a half for Carla, four for Mom, two Splenda for himself. Sometimes our parents sat with us, cross-legged on the sea-grass carpet and hunched over their bowls. We listened to the fire-crackle and slurped on our milky chestnuts with the Christmas tree flickering."

Ruben leaned in a bit closer, gesturing for Prune to give him her other hand. Tears pearled up on the corners of her eyes. He began to massage both of her palms, one in each expert hand, saying, "Holding back your tears is the worst thing you can do for yourself, *chica*. What would that make you if you told a grieving friend to go away and leave you alone? Your feelings are your friends. Don't shut them out." Prune's shoulders dropped about five inches. She squeezed her eyes shut to wring the tears out of them. She wished his kindness didn't feel so genuine, his touch so ingenuous. It would have made it easier to forestall. The tears tickled and she wanted to wipe them off, but she didn't want to take her hands away from his.

Ruben squeezed the sorrow out of the tissue and bones

inside the palms of Prune's hands. A lifetime of destiny ironed out, energy pathways reset like after a summer storm. Then he said, "Carla remembers too. She remembers you, your parents, the good times. Of course she does. I believe it's possible she even remembers memories that aren't hers. That is the way with some of us. It must be how she found her way into the Dreamscape and how she could tell me how to get back out. She'll find her way, Prune. You watch."

"*Tu crees?*" Absent-mindedly, Prune had started to wail. "Do you think she knows what's happened to our parents?"

"I don't know. Intuition manifests differently for each one of us. If she does, she's not aware of it. Not yet."

"You must take me there, Ruben. I have to see her. I need to hear her." Prune's fingers were unfurling like a new leaf. Ruben held her wrist with one hand and with the other, he pulled slowly on each finger, shaking his hand vigorously and puffing heavy breaths out of his mouth after each one.

"It will take a little work," he said.

"Teach me."

"It will take some training."

"Train me."

"I mean, I need to train myself. I've never done that. Taken someone else. I'm not sure how—"

"When do we start?"

Ruben frowned.

"There's an old tool shed behind the cafeteria," Prune added. "I don't think anyone ever goes there except the kids who want to practice making out."

Ruben's mind raced through the booby traps and possibilities, but he said, "Four-thirty A.M. The doorway between planes of experience is thinner in the hours just before sunrise."

"*De acuerdo.*" Prune snatched her hand away from his and sprung up to her feet. Even standing, she wasn't quite as tall as he was, seated on the cot. She stood on her tippy-toes to peck him on the cheek. *Hasta mañana, hermano. Los quatro y media. Merci.*

"*A demain*," he tried in his bad, sing-song-y French as he watched her bounce away with a fresh spring in her step.

Ruben knew that not everyone came back. Certainly, no one came back unscathed. But since he'd met these kids, a burden had begun to lift—that mugginess that had been weighing down everything like wet clothes since his uncle had written to say that cousin Miranda had succumbed from the after-effects of a rougher than usual trick. And Ruben hadn't been there. He hadn't been there to get Miranda out of the trade, hadn't been there to help her cross over to the realm of the Orishas, hadn't been there to keep heinousness from shattering the bonds between people. But here he was.

By candlelight, Rosa's face took on the gravity that eluded it in sunlight. It was not her heroic—almost saintly—status, her Nobel Peace-prize nomination, not even the exotic shape of her hips that Marc had fallen in love with. Rather, it was all that he would never know and all the silences lingering in the shadows around the perfect Fibonacci coils of her nostrils.

She didn't waver when the waiter brought their undercooked duck breast and spilled the white wine in her plate. As the young man effetely and with many a "*pardon*" dabbed at the mess with his towel, Rosa wondered out loud if the wine's liquid courage might grow the poor dead bird some cojones.

"I am so sorry this happened to you," she'd told Marc, her smile lingering on his lips but the gaze drilling into his. A woman's high heels clip-clopped on the cobblestones a few steps away from their sidewalk table and Marc wondered how they ever did it, these women. High heels on cobblestones.

"Oh, it was a long time ago," Marc said, white-knuckling the towel in his lap. The white fabric had left dandruff on his black jeans and he began to pick at it like a chimp grooming her mate.

"*Lo siento,*" Rosa simply said. She seized her knife to attack the meat in her plate and drew blood without a blink.

Lo siento: I feel it. Only the Spanish language captures the delicacy of genuine compassion, Marc thought. Compassion untainted by contempt. French knows only pity. "*Mon pauvre, je te plains,*" a French well-wisher would have said. An English speaker might have said, "I'm sorry," meaning, "I am sore from hearing it." In response, you're left to swallow your own suffering and tend to the one you've caused simply by feeling what you feel. But Spanish is different. *Lo siento*: I can feel your pain, yet it is still yours. You can feel mine, yet it is still mine. And that's the end of it. No judgment about how anyone feels, about how anyone should or shouldn't feel. No enmeshment, no transference, no projection. Spanish is clean that way. Perhaps that is why in Spanish, feelings are allowed to be big, dramatic even; why sobbing, and revolutions, and poetry happen in everyday Spanish—never in English. The French language, well, it likes to theorize about the sobbing, the revolutions, the poetry. It systematizes them. It creates fashion movements and schools of thought out of them. It makes "isms" with them: Rationalism, Existentialism, Deconstructionism. And there is always at least a hint of contempt sneaking into the distancing needed for the making of theory. Even the best-meaning theorizer adopts a posture of objectivity which, by implication, degrades feeling as inferior—weak, at worst; and at best, a source of unwelcome confusion.

That night, the French philosopher and the Mayan freedom fighter finished their mediocre dinner in silence. After, he took her arm and rested it on his as they walked up the steep *Montagne Sainte-Geneviève* toward his tiny apartment. Marc noted that it was the first time he'd remained silent with a woman and didn't feel the need to entertain, to impress with his charming *bon mots* and obscure anecdotes. He was sniffling a little as their steps echoed in the narrow street. And without questions, Rosa let him.

The shed was all shadows, pokey things, and spider webs that linger on your skin like bad dreams. Prune propped the door open to let in the moonlight and birdsong. She told herself that this was the safest place she'd been in awhile. No harvesting machines or watch nurses here. Most likely, no turtlenecked commandos ready to storm in to break her jaw and drag her mother away. Still, where the hell was Ruben?

She felt her way around the jumble of shovels, snippers, broken pots, and sacks of god-knows-what. Her eyes were getting used to the penumbra. On the wall, a large scorpion-shaped dot revealed itself as the grinning face of a jade Buddha encrusted in the adobe. Prune noticed huge earlobes on either side of the puffy cheeks. It reminded her of her father's ears.

"You ready?"

Prune jumped, knocking her forehead against the corner of a metal shelf. "*Aïe!*" Something sharp bounced against her shin and shattered on the floor. "*Merde*, Ruben! You freaked me out, man!"

"Sorry. Are you alright?" Framed in the backlit doorway like an Orthodox icon, Ruben's silhouette glowed around its edges.

"I'll be fine. That's a way to start my training. Some kind of hazing."

"No, no haze: clarity. We start with concentration." On the hard dirt floor, Ruben cleared the exact space needed for the two wool blankets he'd brought along. He threw them down, and they landed in neatly folded squares. "Sit," he said. Prune sat, legs crossed, heels perfectly aligned in front of her pubic bone. Ruben noted her ease with the posture. Swami John's *Sadhanas*, the daily practice modeled after Buddhist and Sikh rituals, were used mainly to brainwash the kids and increase their Ch'i productivity for the benefit of Chinergy shareholders. But here, they might prove good for something after all.

Ruben squatted down on his blanket and took his time to settle into a perfect easy pose, spine erect, chin slightly tucked in, shoulders relaxed, chest open, hands fanning over the tips of his knees. "The body follows the mind," he began. "And the mind follows the breath. This is the greatest piece of yogic wisdom. If you master the breath, then you master your body, your mind, your emotions, your environment, your energy, your endurance. The impossible becomes possible. The people who made this place, these machines, know this. You must learn it, too. You must teach it. This is how you resist."

Prune nodded, trying to swallow. The gulp she made seemed even louder than the mockingbird outside the shed. She wanted to say that she knew a thing or two about resistance. That her mother had been nominated for a Nobel Prize for the resistance she led in Guatemala after half of her family was burned alive by the paramilitary, and before was abducted in Paris by no-one-knows-who, then dumped no-one-knows-where, probably a carcass for the vultures by now. She wanted to tell him that she'd read Frantz Fanon, and Trotsky, and Simone de Beauvoir, and that of course she knew that they had to take their liberation in their own hands, that they couldn't expect a greedy world which sprinkled bad faith on their Corn Flakes to notice them, much less do anything about a handful of kids being phagocyted in the name of progressive energy policies.

Instead, Prune said, "Sure."

"Concentrate on your breath," Ruben continued. "Close your eyes. Roll them up and in to the point between the brows. Feel the caress of the air inside your nostrils." Prune fought against an urge to sneeze. Suddenly, her nose was a very crowded place, possibly crawling with micro-organisms and the tiny insects that hung around the shed. The monstrous image of a hairy mite Alia had shown her on the library's computer came into focus. She redoubled her effort to breathe smoothly, in and out, as John had taught them to. "Concentrate on your breath so much that you can begin to discern the difference in temperature between the air coming in and the air coming out of your nose... Focus on your breath so much that you can feel the sweet stream of chilled air rise inside your head and begin to clear the inside of your skull... opening the blinds to let in the light now..."

Inside Prune's skull, particles rose in a pillar of sunlight, a bit like the bubbles inside the lava lamp in her parent's living room. "It's to remind us of the nature of existence," her father would tell visitors. "Yes. Funky," her mother would add. "The eternal dance of structure and chaos," Marc would answer. "Like making love, or war," Rosa would conclude.

Ruben's voice was still present, but receding. Inside Prune's head, the pillar of light grew into a top-heavy cherry tree in full, magnificent blossom, each particle an iridescent scarab. Prune had to duck in order to avoid the bugs crashing into her. Lying face down on warm sand, she looked up and saw a large mockingbird perched on a branch. Its long lizard tongue snatched at the passing insects. The bird kept growing larger and larger, until the branch cracked and it took off in a heavy flurry. Prune rolled on her side and the branch crashed like a corpse right next to her. A bark chip got tangled in her hair, and as she reached up to search for it, the branch's coarse bark began to smooth itself into human skin, scaly, dry, the bumps of the hair follicles somewhat puffy. The skin was crying for Prune's touch, but she couldn't bring herself to make contact with it.

"I don't want to!"

"This is only an exercise in imagination," came Ruben's bracing voice. "Remember to breathe."

Prune realized that she'd stopped breathing entirely. She brought her hand to her throat and her eyes burst open. "What the fuck was that?" she gasped.

"Welcome back, Prune" Ruben said warmly. "Nice start. Next

time I come with you, no?"

Alia walked down the gravel path with her book held open like a beacon. *Walking lends itself well to the activity of reading*, she thought. It didn't bother her that the lines jiggled before her eyes. She'd discovered that if she treated each page as a world of its own, the actual order and precise placement of each word in relation to its peers mattered little to the overall sense of that world. Much like dreams, books and their pages are filled with squiggly details amidst which one can easily get lost and in the end, all that remains is a tonality—vague yet all the more evocative. *Revelation, terror, clarity, nausea, excitement, longing. I read books only for the sake of these tones, and the hope that I might encounter brand new ones—or else ones I know so intimately that I'd never be able to put them into words.*

Sure, I stumble upon intriguing information once in a while. Alia had been delighted, for example, to find the exact metric volume of sap put out by a Manuka tree in the course of its lifetime. Some people report adventuresome experiences in the company of Siberian shamans, astronauts, or Joan of Arc. Others point out the delights held in a fresh turn of phrase, an elegant thought—take, for example, Proust's "And each time the natural laziness which deters us from every difficult enterprise, every work of importance, has urged me to leave the thing alone, to drink my tea and to think merely of the worries of today and my hopes for tomorrow, which let themselves be pondered over without effort or distress of mind." But Alia was sure that the magic of books really lay in their empty spaces, all those silent rivulets in which each reader's uncanny mind, forgotten history, or idiosyncratic coveting rush in like albuterol in an asthmatic chest. The result was neither trivia, nor the sublime, but recognition, that momentary relief of her essential loneliness—an impression, an excitation. In short, a surge of life.

Also, beyond the obvious benefit of not having to engage with her immediate environment, walk-reading presented for Alia the peculiar advantage of bilateral activation. The right and left leg alternation triggered the left and right brain hemispheres in turn. This quickened not only the frontal lobe for cognitive tasks, but also the hypothalamus, responsible for proper memory processing. With walk-reading, Alia was therefore killing three birds with one stone. One, going somewhere (in this case, from Swami John's tedious Sparta class to the study hall). Two, understanding the information she was gathering (frontal lobe activation). And three, setting the stage for perfect memorization, cognitive as well as motor, thus multiplying exponentially the chances of instant recall even forty years from now. Put simply, Alia had devised a recipe for never, ever feeling lonely, even and especially when she was alone. *As soon as I figure out how to break out of here, I'm patenting my discovery!* She thought.

With its leather armchairs and radiator heat, the study hall was the most inviting place on campus. Alia had already read most of the books on the shelves—some public school library's refuse ranging haphazardly from Mechanics to Homer. But she loved it here. It looked nothing like her parents' library in their Cairo apartment, but the sweaty paper smell reminded her of it.

Alia's parents had ordered a tiny custom-made desk and chair, perfect replicas of her father's, and installed them in her favorite corner by the window that overlooked Cairo's epileptic traffic. There, she'd spent the happiest hours of her life rocked into a trance by the honking outside, weaving in and out of the classical Arabic tales chanting inside her head to form the template of her mind.

People like to talk about their first memory, usually some kind of humiliating realization of their existence as a separate, and therefore abandonable individual—like when you ingenuously clutched your mother's leg in the grocery store aisle, and realized the lady was a total stranger with a hairy mole on her face. Alia's eureka—what she thought of as her a-ha of self-emergence, her baptism into the Church of Consciousness—happened when she was five-and-a-half years old. Her mother had left her alone on the library rug to go fetch tea and halva. Alia bounced up and down, practicing headstands while waiting for her mother to come back and finish reading her story from the big leather-bound book. Out on the terrace, Alia's father had been playing croquet with some civilian gray-suits. He was terrible at croquet and an even more terrible loser.

When Alia had come upright again, the shapes and colors on the rug had taken on a life of their own. She struggled for balance; her eyes fell on the open book, and that's when it happened: Squiggles no longer squiggles. Squiggles had become sailors with smelly feet and a grand mutiny to organize; they'd become a naïve goat looking for its brother in all the wrong places; they'd become the sailors' outrage and the goat's fever. And at the same time, they'd become Alia's own indignation, her own desperation for a sibling of her own. All at once, Alia knew that her inner world could be translated into images and communicated to hordes of invisible people. Also, because it came to life inside big leather-bound volumes that adults collected and dusted and proudly displayed in their homes, this inner world clearly was a very important world—at least as important as the world signified by her father's firearms collection, which he also dusted and displayed, though less prominently than his books.

Today, Alia had The Center study hall to herself. Summer was definitely over. Just outside the window, a mountain bluebird pecked at things to fluff up its nest. More and more birds were coming from the north. Alia chose the chair with its back to the window, where the bird's shenanigans wouldn't distract her.

The book was called *Trauma and Recovery*, by Judith Lewis Herman, MD. It didn't look like much. The cover had come unglued and, to the touch, the paper felt like Alia's grandfather's foot corns. That must be why it had so far escaped both Anthony's censorship and Alia's ravenous appetite. But it was a fascinating read; she couldn't put it down.

She read, "The more powerful the perpetrator, the greater is his prerogative to name and define reality, and the more completely his argument prevails." Alia recalled how impressed her mother had been with Anthony's syrupy lecture on The Center's progressive experimental educational methods, how proud she ought to be that her progeny was accepted into the program, how they, creative visionaries and ethical innovators (here, Anthony had seized Alia's mother's elbow as if to seal their co-belonging in this glorious caste) needed to hold hands, open their hearts (and Swiss bank accounts) to make the world a safer, healthier place for these children. "And has anyone been thinking of these children's children?" he'd concluded.

Alia read on, "It is very tempting to take the side of the perpetrator. All the perpetrator asks is that the bystander do nothing. He appeals to the universal desire to hear, see, and speak no evil. The victim, on the contrary, asks the bystander to share the burden of pain." Like an omen, a bloodstain appeared right next to 'pain.' *Shit*, thought Alia. *Biting off my cuticles again, and not even aware I'm doing it. I'm going to need a heck of a lot more self-control to bring down the jackasses.* Just thinking about Anthony made her neck seize up. She read on, "To hold traumatic reality in consciousness requires a social context that affirms and protects the victim and that joins victim and witness in a common alliance. For the individual victim, this social context is created by relationships with friends, lovers, and family. For the larger society, the social context is created by political movements that give voice to the disempowered." *Right. And at this point, Pedro and I are basically all the social context I can count on.*

"There you are, *hombre*. Where's your little girlfriend?"

"*Hola, jardinera.*"

"Name's Grenadine."

"*Hola* Grenadine. *Que* girlfriend?"

"The baby-sitter chick. The one you buy tampons for at CVS," she winked.

"I don't have a girlfriend."

"Whatever. Where is she? I think she's in trouble."

"Trouble, *hé*? I don't know where she is. Come, let's find her." Ruben carefully locked the janitor's closet behind him. He closed his eyes for a moment and stood still, muttering to himself. Slowly, he began to rotate in place, stepping one foot, then the other, in sync with slow deep breaths.

"Enough with the asthmatic merry-go-round. What is this, you some kind of oracle? If you're looking for Mecca, I think it's that way." Grenadine pointed her finger at the blue plateau. Ruben opened his eyes and started in the opposite direction. She fell in step after him. "Look at that: the blind leading the blind. Is Jesus (She pronounced it Rresus, the Spanish way) talking to you, Mohammed?"

"My name is not Mohammed. My name is Ruben. And no, Jesus doesn't talk to me, but Her soul does." Grenadine smiled at his broad back. She liked that he'd used the feminine pronoun. "What is the trouble?" Ruben asked the autumn air in front of him.

"I'm not sure." Grenadine was a little out of breath from trying to keep up with him. "Let's just find her."

As they approached the shed, the strumming of their footsteps on parched dirt startled a kid who scurried away. "*Hola, que tal Pedro!*" Ruben shouted after him. The boy glanced back but didn't slow down.

The door banged open and Prune stood squinting in the pink

sun with her hand shading her brow. "How is anyone supposed to meditate with all this racket?" When she saw Grenadine's head peeking above Ruben's, she automatically straightened her stance, pulling down at the hem of her gown. "*Hola* Ruben. What are you bringing me, my friend?"

Grenadine didn't wait for him. "You're in deep shit," she said, shoving Ruben out of the way.

"Who isn't?" Prune grinned. "How deep?"

"Pussy deep, at least. They want to breed you like a sow."

"No way. They don't even know I have my period. I've been super careful." Prune shot a panicked glance at Ruben.

"The bearded nurse, Celeste? She got them your blood, or a pube, or whatever the heck they squeeze DNA out of. It's a matter of hours, perhaps a day or two, before they find out."

"*Merde merde merde merde merde!*" Prune stomped her feet. Grenadine noticed the bronze flush at the nape of her neck. In the back of her right shoulder, the sun was cut in half. It brought to mind a Tarot reading Grenadine had once gotten in New Orleans. The beads on the ends of the psychic's braids jingled as he blabbered on about destiny and God's perfect plan, until Grenadine put her Sun card down and accidentally knocked the deck so that the Hanged Man spilled over, coming to stillness exactly halfway over the Sun's jovial face. The psychic went ashen. He'd tried to make light of it, insisting on the accidental nature of the spill, on how unconditionally positive the Sun card was, but Grenadine wasn't duped.

"What happened?" Ruben wanted to know. "What is F Ward?" Both women ignored him. The knuckles of Prune's fists seemed to shine pale rays in the diminishing light.

"They might not transfer you right away," Grenadine said.

"I can't leave Carla."

"They think you loving on the kids is good for them. Good for Chinergy, I mean. Heightens their productivity or some such crap." The gravel crunched as Ruben squatted down to sit, arms and legs crossed. "I overheard them talking in Dawn's office this afternoon," Grenadine added by way of an apology.

"So, what are you saying? Are they transferring me or not?"

"They're waiting to figure out if you're a bigger asset loving on the existing brats or making some more. Either way, they're using you to make more dough."

"Duh," said Prune. The women smiled.

"They bake bread with Prune?" Ruben had a deep furrow in his brow. Prune and Grenadine snickered.

"Dough is an idiom, Ruben. It means money. And don't just sit there, rattlers love to come out at sunset," Prune said.

"They'll dine on your fine little daybreak ass, and smack their lips too," Grenadine added. The girls cackled as Ruben shot up, flicking imaginary snakes off his butt.

Inside the temple, Swami John was struggling hard to model stillness and not scratch an itch below his floating ribs. This morning, the focus of his Dharma talk was one-pointed focus: total immersion in the Now, meant to give access to the gap between perception and thought—that precise latitude *and* longitude of the Joy of Being. Glancing at his tattered copy of Eckhart Tolle's *The Power of Now*, the Swami spoke in the droning voice that, he imagined, a real master acquires through practiced detachment. Like most people, he had had glimpses of the Joy (which he always envisioned thus capitalized) that blossoms when we realize that there are no problems—only situations, either to be dealt with, or to be left alone and accepted as part of the "isness" of the present moment.

"Problems are mind-made," John recited, "and they need time to survive. They cannot survive in the actuality of the Now." He peered over the rows of children. Most were perfect little Buddhas, with eyes staring down at the tip of their nose, half-smiles, palms together in front of the heart, forearms perfectly level with the floor. He felt a rush of pride—which he skillfully pulled aside—for his little pupils who displayed such docile attention.

Some of the students were too weak to hold themselves up and had to lie coiled up on their side. *Who can blame them?* thought the Swami. Perhaps he would suggest cutting down on the harvesting activities, at least during meditation. But he knew that by activating the pineal and pituitary glands, this practice drastically enhanced the children Ch'i production. *This weakness shall pass,* John told himself. He knew that thanks to the ancient teachings, the kids would soon rebuild their pranic power and play tag or "talk Dolphin" around the quad. *Children's resilience is indeed a miracle,* he marveled. It was in the name of that miracle that The Center had chosen such young subjects to launch the most sustainable energy innovation to date. *What a quantum leap in the evolution of human consciousness! Just think: for the first time in known history, humanity will have to depend on nothing but its own self-generated energy for power and sustenance. No more fracturing of the atom, no more fracking of Mother Earth. Instead: pure light of conscious life-force fueling itself, endlessly regenerating! Finally, the flow of bio-force adequately channeled and sanctified. The infinity of essence properly recognized!*

John's attention alighted back on the stiff pillow under his buttocks, the hardwood floor underneath, the copious notes he'd scribbled in *The Power of Now,* and the right meniscus he'd demolished back at seminary. He released the embarrassment of having allowed his mind to stray. True, he was prone to flights of enthusiasm that sometimes interfered with the cultivation of equanimity. But *you cannot stalk peace,* he reminded himself. At times, Joy still manifested in the shape of thoughts, or even bodily sensations. He was working on eliminating his attachment to those but *That's why they call it practice, no?*

Picking up on the next page, the Swami read, "To alert you

that you have allowed yourself to be taken over by psychological time, you can use a simple criterion." He blushed with delight. This particular passage he'd highlighted in neon yellow, his favorite color. "Ask yourself: is there Joy, ease, and lightness in what I am doing? If there isn't, then time is covering up the present moment, and life is perceived as a burden or struggle." He didn't need to look at the book to continue. "If there is no Joy, ease, or lightness in what you are doing, it does not necessarily mean that you need to change *what* you are doing. It may be sufficient to change the *how*."

A few children began to stir. John glanced at his timer and saw that the zeros were blinking aggressively to signal that he'd gone overtime. He readied himself to wrap it up. "And to c... c... conclude, dear f...f...fffffriends, let me reveal to you Master Tolle's jewel secret to lasting s...suh...serenity!" Here, in the interest of time, John decided to ignore Alia's raised hand. He shut his eyes and brought his palms together in prayer pose. "G...g...give your fullest attention to whatever the moment presents. This implies that you also completely accept what *is*, because you c...c... cannnot give your full attention to something and at the same time resist it. N...Nnn... Nnnamaste."

Before the children had time to echo his greeting, a slow hand-clapping signaled Dawn's entrance. Unsure of what the protocol was in such cases, a few kids imitated her. They'd been clearly instructed that silence was the only way to honor the sacredness of these meetings, but if President Hetherington clapped, then perhaps they should too?

John swiveled around to greet her. "Ahhhh! P...P...President Hetherington would ll...llike to make a d...d...duh...declaration." Solemn as a court clerk, he gestured for the children to rise. Those who could, did.

"Thank you, Brother John." Dawn's stiletto heels smacked the hardwood floor as she stepped in front of the column bearing her effigy. She peered over her audience: rows of ashen children, their eyes struggling to avoid hers. *They don't even see me,* she thought. Dawn didn't like to feel transparent. A small boy with tubes plugged into an IV tower by his side was plucking the hair off his head. Dawn scanned her mind for a joke to crack—it always broke the ice with the generals and executives. But when confronted with innocence, the absolute dullness of it, she seemed to lose her sharp. *Dear God, don't let me catch whatever this is,* she pleaded. Then she said, "Hahem, you children look smashing!"

"You're kidding."

Dawn looked as if someone had just passed really stinky gas and John picked up his robe to scurry down the aisle toward where he thought the remark came from. The shuffle of pillows and whispers stopped when Alia spoke again.

"President Hetherington, it's one thing to rob us of our life-force—our birthright. One thing to have your vampire machines suck us dry day after day after night on end. But this? The lies, the pretending, the naming one thing what it is not and calling horror, beauty? Calling cruelty, kindness? Calling rape, love? I may not be able to stop you from killing us slowly, or convince your generals that it's a good idea to care for children instead of devouring them. But I am *not* going to let you drive us insane with your perversion of reality."

A lone mosquito sounded like an aircraft. Dawn broke into a slow grin. "And whom do I have the pleasure of talking to?"

"Forgive Alia," John cried. "She reads a lot. A bright child, but—"

"I am Alia," the girl interjected.

"I would love to continue this provocative discussion, Alia. Meet me in my office after breakfast, will you? For now, I wish to share some exciting news—"

"No." Alia folded her arms in front of her chest.

Dawn winced, but continued. "Your hard work is paying off, my dears! Our engineers are finding ever-more effective ways to extract precious kilowatts from the raw material you are so generously contributing—" Alia snorted and a few children chuckled. John gazed constipatedly at Dawn. "So I have decided to show you my gratitude by allowing two more hours of television entertainment a week!" A couple of children, too exhausted to stay on their feet, sat down—not what President Hetherington had anticipated. Furious, she spat, "Or not!" Her heels dug tiny dents into the polyurethane as she hurried toward the exit, saying, "Thankless little shits" through gritted teeth.

After the folding doors screeched back into place, John chimed in, "Ok, ch…ch… chhhhhildren. Breakfast is waiting!" Some of the kids started to line up to file out the door, as they had yesterday and the days before. But many didn't, and turned to look at Alia instead. They waited.

"Let's go," she said. It wasn't the usual neat column that snaked toward the cafeteria, but an aggregate, a clumpy assortment of confused individuals. *Good*, thought Alia. *Looks like we might have jump-started them thinking again.*

V

Revolutions Are Easy

*R*osa Tum's Paris had forever been one of limestone façades the color of young creamed maize. Monuments towered from the two-dimensional confines of sister Elizabeth's heavy book. The city's almost mythological people, The Parisians, appeared frozen in their lavish steps and their dogs were so minuscule before the austere *Concièrgerie* that at the end of their leash they narrowed into unidentifiable dots. As a girl, Rosa had assumed that the people's smallness was a function of their great distance, a bit like the peak of Atitlán's largest volcano which, from Santa Cruz, seemed no larger than her own barely-there titties. But to her, nothing that lived in sister Elizabeth's books ever remained two-dimensional. Each face unfurled a world of possibilities; each word, a well of longing. And so, each black and white image of a city street had unspooled in her mind a life, complete with accordion lessons, the butter vapors of croissants, and an introverted man-boy with a Django Reinhardt mustache and the slender shoulders of the poets who survive off of red wine and filterless cigarettes.

What Rosa couldn't have envisioned was the light—what the sunlight did to those aluminum rooftops, shimmying off pigeons, drizzle, and grime. What it did to the creamy Louvre and the cobblestones! No amount of Georges Seurat, Monet, or even sunrises on lake Atitlán had prepared her for the Paris that scintillated in the brand new sun that first morning, after that first night with Marc. Rosa liked to believe that it was for this light that she'd left her comrades behind, rather than her bourgeois love of a man, or the necessity to flee from Guatemala's new bureaucrats—many of whom also happened to be the old exterminators.

The tool shed became a designated sanctuary. Prune was making good progress with her training, and Ruben was confident that she was *this* close to accessing the Dreamscape, that "other" plane where, he claimed, Carla was up and about, grumpy as ever in the company of a narcoleptic wolf and a Czech witch. Prune had no choice but to believe him.

Grenadine sometimes came to join them. She grabbed extra coffees and muffins from the cafeteria and, after their sessions, the three of them watched the sun rise over the mesa. It felt good to sit together, knowing they were meant to become friends, but in no rush to make it happen. Also, knowing there was so much they could be talking about yet not quite sure where to begin.

"We're incubating," Ruben finally said after several days of listening to each other sip on coffee.

Prune said, "My father told Carla and me about the Australian Aboriginals' Dreaming. To them, time is all-at-once instead of linear. All time is a Creation time out of which all beings are born, and back to which they return. Dad made shadow puppets with his fingers against the wall above our beds to explain it."

Grenadine handed her a half-muffin. Before she finished swallowing, she said, "The Dreaming is where our eternal spirit-child lives. Everything we see and smell, every sock lost and every lamb born is a result and a sign of the past, present, and future actions of those shadow beings. Because most of us don't see or even sense them, we consider them to be mythical—symbolically meaningful at best, but demonic deceptions at bottom. To the Aboriginals, though, these ancestors are real. Literally."

"And why not?" said Ruben, tapping the dirt with a shovel.

"Do you believe that this shovel fades out of existence when you're not there to hold it? So how come that just because we can't touch our spirit-children, we believe they aren't real?"

Grenadine said, "I guess you could say the same of personal memories, right? Our present is the crystallization of someone's past actions and choices. Am I not the result of my mother's story, her giving in and giving up, but not enough to make it stop?" She sprung to her feet like a judoka. "Am I not sitting here playing hot potato with whirlpools of resentment, and drowning, drowning, doing absolutely nothing?" She waved at the breathtaking panorama. "And you? What are you doing? Am I the only one who wants to puke just looking at all this fucking glory?"

"*Es facil, hacer la Revolucion.*" With his chin resting on the handle of the shovel, Ruben looked like some Diego Rivera propaganda.

Grenadine said, "What do you mean?"

"Revolutions are easy," said Prune. "Relatively, I mean. With enough imagination, a hunk of bravery, and premium communication skills, anyone can overthrow a system, especially a corrupt one. Ask Fidel, ask Lenin, ask Robespierre. The problem is after the revolution. What then? What do you do once your ideals are smeared in blood, the big wigs are roasting in the bonfires of justice, and the stench of burnt flesh seeps under locked doors?" They stared at her. She was right. Once you throw off the structures of power, who knows what madness or purity will follow? After Lenin came Stalin's Gulag, and after Robespierre, the Terror. Heads chopped off. Thousands of them. Then, dreadful conformity. After the Founding Fathers, the Tea Party.

Grenadine turned to Ruben and asked, "What about Fidel? Hasn't Castro kept his promise of independence after all? Even after the fall of the Soviet?"

"Independence, yes," said Ruben. "Freedom? Food? Fairness? Not so sure." The sun had cleared the mountain and a pale moon still hung above the desert.

Grenadine sighed. "Was it Audre Lorde, who said, 'While we wait in silence for the final luxury of fearlessness, the weight of that silence will choke us?'"

"We have to watch out for fear," Ruben nodded. "It is very skilled at masquerading as the voice of reason."

"Or worse," Prune said. "Common sense."

Gazing beyond Prune at the fading moon, Grenadine bobbed her head.

Ruben said, "I am not afraid to fight. I could survive on protein from my nail clippings for a while. I'm not even really afraid to die. What I am really afraid of is that I will turn into one of Them in the process. I've seen what righteousness can do to a man. And to his children."

"I'm not." Grenadine scowled, arms crossed, feet rooted. "We've been defined by others for too long. For too long our backs, our cunts, all our contained-rage-turned-self-mutilation have been *Their* bridge to *Their* liberty, *Their* pursuit of happiness. And this, these kids' life-force being sucked out of them like strawberry milk-shake, is only the latest of these bridges—as if there weren't enough already. Well, *I've* had enough. No one will hand me my dignity back on a silver platter. I have to reclaim it for myself. And the only way I can see doing that is by turning their own depravity back against them."

Prune said, "An eye for an eye—"

"—Makes the whole fucking world blind," Grenadine spat. "I know. It sounds nice and neat. But the world is already blind, Prune. Look around! Does anyone give a shit about your little sister? Is anyone still looking for your mother? How long did it take them to give up on the pesky Freedom Fighter? Two months? Everyone's relieved that they can obsess about where the next paycheck will come from so that they *don't* have to think about whose life gets syphoned down their Mazda. How do you propose to make them open the eyes that they themselves have put out—from shame, from greed, from laziness? You really think you're going to suddenly appeal to Dawn Hetherington's innate compassion and humanity? Or to some Time Warner editorialist's idea of dignity?"

"You sound like Frantz Fanon, Grenadine." Prune looked concerned.

"I sound like someone who's done waiting. This is not an *exposé* about the merits and dangers of subversion, Prune. This is your life. Wake up!" Grenadine stood so close to Prune that Ruben felt the need to place his arm between them. "Tell her Ruben!" Grenadine shoved his arm out of the way. "Do you have any idea what they do to breeders over there in the F Ward? The F doesn't just stand for Fertility, trust me. How do you think they get the girls pregnant? How do you think that's going to work out for you?"

Ruben stepped in between them. "Pardon me, but I think we are getting off the railroads." Prune took a step back and sat down on the log. *She ages like a butterfly,* thought Ruben. *A lifetime in a day.*

Elbows on knees, Prune stared at the dirt between her feet. She was feeling really stupid. She'd never really thought about what did go on in the F Ward. She'd only been thinking about what would happen to her little sister if she were transferred. Now, the sky was caving in. Clouds gathered in front of the sun and she shivered. *Shit,* she thought, *what do they do to breeders?*

Ruben took Grenadine's arm and led her to sit on the log next to Prune. "I think Prune is right," he said. "The ideas are the key to the liberation. And Grenadine is also right, because the ideas are living things, but only the people can bring them to life." He squeezed in to sit between the two of them. "Now," he looked at one and then the other. "We must each decide if we are going to want to be *more* right than one another, or if we want a real solution to our problem."

Grenadine said, "Solution. Easy. Get rid of Dawn. Get rid of her poodle, Anthony."

Ruben said, "Tempting. But we don't need more enemies. What we need is allies. Powerful allies. Convincing allies."

Grenadine said, "Sure, let's call in the U.N., why don't we? I'm sure they've got a few peacekeepers lying around they could send over while we hash it out with Satan and Cerberus."

Prune sighed. She'd had it with the Xena attitude. She looked up past the great wall of Ruben at Grenadine and said, "Why are you still here anyway? You could go anytime, couldn't you?" She wasn't sure whom her question was meant for.

Speaking to the badlands in front of her, Grenadine said, "They took her." Her friends waited. Ruben had found a humongous bird of paradise, and ribbons of orange petals floated to the ground as he nervously tore it apart. "It's so stupid," Grenadine continued. "All I've ever seen of my daughter is her elbow, dimpled and still glowing with my insides. I remember thinking of a crow's wing, so black it is blue. I felt so proud of her darkness, proof that she is her grandmother's. My Gaia's wing flapped twice, and then it disappeared. I heard her wane down the hallway as she was carried away in someone else's arms." Grenadine lapped at the pearl of blood that materialized on her lower lip. Between her own feet, Prune noticed specks of gold and green in the dust. Ruben moved first, but Grenadine was shaking her head no. "Don't you fucking dare, man. I don't need your pity." Ruben ignored her words and landed his broad hand on the back of her neck, making her lean into his chest.

The silence stretched. Hunchbacked, mighty Grenadine suddenly looked brittle as a taco shell. "Nothing has changed," her voice came out strong, even muffled by Ruben's shirt. "They still take our children from us, like my father's fathers did, swapping us for more profitable seedlings." Then she looked up. "And Anthony... It's one thing to pimp himself out. But he gave away his flesh—*my* child!" After a pause she added, "I need him dead."

Prune wished for screams, sobs, the smashing of furniture— *something* to blow the lid off of this. But there was nothing to smash out here, no walls for screams to bounce off of. Grenadine's heaving remained soundless. Ruben patted her back. Prune looked on, thinking, *I'm just not good with grief. Especially other people's grief. It always seems so… Real. My own grief, I can always reason away, remind myself other folks have it worse, think of the Lost Boys of Sudan, hooked on drugs and forced to impale their own for their fix. But with other people's despair—flesh and bones people in front of me—there's nothing I can do. Feelings just sit there and glare, stupid, immovable. Makes me want to hit someone.*

To Grenadine she said, "You slept with that cockroach?" and immediately wished she could take it back. Desperate for a diversion, she turned to Ruben.

"Perhaps there is another way," he said. "We must find it. Or else—"

"—or else we must make it up," Grenadine said.

Carla climbed to the top of the tallest boulder overlooking the waterfall. On the way she found a small ledge that called to her buttocks. With her big toe she scattered the dead leaves, soil, and roly-polies that congregated there, then plopped down. The cool granite nudged suction cups into her soft parts so her body knew it was being held.

The backwash of her earlier conversation with Anastasia lingered. Why was it so hard to discuss simple questions with adults? What was it about things as common as life and death— what could be more common than *these*?—that made them suddenly go limp and abstract as π? It had been just the same with her father Marc. Talking about death was like bringing up sex, or worse, money. *How strange that it is precisely those things that everyone does that are most taboo,* thought Carla. *Each and every one of us is here because someone, at some point, had sex, right? So that makes a lot of people having sex. Almost as many as there are people dying.*

As she recalled the feeling of being cast aside, Carla's nostrils flared all over again. It was often that way for her: feelings blossoming after the fact, as if the actual event were just a rehearsal for the full-blown experience. Then, when the experience does happen it is so messy: the quickening of expectations stalled, but pushing and tugging all the more; all the memories rush in like waving fingers to say, *I told you so* and *What were you thinking,* and *It didn't use to be this way!*

The tension wiggled its way into Carla's eyeballs, announcing a migraine. An orange butterfly landed on a diaphanous leaf at her foot. She tried to kick it but it fluttered away, paying her no mind.

"I don't matter," the girl grumbled, swatting the flat of her hands at the rock. It felt good, this slapping. Righteous. She did it again, harder. The thump of flesh on rock was bringing her back to herself. Like vines, memories of her mother's hand snaked up her wrists and arms. Just the hand, with the square fingertips and the voluminous blue veins of one who's been up working the maize fields before school.

Most days, Carla couldn't remember her mother's face. But her hands, yes. Rosa liked to brush the inside of her daughter's elbow. Her short nails soothed Carla into a trance that even thumb-sucking couldn't induce. Ironically, when the wound in her neck from the harvesting machine got too swollen, the pale inside of Carla's elbow was the very spot that the Caretakers had to tap in the IV that kept her harvestable on demand.

Caressing the boulder, now, Carla asked what was really on her mind. "How do you know if you're alive?"

Silently, simply, the answer came up through the palms of her hands. "It's about commitment," it said. "Not blood, not breath, not even flesh, or hurt; not truth, or illusion. You know you're alive when you commit to it."

"I would *never* commit to life," she said. "What has life done for

88

me lately, besides auction off my flesh to juice up people's SUV's?" Carla paused and listened for more. Nothing, except for that low hum of nature, like a kitchen appliance. She raised her hand and smacked the granite once more. *Look at me*, she thought. *Talking to a dumb old rock and expecting an answer. Must learn not to count on anything. Must learn to rely only on me.* Carla was thrumming the boulder now, the slaps's pulse shooting up her forearms. *Fool, fool, fool, fool, fool, fool.*

And then something loosened. Her throat, like the knot at the top of her mother's tobacco pouch, loosened. A moan, low and steady. Not her own voice. Definitely not her voice.

"Just keep drumming," it said. Carla kept smacking the rock, fierce as an ape. "See," the voice said, "You're committed already. It's just that you don't yet know it."

Back at the camp, Ruben and Anastasia were at their courting rigmarole again.

"I miss the raucousness of the sea," Ruben said, testing the water with his toes.

Anastasia laughed. "That's it? You lost your *Papa* and your country, but what you miss is the raucousness of the sea? Ah, Ruben, Ruben, I knew it!"

"You knew what?"

"'The raucousness of the sea.' I knew you were a poet! Isn't he a poet, Carlota?"

Carla shrugged and turned on the transistor radio she'd been fixing up. The brouhaha of Celia Cruz's big-band broke up on her convulsive salsa, *Quimbara*.

Anastasia shook her head. "Tweens."

"You're not really asking me, are you?" Carla muttered as if to Celia Cruz.

"I'm not?"

"You don't really want to know if I think he's the new Walt Whitman."

One thing Ruben had learned, growing up in a cramped apartment in which women outnumbered men, was to make himself invisible when the women needed privacy. Pandemonium was near as Celia Cruz's song reached its climax. It took him back to *El Chivo*. On Sundays, assortments of homemade percussion disputed Havana's popular beach's waves to the Havaneros' cackling transistors.

"And what do you miss the most, Carla?" Anastasia asked as she towel-dried the dishes.

Ruben was impressed by Anastasia's diplomacy. Answering a defensive question with a placating one was a bright way to shift from aggression to inclusion. It worked, and Carla was taken aback.

"Mmmh. Highway travel," she said.

Anastasia said, "Is that so?"

"What about it?" Ruben wanted to know.

"Everything. With only an adjustable hood flapping in the wind, the noise was like a head cold, until you couldn't think anymore. Only thing left to do was take in the landscape just as it came. And then there was the leek broth in a paper cup from the gas station machine. Singing harmonies with Dad and Prune while Mom kept the time with an empty can on the dashboard."

"All together. I understand" Ruben nodded. "*Y tu*, Anastasia? What do you miss the most?"

"*Saucisson!*" the crone cried as if answering a game show. This woke up Attila.

Carla raised an eyebrow. "Salami?" Once the wolf had made sure that this was a false alert and no charcuterie was indeed in the vicinity, he gave them a reproachful look, rose his great furry self, took a few steps away from their fuss, and plopped back down with a sigh.

"In the harshest of the winter, our pigs slept with us," Anastasia began. "They took care of garbage disposal and kept the house warm. They were my only siblings and my best friends. It's true what they say, pigs are as smart as people. Cleaner than many, and nicer than most. Even so, I grew up with whole hog legs and salamis hanging off our kitchen ceiling to cure, attracting swarms of flies in August and occasionally dripping grease into my hair. My parents made a name for themselves for their liver sausage, but I wouldn't have been caught dead eating my brothers and sisters. Until the so-called Prague Spring." Anastasia had Carla's full attention, now, and Ruben's forehead curled up like a question mark.

"I was fourteen, and likely the only girl in all of Mělník who'd never tasted pork. My mother always said, 'Either you eat one, or you become one.' Then, Daddy had to go to the city."

Ruben's feet were drawing figure eights in the cool water. Carla crawled over to sit with her back against his. Anastasia hung the dish towel to dry on a bush and came to kneel next to Attila. She dug her hand into his fur. "Now, you've got to understand that my Daddy wasn't a big-city kind of guy. For one thing, he went nowhere without his milking stool. He even had Piotr-the-barber make a special belt for it so he could carry it on his back like an African child, with its legs peeking out on the sides. When I wanted to give him a hug, I had to be careful not to poke my eye out on a wooden leg. Daddy rarely sat down on his stool, though. He didn't even really milk the cows either. Only when talk of politics came up, he would put down his milking stool, sit on it, cross his arms in front of his chest, and hold his breath. He could hold it for three and a half minutes, the longest of anyone in Mělník and even, I would think, all of Czechoslovakia. We thought he should go to the Olympics to compete as a free-diver. His face became red as a nursing sow's teats and it worked. It stopped them partisans talking. A breath-strike might not be as advancing of the proletarian project as a laborers' strike, but it was a strike all the same, they said, and for that, it deserved respect. Also, they wanted my Daddy to keep making his liver sausage rather than collapse dead in the cigarette stubs on the floor."

Attila's snoring became very loud and one of his ears began to twitch. Anastasia started to rub him on the head. The wolf stretched, groaned, and snored even louder.

"I guess you could say that it was a case of being in the wrong place at the wrong time," Anastasia continued. "Less than one hundred men died that day, all of them in uniform. We don't quite know how it happened, or why my Daddy was shot. They sent his body in a bag with a boy in a helmet too big for his head. The boy said they were sorry. I thought he meant about the smell and the flies, but my Mamma said 'No. They sorry he dead.'"

It was getting dark, and the warmth of Ruben's back against Carla's wasn't quite enough to keep her cosy anymore. The girl wished for a blanket, but she didn't want Anastasia to stop, so she shrugged and pressed herself against Ruben a little tighter. Sprawled next to Attila, Anastasia kept going. "After that, I just remember a big pigeon-color sad. I didn't have much fight left in me. I ate what my Mommy put in front of me. A lot of it. I loved the salami. I didn't tell Mom because she would have said I told you so, but I loved it. The powdery ash I licked off of the casing. The small bits of white grease to soften the gaminess. The chewy smokiness. Anyway, soon enough, Mom had to sell the pigs.

"When came the next spring, I was fat as a goose. Vaclav the blacksmith, who'd lost his wife to the postman, started coming around. One day he asked about marrying me. My mother shuddered and shook her head no, but then she looked at me differently after—a burden no longer, something she hadn't considered. The next Sunday he brought extra cash and a heavy wool rug. 'What a nice surprise!' she said. Without another word she ushered me toward his waistless shadow and hairy fingers."

Ruben took his feet out of the water and dried them on the grass, saying, "And you were how old?"

"Fifteen, and Vaclav wasn't half the man to handle a girl like me." Carla moaned for having to resettle after Ruben had moved. She went to lie down next to Anastasia, grabbing the hem of the crone's skirt to cover her legs. Ruben crawled over to the fire pit and busied himself building their fire.

Anastasia kept going. "Vaclav's tears came too early and his blows too late, or vice versa. He quickly knew he couldn't hold onto me, but he introduced me to the drink and took me to Bratislava on our honeymoon. When he left, I stayed, living it up at the Hotel California on skillful fornication and not so skillful fiddle-playing. There actually were mirrors on the ceiling, just like in the song. They were stained with spit and bratwurst grease. I found my true husband Karl there, or he found me, all of fifteen and borderline syphilitic. He had an easel and a funny accent. After a few drinks, he asked if I would come to his unheated studio on Glöberstrasse. It was snowing in his bedroom, and we made a pile of lust and hope under the blanket. He offered me my first ever sip of champagne, which he'd swapped for drawing lessons with one of his collectors' bratty son."

Carla was asleep now, making occasional sucking sounds on her thumb. Ruben and Anastasia watched the fire crackle.

"I think I better go, now," he said after a while. He wasn't sure why, and it was idiotic of him, but he didn't like hearing about this Karl guy.

"Yes, you go." Anastasia got up to poke the embers with a stick and sparkles scattered like thoughts. Her attention still trained on the fire, she added, "Karl is still here."

"Of course he is," Ruben said, getting up to place a blanket over Carla. The girl had her arm around the wolf, who immediately kicked the blanket off. "Those we have loved never really go away, do they?"

"No, I mean he's *here*." Anastasia pointed her finger at Carla. "My husband's soul lives in the girl."

"Look, Anastasia. I get it. I get that spirit is real, more real than matter even. I get that the imaginal plane is the matrix of both, and that individual bodies are not what they seem; that life and death are not quite as separate as we think. I get that this place, this Dreamscape, is a proof of all that, and surely of much much more that I don't understand. And that's the thing. There's so much I don't understand. I don't know what to believe. I don't know what you mean, even."

"You don't have to believe, Ruben." Anastasia was standing close enough to him that the warmth of her softened into his. "Just desire," she said, tracing his jaw line with the tip of her finger.

Ruben reached out to touch one of her thick locks, saying, "Is it really that simple?"

"It really is."

"Will desire help me help these kids?"

"At least as much as belief will. Well, ok, maybe not desire *per se*. But the *energy* of desire. *Shakti* will help them." Her lips were grazing his now. "She is the subtle vibration that underlies everything," she whispered into his mouth. "All of reality is Her dance…" Ruben rested his hands on her hips and slowly, they began to twirl. "… From the biological processes of our bodies, through the force that nudges us toward conscious evolution," she whispered into his ear. "… On to ecstasy."

At that, Ruben tightened his grip, and the crone squealed when her feet left the ground. "I don't quite know what's going on out there, Anastasia. I don't know if you're a crazy *curandera* lost in her meditation, or an ancient powerful goddess."

She clasped her legs tight around his waist.

"You might even be my own demented fantasy, for all I know." He twirled slowly. "But I want your help."

"Of course you do." Her skirt was tickling his thighs. "I am the desire that will save you."

Ruben glanced at Carla, curled up against the wolf. The sleeping child seemed to perplex him, and he set Anastasia back down.

The crone took Ruben's hand and started toward the dark shelter of the canopy. "Walk with me," she said.

Ruben followed.

Grenadine felt around the nightstand where she kept the music box with the screechy ballerina on top and the blade inside. In their half-sleep, her fingers stumbled, knocking over the glass of water. *God damn!*

The spill didn't really matter, only her awkwardness. *Where'd the Kleenex box go? Shit, where did the fucking ballerina go?* Propping herself up on one elbow, she fumbled for the light switch. *Must get to the blade.*

At the oddest moments, the mental image of Prune's bare chest had been insinuating itself into Grenadine's daily landscape—from the potted box tree to the shower handle. Grenadine pictured Prune's breasts riding high and proud, the teat almost pink. *What feelings are these feelings anyway?*

Lust, Grenadine understood. There was the discomfort, like the tag inside her shirt biting at the back of her neck. Even if she cut it out, some hard little seams remained, often sharper biters even. But Grenadine was used to having invasive thoughts, and those weren't what bothered her. In fourth grade, she couldn't walk by the boys' bathroom without envisioning boy nakedness, the tennis-ball-sized buttocks and the funny little Ping-Pong sacks.

Grenadine had always known she was dirty. "Brown is the color of soil, of that which is soiled," her father liked to remind her. And she'd been *born* that way. But by the time she'd reached puberty, sexual thoughts became scary. As it became a matter of choosing to act on them or not, the question cropped up of whether they were normal curiosity, or abject fantasy. Pretty soon, the boys at school knew. They could tell, they said, which girls were *like that*. Then the boys from Booker T. High knew. Word got out that Grenadine didn't mind being roughed up once in a while. The good thing was, bruises didn't show that much on skin as dark as hers. Or you'd have to look real close, and no one really did.

No, what bothered Grenadine now was that along with the familiar lechery, there were much more confusing images cropping up—like, Prune laughing, arms wide, face lit by the reflections off the clouds—instead of how Grenadine was used to envision the objects of her want: on their knees, head bent, begging for a forgiveness she wouldn't, under any circumstance, grant.

In the shed, Ruben's voice reached Prune as if through water. "Offer yourself up," it said. "Become anything you encounter."

The paw print was of a large cat. *Too large to be a leopard's,* she thought.

"Free yourself from the tyranny of the literal." The voice was unrecognizable now, and far, far away. Prune's taut thigh felt the urge to set foot in that paw print and as it did, soft soil engulfed it. It fit. Prune pushed at the ground and the propelling power of her haunches was a shock, the spring in her step a soaring. *I am light: pure power. I am an Alvin Ailey dancer. Gravity is a mere excuse for suspension.* Mammoth tree trunks, fat lianas, plush blossoms the size of her skull buzzed by. She noted how shiny was the black fur on her paws that clawed at the air between her throat and the ground. Effortless.

I don't stay. I can't stay. I touch earth only to rise, I tumble, I pounce, there is no landing, no landing, no land. There are smells. Weightless, green sweat of sprouts, heavy smell of carcasses, all matter equal before decay, all food, all food. I'm hungry, so hungry! Gravity is only an excuse for expansion. I reach the edge of the grove— sniff... Overload. Overload. It's Christmas at the mall, the Musak all electronic. There's been pheasants here, drum machines of them, thump thump thump, ground mice, moles, roaches, I'd eat anything, anything! Gravity is only an excuse for suspension. I slow down, the pulse in my thighs shortens, I sink, sand, what is this called, those sands that suck you in, suck you down like Lawrence of Arabia. The parachute in my diaphragm collapses on itself, tight, tight like those pantyhose I tried on once, when I wanted to be woman, when I didn't know it would mean loss... Gravity is only an excuse—do I still have eyes?

"The poetic consciousness..."

—Whose voice? Is this my mother's voice? My mother wouldn't have said 'consciousness,' my mother wouldn't have... Do I have a mother? It is so dark in here that it is all space—no empty, no full. No container, no contained. No self, no mother. It takes light for differentiation. Gravity is only... My feet! My feet are feet again, suction cups rooting me to cold stone. And the music, I think I hear music, but no musicians, just drums, drums, a wooden spoon, clank, clank, *the insides of the cauldron spill, sparks spit, the bonfire licks at my calves. This is dancing! Like Alvin Ailey's naked bodies, this is me, this is my hips, tight boyish hips, tight. Gravity is only an excuse for suspension—I hold myself: arms crisscross chest, like making out but no one else here, no one to hold my hips, and the cave widens, and the moss drips with the sweat of drums... there were drummers here, I see white paint on their black faces, war paint. This is no war! This is me dancing, this is my navel, this is the center of the universe... Gravity... an excuse for... strength, pulse, flight! What do you mean, what do you mean, you're not coming back, what do you mean, you hate our mother... you have hate in your mouth, who are you, Carla? You were my little sister. Who are you? I want to dance, will you take my hand, Carla, will you dance, will you wipe the white foam hate from your lips?*

"What is she talking about, wiping hate foam from lips? Prune! Open your eyes!" Carla's face was huge right up against Prune's. There were specks of copper in her sister's pupils. Something smelled delicious.

Meat. I think they're cooking meat. Here's an old woman stirring a huge pot. There's Ruben. His lips move but I hear no sound.

"Carlota!"

—Whose voice? It sounds too close... clank, clank *against the walls inside my head—a sinus cold? I wish someone would give me*

something to eat. Beef Bourguignon, with carrots and shallots candied in the wine. The giant panther head flashed by, its eyes making yellow streaks. *It wants to bite my head off, why do I feel so calm?*

"Prune, you made it!"

I just want to go to sleep. Clank, Clank. *Let me go to sleep.*

"Prune!"

Rumbles, like an empty stomach inside my head. Mmmmmh, it's so warm here. I could stay forever. If only they gave me something to eat. Salt. Water. I'd do anything for a glass of water.

"What have you done to her?" Carla scolded Ruben.

"Here we go, coming through!" Anastasia handed Prune a bowl and a glass of water.

I have to sit up but the moss is so snuggly on my back!

"Red meat. It will ground you," said Anastasia. The bouillon was reddish brown.

Dried blood. Ahhhhhhh. Burst of life, death, sweet! Mother-of-pearl claws gleam from the bottom of the bowl.

"Prune!"

My sister looks so old with that crinkle in her brow.

"This is it, Prune, we made it." There was the sadness of the obvious in Ruben's voice. Carla held out the smoking spoon for Prune, who slurped on it loud and long, the way it used to drive their grandmother crazy.

Finally, Prune said, "I missed you like the sun, Carlota."

The grounds looked particularly eerie when Prune came out of the shed. Tall grasses sashayed in a *mille-feuille* sky—sheets of clouds moving at different speeds: round fluffy ones on the go and thin stretchy ones stretching easy. It brought to mind nature shows set in Kenya, and Prune half expected an impala to come bounding across the vista.

Seven thirty-six A.M. The kids must be done with Satsang, she thought. *I'll go catch up with them and grab myself a biscuit. Hope it'll stop this wicked growling in my stomach.*

98

"Prune!" Standing in the vastness, Ruben looked small.

"What?" It came out more blunt than she meant it to.

"It's like Anastasia said. You can go back and visit anytime, you know."

"I know." She didn't want him to witness the sobs that were coming up so she started to walk away. Relief, joy, grief, fear, hope, worry, worry, worry. Too much un-fucking-certainty.

Prune was glad to hear Ruben's footstep crunch after her. She wanted to be alone, but it was nice to feel him nearby. The air was cool, the breeze balmy. Over the quad hung aluminum clouds, maybe some afternoon showers on their way.

"Why not go look for your parents?" Ruben called after her.

Prune stopped. She tried to swallow, but couldn't. When Ruben caught up with her, he put his hands in his pant pockets and for a moment, they both stood there, frowning at the clouds.

Again, Ruben said, "Why not?"

Studying the dirt between her feet, Prune said, "How?"

"What?" He had heard, but he wanted her to think about it.

"How?" She said, louder. "How do I leave my sister alone on a cot with tubes stuck inside her? How do I get out of here? How do I even begin to figure out what happened to our parents? All I know is that two years ago, my mother was kidnapped in broad daylight, in our home in the center of Paris by *very* professional-looking assassins, and my father went missing shortly after he went batty with the grief. I have nothing, Ruben!" Prune realized she was practically shouting, and it felt good. She glanced around at their surroundings, noticed a straggling child across the quad. "Nothing," she repeated, as if to herself.

"I'll take care of Carla, Prune, you know I will," Ruben said softly. "You heard what she said. She won't come out of her coma Dreamscape unless you find out what happened to your parents."

"No, she said she won't come back unless I *find* them." Prune stood squarely in front of Ruben. "All or nothing," she added.

"You have to try, Prune. Who else will if you don't? How will you live with yourself? You can't stay here anyway. You heard what Grenadine said."

"I know. Dawn wants to breed me like a sow."

"How alive can you stand to really be, Prune?" She looked as if she'd been whacked. "That's really what this is about and we both know it," Ruben added. "You can choose to stay here and hide behind your good sentiments for the kids, be a martyr for your little sister, yaddi-yadda. But it would all really boil down to fear."

"You're damn right, I'm afraid," she protested. "I've only got a transnational corporation with Pentagon backing keeping me and my only remaining relative parked like industrial poultry, and parents who may be either dead or barely alive in some terrorist dungeon somewhere!"

"But what you're really afraid of is not Dawn or the powers-that-be, Prune." Slow tears rolled down her cheeks as children trickled out of the cafeteria. "Am I right? What you're really afraid of is—"

"Being fully alive, I got it," Prune sniffled. "Shit," she added, wiping her nose with her sleeve. "You're pissing me off, Ruben."

"I love you too, Prune." He slapped her back, and headed for his scrambled eggs.

Satsang must have run over. When Prune got to the cafeteria, Ruben had already left and no one else was there—although the steel platters of tofu sausage and kale grits were set out on the counter, smoking underneath their heating lamps. Prune heaped it up on a plate and squirted too much *Valentina* hot sauce on top. With neither live bodies nor babble to dampen the towering Dawn and Trump staring her down from their mural, this place gave her the heebie-jeebies.

Out front, she happened upon little Lou, who was squatting down by a pink plastic flamingo. Lou was such a sparrow, Prune had to look closely to see the tiny trail she'd left in the flowerbed. But the IV tree she now had to drag around everywhere gave her away.

"... 3, 4, 6, 8, 9, 12...uh...16—"

"Hey Lou!"

"Hush....14, 18, 19, 20, 20—er... I forgot what's after twenty, but I've counted and there's a little bit more than twenty beds in our room," Lou announced.

"Yeah, I think that's right. Great j—"

"Hush. Now I count in my head the harvesting machines behind the curtain." Lou shut her eyes. "1, 2, 3, 5, 8—"

"Why?" Prune squatted down next to the little girl. Their hands almost touched on the IV tree.

Lou squeezed her eyes tighter. "Hush. How am I supposed to count if you interrupt me all the time?" Her long eyelashes flapped open. "Well, I've lost count now. Happy?"

"I'm sorry, sweet pea. But why are you counting the beds and the machines?"

"I want to know how many more days I'm alive." Prune looked puzzled. Lou sighed, but she indulged her. "Pedro said, if we stay here we won't live much longer than there are beds divided by the number of machines in this dump. Prune, I wish you'd bring me something back."

"Back from where, pumpkin?"

"I'm not a pumpkin!" Lou meant it so earnest that there was a lag in her petting of the flamingo. "Pumpkins get holes cut out of them, and they end up with raggedy teeth like the people who live up in the hills and don't never brush their teeth after candy. And then the pumpkins get all saggy, and their heads all squishy, and they look old old, like Mr Augustine except older, like the planets we can't see because they're so old they don't even light up in the night sky anymore."

Prune wanted to grab the sprout girl and squeeze her tight. Instead, she smiled. "What's your flamingo's name?"

Lou had to think for a methodical petting-of-the-head moment. Finally, she said, "Sam."

"Hi Sam!"

"Sam don't talk. His tongue got eaten up by ants and it was all my fault."

"How could that be your fault?"

"Alia said I couldn't cut the flowers, but the ants needed pillows so I *had* to make blossom pillows, because the concrete is *too* hard."

Looking down at where Lou pointed, Prune noticed small clumps of discolored Mum blossoms arranged along the thin line of ants that was snaking its way across the concrete pathway. Determined not to stray from the shortest path, the ants were crawling all up and down the blossoms. A fat one was working on loading up on its back a blossom twenty-five times its size. "I don't understand," Prune said. "Will you explain it to me?"

Absorbed by the black specks of mildew encrusted in the sun-faded plastic of Sam, Lou was now patting the molded wings of the flamingo. She looked concerned. "Pedro said you go to Dream Cape to visit Carla. They have skateboards there? Will you bring me back a skateboard? He says Carla's not dead because she's too tired to be dead, so that's why she sleeps all the time. But in the Dream Cape she all the time skates… Prune? Those who don't sleep at night, what do they do with dreams when they come?"

"I'm not sure. I think that sometimes, when people don't sleep, their dreams go to other people—people who are asleep, or who are so quiet that the dreams think they're asleep, and it's safe to go to them."

"Sam is sleepy. I have to put him to bed." Lou stood up, pulled the flamingo's stick legs out of the ground, tucked the hard plastic body under her arm, grasped her IV tree with her freed hand, slipped her other hand inside the sheath of Prune's, and led them down the way to Ward Q.

When Marc unlatched the passenger's door, the wind banged it wide open and Ocean spritzed Rosa's face.

Having grown up on the escarpments of lake Atitlán—so gorgeous that someone famous said it was 'too much of a good thing'—Rosa had assumed that the ocean would be pretty much the same, only bigger, and without the napping volcanoes to hold it in like a belt on a beer belly. But on her cheeks, along with Atlantic's sputter now alighted volumes-worth of sister Elizabeth's Encyclopedia Britannica. It brought to mind etchings of monstrous crustaceans and stories of Caribbean shipwrecks, *conquistadores* drowning on their knees.

"My folks can appear a bit harsh," said Marc. The two lovers had spent three-and-a-half months walking across the bridges of Paris into dewy dawns and knitting up passionate plans for saving the mind and its avatars from imperialism. Now he had invited Rosa to spend Easter at his family estate. "You know how people are a function of the landscape that nurtures them?"

Rosa glanced around at the vertiginous white cliffs and their waves, furious as a childless mother. She nodded.

"Say, you." Marc wanted to explain anyway.

"Me what?" Rosa smiled. "Too much of a good thing, or mountain goat?"

"Do they have mountain lions in the Guatemalan Highlands? I can't picture you as a goat."

"You bet they do," she growled, making a claw with her hand. She took off up the steep trail.

"Perhaps a goat-lion, then," he puffed after her.

As usual, Rosa kept a good twenty steps on Marc. This would continue to baffle him. Each day, Rosa smoked five or six baobab cigars. Marc relished the campfire hint it left in her hair, but he'd never understood how it was mechanically possible to inhale smoke without gagging. Every Thursday, after his lecture, he walked the kilometer or so from the *rue Descartes* to the *Piscine Saint-Germain* to swim laps for an hour. She, on the other hand, made a point of never exercising, and openly laughed at those adult couples who held hands on their roller-blades along the river Seine. And yet, he was the one holding his chest, trying to keep his lungs from tumbling out, and having to set mustard-seed poultice on his knees after their races.

"You know what I mean," he puffed.

"I do," she said. "And I win."

At the top, they had to hold onto each other not to be blown off by the wind. They listened to the crashing waves until they couldn't feel their earlobes anymore.

And to be sure, Marc's mother was a bit, er, challenging. For one, Alma insisted on calling Rosa, Rose. She couldn't get used to the idea of her son's fiancée (she also insisted on calling her that, even though there hadn't been any talk of engagement between them) being a foreigner.

"To her, you'd be a foreigner even if you'd only driven the fifteen kilometers from Caen," Marc's brother Loïc noted softly around coffee as Alma dozed off in her late husband's armchair. Alma also kept referring to Rosa's native Guatemala as Ecuador, or Peru, alternatively. Apparently, she was unaware that any piece of land south of Dallas, Texas (identifiable solely thanks to its eighties namesake T.V. series) had separate histories, oppressions, or aspirations. When Marc tried to explain, Alma put a lid on that conversation with a curt, "They're all socialists with mixed blood, aren't they?"

At night, from across the chasm of their twin beds in Marc's adolescent bedroom, Rosa said, "You are my first *ojo azul.*" Her face looked queerly small underneath the movie-size poster of Friedrich Nietzsche's.

"Your first blue-eyes, huh?" Marc was trying to decide whether he should be flattered, or something else. In the pillow, his fingers clasped under the base of his skull. He sighed. The stretch in his armpits and shoulders felt good. "So?"

"So *que?*"

"So, how is it?"

"How is what? Lying down with a skinny man who speaks with his hands and asks too many questions?" Rosa's bare breast plopped out of the covers as she reached out to poke his upper arm.

He unclasped his fingers and raised his hand, waving it in the air between them like a ballet dancer—middle finger slightly in, pinky finger raised. Rosa's breast quivered with her laughter. She pinched the tip of his manicured ring finger and held it in place. Her knuckles were like tree roots, dwarfing his own, which were blue in the glare from the white lampshade on the white wall.

Regardless of how tightly they hung onto each other, how far apart would they have to remain? Her childhood, picking coffee at La Finca. Her baby brother stiff, life gone, from inhaling the pesticide they sprayed right on top of their backs. The stomachs swollen under thin blankets ornate with bright suns rising above conquests. His, snuggled under his hypoallergenic duvet with Jules Verne and a flashlight. *Can common ambitions and shared diaper duties fill in that rift?* They wondered in silence, watching each other's fingers walk on air.

No sooner was Ruben done with his shift than he ran to the monkish room where he spent the night when he was too tired to drive back to his Albuquerque home. He sat on the bare floor and meditated.

For privacy, Anastasia had conjured up a lovely Dreamscape log-cabin a little way away from their camp. It had been a long time since Anastasia had wanted walls anywhere near. Once her husband Karl had transitioned on to the next plane, the gurgling of the waterfall and the shade from the coconut palms were all the containment she ever wanted. So this was new. This was momentous. And it was where Ruben and Anastasia liked to *rendez-vous.*

She encouraged him to rehabilitate the masseuse skills his cousin Miranda had taught him and he'd allowed to lapse.

"The spiritual practice that has led you to us," Anastasia explained, "is bound to dead-end if you don't bring a deepened understanding of the body to bear on it. Humans don't transcend by leaving the body behind, as if it were a roadblock on the path to Nirvana. Our body is our vehicle to enlightenment. Our breath is the road *and* the horizon. Our mind is the trailer, with all the extra baggage." She set out a large sheepskin directly on the rough floor planks. Although it was warm enough to want your skin bared, an old iron wood-stove glowed in the corner. "For atmosphere," she said.

"*Atmosphère, atmosphère…*" Ruben recited.

"… *est-ce que j'ai une gueule d'atmosphère?*" She jumped in. When she spoke, Anastasia's head bobbed, like the Indians with whom Ruben sometimes practiced yoga at the Albuquerque India Cultural Center. He found it irresistible.

"Arletty, *Hotel du Nord.* So you're a fan of old French movies too?" Ruben got up to check on each of the seven volcanic stones he'd laid out to heat on top of the stove.

"Not all French movies," Anastasia said. "Only Arletty. I think I might have been her, in my last incarnation. Always been fond of playing the no-nonsense, romantic prostitute."

Satisfied that the stones were ready, Ruben gestured for Anastasia to lie, face down, on the sheepskin. She let her silk robe drop limp at her feet, and shivered as the skin of her belly released into the tickle of the fur. She moaned, stacking her hands underneath her chin. Ruben kneeled down beside her, cupped the back of her skull in one warm hand, and ever so gently, guided her head to rotate so her right cheek could rest on her hands. Anastasia let out another moan, and when he began to run light fingertips up and down her entire back-body, she felt garlands of glee lighting up the sides of her spine, scurrying from the tip of her heels to the crown of her head.

"What do you mean, deepened understanding of the body?" His whisper was a feather inside her ear. He set a hot stone on her lower back. Goose bumps all over.

Unwilling to speak her answer just yet, Anastasia groaned, thinking. *Deepened: more than dumb meat. Pleasure. Pain. More than matter's eternal present: the entirety of the past. More than time: energy and infinite potential. Desire. The totality of creation and destruction. Eros and Thanatos. Life, death, rebirth. The soul substance adheres to fingernails, hair, excrement, saliva. It sticks to all the things the soul has ever touched.*

Later, when they both laid, entwined and sticky, Anastasia felt ready to speak again.

"Karl was the sweetest of hearts most days, but a little macho man on the edges. Lakota men are harder-headed than the billy-goat my Dad kept on our land. Renegade was his name. His locks had grown over his eyes, so for all intents and purposes blind, and crazier by the day from bumping into trees, he was in a constant state of fury. Piotr-the-barber once tried to give him a shave, but he hollered, and kicked, and there were vapors coming out his nostrils. Even I was scared."

"The barber tried to give the billy-goat a shave?" Ruben played with one of her locks.

"No! Karl did not once in his entire lifetime let anyone cut his hair, facial or otherwise. He said no human being other than his own dead mother and myself was ever allowed to touch it. I know he lied, because the man was definitely not a virgin when he came to find me in Bratislava!"

"How would you know?" Ruben drew circles around her navel

with her lock.

"Well, he had this way with his tongue and my—"

"Shhhhh." Ruben started to snake down along the side of her, his body hair bristling against her skin. He pressed his face into her Venus mound, mumbling, "Your juicy papaya?"

"You're tickling!" She prayed he wouldn't stop. "Sorry to disappoint you, *hombre*, but my papaya hasn't been juicy in a while. And I think it's time to feed the animals." Gently, she pushed his face away and hopped to her feet. "Believe me, you do not want to mess with Attila's dinner habits."

When she walked away from his naked body, Ruben fell back onto the sheepskin and sighed.

"You can't shock me, you know. I'm a body mechanic," he said.

She opened the door to let the wolf in. Attila glanced distractedly at Ruben, and went straight to his empty bowl. He sat, gazing up at his mistress as she carved out white bits from the smoked ham that hung from a butcher's hook. The wolf let out a whistling yawn and licked his chops.

"I work with bodies," Ruben said, rolling on his side to prop himself up on his elbow. "Their twisty rods and crinkles, their wet membranes, their smells. It's all—"

"—Dumb meat?" Anastasia offered, throwing a long piece of shiny rind to the wolf, who immediately began to chew, with an anxious eye still trained on the shank.

"No! Actually, it's all light," Ruben said. "Grosser or subtler concatenations of spirit, pneuma, Ch'i, whatever you want to call it."

"Kundalini?" She squatted down to leave shreds in Attila's bowl. She patted the wolf on the collar, and finally looked at Ruben, whose pectorals had turned waxy in the stove's glow. He nodded, and she floated toward him, wetting her lips. "Well, you're certainly getting *my* Kundalini awakened with that look and all the hunky mechanics talk." She mock-fell down by his side and rubbed her bare back against the sheepskin, groaning like a bear.

Ruben brushed the locks off her forehead and tucked them behind her ear. The motherly gesture felt uncanny coming from a man who, just a few weeks ago, knew nothing of her, or the world she inhabited. He watched as a small seizure took her nipple, and joy rippled from her navel like a pebble in a lake.

This is how bodies come alive with age, he thought. *More ocean than pool.* Mesmerized, he peered at the rising waves of her, the silver bushiness at her pubis unbothered by the storm. He recalled the fourteen-year old belly of *La Flaca,* smooth as the low tide, glistening in the beach bonfire's *chiaroscuro.* How he, at fifteen, wasn't *honcho* enough to be noticed by her.

"Have I lost you?" Anastasia asked.

Ruben's response was to bury his face into her. The softest of her yielded to his stubble. "No." His words bounced like moths against the walls of her insides. "I think you found me, *mi amor.* You found me."

Prune didn't own much, so how hard could packing be? Over the four days that Ruben and Grenadine had spent pep-talking her, they'd all collaborated to smuggle her things, bit by bit, into Grenadine's room to avoid triggering the children's anguish and the staff's suspicion.

"I don't want to go," Prune said, collapsing into a mole hill of her clothes on top of Grenadine's bed.

"Of course you do. How the fuck else are you going to find your mother? Google her up? Dear Google, Please help me find my mother who's been abducted I don't know why by I don't know who after having been on the run from mysterious assassins for fifteen years." Prune chortled.

"Aww. Come here!" Grenadine pulled her close enough to lap at the tears off the corners of her eyes.

"It tickles."

Grenadine's tongue lightened its touch, but kept going—now tracing the edges of Prune's nostrils.

"Stop it! Gross!" Prune wiped her face with her sleeve. Then quickly, as if by accident, she kissed Grenadine. It was furtive, a non-committal kiss—almost a question. Grenadine answered with a full, frank, unequivocal kiss. It was the most stupefying thing Prune had ever experienced, and she wanted to know if it might just be a fluke, or—

The second time they kissed it was even stranger. Not that Prune had much experience with kissing. There'd been a couple of boys, one with velvet above his lip. That felt like when she was too eager to get to the artichoke heart, and forgot to remove the tiny hair. It made her gums itch. One boy told his sister, who told Prune, that she turned her tongue too fast.

Grenadine's kiss happened too hastily to worry about tempo, and too softly to think about tongues. There was stillness. No bumping into teeth, no nibbling. Their lips simply forgot to end where the other's began. They became live membrane. The light and the fluttering of an eye. Grenadine's fingertips smoothed out the contours of Prune's face. Jawline, brow, the pulsing in her eyelids: rewired. *My face no longer a face, but the map of a treasure hunt. Somewhere near the south pole of me, there is a will.* But Prune's body took its time to respond to intent and when it did, Grenadine stopped her with one hand.

"Let me," she breathed into her hair. Grateful, Prune let her.

Then it was late, and Prune's backpack was a porcupine. She picked it up to try it on, saying, "What if I can't find her, Gren? Or worse."

"You'll find her. I wouldn't want to be a CIA, or DST, or Mossad, or whatever so-called Intelligence pawn out on the prowl right now. If they knew that Prune Michaux is on their tracks, I bet they wouldn't sleep too soundly tonight." She raised her voice to address an imaginary crowd. "You hear me, dickheads? My woman is coming to get you! You better stock up on TP 'cause some of you are gonna be shitting your pants!"

"What if she's dead?"

"Well. You need the truth, don't you?"

"That's what I think."

For the nth time, Prune unlatched her pack and reran her inventory. Five pairs of grayish underwear, one colorful sweater knitted by Rosa, an old Catholic-school skirt that had grown too short, books—too many, they agreed, but Prune couldn't part with any. A bottle of dark-purple nail polish. A Swiss Army knife. A palm-size felt owl that Pedro had made with superglue "for good luck and clear vision," he said. "When you don't know what to do next, ask the owl," he'd explained. Prune smiled at the thought of him. In just a few months of captivity, puberty, and heartbreak, Pedro had acquired some kind of ancient wisdom. The unbearable will do that, if you let it. It has a way of fast-forwarding you through the centuries of grief out of which old knowing rises.

The bell rang curfew. In less than four hours, Ruben would be waiting for Prune at the shed. He swore he had a foolproof plan, and that if he told her any of it she might bust it, awful liar that she was.

Grenadine reached for the kitchen matches she kept on her bedside table, and lit the candle she'd planted in a tiny terra-cotta pot. "I guess it's too late to go back to your Ward," she said, patting the bed cover next to her with one hand and switching the lamp off with the other.

"Will you hold me?" In the dark, Prune's voice sounded cavernous. "Just hold me?"

Grenadine slipped under the covers in her Wonder Woman PJ's. "Come here," she said, the open sheet an invitation to safety.

To take the edge off, Dawn Hetherington had a couple small glasses of sweet Port wine before she got to the Happy Goose. General McMitt had been breathing down her neck more than usual lately, but it wasn't like him to call in an emergency meeting like this. Dawn barely touched her moo goo and had three Tsingtao while he scarfed down mounds of bean-curd tofu and wilted broccoli. When the neolithic restaurant owner expressed surprise that he'd foregone his usual twice-roasted duck, McMitt explained that his new wife was a pilates instructor who had made it clear she couldn't envision kissing—much less doing you-know-what—with a man who ate food-with-a-face. When came time for the fortune cookies, McMitt still hadn't shared any meaningful information, and Dawn had done all she could not to let him read her less-than-flattering thoughts.

"Right or left?" McMitt held both fists out for Dawn to pick a fortune.

"Oh, get on with it, Nathaniel. You know I have no more tolerance for rebuses than I have for men who wear white socks."

The General glanced at his immaculate socks. "Well, I guess that puts me on your shit list."

"Honey, you've been on my shit list ever since you showed up with a lowball offer and the scorn you usually reserve for those who survive on cowpats south of the equator."

His blade-thin lips flattened into what must have been a smile. Absorbed in the task of unwrapping his fortune cookie he said, "Well, that didn't keep you from asking for more when I— how should I say—"

"When you ate me out? I must admit, Nathaniel, you are moronic with your fingers, but your tongue knows how to make a vulva salivate." The rim of his scalp, where the buzz-cut drew a fuzzy shadow, flushed with delight. Over the course of their two-and-a-half year-long on-and-off "partnership," McMitt had learned how to hone a compliment from Dawn's peculiar affections. Indeed, he prided himself on his cunnilingus skills, which he'd practiced assiduously on the bruised peaches that, back on the farm, his father threw aside to feed the hogs. Alternating between tongue taps and full-lipped sucking, knowing when to alter the tempo, surrounding the target without overpowering it—a good cunnilingus boiled down to what Sun-Tzu commended in *The Art of War*: always leave the enemy an escape route. *That way*, McMitt inferred, *when he does surrender, you know your victory is total.*

"Sure you don't want it today?" The general pushed toward Dawn a mangled cookie with the white slip sticking out.

"I have little time for your maladroit flirtation, dearest. Nor do I believe in luck." She pressed her hands into the tabletop to help herself up. He reached out to pull a strand of hair off her forehead and she swatted at his hand. "Don't talk bollocks, Nat. You know that wealth, not fortune, is what I care about. So just tell me how much."

"Well, the President has given me little leeway for negotiations. I will have to—"

"How much?" She yelled. Several heads turned away from the pile of crab Rangoon on the buffet to glare at them. The fortune drifted out and as it floated on down, Dawn read, "Your respect for others will be your ticket to success."

Her laughter started with a shiver below the navel. It gathered in spastic waves round the throat to rush out of her mouth all at once, like vomit.

Once home, Dawn leaned the small of her back inside the front door. She winced when the Louboutin stilettos came off and her toes stirred back to life. With one shoe in each hand, she trotted across the luscious carpet, pausing to dig her feet into the wool, enveloping as a lover's mouth. Through the netting of her tights, the sheep skin awakened those hungry spaces between toes that shoes cancel out. Aiming at the full-length mirror across the room, she tossed the Louboutin, one on the heels of the other. She thought she looked palsied as she hopped toward the bar, trying to extract herself from her tights.

Thankful for the cool thrust of the countertop against her pubic bone, Dawn reached up for a martini glass, opted for the one with a zigzag stem, and pulled the refrigerator open with the tip of her foot. She frowned at having to straighten the Perrier bottles, which had slipped out of alignment. She reached inside the door for a Miller High Life, slammed bottle and glass down on the counter, swiveled around, and unzipped her skirt. She wiggled out of the Armani sheath and started to hum La Callas. The jacket landed in a heap at her feet, on cue with "*jamais voulu de roi.*" She reached under the loose back of her shirt to unclasp her bra, then pulled it out of her sleeve, like a bunny out of a hat. On the tremolo of "*L'Amououououour, l'amououououour* " (Dawn was finding her opera voice now), she waived the bra at the empty room, and tossed it toward the empty couch. The bra flopped down three inches from her feet. Dawn couldn't remember what came after *l'amour*, so she started whistling along, turned back around, popped the beer open, and poured it in the martini glass. She loved that it looked like Champagne, but tasted like watered down piss. *Just like me*, she thought. She gulped a swig that spilled out of the wide rim and lazied down along the line of her jaw.

The beer acted fast. Soon, the humiliation of the White House's underhanded reluctance to support her project in the only way that truly mattered, i.e., le moola, would melt away in the Dead-Sea-salt gurgle of her whirlpool. For all his four stars and two-thousand favors owed on the hill, Nathaniel McMitt was a douche. She would just have to bypass him and go straight to the media—weren't they the only ones doing the actual governing these days, anyway?

Of course she'd lied to the General. She couldn't care less about money—as long as her yacht's fifteen-hundred dollars-a-day anchoring in the Monaco marina could be maintained. What

Dawn really wanted was what no one had been able to give her so far: the Truth—that is, public recognition that she, Dawn Hetherington, had risen above her father's mediocre fiddlings with the kind of third-rate hedge-funds that precipitated the City to the rim of total collapse back in the nineties. Forget Margaret Thatcher. Forget Dick Cheney and Robert Oppenheimer and Mark Zuckerberg. Dawn Hetherington, of Clubmoor, Liverpool, owned the means to transmute the world in a time when transmutation was the only chance at survival. She wasn't going to let some bling-bling pussy-eater intimidate her out of it.

In the den, Dawn walked over to the hot tub, turned on the massive faucet, and proceeded to crack open all six sets of blinders just enough to invite in the sunset. She slipped out of her panties and dipped her toe in the vortex. It burned. The anemic skin of her calf flushed. It raised a rash on her shin, but she ground her teeth and thrust the rest of her leg in. When the phone hooted its train whistle hoot, Dawn had no intention of answering it, but she couldn't help glancing at it. "Tony" flickered like Las Vegas on the screen. *Shit.* Squinting in the sun slats, she turned off the gushing faucet, stepped out of the tub, and dried her hand. Vapor was rising out of her crimson calf and she cursed the water stain it made on the Australian carpet. The heat was making her dizzy. She went to sit on the French porcelain bidet, cold and cutting against her bare ass. She took another swig from the martini glass. The whirlpool burped angrily at the water shortage. Again, the phone hooted, and a green bubble flashed onto the screen. "French pest gone," it read. "I was right."

This time, laughter mingled with the vomit, and the heaving lasted until after the moo goo was done swaying in the carpet.

VI

Kundalini Rouses

Prune felt that always familiar and always surprising settling of the breath as soon as she found herself inside the airport's automatic glass doors. A hysterical Bichon with the under-bite of a piranha came bouncing up and down her calf, and her numbness dissolved into the kind of laughter that breaks the waters of the unfelt. This worried the dog, who snuggled back inside his master's tote. The master shot an indignant glare at Prune, and she flashed her brightest I-don't-care-if-you're-a-dick-I-adore-everyone-today grin. The man clutched purse and Bichon tighter under his arm, and squeaky-wheeled onward.

It took her eyes a moment to adjust to the pulsing light of the departures screens. Atlanta, Anchorage, Dubai, Houston, Kansas City, Las Vegas, Portland, Shanghai. Of course, no direct flight to Paris. She fingered the money belt that Ruben had made her strap under the double layer of her mother's hand-knit sweater—too warm for New Mexico's September but too chunky for her bag—and the silk undershirt that Grenadine had made her put on as a lucky charm.

Four-thousand-four-hundred-seventy-three-dollars-and-eleven-cents: The total sum of Prune's, Carla's, and Ruben's life savings, combined with the proceeds from Grenadine's pawned family heirloom—a designer necklace from her grandmother that turned out to be a nickel-silver blend instead of the white gold it claimed to be, and her mother's engagement ring. The crisp passport showed Prune to be one Virginia Lavender, eighteen-

and-a-half years of age, born in Taos, New Mexico. Ruben had scored it for nothing because his housemates from Honduras were running a successful printing business from their cellar, and they had somehow decided that the nature of Prune's journey was of the pilgrims' kind. They wanted in on the meritorious— wouldn't take no for an answer.

Four-thousand-four-hundred-seventy-three-dollars-and-eleven-cents. With that, Prune was to make her way to Paris, find her missing parents who, for all anyone knew, might be buried inside the concrete foundations of some Luxury Hilton in Dubai, and then… Well, then Rosa would know what to do, Prune hoped.

"Eleven cents is a sign." Ruben was adamant. "It's the number of spiritual mastery."

I'm going to need more than spiritual mastery to get me through this one, Prune had wanted to say. But she'd taken the belt, strapped it on just like Ruben said she should, over one arm and under the other, and when the airport traffic control drone had shouted in its loudspeaker that this lane was only for passenger drop off, and would the sir please remove his vehicle from the area, Prune had hopped on out. This was a good thing, because she really wanted to bury her face in Ruben's lap and clench her arms around his leg until he'd say, "Let's go back," like Marc had done when she'd refused to get out of the car on her first day at the *Lycée Louis-Le-Grand* and he'd taken her for hot chocolate at *Angelina's* instead.

As Prune hurried toward the sliding doors, Ruben shouted something after her, but it drowned in the drone's reprimand.

"Stop worrying." The voice was raspy like E.T.'s, and Pedro had to stretch his eyes wide to make out where it came from. The Ward Q bamboo danced psychotic shadows against the moonlit ceiling. Back home, Pedro had learned to tell himself, "Plants, just plants" when the giant palms whistled about his hammock. He'd taught himself to see them as co-pirates rather than the angry ghosts of ancestors.

"We don't need her to save ourselves." The voice was still disembodied, but less foreign. Pedro gathered his pillow in front of his chest and propped himself up in his bed. He searched the nightstand for his glasses. Suddenly, eyes flickered right in front of him.

"I know what to do. Come." Alia, of course.

"Shoot, you scared the Jesus out of me!"

Under normal circumstances, Alia would have gloated her triumph. Instead, she gripped his wrist too tight, and pulled hard enough that the pencil he'd armed himself with dropped to the floor.

"Let go!" Pedro hush-cried. "Aw!" Inadvertently, Alia had clawed the back of his hand. Tears welled up, and his eyes shone like imminent roadkill's.

Alia's "I'm sorry" rolled over the moonlit rows of beds that were beginning to stir. She pointed a finger at the gash where black blood was pearling, seemed to hesitate, and then, swift as a millipede, she tapped at the droplet, brought it to her mouth to taste, and was gone. Her blanket was still jittering when the overhead lights snapped bright, announcing Anthony's wrath.

After Dawn had slurred her most scornful admonition to date, blaming him for Prune's escape in addition to bad weather and the failure of the War on Terror, Anthony had come to the conclusion that unless he found a way to redirect the flux of authority into a flow chart that effectively placed him at the top, he might need to reexamine his professional options. But that would mean admitting to his fraternity brothers that he'd been wrong, or at least misled—might as well say naive and delusional. That did not sit well with Anthony. But since the thought of taking a stand before Dawn—or worse, McMitt and the United States institutions he represented—made Anthony's psoriasis flare up, he decided someone less perilous should pay. So he stomped directly over to Pedro's bed, seized the downy hair on either side of the boy's face, and lifted him up out of bed, bare buttocks and skinny legs all a-pedaling.

"Ay, ay, ay, ay, ay!" Pedro was trying not to scream.

"Look at that, Mr. Alvarez *almost* all grown up down there!" Anthony waved the boy around like a trophy for all to see. The cot's springs squeaked when he dropped him, and Pedro crawled under the blanket. Someone sobbed. "I can see why your sweet friend Prune decided to escape and leave all you snotty-noses behind. I have a feeling this little guy here wasn't quite enough of a man for her. She had to go out into the wide world and find herself a real mate. Don't you take it personally, Pedro, it's just hormones, you know. Girls reach a point in their lives when that's all they can think of. They *gots* to get themselves a *real* man."

There was silence, but for the intermittent lament of the harvesting machines. The children were too embarrassed to look at Pedro, and too scared to look at Anthony.

"You lie. Prune didn't leave us." Alia stood up, jaw clenched. "What did you do to her, you freak?"

"Ah, there's the clever girl." Anthony was genuinely amused. "You're right, we did have plans to take her somewhere else, make her less of a leech on you guys. Not fair, having her strut about, never being harvested because she's too old to produce anything worth our while, while you upstanding citizens of the Earth are lying here, sacrificing yourselves for the greater good."

Ambling toward Anthony in her nightgown, Alia was Joan of Arc, unflinching towards fire, armies, or purgatory. Behind him, Pedro reached for his pajama pants.

"But you're wrong," Anthony continued. "Prune really did leave. She really did get tired of you."

"Or you," Pedro spat, up on his feet now. He was only a third of the man's bulk, but stood at about the same five-foot-eight.

"Yeah, Prune doesn't put up with bullies," she said, close enough to punch Anthony in the nose, and wondering what it would be like to feel his cartilage ply against her knuckles. The thought made her sneer.

"Yeah, Prune is not escaped," squeaked Lou. Standing on her bed in a fierce warrior posture, she was waving Sam the pink flamingo like a sword. "Prune loves me. When she comes back you be dead asleep and never wake up, like Carla."

Anthony flinched. He started toward the curtain. In the doorway he turned around, fanned his gaze across the Ward, and as he switched off the lights, his baritone echoed against the dark. "You spoiled little shit-heads think this hasn't been a walk in the park? You're in for a treat. And go wash. It smells like piss in here."

A roar scurried toward him. He fumbled for the switch, but in the second it took the fluorescent lights to stutter back on, the sharp beak of Lou's flamingo hit him in the center of the chest. It hurt. It would bruise. Sam got tangled in the little girl's hair as she went to stab Anthony again, and her shriek hit the sound barrier. With one hand, Anthony seized the flamingo's neck and snapped it in half. Caught in Lou's hair, the head dangled in front of her, pitiful. This stopped her dead in her tracks. She cradled the rest of Sam's body like an infant, and drifted back to her bed, petting its wing. The flamingo's head still dangled in front of her face and when Pedro stepped in to untangle it, Lou pushed him away, climbed back into her cot, pulled the blanket over her legs, and began to rock her flamingo's remains to the soft tune of *Frère Jacques*. Several children began to hum along with her the song that Prune used to sing to them. Anthony turned off the lights and walked away.

At five-fifteen A.M., when Augustine-the-Squeezer— morning shift caretaker—arrived at Ward Q, he grumbled, "What in the Good Lord Mr. Potato Head is going on here?" Chatter hung in mid-air to acknowledge the grown up's entrance.

Someone turned down the volume on the radio, then the beehive buzz picked right back up. Small arms spiked the white beds like knitting-needles in soft spools. Augustine bounced between bed rows, shakily shaking his finger at those who'd piled up pell-mell in threes and fours on top of the covers. A few guffaws erupted here and there. It was hard to take him seriously, with his convex forehead squeezed between yellow lion-eyes that melded with frothy sideburns. Lou did, however—take him seriously. She took seriously the swirls in her tummy when he came around. Like an indigestion, but pinker.

To Lou, feelings came in colors, and pink meant happy. Green meant sad. Blue meant scary. When purple came, Lou usually lost consciousness—purple was: no feel. But when the Squeezer came, Lou's tummy went pink. She knew that, under cover of monitoring the Ward's equanimity (one of the few items on his guidelines checklist that left room for interpretation), he was looking for her. She hid under her blanket, but her grin paraded all four of her teeth. She couldn't wait to show him the fifth, tiny arrowhead peeking through soft red gums on the bottom. He would be so proud that he would hold her against his bony chest. He would hum, and she would feel the bass boom of his heart, right there on the other side, rippling through her cheek. Slow. Slower. The clicking sound of the machine's compressor would grow faint. All the cackling in the Ward real quiet. Everything real quiet, and warm.

All pink.

They had agreed that it would be safer to avoid email, and for obvious reasons cell phones were strictly forbidden on campus. For Grenadine, the elation of the first days after Prune's escape gave way to nail-biting alarm by day five. By day ten of no news, worry had wormed its way into graphic, terrifying, and ritual-ridden insomnia.

"What is wrong with me?" Grenadine asked her reflection in the bathroom mirror. "Calling Prune my queen, and invoking Goddesses like the hoodoo witch all those white pundits expect me to be. Get ahold of yourself, Grenadine Annabelle Marigny!" She slapped her own cheek. The surge of energy was immediate. Breaking things didn't do it for her anymore. Shattered porcelain, with its cat-in-heat pitch, had once brought Grenadine some relief from her most abject feelings. In fact, she had become a liability at her thrift-store job in Yazoo City, and so the washed-out blond with the permanently plucked eyebrows (what was her name? Mary-Lou? Mary-Jo?) had told her to hit the road. It was too bad because Grenadine had actually loved that job. She loved the old wax; the citrus, and pine, and Clorox smell at Wild Thangs. She liked giving old stuff another chance. She even liked listening to Mary-Something drone on about what a lowdown motherfucker her ex was.

Grenadine slapped harder, more methodically, making sure her fingers bounced right back for better effect. *It's like playing drums, or my cheek against a horse's belly.* Grenadine braced herself for another slap, a harder one, or perhaps one closer to the temple and the delicate eardrum.

Ruben's joyful Rumba knock on the door made her jump. In the mirror, she eyed the rosy splotches on her cheeks. *Good thing me Neruba princess*, she told herself, *or some nice guy might have to rescue me from myself.* She went to unlatch the door.

"Yo, Ruben. *Que tal*, old man?"

"*Hola, muñeca!*" Ruben went to kiss her on the cheek.

She punched him just a bit too hard in the shoulder. "How many times do I have to tell your macho Latino ass that I'm not your fucking doll?" His gaze lingered on the inflamed cheekbone.

"I need to show you something. Come." And he tugged her after him.

Night happens fast in the mountains. It was so dark in the shed that Grenadine could barely distinguish the outline of Ruben's body. She kept her eyes focused on the stars that blinked through slits in the walls. Those memories of light made the memory of Prune more alive, less of a mirage. Sitting on Prune's meditation blanket was better than reading and re-reading that note with the faded daisy taped to it that she'd left under the pillow. For the first time since Prune had left, Grenadine could actually feel, not just some dead slabs of worry, but the warmth of the girl, the trust she poured in that broad-toothed smile of hers.

Without a word, Ruben had dragged Grenadine here, sat her down with hands on her shoulders, plopped himself down in front of her and, with the unwavering white of his eyes glistening in the dusk, he'd said, "Prune loves you. She has magic. She will be back for you. You are too much sorrow to travel now, but tell me your sorrow. After, you will be more light, and I can show you the magic." And somehow, that had done it.

After her father had been acquitted by an all-white, eighty-percent male jury, but ordered to stay away from fifteen-year-old Grenadine and her sister, Grenadine's mother had tried to get them to a therapist.

"Therapist: the rapist—can't you see?" Grenadine was adamant. "It's the same fucking word, same fucking scene. The rape of my body has barely ended, now let the rape of my mind begin, why don't you!" Grenadine knew quite a few of Hell's backstreets by then, and there wasn't any way in hell she was going to go lie down on some couch with some mind rapist to offer up her sick insides for augury. "I ain't no Greek bird. What kind of omen would come out of that reading, pray you?"

But here, in the dark of the shed, with only the thin layers of Prune's blanket between her ass and the cold earth, what was there to lose?

So she did. Grenadine agreed to speak about her father.

"The last time I saw him, he was old. The rage in his face had withered and what was left was weariness. There was ash in his hair, and fog in the gaze that used to petrify me. A patch of stubble wandered along his imprecise jawline. Dandruff perched on the collar of his tux. He did not open the dance with his daughter, my sister the bride. Instead, he limped back and forth for seconds and thirds of crawfish étouffée between the buffet and a side table where he'd been parked with the second cousins. He spent the toasts avoiding eye contact and nibbling on crumbs off the tablecloth. He did not talk to me. Didn't ask how my mother had died. I wish I could say he was pitiful, but it would mean I felt pity.

"I saw death crawling up on him like lice. I saw impotence. I swear, I even saw repentance. I wish I could say his decay gladdened me, but it would mean I felt glad. All I could feel was the weight of time's stillness—the barb of his hipbone forever digging into my thigh, his wet mouth against the side of my neck, the hot relief of my piss spreading down the leg of my pajamas after my body had betrayed me with its curiosity."

Grenadine searched for shock, disgust, a blink of Ruben's glimmering eyes. She found only steadiness, unwavering. She kept going.

"It is not true that time heals. Time freezes, and grips, and stiffens. Time is arthritis. Look at old folks." She thought she saw him smile, but it was too dark to tell. "Ruben, I am no more capable of saving my Gaia than my mother was of saving me. What does that make me?" She surprised herself by hoping for an answer—something other than reassurance, more genuine than pity. She listened for his breath: long and deep, a poor measure of her impatience.

Finally, Ruben said, "It is good. It is ok to be angry *and* to love at once time. This is important. I think maybe Anastasia will help with you and Gaia. I will introduce."

"Introduce? I thought Anastasia was in that coma world of

little Carla's. Prune had to train like a Special Olympian for this shit. How do you suggest I get there?"

"Maybe I ask Anastasia to come here?" Ruben didn't sound too sure of himself. Or else he'd been spending too much time with those American pre-teens who inflect every sentence with a rise in their voice. Some weird generational thing?

Grenadine couldn't remember: at what point had everything become a question?

"There he is! Attila, you tramp, I can't leave you alone, can I? One minute you're with one girl… I barely turn my back, and there you are, curled up beside some stranger and groaning like a Swedish porn-movie star! Excuse my wolf, Ms. Did he use fang-persuasion to pressure you into petting him?"

Grenadine yanked her hand away from between Attila's ears. She shook her feet dry and gathered her socks and boots. "He came out of nowhere and just plopped himself down. I could have sworn it was a dog." She glanced at the wolf's balding pink belly. With his head raised off the ground and his tongue hanging out the side of his mouth like a cartoon K.O., Attila shot Anastasia a reproachful look.

"Don't you blame me, Mister. I couldn't turn you into a Pomeranian even if I wanted to." Anastasia watched Grenadine lace up her boots, then she hop-scotched her way across the creek like a schoolgirl. Her bare breasts bobbed up and down.

Grenadine tried not to stare, and failed. Long locks tangled around the crone's head like a snake's nest. White folks with dreadlocks peeved Grenadine. *It wasn't enough to wrench us from our land and toss us about this one to eradicate our bonds, language, meaning. Now they have to ape our roots?* But trying to sound civil, she said, "Ruben said you wanted to meet me?"

125

Absorbed in whatever transpired below the surface, Anastasia squatted down by the creek. The old witch had no trouble keeping her feet flat on the rock and the bounce in her knees, the long fingers interlaced on the end of her stretched arms, gave her a pubescent air. "Me, want to meet you? Why would I? He told me *you* were dying to meet *me.*" Anastasia found a stick and drew figure eights in the water. "He had to do quite a bit of convincing, I must say." She blushed a little and threw the stick in the water. Both women watched it scuttle downstream.

With no visible effort, the crone stood up. Grenadine stood across the creek from her, barely beyond arm's reach. She had on one boot, and was holding the other in her hand. The legs of her pants were rolled up and darker where they'd gotten wet. There were goose bumps on her calves.

"How do you think you got here?" The crone sounded defiant. Grenadine was starting to like her. Wrinkly at the base, her boobs drooped low, but round, and proud, and hypnotizing. It made Grenadine want to palpate them, like exotic fruit at the Asian market.

"I see," Grenadine says. "He played us."

Anastasia's sudden smile cleared up all the shadows that the fast clouds had been hurling at the ground, and the temperature rose notably. Attila startled Grenadine when he leapt across the stream to come standing next to his mistress.

Hopping on one leg while struggling to boot up the other, Grenadine looked like she might fall. "He said you could help," she said. Anastasia gestured for her to sit down. The rock felt snug at her sit bones, and Anastasia lowered herself down too.

Some people move the way others sing. There is no monotone. Everything lilts, even in the straightest of lines—a wink in the hip, a vibrato in the shoulder—and you, too, are suddenly pulsating, just from watching them. Anastasia was one of those people.

"Bring your palms together in front of your heart." The thrum lived in her voice, too. It spread all the way into the rock under them. And when she closed her eyes, Anastasia's paintbrush eyelashes lengthened toward the throbbing water.

There we go. The old hag is going to make me atone for my sins, Grenadine thought. She shifted in her seat, yet did what she was told. *Mmmh, what is this, this yielding without feeling like I'm giving in?*

"You have been given the opportunity to learn and practice this technology of self-elevation as a dispensation of Grace in answer to the longing of your soul. Use it to strive for progress, excellence, expansion, healing." Anastasia's timbre was gravelly, like it came from below the creek's bed. "Press your palms together. Touch your thumbs to your chest. Roll your shoulders back. Lengthen the back of the neck. Breathe."

The words lulled Grenadine inside the body she'd spent most of her life tugging about with as rarefied an awareness as possible. She began to sense a warm glow undulating up and down her spine. It called to mind the jellyfish exhibit she'd once seen at the Aquarium in Monterey Bay. The fish tanks had been framed with ornate gold frames and, with the room in complete darkness but for the glow from the tanks, the monstrous morphed into a sublime work of living art. Delicate blue and red threads veined the fish's translucent bodies. *Life is electric,* Grenadine had realized. She'd tried to tell her sister, but by then Evangeline was on six Vicodin a day and non-reactive. So Grenadine had written the thought down in her notebook. It seemed she might want to go back to it sometime. She hadn't, so far.

"Kundalini is one of the many names for creative energy, primal force, élan vital. This vital impulse is always dual. She is Shakti, the manifesting power of the universe flowing from spirit to matter. In her reverse flux, she flows back to her source, in spirit. Through Kundalini's flow, matter and spirit—the gross and the subtle—manifest as opposite ends of a single continuum: as One." As she said this, Anastasia's entire body began to throb. Grenadine couldn't tell if it was the motion, the words, or some invisible drug in the air they breathed, but she started to feel—what should she call it? Ease?

"Close your eyes," Anastasia continued. "Roll them up and in to the third eye, the eye of intuition, of inner knowing. Go within. Let this be your own experience. The path of Kundalini is the path of return to the higher self. On this path, the body becomes a participant in spiritual awakening, a conduit to energies of a high spiritual nature. Your subtle body holds the key to your victory, Grenadine." Grenadine didn't understand what the crone was saying, but she didn't mind. She just wanted her to keep going.

"Now, bring your hands to your knees and begin to circle your navel around, counter-clockwise. This is the direction of self-initiation. Ignite yourself! Stoke the fire at your navel. Remember to breathe. Remember to remember. Wake up. Wake up. Wake the spinal juices pooled at the base of your spine!"

Grenadine's racing thoughts slowed down, but it wasn't like fatigue, when the mind has to wade through molasses of frustration and numbness. She felt herself growing taller, and crisp; her spine loosened as it reached for the holes in the clouds.

"Now, come back to center and circle around the other way. Notice the field resisting this new direction—this new choice you have made. Now notice the resistance easing up as you commit to your new direction."

For a split second, Grenadine blinked her eyes open—an old hyper-vigilant reflex. Modeling the posture, the crone was making love to the ground, but there was nothing obscene about it—none of the awkwardness or self-consciousness: just bliss. Grenadine decided she wanted whatever Anastasia was having. She closed her eyes, and kept grinding.

"Plug your sacrum, that sacred tail, into the Earth. Imagine your spine is drilling down into the rock, down through the water below, and the sand, and silt, and gravel, deeper, deeper into the fiery core of the Earth."

The creek thumped. Anastasia's words wove in with Grenadine's heartbeat like a safety net into which she could collapse. *Paradise is, perhaps, to be defenseless without feeling threatened.* Thoughts sprung from another part of Grenadine's, a part she'd thought dead but that was coming back to life now—the only part of her capable of this experience: perfect, untouched innocence. *Could it be that it has never left me?*

"Back to center, begin to flex your spine forward as you inhale, and round the back as you exhale. Keep going. Do not fear hearing yourself breathe. Breath is life. Breath is pure vitality. Move. Rustle in the wind. You live by your breath and you die by your breath."

Shuuu, thump, ta-tum, ta-tum, shuuuuuuu… Puff of life asserting itself like a suitor. Chest balloons, wings shooting out, respiration of water rush, aspiration. The guide inhaled, exhaled. All was quiet and breath, like a cello solo exhuming arpeggios from the silence.

Just when Grenadine was sweatily pumping her left foot behind her raised buttocks to the intoxicating groove of Anastasia's cheering, Ruben appeared from behind the crone's boulder. Attila stirred to make some room next to Anastasia, and Ruben sat down like a perfect yogi, legs crossed, chest out, chin impeccably level with the ground. He took a moment to center himself, then came right down on all fours to pump his leg behind him, twirl his arms, and pump his navel along with the women. He and Anastasia were in sync, radiating the kind of eye-of-the-storm serenity exhibited on the cover of self-help books. Maybe it was the crazy amount of deep breathing, or something about the fast-paced rotation of her limbs, but Grenadine had to admit that she was feeling more alive than she had since she'd gone canoeing with her family at Tickfaw Park and bonked a napping alligator on the head with her oar.

Anastasia led them beyond exhaustion, to the place where pleasure and pain meld. They lay down on their backs, palms up.

"Relax… Relax and let the healing begin. If given half a chance, the body will repair itself on its own. Like you—like every thing and every process—your mind-body-soul seeks homeostasis—perfect, dynamic equilibrium. Give it that chance now." Anastasia's voice was reaching Grenadine in sheets through the bubbling of the brook. "Open up to the experience of the infinite in the finite. You are not a human being having a spiritual experience, you are a spiritual being having a human experience."

With the pulse of the water under her rock, and the pulse of the fire under the water, Grenadine saw herself spiraling up a funnel of light. Up and up she went, slowly flapping her indigo wings—the exact hue of the umbilical cord that had once tethered her to plump Gaia.

"Ask for what you need. Ask for anything. If not now, then when? What are you afraid of? Why hold back?" Anastasia's words opal crisp.

If not now, then when?

Convulsions seized Grenadine's midriff. *Don't hold back.* Gaia's gray eye, blind with infancy. Grenadine's father's gray skin, so close that the pores are planets, the man is a galaxy. The parachute at Grenadine's solar plexus palpitates like jelly fish in a Michelangelo frame. Inside her abdomen, the tornado rises and falls, rises and falls. Gaia's tummy is warm marble against her cheek. *Don't hold back.* Grenadine's arms are glued to the rock, but her legs! Her legs are free and mighty. Grenadine kicks, so hard her hips bounce back. Kick, bounce, kick, bounce, kick… *Rhaaaaaaaaaaaaaaaa… Don't hold back… Rhaaaaaaaaaaaaaaaa…* Her father's severed head drops, blood gushes… Her wings! Blotches of her father's blood on her wings. The stains grow and blossom into Anthony's face, a flash of his gorgeous smile and then the strain of selfish sex, the O mouth of orgasm. *Nooooooooooooooo…* Grenadine shakes her head no. Her pelvis follows, *no, no, nooooooooooooooo,* and collapses.

Easy, the breath slides down and across the chasm of her solar plexus. A golden spiral gently pulls Grenadine's awareness deeper into the subtle, the exquisite non-space behind her navel. Three slender beings await there. Neither male nor female, but Enoki mushroom-like in their togetherness, they radiate. Grenadine is positive that she's never seen them, yet they know her completely.

"Of course," they explain, "You are of us." The knot between Grenadine's shoulder blades lets loose, like a ballerina's bun after the concert. Her tears tickle inside her ears.

Then why? She wants to know. *Why did you let him?*

In chorus, they emit, "Because your soul wanted to know. So you could help others." Sarcasm comes to mind, then dissipates. Grenadine's fingers and toes begin to stir. She's confident that she'll know what this means, later. Deep breath in, deep breath out.

Steady, Anastasia's voice trickles in. "Bring your arms above your head for a nice, long stretch. Fold your knees into your chest, and give yourself a nice hug here. I love you, I love you. Hold under your knees, and begin to rock-and-roll, rock-and-roll forward and back on your spine, then all the way up to sitting."

Still following instructions, Grenadine touched her palms together in front of her heart. There was a world of a difference between how she felt now—who she was now—and who she had been an hour ago.

"And to seal the energy of our practice, we will sound together the mantra *Sat Nam*. It means Truth is my name. Truth is my identity. The truth is inside of me. In truth, we are one. Take a deep breath in… Saaaaaaaaaaat—" Their voices linked. Anastasia's, brightest, vibrated at the brow. Ruben's curled up around it—a spoon. Grenadine's lay underneath—a low, flat bed, but swelling like the tide. Off to the side, incongruously, there was teeny crystal—*Carla?* Attila howled, and their collective "Naaaaaaaaam" wound up one unified hum, pulsating from within each of their chests.

With Prune gone, the ficus dispatched its sadness to the whole building. Every time Pedro came in and out of the Ward, he pulled on a scrawny leaf, like girls pull petals off of daisies to count the ways they are loved. Except Pedro was keeping track of nothing—no alternatives and no choices. For a few days, he tried to read to the little ones stories from the tattered Hendersen book Prune left on his desk. But the little match girl had used up her last spark, and there were more yawns than questions in Lou's or Hakim's eyes.

This morning, Alia caught up with Pedro in the boys' bathroom. She crawled under his stall's door, brandishing a smart phone between her teeth. She wouldn't tell him where she got it, but the screen saver displayed the green and red Portuguese flag, so he guessed she'd swiped it from Squeaky-the-nurse, alias Ms. Pereira. How and why the night-shift nurse had managed to sneak a phone into The Center was another question.

Alia had an escape plan. It was full of holes. It involved a monastery which, according to MapQuest, was only fifteen miles away, deep into the desert. Everyone there, she said, had vowed total silence for all eternity, even the cooks. They had a brief argument over whether communal silence was either possible, or desirable. Alia swore it was both. Pedro pointed out that she wouldn't be able to hold her tongue for a whole minute if a good argument was to be had. She retorted that as long as there was no one around to expound stupid opinions needing redress, she'd be fine without having to talk, thank you much—especially with a good library around, which a monastery was bound to have, wasn't it?

In fact, Alia's only experience with monasteries stemmed from Umberto Eco's *The Name of the Rose*, which she'd read two-and-a-half times.

Pedro wanted to know how silent monks were going to help them spread the word about what was going on at The Center. Alia assured him that at least, the monks wouldn't rat them out to Dawn. Point taken. Once there, she said, they'd figure out the next step.

"What about Lou?" Pedro wanted to know. "Prune gone. Now us. It will break her heart."

"There's only one Paki here, as far as I know." She relished the worsening of the Swami's stuttering with each easy humiliation. "You know, the one who almost walloped Anthony."

Anthony damned himself once again for having told Dawn of the Ward Q incident. He said, "That wasn't…"

"I know. It was the four-year old, who socked you with her plastic flamingo. My bad."

"I m-m-meant whi-whi-whh…"

"Which nurse, Dawn?" Anthony sighed. He felt a bit queasy each time he watched her jubilation at undermining people. It wasn't so much a matter of moral conscience on his part. Envy, perhaps? The ease—almost grace, really—with which she projected shame was exquisite.

"If I may, I think the mulatto man can't be trusted," Anthony said.

"Old Augustine? A bit senile, isn't he?"

"Maybe. Mostly, I'm afraid he's getting too attached. I heard him sing a lullaby to the comatose one."

"That wouldn't surprise me. Augustine is a softie. I should know, he just about raised me."

"That o… olll… old man?"

"He raised you?" It was hard for Anthony to picture Dawn as a small girl having to be raised.

"Well, let's say he was around a lot when no one else was. Not that I have anything to complain about. Posh boarding school, summers in Ibiza, Christmases in Mégève, and Augustine shadowing me like some bloody Dorian Gray. He must have uttered a total of fifty-five words in the eight or nine years he worked for my parents. I could never tell if he was a cretin or a genius. You know how those things are."

John nodded.

Anthony said, "No, actually I don't know. What would make you think he was a genius?"

"When I was twelve or thirteen, I became quite angry at my

mother—typical teenage girl witlessness, I suppose. The poor woman had better things to do than attend to a needy, self-centered, acne-covered girl. She was busy pioneering progressive energy policies at Davos so that the world would be ready for *us*—for Chinergy. She trail-blazed so that girls like me could break the glass ceiling." Absentmindedly, Dawn sucked on her teeth. "My mother was busy saving the world, and I, dopey teenager that I was, was busy resenting her for it."

This promised to be juicy. Anthony gestured for John—fidgety as if he had to pee—to take a seat next to him in the armchair across from Dawn's colossal desk.

Dawn continued, bolstered by her audience's full attention. "So, I began to nick stuff. It started with shoes, of course. Obsessions have a way to get handed down from one generation to the next."

"That's why we prefer to start with a blank slate here," beamed Anthony. "Without parents to pass down their neuroses, children maintain their purity and the concomitant quality of their vital energy. No expectations means no resentment."

It was impossible to tell if he was being sarcastic or not. Dawn didn't care.

But John nodded, exclaiming, "Karmic freedom approximated!"

"Well, Mother bought a backup of everything, so she didn't notice I was stealing from her, even after I showed up for tea with her Chanel flats two sizes too big. But Augustine noticed. Without saying a word, he picked up the shoes from under my bed that night, and replaced them in her wardrobe exactly where they belonged, on top of the box they came in. Next, I got into her underwear… John, that will be all, you can go now." This, Dawn added as if awakening from a dream.

John began to protest, but Anthony motioned that he'd better get moving. After the Swami mouseyly closed the door behind him, Dawn cleared her throat. "My mother had the most amazing collection of underwear. You would have loved it, darling. All black lace. Small silk roses threaded into the trim—gold, silver, white. Bustiers, garter belts. No thongs—father felt they were only for harlots, or Brazilian gymnasts. Eventually, mother took note that some were missing. When asked, I blamed it on Augustine. Of course, no one believed me, but he got a scolding all the same. Threats. He didn't even try to deny anything."

"That's just moronic. Some ridiculous martyr complex black people need to get over. Or plain cowardice."

Dawn glared at Anthony. It always puzzled her when he spoke about black people as if he wasn't. She said, "No, I don't think that's it. I think it's the genius of not caring what others think of him."

"Well, that's just unconscionable."

"And of carrying on loving no matter what. I assume that's what they call Unconditional Love?"

"Whatever." Anthony stood up. "Sounds like I was right, though. The old fool can't be trusted."

"No one can." Dawn smirked. "Have you found the girl, by the way?" She fidgeted with a ponderous lighter.

"On a flight to Paris, as expected."

"How cliché. I take it we have people waiting for her at Charles-de-Gaulle?"

"Yes, but not to bring her back. Right now she's more useful roaming around the City of Lights."

"Free publicity?"

"Yes, that. And if all goes well, she'll stumble upon helpful information about her parents."

"What about them?"

"We don't know, yet. But if the secret services are involved in their disappearance, as I suspect—"

"That may give us a bit more clout with the White House?"

"*Exactement.*"

"Won't it backfire?" Dawn licked her lips, puffy with excitement.

Political maneuvering gets her off better than I do, Anthony thought. He expected her to start moaning anytime, now. "We can't know," he said. "You wanted a revolution? Revolutions are unpredictable, my dear."

VII

The Origin of the World

Butter in the air. Crisp, flaky, croissant kind of butter—the kind that conquers you in layers. First, the flavor of dawn, of waking up to the groans of the grinder and the victory smell of coffee. Then, the merging with tongue, like an adoring kiss. At the end, the rubbery need for more.

Like all international airports, Roissy Charles-de-Gaulle is a no-place, that utopia of postmodernity. But Prune knew she was home when, looking for a bathroom, she had to climb down narrow blond steps and whisk by a counter where naked croissants lounged about in a straw basket, exposed, obscene, to germ-free international transit and dank alcohol on the red-eyers' breath.

Prune deflected her first impulse to order two of the gold prizes and an espresso, hurried through two more turns, and stood in line for the one stall that six women were tarrying for. In front of her, one very tall woman cased in a black burqa from nose to toes was powdering her forehead in a hand-held mirror. It made Prune smile, this indefatigable display of self-care that women relish in France—a sort of universal right of woman to enhance her beauty without having to name it vanity, or seduction, or even oppression.

"Don't let those puritans disguising themselves as feminists tell you otherwise," Prune's grandmother Alma would tell her taffeta-clad granddaughters lined like macaroons for the wedding of a second cousin. "Women's beauty is God's gift to the stinky streets of our cities. To embellish ourselves is neither vanity, nor insecurity:

it is pure generosity. An elegant woman is a general amnesty in the maximum-security prison of our daily grind. See how everything brightens up when she walks down the street! Hammer-drills go quiet. Men lift their noses from their newspapers. Boys finally find a reason to grow out of boyhood, and girls grasp something other than diaper-changing to look forward to."

The burqa-clad woman caught Prune's gaze in her tiny mirror. She said something Prune didn't understand, something at once harsh and reassuring. To Prune, Arabic sounded like English does when addressed to a misbehaving pet. You'd expect one who speaks it to wag their finger at you. God, how she'd missed hearing those sounds, packed with golden domes, the call of the muezzin, and orange blossom water.

Prune risked a vacant smile and, feigning an urgent intent to wash her hands, she squeezed by a stout Anglo-Saxon who glared at her suspiciously. Above the sink, Prune thought she'd caught a glimpse of Rosa in the mirror. With eye-bags and hair dulled by lack of sleep, the girl seemed several years older. She'd never noticed how much she looked like her mother.

The hand-dryer was supersonic. It was aptly called Blade, and urged you to dip your hands in and out of a robust sheet of air.

Now there were eight of them waiting in line, not counting Prune. All were staring hypnotically at their feet. All had weary skin, courtesy of excess AC and overhead lights. No one said anything, but you could see most would go for the jugular of whoever tried to skip out of position. To be fair, French people are indeed prone to do so—skip lines, that is—and Prune briefly wondered if *Lonely Planet* had put out a warning.

"*Excusez-moi,*" Prune said a little too loudly as she squeezed herself back in line behind the woman in position number 6. The back of the line receded, but the front didn't budge—each link a live oak.

Back at the café area, travelers stood in thickets around tall aluminum tables. This year, traders were identifiable by their pointy leather shoes and skinny pantsuits. At six-o-two A.M., everyone was sipping on a tiny paper-cup espresso and staring at a tablet or phone—with the exception of three Arab men in ill-fitted suits, who were drinking Heinekens and ogling women's calves. Probably, their wives and sisters were sheathed in black and their sons forbidden to touch alcohol. Prune turned her attention to the counter where lay the croissants.

"Bonjour mademoiselle! Qu'est-ce que je vous sers?" First smile on French soil.

"Bonjour! Un café et deux croissants s'il vous plaît."

"Et voilà! Ça vous fera sept-euros-quarante. Et une bonne journée à vous.

"Merci!" Inside her mouth, Prune's tongue went festive like a disco ball. How long had it been since she'd spoken in French? How long since she'd heard that Parisian accent, with each end-syllable dovetailing into the next, urgent word? With the greasy napkin that the croissants came on, Prune dabbed the corners of her eyes. She tossed in the trash the six empty Heineken bottles that the Arab men had left behind, tucked her bag between her two feet, and took her first bite off the first croissant.

On Rosa Tum's first day, City of Lights waded in litanies of sirens—Existential sirens. Rather than their routine, "Get out of my way, someone's need is more urgent than yours!" they cried a new refrain: "Who will you be now, stranger in a strange land?" Branches blurred in stained autumn skies. Heavy-lidded, river Seine draped herself over green bottles. Even in the rain, the *Pont-des-Arts* didn't disappoint. On one side, the Venus mound of the *Ile-de-la-Cité*, tight between two river thighs, harbored the matching red umbrellas of a Japanese tour that popped like poppies at the feet of the horseback-riding statue of a king.

Francis-the-First had impeccable taste, judging by the looks of the *Pont-Neuf*, the bridge he'd commandeered. In the background, rows of voluptuous stone-arc after arc fanned out like so many portals.

The wind made Rosa's earflaps flap when she turned to take in the opposite vista. Here, the Seine was wide as an American highway, with the formidable range of the Louvre on its right. In the distance, the Eiffel Tower stretched its neck to hide a rusting head inside a cloud. Limestone façades and slate roofs harmonized seamlessly with the nuances of cloud. At one end of the bridge, the cobblestones of the *Collège de France* gleamed with proud brine. Twenty feet above, the magisterial clock made nine-forty A.M. seem like a permanent edict from a golden god. Under Rosa's feet, tour-boats touted in Dutch, Italian, and Russian the merits of this temple to the human intellect, the French Academy.

Rosa started toward the Louvre and the blue, white, and red flag whipped the air behind her. She stepped off the bridge and came to the edge of the Louvre's *Cour Carrée*. In perfect perspectival alignment with the bridge and the gate, an ample one-jet fountain beckoned. She risked a foot onto the pedestrian crossing, and inside his zooming BMW a silver-topped suit grimaced as if to say, "I can make this red light turn green on command!" He came close to running Rosa over, but his eagerness made her smile as all the other cars, scooters, bikes, and buses did stop in a flurry of exhaust fumes not unlike Mexico City, where she'd found refuge after the latest Guatemalan elections.

Then, Rosa was inside the *Cour Carrée*. She set her buttocks on the damp fountain ledge to take in the view. Austere indeed. Square indeed. And disarmingly poignant, with its sudden silence. Large stones absorb noise as if their solidity depended on it. The Louvre shares that with the Guatemalan high plateaus.

Five Americans in flashy sneakers were posing for pictures. They asked her to take one, and handed her one camera after another to make the same five shots of their weary faces under soggy baseball hats. They thanked her profusely in English, and disappeared under the dark portal that framed the pyramid of the vast *Cour Napoléon*.

From the depths of the alley rose a cello sonata. The drizzle had stopped, but Rosa shivered. She pulled in the flaps of her hat and tied them into a knot under her chin. Wrapped in an impossibly small-waisted raincoat, a narrow bust perched on stiletto boots glided by with a glance at her knitted hat. Rosa envied that woman, who assumed permanent immunity from being either judged by a stranger, or abducted by heavily-booted boys. Rosa recalled feeling similarly invincible when she'd quietly picked up her machete beside *abuela*'s stove, then led her goat down the slippery trail to stay with Carmencità, the only other girl to attend the French Nuns' seventh-grade class—otherwise reserved for the boys destined to represent the community's interests in the Quiché's workers union. After a tight-throat hug to the goat and one quick kiss on Carmencità's cheek, Rosa had kept on walking towards the tall shadows and naked roots that, she hoped, would scramble any trail the paramilitaries might want to follow.

Once on the RER train from the airport, Prune realized she had no idea where to start. From the other side of one whole ocean plus one whole continent, it had seemed that getting out of The Center was the challenge, and getting to Paris the destination. But Paris now felt like a beginning— of what? Prune prayed that the answer was less dreary than the concrete of the suburbs they were zooming through. She stared out the window at rows of makeshift huts and fast disappearing Gypsy children who kicked a soccer-ball into puddles.

A stab of missing Grenadine made her wince. Prune wished for her lover's poised outrage. She wished for her friend.

At *Saint-Michel-Notre-Dame*, Prune got off the train. Their old *rue Saint-Jacques* apartment was only a few blocks away. She blinked like a miner when she emerged on the *Quai Saint-Michel*, with its ivory façades glaring in sudden sun. The roar of converging traffic, river barge, and steel-cutting metro workers merged in a momentary deafness. Prune pinched her nose and blew hard to relieve the pressure of the jet landing. The racket returned, and it took a minute for her eyes to adjust as she swiveled around to face *Notre-Dame*.

It was one of those mystical cloud-piercing moments, when gleeful cherubs are about to slide down brassy slants of sun. The cathedral's twin towers unveiled Gothic demons enlaced about the gargantuan rosette window. Prune blushed. Their family scorned chauvinism, patriotism, the pride of unearned privilege. But by God, she was French, and in that moment, standing on that corner in this perfect slice of monumental Paris, she felt damn pleased to be so.

The light turned green. Prune slipped on her Parisian stride like a well-worn pair of jeans and trotted up the *Boulevard Saint-Michel* toward the apartment where she and Carla had learned to set a dinner table worthy of a countess and sing Cuban revolutionary songs in canon. Of course, someone else would be living there now. Someone else's book piles, and guinea-pig litter-box, and dirty laundry. Someone with no assassinated relatives.

Pedro was sure they'd been through this *arroyo* before, and even the cactus looked thirsty. Red dust and juniper sprouted out of cracks in the earth. He slowed down to scan a nearby bush— for what, he didn't quite know. Maybe impulse? Not intelligence, not even consciousness—with these came too many unpredictables that often leaned toward self-absorption, if not outward evil. But watching mere billows of dust in the bushes' prickles wasn't doing it anymore. Maybe what Pedro was after was—what had Prune called it? The Prime Number? Something like that... No! The Prime Mover. He leaned in to regard a blue scarab lumbering up a twig, and realized that what he was really after was a sign of God.

"Hey, hog face! Ever heard of Gyges' ring?"

Bug-eyed from an unseasonable sun-trance, Pedro didn't bother to respond. Alia was going to tell him all about whatever chatter topic she'd picked anyway. He might as well save his precious saliva.

"It's pretty cool," she said. "If you put it on, you become invisible. So the question is, would you use it to maim and steal, knowing that no ill consequences would befall you—or would you act normal?"

Pedro shrugged. Against his kidneys, the bounce of the water jugs felt dangerously brisk and the sky was going lavender above the mesa. "Normal, I guess."

"That's so boring."

This time he knew better than to reply.

"You see, in the famous *Robinson Crusoe*, the Scottish version, Robinson ends up recreating the most regimented, oppressive order, even though he's all alone on his little island. And sure enough, as soon as the Black guy Friday shows up, Robinson takes pains to reproduce all the Neo-colonial injustices he's witnessed back home. Isn't that insane?"

No, not really, Pedro thought. *Stupid, maybe. Unimaginative, for sure. But not insane, no. That's what he knew. Maybe that's precisely how come he didn't go crazy.*

The crimson skin on Alia's nose was peeling off, but she was on a roll. "But the French Robinson, he's cool. He builds things that make music when the wind howls through them. He has sex with the mud. Not just *in* the mud—there isn't anyone else there—but *with* the mud. Isn't that cool?"

"Uh, no, not really?" Pedro said prudently.

"Of course it is! It's a metaphor, don't you get it? Left to his own devices, forced to start anew, he becomes *elemental* again. He is God again, not some boring little human coddled by his neuroses."

"Well, I don't know." Pedro was really wishing Alia would shut up, so he could focus on finding a way for them to avoid sizzling like Chinese roaches in the desert sun. On the other hand, he really wanted her to keep talking because as long as Alia talked, she was thinking, and as long as she was thinking, she was hoping. And as long as Alia was hoping, Pedro had something to fight for. So he said, "I'm not an expert or nothing, but I think someone could argue that having sex with mud is a bit neurotic."

Alia mimicked his sousaphone voice. "Someone could argue that having sex with mud, gnagnagnagnagna. You'd have to be at least as neurotic as Freud to think that!"

"Well, maybe I am!" Pedro was starting to find it very hard to breathe. He reached behind into his backpack, feeling around for his inhaler. Alia's stride had not slowed a bit all day. If anything, she was walking with more vigor. Outrage was her fuel of choice, and she currently had enough to power her to Ciudad Juarez and back. Pedro was falling behind, and he detested seeing the distance between them grow any further.

"Alia?"

"Mmmmh?"

"What does neurotic mean?"

"It means, ruled by fear rather than love."

"How so?"

It worked. Alia turned around to face her friend. Walking backward, and slower, she raised her hand to shield her eyes from the sun. "Well, if the Scottish Robinson makes those rules and writes them down even though no one else is there to read them, or if he sounds the bugle to call himself to lunch, and stores large quantities of food even though he lives alone, it's not out of love for the human civilization that he misses. I think it's out of fear—

fear of change, of lack, of loneliness; fear of madness—all petty rehearsals for death, of course. All our fears boil down to that."

"Well, death *is* scary."

"Is it? Why?"

Pedro sighed. "Ok, never mind. Keep going." The inhaler must have fallen out earlier. It wasn't where he'd left it. The drawstring inside Pedro's chest tightened. Laboriously he added, "Let's find your hush-hush monks. I'm not rehearsed enough to become the Mexican Robinson Crusoe."

"You wouldn't have to be." Alia flipped around to face forward again. "I'd be there to watch over you."

After her first Kundalini yoga lesson, Grenadine was sweaty, but clean. The sensation was new and strangely uncomfortable, like a compliment. She was used to gagging on her own smell and ever since she'd been tall enough to operate the hot and cold faucets, she'd taken two to three showers a day, four when she'd been running.

Among friends, her father had liked to compare her body odor to Yosemite's least treaded trails, which he'd backpacked alone at seventeen in the moonlight. "Best times," he'd said. "The Origin of the World offering itself up to me." For years, Grenadine hadn't known what Yosemite was, but the Bible they'd had her read at the Sacred-Heart talked about Semitic tribes having to flee from Egypt to cross the desert. She'd assumed Yosemite referred to the Semites and that it was her father's roundabout way of alluding to her blackness. After everyone was gone, he'd make her fetch his mold-stained army surplus pack, the one that made her sneeze. Made her open it, take off her pajamas, and put on instead the Boy Scout uniform he kept there. It smelled like wet laundry forgotten in the washer. The shirt slid off her stiff shoulders and she'd tell him she was cold, but he'd say, "Come here, I'll hold you. Come here, I won't hurt you. Come here." Too big, the shorts kept sliding off and she held them up with her left hand because she was right-handed and she thought she'd need her stronger hand to push her Daddy's face away when he brought it right up against her to breathe in the Origin of the World.

Once, when she was nine years old, Grenadine had said no to her Daddy. With her fists held so tight that the short nails bit into her palms, she'd said, "No Daddy, I don't want to." And her Daddy had fallen to his knees and there were tears coming out of him. Grenadine had never seen her Daddy cry, but on T.V. she'd seen black men cry, sometimes. Mostly, black men cried when kind white men freed them from slavery. But Grenadine had never seen a white man cry. She didn't know white men could cry.

I have been afraid even of trees, she now realized. *Their lizard skin and constant erection, their drying out and forever rebirth, their naha at the sky and sucking from earth, air, hurricane all that they need—exactly enough, never too much, too little only when the choice isn't theirs. Trees have been the blond sister of my childhood, the one so beautiful that over her, dozens of boys got to copy one hundred times, "I will not climb up toilet stalls to peek at girls in the bathroom."*

When it cools off the skin lets go of its burnt chicken smell and scar tissue starts to grow, like moss. After a good burn, Grenadine was no longer afraid of trees: she became forest—one with tall oaks and bushy undergrowth where unknown things crawling feel like life instead of rape.

Now, watching the flames of Ruben's bonfire dance their shadow puppet's dance, Grenadine noticed that her hand wasn't hungering for that burn blister. Her hand lay still, palm warm on stomach that ebbed and flowed, ebbed and flowed, in sync with the bonfire's shimmy. Anastasia hummed a Transylvanian wedding march as she raked her fingers through Carla's hair.

I am here, thought Grenadine. And it wasn't home *per se*. But it was a place to be.

Grenadine must have fallen asleep. When she woke up it was completely dark but for the shadows' drama on the canopy's underbelly. Ruben looked up from the skillet he was holding over the fire when she blurted out, "Why am I here?"

Anastasia kept on humming. Ruben stirred the sizzling bacon with a stick, and across the bonfire there was a slight stir of Carla's silhouette.

After a while Ruben said, "Because you've been chosen to save the world."

Grenadine said nothing. The fire crackled, illuminating the clearing like slow lightning. The serenity of the scene was shocking. Ruben squatting down by the fire, Carla cuddled with Anastasia and the wolf—the homeliness of it all, in a sweet caveman kind of way, was triggering images from an awfully dated French film Grenadine watched years ago.

Conveniently, Grenadine remembered neither the plot, nor the ending of most movies but, just like with her dreams or childhood memories, she was randomly assaulted by evasive impressions and crude fragments—often the crassest of moments at the most dissonant times. The image was of a cavewoman squatting down by the river, and a caveman surprising her from behind to lift her fur-throw and copulate like a dog, quick and choppy.

I hate quiet, thought Grenadine. *This is what quiet does.*

Then to the happy Dreamscape faux-family she said, "You've got to be fucking kidding me."

Anastasia said, "Like love, tornadoes have a way to spit out the things they've caught—sometimes undamaged, only elsewhere. My late husband Karl would sometimes lull me to sleep after love with the list of random things that dust storms had brought to his door. A black sock, guitar picks, a real fox tail, a miraculously unscathed thirty-five mm lens, several pairs of designer sunglasses in divers states of disrepair, a corn pipe, a tuna sandwich in a bag, half unwrapped lollipops, deer horns, a flip-flop. He called it his

Random Abundance Bounty. Made an altar around the chimenea that collected sage dust and prayerful ashes. To him, these things were a visual poem, a material ode to loss and recovery. In my ear he hummed the stories they carried, all the things' ancestors' stories. It sent shivers down to my tailbone."

Ruben stood up. He'd wrapped the bacon around some kind of pleated leaf with a peeled cactus ear nestled in the middle. In a flash, Attila was right in front of him, slobbery tongue hanging, ears pricked, tail wagging.

"Here you go. Wolves and feral children first." Ruben tossed one wrap to the wolf, and another to Carla. He bent over to pick up another wrap and toss it to Grenadine. "You see, Anastasia's Dreamscape is modeled after tornado physics. At times, checkered blocs of reality become too heavy—with un-grieved grief mostly. This generates enough pressure against space-time's fabric to tear sinkholes into it. When the edges of the fabric rise fast—a sudden shock of hope, an old friend's cursive on a postcard—they begin to twirl, *los bloques de realidad*, caught in the vortex of high and low pressures of distress and gladness. Unable to choose, they might twirl endlessly, until the centripetal force tears a block away from the swirl to actualize it."

"That's right," said Anastasia, grinning. "And with the momentum, the swirl eventually sucks in everything to spit it out, mostly undamaged, only elsewhere. 'Displaced, never misplaced,' as my Karl would say. *Et voilà!*" Bound with the smoky crisp of bacon, the tender cactus was amazing. "I believe that's how come Carla strayed and ended up here. But me and Ruben can take her back." She winked at him. "*Verdad, cariño mío?*" Grenadine's gaze darted back and forth between Ruben's awkward grin and Carla's frown.

"Oh come on, Grenadine. Don't tell me you didn't know those two had a thing," said the girl. "Why else do you think your buddy Ruben would have journeyed so often inside my comatose little mind? He may be wise, but he's still a man. *Verdad, cariño mío?*"

Oblivious to the sarcasm, Ruben was still beaming.

Grenadine said, "Fine, I'm glad you found love, even if it's inside Prune's little sister's dreams." For Anastasia's benefit she added, "He's a good man and you better—" Anastasia nodded, amused. After a pause, Grenadine said, "So, tell me again Anastasia. What's the difference between what you're doing and what The Center folks do? Aren't you preying on Carla's *Prana* the same as Dawn is fattening her Cayman Islands bank account on the kids' Kundalini?"

Ruben opened his mouth to speak, but Anastasia raised her hand. "Woman, you are putting your finger on the essence of relationships here. There are really only two kinds, you know: giving and taking—biophilic and necrophilic; vital and morbid. Carla and I have a symbiosis. We give each other life: love. Like a good marriage, if you will—the rare kind, you know, that doesn't become nights on end of bad acting in a predictable drama? The girl carries the soul of the man I loved. He revealed myself to me, and taught me that to love is wanting to live, and wanting our beloved to live as fully as one does. He showed me that I didn't have to sell either my pussy or my soul for affection. That love could come for free."

"So, aside from the disturbing marriage analogy with a ten year-old girl, what does she get from you?" Grenadine moved in closer to Carla.

"Duh!" Cried Carla. "Like, a life?"

"You call that a life, slouched on a bed, hooked to a sap-sucking machine? No eating, no talking, no playing? A kid her age should be running wild. She should be punching boys and tearing off flies' legs, and—I don't know, baking stuff! She should—"

"Stop, Gren," Ruben said softly. Grenadine had been the only one not to notice, but her voice had steadily risen to a scream. The tendons in her neck formed a V. Carla took her hand in hers, pointing at the humming lushness and the bubbling waterfall. A pair of bunnies were chasing one another in the thick clover.

Attila, yawned. He'd been sitting on the edge of the clearing and came to lie down with his head resting on Carla's foot.

"This is my life, Gren," the girl said.

"So, you're just going to let The Center suck you dry? Be the good conscience they can flap about like a standard before their bad faith—*Look, those kids may not look it, but they're thriving!*"

"They're not sucking me dry, Grenadine. The energy that courses through me is infinite in supply because here, I am happy. Here, I feel loved." She ran her fingers through Attila's fur and he rolled on his back to offer up his belly. "Here, I am safe. Can you say this much of your 'real' life?"

Grenadine looked at each one of their faces throbbing in the bonfire glow. "You're all fucking nuts!" She stomped away and disappeared inside the black thick of the trees she used to fear so.

Carla woke too early and decided to go for a hike, cogitate a bit—or maybe not cogitate, for once. Attila trotted drowsily behind her as she tip-toed by the zonked mess of Ruben and Anastasia tangled in their hammock.

In the virgin forest, green blends with green. Layer upon layer of sap-swollen leaf, moss, iguana, pistil, spider egg. Leaning into a leaf the size of her thorax, Carla squinted to regard the white pearls that an agile spider had suspended. Just above the leaf's central nook, the spider's eggs trembled in the girl's out breath.

"*N'ayez pas peur,*" she reassured them. The tremor revealed silk threads fanning out to infinity against the hole in the pocket of sky above. Carla wanted to know where the web began— or was this the beginning and the other end—well, the end?

She was learning to move slowly, not because she must be vigilant, but because she was registering that nothing in the jungle was out to get her. This had taken several nights of wide-eyed stupor, straining to diagnose the precise distance between her tragically exposed body and the cacophony of frogs, bats, and hard-shelled things. It gave her plenty of time to question this choice of setting for her own Dreamscape, and decided it had to be blamed on Rudyard Kipling and television—particularly, her father's inexplicable love for Johnny Weissmuller's Tarzan movies.

For Carla to start sleeping through the night, it took a torch-lit tour during which together, she and Anastasia named every batrachian (Sidonie, Carmelia, Liam), insect (several Georges—the First, the Second, and so on; one Aurelia, a Hope), and bat (Louise and Marsha) that happened to flap about their heads. It turned out that each and every one of these dream-mates was much prettier in person than in Carla's imagination. Also, the beasties showed less interest in girl and crone than they did in smaller, generally very un-mammalian-looking things with wings and umpteen legs.

The real reason why Carla slowed down in the jungle was that the Earth magnetized her bare feet. This was no New Age hooha; it was the real, white-coat truth. When there isn't a slice of plastic between your skin and the naked ground, then Earth's magnet and your own harmonize. They de-polarize, like school kids who finally kiss after wasting half the semester bickering over who's the doctor and who's the nurse.

One foot, heel first, then ball, then toes. Other foot: heel, ball, pinky-toe, next-to-pinky-toe toe, middle-toe, other middle-toe, big-toe. And another. Carla held her breath, arms close to her ribs. That, she'd learned from watching Attila. When following a track, the wolf knew to take up barely any space. There was no question that he would claim elbowroom aplenty when the need arose—when the time came to parse their moss cot, for instance. But when he trotted on the narrow forest trails, Attila's paw prints followed one single thread. He was a funambulist, Attila was.

With the Tyrannosaurus palm's canopy for a background, Carla could observe her spider web again. Another step. The wolf so close to her knee that the warmth his body emitted rippled through all her joints, loosening even the knuckles in her fingers, so tired of holding on to invisible threads. So tired…

Maybe the mystery of the origin of the spider eggs could wait. It'd be another twenty hours before they'd be ready to hatch anyway. Carla liked to think that if she were to follow the thread far enough, she might find her mother. Perhaps her father too? But for now, a nap was in order. She spied a welcoming patch of moss in the tangled roots of a giant Catalpa tree, untied the sarong Anastasia had shown her how to wrap, draped it around her shoulders, and coiled herself, snake-like (Bernard), inside the hollow.

Attila sighed and sat in front of the tree, waiting. When he realized she wasn't going anywhere, he whined a little. Already asleep, Carla reached for the wolf's soft, but he stood up, took a few careful steps along the spider web, and whimpered again. When Carla didn't react, Attila decided to go on and thread his own way down the trail.

It was a crisp day in Española and for once Swami John woke up with unobstructed sinuses. It made him feel expansive, so he brought to class the bounty of his mother's Thanksgiving care package to share with his pupils.

"Why does divinity have to stick to your teeth? I hate that!" Luther muttered. He slid a finger inside his mouth and proceeded to scrape the bits of nougat lodged there.

"What is it, Doctor John, you've never seen a *demoiselle* pick her teeth?" Hakim's blond curls bounced to the nervous jerk of his knee under the desk.

"No, I'm just ttttttt-trying to understand what aspect of God would ddddddd-do that."

"Do what? Pick her teeth?" Luther picked away liberally.

A quick survey of the classroom informed the two boys that no one was really entertained.

"No, sssss… ssstick to your t… t… ttteeth." John seemed genuinely intrigued. Clearly, the Swami was starved for theological conversation. This was his own "God: One or Many?" class, and lately the children had been inquiring more about Prune than First Causes. He said, "Doesn't that binding quality bespeak the Ddddd-tt-divine substance? Lou, what do you think?" Lou was gazing at something faraway. Her two middle-fingers vanished inside her mouth and she absent-mindedly petted her plastic flamingo's beak.

John had tried dipping Lou's hand in vinegar, like his mother had, to stifle this thumb-sucking. But it so turned out Lou was fond of all things vinegary. "I taste like pickles!" She'd cried, elated and suckling with redoubled vigor. No other solution came to John short of physically restraining the girl, so he gave up. Presently, Lou tried to form words that no one could make out.

"Yes? Yes, what, Lou? Go ahead, I am cccccccc-urious to know what you thhthhthink." When he addressed her, John's voice always rose an octave, as if talking to a small pet.

Lou pulled her fingers out, though it looked painful. "Yes, I like divinities too. They're sweet like angels' milky teeth. Does the tooth fairy come for angels?"

"Why?" John asked in his falsetto.

"Because I'll be an angel soon but I don't want to be an angel if they don't have the tooth fairy." Lou plunged her fingers back in her mouth.

While John was fishing for a comeback, Hakim squawked, "Hey, Doctor John! Is it true that angels don't have a sex?" A couple of boys chuckled and John frowned, but Lou had all his attention. The girl's cheeks had remained cherub-rosy through the frightful withering of her health, but her hair was falling in clumps. Her eyebrows were almost entirely gone, like in those emaciated Nativity scenes from the Middle-Ages. It was hard not to read "martyr" into this, and John was relieved when the bell rang the end of class.

The gym bathed in light and the dirty-snow smell of central AC. The Swami shifted the shutters, making sure to keep enough light for reading. At almost twenty-eight, he knew it was too soon, but felt a strain within minutes of peering at small print. It bothered him to think he might need glasses. John knew that his looks weren't his strongest suit, and his green eyes were definitely his best feature—Megan, the largest-breasted exchange student at the Ludwig Maximilian University in Munich, where he'd completed his doctoral work, had told him so.

In the wall-length mirror, John caught a glimpse of himself standing between the rowing machine and the elliptical. He ran his hand through his hair and tried a slanted smile à la Orlando Bloom. A few frizzy strands stayed up. He adjusted the collar of his robe and congratulated himself for having freckles that matched so perfectly his saffron habit.

Feet shoulder width apart, the Swami began his light stretches routine. *Aaaand inhale, exhale, lunge to the right. Knee above the ankle, shoulder blades gathered behind the heart, the neck an extension of the spine. Aaaand inhale to center, exhale, lunge to the left.* He was taking care to flex his feet and ankles as deeply as his bunions allowed, for he wanted to test the pliability of the new sneakers his mom had mailed with a note on the same lilac-scented stationary she'd used for Easter. The note read, "Because your health is in your glands, and your glands hate what is bland." John wasn't crazy about the neon orange accents on his shoes, but he had to admit that it accorded nicely with the rusted mustard of his robe. In fact, gazing at his own feet and absorbing the sunny complexion of his attire promised to be a mood-lifter almost as effective as the Nutella Megan had once fed him with her fingers. "Thanks, Mom!" he called cheerfully to his reflection in the mirror.

Last warm up. John planted his feet right under his hips and began to hop up and down to oil the joints. On the tatami, the sneakers felt bouncy as Megan's bosom. He flung both of his arms to the left (inhale) and to the right (exhale). At first, his arms flapped about like basset ears but eventually, momentum built and they began to hover waist-high, swiveling about the dancing pole of his spine. It sounded like when birds pour by your face. John's shoulders and ribs were spinning so far to each side, now, that he wondered if he might end up wringing himself all the way around. *Then I could screw myself into the ground, tap directly into the fiery core of the earth—or else, why not, and maybe at the same time—why not?—wind all the way into the ceiling, on through the ozone layer, to the mesosphere where meteors combust, and finally to the exosphere where matter merges with void. Pure. Space.*

After he'd caught his breath, he went to dig Saint Thomas Aquinas' *Summa Theologica* out of his bag and climbed on the treadmill. It was an older model, which meant less electronics on the dashboard and more room for the book. The *Summa* still reeked of the garlic that hung in the air of the used bookstore off Wildermayerstrasse where as a student, John liked to meditate between seminars. The store keeper, a disabused investment banker from Turin, kept zabuton pillows and singing bowls scattered about crooked book aisles for the Zen sangha who had plucked her off of *Samsara*'s delusional wheel of duality. Thanks to this, Francesca had realized oneness with her hamster Gustav, whom she set free in tribute to her own liberation. Gustav was a pro at the litter-box and he came scurrying squealingly each time the words "batavia" or "pumpkin" were uttered. To combat an egregious form of nail-fungus that kept her wearing white gloves at all times, Francesca noshed on raw garlic cloves between meals.

It was a bilingual edition, with the Latin on the left, English on the right. The spine had been beautifully broken, so it was no trouble at all leaving the fat volume to hold itself open. The pages were heavy enough to seem moist, their edges rough from the hand cut. Page iii, the first of a thick table of contents, was missing its bottom right corner where the knife had slipped. Or else, Gustav had mistaken it for lettuce.

John punched in his usual on the treadmill and for several minutes, he concentrated on his day-glo orange heel-to-toe swagger. Then he grew confident and picked it up to a cruising stride. Scanning through the twelve-page long table of contents, he quickly found what he was looking for. "The Treatise on the Angels" (Questions number 50 to 64 of Part 1 of the *Summa Theologica*) came right after Question 49, "The Cause of Evil," article 3, "Whether There Be One Supreme Evil Which Is The Cause of Every Evil."

Saint Thomas answers the question of the corporeality of angels with a classical Aristotelian argument based on the certainty of God's goodness. "There must be incorporeal creatures," Thomas writes, "for what is principally intended by God in creatures is good, and this consists in assimilation to God Himself. And the perfect assimilation of an effect to a cause is accomplished when the effect imitates the cause according to that whereby the cause produces the effect; as heat makes heat." Heat was indeed building inside John's psoas muscles. He resisted the temptation to climb off the machine to go turn up the AC as one of his mother's lilac inspirationals—"*A good sweat each day will keep you sweet through dismay*"—rung in his mind.

"Now, God produces the creature by His intellect and will. Hence the perfection of the universe requires that there should be intellectual creatures. Now intelligence cannot be the action of a body, nor of any corporeal faculty; for every body is limited to 'here' and 'now.' Hence the perfection of the universe requires the existence of an incorporeal creature." One click, then on to five-point-five mph—optimum cardio fitness for his bulk. The Swami wiped off the sweat that was dripping onto the page.

Next, Thomas went on to explain that angels are not merely vaporous, ethereal kinds of material things, since they're not material things at all. Nor are angels the souls of dead humans. Click. Back down to four-point-five mph. John wheezed a little, but this news made him take in a smooth lump of air. *Glad we cleared that up,* he thought. *Even if a child dies while in the care of The Center, it doesn't make The Center an angel-maker. Therefore, working for The Center does not necessarily make me an angel-maker. Lou is mistaken.* John sighed. *Besides, the kids are clearly material creatures. How else would they be producing so much Ch'i that fracking is becoming as obsolete as coal mining?* He was feeling springier. Click, click, on up to six mph!

Thomas also surmised that even though angels are completely immaterial creatures, they sometimes assume bodies—*or else, how would we mere mortals ever be able to behold them?* In short, angels manipulate matter—actually, air: they condense air "so far as is needful for forming the assumed body." *Ok, so back to square one. The kids could be angels in disguise, and so could anyone else, for that matter. Hell, Anthony could be an angel!*

Sweat was dripping into the Swami's eyes. It stung a little, but this was juicy. Click. Six-point-five mph. *Let's get that heart pumping. Those Nikes must be nuke powered. Ha! Maybe I'll write that in my thank you note, Mother!* The breath was still catching in places but John felt like a Norwegian Strongman. Click. Click. Six-point-eight mph. *What's that? Seven percent incline? Bring it on!*

Of course, John thought, *this raises the question, Why the heck would angels assume human form?*—or, as Aquinas puts it, What is the purpose of angelic "conversations"? Thomas is clear that angels' bodies are meant neither to sense, nor speak, nor eat. More likely, the purpose of the appearances of angels is to inform humankind of divine realities, and so to lead people to God. Click. Click. Click, click, click, click. The treadmill bolted. *How the heck do you stop that thing?* Click!

Fingers clawing the handlebars, elbows hanging, head bent, John struggled once again to catch his breath. He watched his sweat gather at the tip of his nose and drip onto thick pages that drunk it in like thoughts. Suddenly, the door burst open behind him. He glanced up in the mirror. "Anthony, my man. Thinking of the devil!"

"I thought I'd find you here." Anthony sounded grave.

"Seeking me out, huh?" John toweled his hair dry, peeking at Anthony's reflection. "But I'm glad you're here." He combed his hair with his fingers. "Let me run this conundrum by you."

"When did you quit sssss....ssss.... stammering?" Anthony taunted.

"I only falter in my speech when forced into unnatural situations. Now, let me ask you this." John took his time to lift the hem of his robe, step off the treadmill, and plant himself in front of Anthony. The Swami was noticeably taller, and Anthony had to take one step back.

"It may strike you as strange. Remember that I'm a Buddhist, I don't believe in a transcendent God. Nevertheless, I must ask you—and please answer me as candidly as you can." John brought his hands to his waist. "Which divine reality are *you* here to reveal to me?"

Anthony pinched his nose. "Man, is that some kind of hormonal imbalance or something?"

John became absorbed in the bright ribbons of orange on his sneakers. The ochre hem of his robe draped over the electric blue of his shoes like a lagoon. He thought of sunrises in the bay of Madang. Mud-painted men, spear in hand, asking somberly that he put in a prayer for their hunt.

Without looking at Anthony he said, "Because little Lou, yes, I can see it: love, mercy. Prune, I can see it: compassion, courage. But you? Me? Hetherington? What do *we* have to show for ourselves?"

Anthony peered at his reflection next to John's in the mirror, licked his fingers, flattened his hair, and said, "Omnipotence?"

John stared. "Is... is... is that it? Is that whu... whu... why we do what we do?"

"Oh, don't start acting all saintly on me, mister monk. You're just as starved for power as I am. I see you pecking at the crumbs that the Queen Mother casts for you. I've watched you elbow your way into one more class, one more report, one more meeting, sucking up to everyone on the way, from the pups on up to the super. You want to be a graduate assistant for eternity? Fine. You think *that's* my retirement plan?"

"But Chinergy. The eff... eff... efffficacy. It b... b... burns clean. It's one-hundred-and-eight times more potent than f... f... fossil fuels, fifty-six times safer than f... fffracking. No cumbersome solar ppppp... panels to recycle."

"I know," Anthony beamed. "And best of all, as long as there are humans around to stumble about on this silly little planet of ours, we will never run out! Ok, so you're with me now, brother. Are we going to let all this perfection go hogwash because Missy I've-Got-Everything-Under-Control-Hetherington has delusions of grandeur? I don't think so. I think you and I are the smart ones here, and we've got to take care of ourselves. The healthy kids are fleeing like fleas and the other ones, well." Anthony walked past the Swami and climbed on the treadmill. "I think there's trouble brewing, mate," he said, punching in his settings. "This whole enterprise was built on compliance and complacency, but we might not be able to count on that for long." Anthony punched a few buttons and launched into an easy jog. "As long as Hetherington's in charge, neither you nor I have the authority to unlock the funds we're going to need if we want to maintain the kids' safety."

John was getting agitated. He planted himself in front of Anthony. With his huge mitts resting on the belt of his robe, he called to mind a young Merlin.

"If push comes to shove," Anthony explained, "we might need to be ready to call in a little help from our friend the General."

John crossed his arms in front of his chest.

"You know," Anthony continued, "in case something

unexpected happens. But most importantly, you and I need to stick together, brother. Union makes strength, right?"

Still jogging, Anthony held his hand out for a handshake, but the Swami ignored it.

"Here I was, thinking you and President Hetherington were in love. Weren't you? No, never mind, don't answer that." With a sad smile, John slowly raised his hand to shake Anthony's. "I'd rather not give you any more opportunities to betray your soul. I will pray for you, my man." Then the monk wiped the sweat off of his face with a towel, and quietly left Anthony to his puffing.

It was too early for the stores to be open. Some had their metal curtain drawn, but on November 24th, H&M and Zara were displaying next spring's collection in splashes of pastel. Low-cut cowboy boots, poofy skirts, and native print T-shirts were going to be in order next year. Prune glanced down at her worn-out sneakers and oversized sweater, feeling lame. In Benetton's display window, the price tags indicated nothing under eighty euros, so she tucked her thumbs inside the straps of her backpack and picked up the pace, bracing herself for the ascent past the *Jardin du Luxembourg* and on to the Pantheon Palace.

Rue de la Huchette, rue Sarrazin, rue Saint-Séverin. Rosa claimed that the streets in this neighborhood had been named after fantastic birds. For the first time, Prune realized what her mother meant. *Rue Serpente.*

At the bus stop, an old woman with a black headscarf took over the bench to transfer the contents of one large plastic bag into another, identical-looking bag. Standing dangerously close to the curb, none of the other bus-waiters paid her any attention. A teenage girl in dark sunglasses and a crimson pout poked fast thumbs at a tiny screen. A middle-aged man in an impeccable suit and turquoise headset soundlessly moved his lips, one foot tapping on the asphalt. The bus sighed its asthmatic sigh as it slowed to a stop. On cue with the tinkle of the opening doors, the bag-lady picked up her pace, as if scrambling to get on the bus. A lanky African man in traditional dress climbed out as the pouty girl and the foot-tapping man climbed in. The bus took off without the bag lady, and when she caught Prune watching her, she grinned a beatific grin. Then, as if she'd just remembered some vitally important thing, she got busy transferring the contents of the new bag back into the old one, like Sisyphus, the absurd hero condemned to carry a boulder up a steep slope only to watch it roll back down once he reaches the top. Over and over, Sisyphus begins again, his entire being absorbed in the useless task. Prune pictured his strong Greek body, the hard muscles strained toward the goal, the face screwed up, the pearls of sweat at the hairline. And she saw herself, thumbs crushed against her ribs, leaning in the slope of the Boulevard Saint-Michel like a Himalayan sherpa. She thought that the irony should make her laugh—that it would, no doubt, make her father laugh. What was that line from Albert Camus's essay on Sisyphus? "*Il faut imaginer Sisyphe heureux.*" Marc loved to quote it so much that it became a joke among all of Rosa's Marxist friends. They tossed it around like a mantra every time they reached a dead-end in their subversion of imperialism. Surreptitiously, it had become their motto. "One must imagine Sisyphus happy."

The *Place de la Sorbonne* cropped up on Prune's left. She walked over to a bench next to a defunct fountain. The rusted jets at the bottom of the tank glared a one-eyed glare right back at her. Oxide deposits along the concrete sides glowed like pine saplings. Prune carefully set her pack down and plopped down next to it. She began to massage the pinched nerve in her shoulder and it ignited a bonfire inside the sole of her foot. She wriggled her seat bones into alignment and landed both feet flat on the asphalt, knees at a ninety-degree angle. She took a deep breath in, closed her eyes, nestled her left hand inside the right in the crease of her lap, and let all the air out, thinking, *I have arrived, I am home,* like John had taught them.

When Prune opened her eyes, there lay familiar baby-blue-cover books, barely visible behind the glare of the clouds in the display window of the *Librairie Philosophique* J. Vrin. In her solar plexus, something gave. Warmth.

Often, Marc would leave his books lying open, face down on the kitchen counter. The paper was so grainy, he could have made cornmeal sacks out of them. He ouched after half-burnt toast inside the toaster, then buttered up the *tartines* for his girls. Inevitably, *The Grammar of Phenomenology* ended up with coffee stains and sticky streaks—the kind of "addendum of surface matter" which, Marc claimed, "made up for a lack of real substance in the depths."

At the *Café de la Sorbonne*, loud women with empty strollers huddled around a table. They'd just dropped off their toddlers at daycare—the very one Prune and Carla used to go to. Maybe *Mademoiselle* Ponin still worked there, with her huge freckles and ukulele songs? It felt good to see them looking so normal, these mothers, with their purses and Ugly Dolls filling in their child's seat. They knew they'd go back at five and find the little ones, perhaps red-eyed or runny-nosed, but otherwise unharmed.

Time to get going. Their old apartment was only a few minutes away. *Talk to the gardienne? Neighbors? The Chinese to-go across the street?* Someone was bound to have seen something. Prune stood up, tossed the backpack on her sore shoulder, and started across the square toward the *rue de la Sorbonne*. Right as she passed the empty fountain, the whole row of jets started to sputter and great big geysers rose out of a rusted hole in city cement. Prune stopped to search for a rainbow—old family habit. She spun around as she kept searching. From here, she could see through the window of J. Vrin. Amidst broken reflections of the water jets, one soft blue volume jumped up at her. In red blocky letters the cover said, "*Vitalité: Une Vie*" *par Marc Michaux*. A white band of paper—

the kind they add to catch the customer's eye—had been wrapped across the bottom of the cover. It read, "Life: Truth or Dare? Questions for the Disappeared."

The glass door of the *Librairie Philosophique* J.Vrin tinkled when Prune poured it open.

Alia heard a thump when Pedro collapsed behind her. The boy's coughing got so wretched that he vomited all of the lone pack of beef jerky he'd ingested in the last twenty-four hours. Alia turned into her own mother, holding his forehead and whispering calming Arabic words. When the coughing abated, Pedro tried to talk but without air, the words aborted on the edge of his teeth. He looked like a calf lassoed in the ring.

Alia remembered, as one does in emergencies, that keeping him upright was foremost. She kneeled behind him on the ground and wrapped her arms under his chest. She undid his belt and unbuttoned the polo shirt he liked to keep buttoned up. She told him to lean against her. He did. It seemed to relieve his anxiety for a time, but then he became agitated again, wanting to see her. The heat between their torsos became moist, the weight of him a strain on her back. Her new breasts felt sore against the blades of his shoulders.

Alia searched around, but there wasn't much to lean on—Cactus pears; juniper bushes; spindly rocks. In the distance she spied what looked like a heavenward boulder, one of those monoliths erected at Stonehenge as offerings to the fertility Goddess. In the dusk it could have passed for a black hole. Finally, Pedro's wheezing dwindled to a sigh and he was able to get up. They stumbled toward the thing, the boy weighing on Alia's arm.

It was further than it seemed. *Allah Akbar*! thought Alia eventually. Oh, the sweet sound of rushing water! She tried to ignore the scampering underfoot as she dug out her scarf, unfolded it carefully, set it down on the ground, and laid out the contents of her bag. A toothbrush with tiny toothpaste fitted in the handle from an airline business class kit; a tiny nail file that looked like a matchbook; the Boy Scouts of America's survival manual; Hafiz' book of poems, *The Gift*; a palm-size turquoise scarab—good-luck charm from her father's driver Rachid; two pairs of Center crew socks; two pairs of basic white underwear, folded; a flashlight; a ballpoint pen.

When the little altar was ready, she dug a bath-towel out of Pedro's pack and set it out. She pointed at the towel as Pedro struggled to hold himself up against the stump.

"Now you may sit."

They cupped their hands to drink from the stream and felt better. They took off their clothes and washed off the day's dust in the frigid water, shrieking in the moonlight. Trembling, they split a granola bar. With her balled-up night-gown they vigorously rubbed each other's back to make heat. You could have sworn there were sparkles. Then they put their clothes back on and tried not to go to sleep.

Pedro gave in first. His snoring was a jet engine. She woke him once, twice. The third time, she noticed that he quieted down when she placed the palm of her hand in the center of his back, just behind the heart. So she set it there and the rasping inside his chest tickled her palm.

VIII

Like the First Breath

Leaving the Dreamscape turned out to be harder than getting in. Grenadine wandered about that forest for hours, searching every tree hollow and surveilling the rapids for some kind of—what? She didn't even know what to look for, but hoped she'd know it when she saw it. Her steps kept taking her back to the clearing where Ruben and the witch were snoring away. Carla was nowhere to be seen, but the wolf kept prowling the edge of the glade. Twice, Grenadine found herself face-to-face with the beast. Each time, the fur around his collar swelled like a full moon tide, all silver and bristle. Each time, Attila glared at her from below, head lowered, ears pricked, tail tucked. He didn't seem bent on attacking, but he was not going to let her near his sleeping beauties.

Eventually, the silence grew deep, broken only by the hum of the waterfall and an occasional frog kweeka. Grenadine could have sworn someone had put bricks in her boots. When she found a patch of moss by the roots of a tall oak, she decided to wait it out there.

She woke up to Ruben handing her a smoking mug of strong coffee. When Grenadine sat up to drink it, Carla was broodily traipsing up to the clearing. Attila jumped up, stretched, and trotted away to take a piss before going over to nuzzle the girl's legs. In the chill dawn of the primal forest Grenadine could still feel the warmth that the wolf's body had left in hers. He must have lain down with her after she'd fallen asleep.

Ruben said, "Attila likes to make sure we are cared for." Then without asking, the janitor sat down next to Grenadine and made her scoot over so he too could lean against the trunk of her tree. They sipped on their coffee and listened to each other's breath. Then Grenadine began.

"My father came to kiss me good night. I was so excited: Daddy was home! So happy that he came to my room instead of my sister's. For once, he'd picked me first.

"There was wine and meat on his breath. Business-dinner breath. His goodnight kiss felt a little too wet, but I didn't think much of it. Then there was this tremendous weight crushing my hips. I tried to move my legs but they were paralyzed. This big, dark mass hovered over me. Grasping for air I turned my head, and a hand crushed my neck to the side, my cheek into the pillow, digging. His stubble rammed into the skin of my cheek, my chin. I tried to scream but my throat was crushed. Where was my Daddy?

"Next thing you know, I peed. He must have felt it when he put his hand there, struggling to undo his belt. 'Ew, you're disgusting!' he slurred. Then he just hopped off of me and was gone.

"I got up out of the wet bed to sit on my little-girl chair at the end of the hallway—the one mommy and me had painted pink. I think I was whimpering, hoping my sister would wake up, or my mother. Someone.

"I heard him flush the toilet and saw his shadow stumble toward my sister's door. I grew very quiet. I don't think he saw me. Would he have cared? He disappeared into Evangeline's room. This is when I started to scream. I screamed an ancient, animal, interminable scream. I screamed a scream to wake the dead, a scream that woke my mother, even. She came running down the dark hallway, naked but for her slippers, crying "What, what, what?" I just pointed my finger. I didn't have the words.

"Mom rushed into Evangeline's bedroom. Shouts, shouts, I plugged my ears with my fingers.

"We saw him rarely after that. He kept sending money. He was a lawyer.

"My sister shot herself in the throat four months after her wedding to an addiction counselor. She was three-and-half months pregnant. Her note said only, 'Sorry, I cannot keep her safe.'"

When he was sure Grenadine was done, Ruben stretched his legs out and rested his head into the oak. He sighed a long sigh and said, "When I had no more strength left to suffer, finally I agreed to become a shaman. You are ready. Now we go."

Anthony swatted at the fly and rolled over with a yawn. The memory-foam pillow adjusted punctiliously to the new angle of his jaw. He sank deeper, his head at once floating and anchored. Pure peace trickled, warm, down the corner of his mouth. He tried to guess what time it was, but didn't want to bat an eye. *Twilight. Dark enough,* he thought. The fly landed on his shoulder but Anthony didn't want to move, so he bore the tickle.

Suddenly, there was a blaze inside his shoulder and his arm was in a pretzel behind his back. Someone sat on it. His face sank further into the pillow, his neck kicking around like a palomino, one nostril completely buried in the memory foam. His mouth twisted open to curse and a dry wad was stuffed inside. Greedily, his one nostril flared. He tried to lash out again and something snapped in his elbow. Surely, it was broken. His one available eye rolled back inside its socket to search the dead angle. Found nothing. *Just breathe*, he told himself. He tried lugging his racing mind back to that one, infinitely precious nostril.

Of course, that little Swami twat was going to be a snitch! Already, Anthony was preparing his defense. *I needed to test his loyalty, Dawn! I worried we'd come under tighter scrutiny and... Yes, I should have told you. Forgive me. Will you forgive me?* It might cost him a heavier spanking than he was comfortable with to indulge her dominatrix bent, but Dawn would come around. She would. Just wait.

After what seemed like several minutes, the whisper inside his ear was a shot of nitrous oxide.

"I hate to interrupt this. I had no idea your fear would be so elating, Tony." Grenadine's voice made him heave. Snap! This time it was a torn tendon. The vise around his ribs tightened. "But there's something I need you to do for me. I'm going to take this smelly sock out of your mouth, Anthony, and there's only one sound I want to hear out of that mouth, you hear me? And that sound is Yes. I want to hear you say Yes. Do you understand me, Anthony?" Her grip on his arm was getting slippery so she brought in her knee and put her entire weight into his twisted arm, his back. She could tell that the only resistance now was that of bone and tissue. She was hoping something was irreparable.

"I want to see my daughter." She cleared her throat and said it again, louder this time, "I want to see my daughter. So you are going to take me to her. Ready? Yes. Remember, one sound. Yes. Or you can say bye-bye to what's left of your arm."

When the sock came out of his mouth, Anthony took the longest, deepest, most delicious sip of air. The frantic feeling inside abated a little, but his arm and shoulder had gone numb and his neck followed suit. *Anything to be able to move my neck. Anything!* He managed a weak, "Let me go." Another twist. Snap in the neck. *Shit!*

"Yes!" he cried. Immediately, Grenadine's vise eased up. "Yes! I'll take you to her. She's doing fine. I'll take you. Let me go now."

Grenadine eased up a little more. With a roar, Anthony snapped out of her hold and reached around to grab her arm, pulled her off of him, and tossed her to the floor. He had one heel in the center of her chest. He said, "I will crush you like a sparrow." Their eyes glistened in the brightening day that seeped through the cracks in the opaque curtains. Grenadine reached for his ankle with both hands. He was bracing himself to pulverize her ribcage with his heel, but—

He heard the whack before he felt it, fireworks in the clavicle, then all black.

Anthony woke up to the looming chins of Grenadine and Ruben. He lay flat on his bed. As far as he could tell, all of his limbs were still there, but when he tried to move he couldn't. The fuckers had tied him up. *Fuck.*

He said, "What's the mop-man doing in my bed?"

Ruben got up and went to the door. "I'll leave you two to it, then," he said, slipping away.

Grenadine grinned. There was a small pocket knife in her hand. She held it up to admire, then brought it very, very close to Anthony's eyeball. His eyes sealed up tight.

"How many ways do I need to tell you?" She grinned no longer. "If I don't get to see Gaia now, you won't get to see anything ever again. You'll finally have a use for those overpriced Wayfarers I got for your thirtieth. They'll have to become a permanent accessory. Not that you'll have a chance to appreciate how stylish they make you."

At five o'clock every evening, Sister Ana Maria's feet swelled.

She'd first noticed it when she turned twelve one January, peak of summer in São Paolo. Ana Maria had been walking home from rugby practice when it became imperative that her feet ditch the shoes. She took in the bumpy vacant lot with its two yellow cranes that had been listing there for as long as she could remember. Scattered at her feet were chunks of broken glass. Just ahead was "the creek"—dirty water trickling out of a concrete tunnel. The rugby team liked to run inside its coolness, banging on the walls with sticks and shouting things that their mothers wouldn't approve. The gray walls shouted those things right back at them and, together with the banging and the stomping, it made for hip-hop just as catchy as MTV. The buzz from the marijuana cigarettes that Ramón stole from his stepfather helped weave it all together smoothly. The creek was how come Ana Maria discovered that cold water is the only remedy for her swollen feet. So to this day, everyday at five o'clock, whether her Saint Clare orders had her tend to tungsten-mining guerrillas in Cartagena, refugee camps outside Abidjan, or sustainably raised goats in Vaulx-Le-Vicompte, Ana Maria arranged to be near a cold-water creek—or, at the very least, a French bidet.

Here, in Rio Arriba county, New Mexico, Ana Maria usually had her feet sloshing about Cañones Creek before she had to be back to the kitchen helping with the convent's dinner.

It was five-o-five when Ana Maria sat on her favorite boulder to undo her bootlaces and a lizard with an indigo tail scampered off. She said a silent long-life prayer for it and its family. She pinched off the toe end of her socks, leaned back, and pulled both legs up and out to slip out of two layers of socks at once. This made her roll on her back, giggle like a toddler, and come eye-to-eye with a Mexican jay hiding in a juniper tree. The bird swiveled its head about like a tennis fan. *Heya,* thought Ana Maria. The bird answered with a squawk, fluttered down, jabbed at a piece of lint from her socks, and fluttered back up to disappear in the bramble.

Ana Maria rocked-and-rolled up to sitting and, with one sweeping roll forward, she plunged her feet into the creek. The icy water shot up her legs like a snakebite. It made her cringe, but she slipped the palms of her hands under her thighs and placed one foot in the current for a massage. *Ahhhhhh!* The other foot came up and out to sponge up the sun stored in the boulder. Her eyelids closed.

When she opened them, about midway through the creek she noticed a blue plastic bottle shaking between two rocks. On either side the water shot out in two parting jets. Sister Ana Maria cursed whoever had littered her creek, complete with fantasies of shooting their knee-caps with her BB gun. Then she crossed herself for atonement and reached over to grab the bottle. *No, not quite.* She scooted forward and, when the hem of her robe dropped in the water, the permafrost bit right into her thigh. *Damn it!* Cross sign.

Ana Maria wrung out the corner of the robe, then rolled it up to wedge it good and tight under her buttocks. By the time she found firm grounding for her feet, she could no longer feel her shins and ankles. Finally, leaning in as far as she could, she was able to graze the blue bottle-top with the tip of her nail. Her loose sleeve dipped in, trying to drown her arm, and permafrost bit into her elbow. It felt like a bee sting near the heart, but Ana Maria's finger kept flittering at the bottle-top. *Almost. Almost!* The bottle teetered. Suddenly, it sprung forth and tumbled downstream. *Hell!* Cross. But as the bottle flew up, Ana Maria knew she'd seen something rolled up inside—*a message in a bottle?*

Ana Maria had been sent from France to Española on account of the unusual depth of communication she'd achieved with animal life. In fact, after she'd established herself as a talented goat-interpreter, her presence in Vaulx-le-Vicompte had led to major changes in goat-cheese making.

"The goats are feeling traumatized," Ana Maria blurted out one day to the Mother Superior, who was bemoaning the drop in quality of the convent's goat-cheese production after two eminent Parisian restaurants had suddenly decided to start procuring their *chabichou* from *le Père Marcel* down in Savigny. Émile, the billy-goat, had been struck by a mysterious illness, which Ana Maria had correctly diagnosed as acute melancholia, but for which no treatment seemed to work. After the third failed attempt at having Émile impregnate the herd, the Mother Superior had him donated to a petting zoo near the Castle, where he had to be restrained after he'd gnawed a festering hole into his own leg. In his stead they brought in Roland, all frisky and self-important—"a real male," the Sisters chuckled. But the she-goats were missing Émile's sensibility, his pensive cuddles after intercourse. Roland just did his affair and fell right away into an agitated sleep. The goats felt cheapened; their self-esteem dropped. Of course, it showed in the quality of their milk.

Eventually, Émile was returned to Ana Maria's French convent. Although his performance as a breeder didn't improve, his gentle presence among the herd alleviated the goats' anxiety. Ana Maria insured that a sample of goats were consulted in the selection of Roland's replacement, and in a few months, restaurateurs from Brussels, Saint Petersburg and Brazzaville were emailing their orders for *Le chabichou de Sainte Clare*. But the Mother Superior grew tired of hearing about the goats's états d'âme, and she'd always thought that Ana Maria was a little odd anyway. However, she did recognize in the novice a potential— perhaps even a Gift of Grace?—that deserved to be cultivated. So, when Mother Superior received a congratulatory text message from her old seminary cellmate Carmen, head mistress of a convent in the Native American territory of the Western United States, it occurred to her that it would be an apt place for Ana Maria. Didn't the Indians talk to animals too?

In the four months since Ana Maria had arrived at Santa Clara, there had been little excitement except for her interactions with the local fauna—prairie dogs, in particular, and a geriatric cat named Stigmata. She had cheerfully agreed to commit to complete silence, speculating that to relinquish communication with her peers would only strengthen her ability to hear what other creatures wanted to tell her. She had speculated right, but as fascinating as the inner world of birds and bees was, Ana Maria was feeling starved for human drama—the little daily cruelties, the loud feelings, the senseless wants. So needless to say, an enigmatic message-in-a-bottle was hard to resist for the young nun.

In a heart-beat, Ana Maria picked up her robe and hurried downstream. Gravel chewed away at the soles of her feet but she kept her pace. She knew of a hairpin bend a little ways downstream. There was a chance that the bottle would catch in the bramble there.

Bingo! There lay the bottle, bobbing on its soft bed of river grass. Ana Maria tip-toed onto the sandy bar and stopped at arm's length of the prize. Sure enough, there was a piece of ruled paper rolled up inside. Ana Maria folded her sleeve all the way up to the shoulder and slowly approached the trembling bottle. Pluck.

Standing right where she was, Ana Maria dried her hands on her robe as best she could and unscrewed the blue top. It was on real tight so she had to use her teeth. Inside, the paper looked a bit wavy, with blue ink bleeding through. The roll was too loose to come out, so she reached in with her longest finger and wound the note tighter around it. It worked. She pulled out the roll and wedged the empty bottle between her knees.

In round, slobbering letters the note read, "Help!! Boyfriend K.O! We are dying next to lightning-struck stump! Bring alboterol [sic] and food ASAP! Please hurry!!!" It was signed Alia with a heart-shaped dot on the i.

The Friday before they stole Rosa was the best day of Marc's life. He didn't need to add, "Except the day I met you" to Rosa, who relished his joy. Via senior editor Michelle Briens, the prestigious Parisian publisher J. Vrin announced that he'd accepted Marc's latest manuscript for publication. This was Marc's third monograph but it was *his* first book—the first that wasn't about what other thinkers thought. After a few glasses of *Boulaouane*

gris at the reception organized by his boring friend Dieter, Marc declared, "My hope is that Vital Ontology does for teleological thinking what international finance has done for the Nation-State. Only with a radical ungrounding of the necrophiliac 'us vs. them' morality that capitalist democracies promote may our children have air to breathe, free water to drink, a planet to—" At that point Marc's words had gotten lost in the scuffle as a paparazzo had to be manhandled out of the restaurant by the portentous Moroccan bodyguard Dieter had hired after his philosophy talk-show earned him accolades in the national press.

Damned jet lag. Prune's stomach growled. She remembered resenting having to share her candied-lemon lamb *tagine* with her mother that night. Always eager for the most luxurious sample of flavors possible, Rosa had demanded to share platters and she had, as usual, eaten more than her arithmetical half. There had also been Dieter's impossibly red nose as he kept whispering things in Rosa's ear. Rosa's elbow, finally, so sharp between Dieter's ribs that he had spilled his red wine on his model girlfriend's lap. The girlfriend storming out, and Dieter calling her "*sale pute*" through his teeth. Marc, glowing at the far end of the table, impervious. Michelle Briens finger-drumming on her heart, drinking his words. Rosa and Marc, silent on the walk home, with Prune in the middle. How grown up she'd felt with one parent hanging on each arm— and also a little bit proud.

The next Monday, Marc had put up a handmade sign on his home office door that read, *"Je vis, donc j'écris."* I live, therefore I write. Vrin wanted the completed manuscript in no later than Christmas. That left four months to perfection.

Marc had never finished. In the seven weeks between Rosa's abduction and his own disappearance, he'd barely set foot in his office. The door, which they'd been used to seeing either wide open, when he wasn't in, or sealed shut, when he was working, stayed ajar with the leather and man smell spilling out. The television, which had always been more philodendron shelf than entertainment center, babbled on all day and night. In the morning, before leaving for school, the girls found their father shriveled up in his armchair in front of pet-grooming shows. A few times he'd snapped awake to Carla brushing his hair with a toothbrush.

The woman at the Vrin bookstore approached Prune from behind. She was trying not to hover, but the girl was fondling the book with such intent. She knew little about Marc Michaux. Only that his book had grazed the best-seller list in its first weeks.

"His wife disappeared not long before he did, you know." She spoke fast, surreptitiously. "People talk. Mad love, they say. He killed her, then killed himself. Crime of passion. But I don't believe it. They'd have found bodies, don't you think? Scholars are the worst gossips, you know." She pointed her chin toward the ornate gates of La Sorbonne. "I see it all the time. They come in here, and yabbery-yab!"

"When did it come out?"

"Huh, let me see." The woman glanced at Prune's white knuckles on the book's spine. She decided her book was safe enough and walked over to the cash register, rummaged underneath, and pulled out a catalogue. She licked her finger to flip it open, used her other finger to scan top to bottom, flipped to the next page, scanned bottom to top. "Ah, *voilà*! It says here August 7. Yes, that seems about right." Her eyes wandered out the window toward the square. "The *place* was deserted. The scholars all at the beach playing racket ball. It was only the pigeons, the tourists, the bag-lady, and me."

"Do you know how I can get in touch with Michelle Briens?"

"Michelle? She's long gone. I think she got a job with *Actes Sud* in Provence. Dream job too. With real writers—you know: creatives. How do you know Michelle?"

Prune was standing in front of the cash register with five copies of her father's book in her arms. "How much do I owe you?"

The stump that Alia had come to think of as theirs had turned into iron from being struck by lightning. There were even rusted bits. But the dirt around it was soft, with tufts of tiny flowers peeking through. Alia was sure she'd read somewhere that lightning fertilizes earth. Charred plant matter turns into nitrate fertilizer and growth is even stronger after a forest fire.

Tongue sticking out, Alia applied herself to sketching the flowers in her notebook, hoping that she'd eventually be able to look up their names. She had not chosen this place for their last resting place, though she would probably have chosen a place just like it. The creek brought fresh water for bathing and drinking, and also plenty of carp. They had yet to catch one. All sorts of birds were magnetized by the berries that grew like weeds.

The first days, Alia tried talking to the birds, asking for guidance. Then she got upset that they kept pecking mindlessly instead of wanting to help, and she decided to ignore them. Finally, after the last of the jerky and granola bars were gone, the berries became a matter of subsistence for her and Pedro. Alia engineering a scarecrow out of some driftwood, a half cow's skull, and the only change of socks Pedro had packed. But by day four, there wasn't much else than the birds to look at. Sky, cloud, sun, Pedro motionless under the flimsy shelter, dirty backpacks, her best nightgown with the pink lace browning with dust. Sky, sky, sky.

Alia elaborated thirteen plans to free the children, only one of which didn't involve leaving Pedro alone while she went to look for help. The shame over wanting so badly to walk away, she warded off during the day by caring for him smotheringly. But it came back at night to haunt her fits of sleep. Again and again, Alia spasmed awake to the small smile of her mother in the rear window of the taxi cab that was taking her back to the airport. For the first time, it occurred to Alia that after her father had left them with a note and a bottle of French perfume in the midst of the Arab Spring, bringing Alia to The Center may have seemed a matter of survival to her mother. *Still, I'll never forgive her*, thought Alia. And so, even for the sake of seeking the help they desperately needed, Alia could not resolve herself to leave her barely conscious friend in the middle of this nowhere-land.

Truth be told, the one plan that didn't involve leaving Pedro to dry out like a Turkish fig turned out to be Pedro's—sort of.

He was playing with a dead branch in the creek when a coughing fit overtook him. The branch took off like a groundhog and disappeared around the bend. "Too bad we don't have a bottle," Pedro said casually after he'd caught his breath, "or we could send a message in a bottle. It'd be bound to get somewhere. Don't all creeks lead up to a river, and don't all rivers get to... I don't know, places where people live, not just turkey vultures?"

Their jugs were too cumbersome to do the trick. They kept getting stuck in the nests the rocks made. It took Alia but fifteen minutes of hiking upstream before she spotted the right workaday blue plastic bottle beached on a tiny sand bar. The tag was gone but the bottle was undamaged. For once, Alia wanted to throw kisses at the anonymous litterer instead of kicking their shin.

By the time sister Ana Maria found them, the skin on Pedro's nose had bubbled, burst, scabbed, and peeled off again. Having vowed silence, Ana Maria couldn't speak her concern and comfort, but her appearance triggered a cataract of explanations from Alia. Eventually, Pedro found the strength to crawl over to them and pull hard enough on Alia's gown to make her let go of the nun, who kept pointing at the horizon and making wide circles with her finger as if to say, "I have to go get help but I'll be back!"

Alia spent the next hours sweeping and swatting, folding and re-folding, turning their packs inside-out and whipping every speck of sand out of their things. Then she squatted by the creek, her back to Pedro. She didn't want him to see how scared she was.

He didn't try to reassure her. He worried he'd jinx it if he said how much faith he had. Of course, the nun was coming back. Of course, she wasn't alerting Dawn, or the CIA, or whoever wouldn't want them to make it.

The moon was rising over the mesa when the Range Rover halted by the stump. The slamming doors woke up Pedro. He barely had time to take in sister Michaela's ogre boots before her miner's flashlight blinded him. Without a word, she slid one arm under his back, another under his knees, lifted him up as if he weighted twenty pounds instead of one hundred-and-ten, and carried him over to a makeshift cot in the back of the truck. Less than a minute later she had a respirator pressed against his face and a rubber band was pulling on the hair at the back of his head.

The first full breath was a long-held scream.

The line in front of the *Musée d'Orsay* was long, but fast-moving. The Senegalese guard at the door paddled people through, whistling "Don't Worry, Be Happy." Prune grinned as he waved her through, and he grinned back. In an accent-less French he cried, "*Ah ben voilà, enfin quelqu'un d'aussi heureux que moi!*" meaning, Ah, finally someone as happy as me! "*Elle est pas belle, la vie, mademoiselle?*"

"*Magnifique!*" chirped Prune. She was elated: Her father *had* to be alive. How else would his three-hundred-and-seventy-two-page monograph be sitting on the main display table of J. Vrin?

At dinner, Marc had loved to make Rosa and the girls place bets on how many pages he'd written that day. Whoever came closest won a foot rub, so they were pretty serious about trying to figure it out. Prune knew for a fact that he barely had two-hundred pages written when they took Rosa, his mind went into shut-down, and then one night he just didn't come home, not even after Prune had fixed Nutella toasts and hot cocoa for supper, and Carla crashed on the sofa with her face smashed into Rosa's orphaned crochet.

The lady at the museum coat-check didn't say a word, but she took the behemoth backpack, the five-books-heavy plastic bag from Vrin, and the frayed coat without a blink. In exchange she handed Prune a tiny ticket with the number thirteen printed on it.

The main hall was narrower than Prune remembered. Harrowed faces shuffled among the naked bodies of bronze ghosts. A lustful Sappho. A "Young Aristotle" of about ten who held a ball in his hand but was not playing—absorbed in his reading instead. David, his delicate foot casual on Goliath's severed head. A carefree "Pan with Bear Cubs," young boy on his stomach with his goat-legs playfully beating the air. Everywhere, reminders that goddesses, heroes, and sages too had once been children.

Orsay was Rosa's favorite museum, not so much for its famed Impressionists as for the lesser-known surrealist pastels of Odilon Redon and the hilarious caricatures of nineteenth-century bourgeois by Daumier. "Social satire from the antediluvian times before political correctness—priceless!" she'd say.

Prune set out to find Redon.

For her daughter's fourteenth birthday, Rosa had insisted on taking her alone to the museum. The view from the café's balcony, with the fast clouds, the *Tuileries* gardens' splashes of tulips, the Ferris wheel, the *Grand Palais* skylight, and all the tiny people going about their important lives, was Prune's favorite. So was the lemon-meringue pie. But before Prune was allowed to squeeze in the elevator to the fifth floor, Rosa set them on the trail through oversized hunting and war scenes.

Prune's excitement had started to falter when, out of breath, her mother asked a bulbous-nosed guard where they'd been hiding The Origin of the World. He pretended to think, then winked, pointing beyond the striking Turkish painting of an old man gazing at children's tombs.

"Ils l'ont planqué là-bas derrière," he whispered, conspiratorial. *"Pour pas choquer les gens"*—meaning, They hid it back there not to shock people. "Though if you ask me, kids see worse everyday on the computer, and not quite as pretty."

Rosa said *merci* and took her daughter's hand. They turned the corner, crossed two rooms in a row, and there it was, right smack in the center of a big white wall: the meticulous, Victorian-era close up of a pussy. Gustave Courbet's The Origin of the World.

Rosa planted herself in front of it. She planted Prune, as tall as her already, right between herself and the folds, hair, vulva on the wall.

One white breast glows in the corner, invites you in closer to the smooth belly. The milk of the thighs draws you toward the mess of hair in the center, parted by a slit of the richest pinks, shiny clitoris peaking through.

Rosa declared, "Whatever anyone tries to say to you about your cunt, your woman's genitals. Whatever they whisper, shout, mutter, draw, paint, sing, photograph, grab, caress, bite, evoke, advise, or regiment about your vagina—and believe me, daughter, they will. Do not ever forget. *Do. Not. Ever. Forget.* You are a work of art. Your entire body, each and every cell, cartilage, and pore is a work of art."

A few visitors ghosted by, none daring to stop and look squarely, like they did at the eviscerated deer next door. From the corner of her eye, Prune caught the same chubby boy orbiting about a few times, but hurrying away as soon as he came within the painting's gravitational pull. Rosa felt Prune's evasion and weighed on her shoulders to anchor her down. "And I, I made you. You know what that makes me?"

"My mother?"

"It makes me a great artist. The greatest. And you, a woman, are the greatest artist, too. You are making and remaking yourself, constantly. With each thought, each choice, and each non-choice. You are making and remaking the world with your words, your touch, your gaze. Maybe, one day, you'll give birth to another human, if you so choose. Maybe you won't. But each one of us, each little human"—Rosa fanned her arm out to include every straggler in the "Realism and Nudes" aisle of the Orsay museum— "is a universe!" This, she cried just as a German senior tour-group was clustering in front of a series of washed out nudie photographs from the nineteen hundreds. "Each an entire cosmos, and comets, and black holes, and birthing stars, and dying cells. But you, *mi hija*, are a woman. Look!"

Prune was looking. She was staring into that vulva, the vertiginous layers, the pleasures and the hurts, the claims of the artist and the man over it, the reclaiming by the model of her own nudity, and by the viewer, by her, Prune, by her mother.

"You are a woman!" Rosa was shouting now. The Germans tried to avert their eyes, except for two blue-haired ladies, who broke out of the herd and pointedly came to stand right next to Rosa and her daughter. Rosa ignored them. "And that makes you God-seed. That makes you, *mi hija*, the Origin of the World. With that comes great power, great potential, great responsibility. Don't screw it up. Love yourself. Love all of you. Love the ugliest and the sweetest, the frailest and the mightiest, just as I love you. Love your failures, your wounds, your doubts, your hopes, your lovers, your friends, your work, your pussy, your breasts, and even your thighs—yes, even your thighs, *mujer!*" The German ladies clapped a polite little clap. Prune tried to protest. Her mother's fingers burrowed deeper into her shoulders. It hurt but the girl said nothing. There were times when Rosa could not be moved and they were rare, but this was one of them.

Rosa continued, her voice low inside Prune's ear. "Hell is the absence of love. That's all. That's all it is, Prune. Hell is the absence of love. Don't make a hell for yourself; not even for your enemies. Make heaven. Bring heaven on Earth. You can. You must. Love. Even if I'm not here—especially if I'm not here. Love yourself just as I love you. Love yourself better than I love you. Love yourself like you are God. Because you are, Prune. You. Are. The. Origin. Of. The. World."

As soon as Anthony closed the playroom door to leave her alone with Gaia like she'd asked, Grenadine wished that he hadn't.

The baby held onto the bars of her playpen with both hands, trying to pull herself up to her feet.

"Hello there!" Grenadine said as cheerfully as she could. The baby frowned and pulled herself up high enough for the top of her head to bob above the guardrail. There was a squeak when she toppled over on her diaper. Grenadine lurched in, "Oh my god, are you ok?" Gaia's brow rode up her round forehead, her perfect mouth drawing an O. Suddenly, an ear-piercing siren rose out of the toddler's body. How could something so big come out of something so small? It stopped Grenadine in her tracks. She plugged both her ears with her fingers, thinking, *This is not going so well.* She tried to think of something that would stop it, but nothing came.

Grenadine had always been the youngest everything: sister, cousin, summer-camp-kisser, master gardener. It had earned her the privilege of deciphering the names on Christmas gift tags and bringing the bow-wrapped packages to their due recipients. But it also meant she'd never been around kids, really. Not until The Center. And even then, she'd tried to stay away. She had to admit, kids grossed her out. The tenuous control over bodily functions; the absence of volume regulation; the general lack of self-awareness; the snot. Grenadine thought, *Children are just tiny madmen, and somehow you're expected to put up with it because they have those big round eyes and they cry easy?*

When her moon cycle hadn't come and her breasts had kept on swelling sore like abscesses, Grenadine had assumed abortion was the only way. The Planned Parenthood lady asked the most personal questions in the least personal way. She was good, her eyes moist like a Golden Retriever's. She told Grenadine not to mind the stomps of the haters outside. "God will recognize his own," she said, confident, as she pumped the blood-pressure brace tighter and tighter, until it strangled Grenadine's arm, and words got stuck in Grenadine's throat, and Grenadine had to run out of there.

Grenadine took one step back, squatted down, and the baby's screams abated. The mother eased up on her ears and tried to smile.

"Hello Gaia. I know you don't remember me, but I gave birth to you." The baby's screams redoubled. They came in sheets, like vengeful rain. Grenadine glanced back at the closed door, hoping Anthony would be there, peeking through the peephole. Even his creepiness would be better than this being alone with her daughter for the first time, and sort of hoping it would be the last. Nope, no one was watching. *Fuck. Fuck fuck fuck fuck fuck!* thought Grenadine as Gaia screamed herself purple in the face, her chin a Parkinson's. *Fuck.* Hiding her face in her hands, Grenadine told herself, "Think!"

Aryan Iceberg. Most people would call that the start of a pretty day, the moon washed-out and a few perfect stars still sprinkling the zenith. It was that kind of scrubbed-clean morning, with watermelon on the horizon, when my waters broke. It's not what I'd planned, this puddle on Anthony's bathroom floor and a sky pale as my father's eyes. The doula had warned me about sex in the twenty-sixth week. Something about the Kabbala—I remember now: 2+6=8, number of infinity— which I naturally cast aside as witch's crock. I must say it was hot smut, on my knees, Anthony riding me from behind—more gentle than I would have wanted, motions mindful, everything a little bit too real.

When the walls stopped shaking, the silence felt numb. Through her fingers, Grenadine saw that Gaia was watching her, curious. Grenadine pulled her hands away from her face and

Gaia's chin started to shake again.

"No, no, no, here!" Grenadine cried, rushing her hands back in front of her face. Gaia lit up. Grenadine knew this game. She'd felt inconsolable when her sister Evangeline's face would disappear, elated when it reappeared. There. Not there. There. Not there. Just like that, with the simple motion of one hand, five fingers.

With Grenadine's face there again, it was as if a switch had been turned on. Gaia began to whine, all scrunched up like a newborn. Grenadine turned around, her back hunched over to forestall the assault of sound, fingers at the ready next to her ears. Her mind shouted, *Walk out of here, go stab Anthony in the balls, Dawn in the chest, then keep walking, keep walking, keep walking.*

"Ba... ba... ba... dadadaaaa."

Grenadine glanced back at the baby. Propped up on her diaper as on a throne, Gaia sat in the exact center of her playpen, hands over her eyes, beaming. Grenadine noticed the perfect little nails on the end of perfect little fingers, the plump folds at the wrist, the forearms shaped exactly like her own.

"Ba ba ba dada?" Grenadine offered. "Do you want your daddy?"

Gaia snatched her hands away, shaking her head no. "Ba!" she said, insistent.

Grenadine took that as an invitation. She risked a few steps toward the playpen. Gaia observed closely. She seemed to be counting her mother's steps.

"I don't know what you're trying to say, little one. I don't speak babble." Grenadine squatted down by the playpen. Gaia's face was inches from hers across the wooden bars. She smelled like curdled milk. "Will you teach me?"

Gaia raised her hands over her eyes again. Her grin uncovered shiny gums. Through the baby's spread fingers, Grenadine could see eyelashes so long and curled, they could have been fake. Grenadine's mother had eyelashes like that. She'd never needed to wear mascara and everyone envied her for it. Grenadine's father said it made her look like a cow.

Grenadine covered her eyes, too.

They stayed there, mirror images of each other, grinning and batting their eyes behind their fingers.

After a while, Grenadine cried, "Where in the world did Gaia go?" It was coming back to her, how the game went.

"Ba… Ma!" Gaia's hands flew up in the air.

Grenadine's hands shot up too. "Maaaa… That's right, Gaia. Ma! Ma… Ma … Mamamamama…"

Gaia bounced gaily up and down on her diaper, arms aflutter. "Maaaaaa… maaaaa…mamamamamamamamama." Together they sang, until there was a loud knock and the guard's voice came in muffled through the door.

"Ma'am? Time's up. I don't want no trouble. I got a call. President Hetherington is on her way."

"Eggs have always made me sad." Carla prodded the yolk and watched it jiggle until it came to a rest. Attila was watching her fork with his entire body.

"Don't you even dream of tossing those out to him," Anastasia mumbled through her toast. She took another bite, then proceeded. "They make him fart." A few crumbs shot out of her mouth. "Have you ever been exposed to Attila's flatulence? It's Tchernobyl! It's the Huns rampaging the Mongolian plains! Where do you think he got his name from? Just eat your eggs, child."

Carla slipped a minuscule bit of crunchy white past her lips. Without looking up from her plate, she said, "I bet Prune is eating croissants with our Mom and Dad right now."

Attila's ears pricked up. Carla scanned her surroundings for an identifiable cause and settled on a creeping ginger blossom. "I just wish this flower would grow less noisily," she said, covering her ears with her palms. "So I can hear the song of the sirens." A pained furrow was splitting her forehead. She wasn't pretending. It hurt.

Anastasia said, "Tell me about those sirens, squirt. What do they sound like?"

Carla's eggs jiggled again when she got up to go lie on the ground. Splayed out in the grass, she was still holding her head, an aura of clover blossoms fanning their purple about her body. "They don't sound like anything. Or maybe they sound like everything—like crows, lawnmowers, Aerosmith, mother's love-making, Italian tourists at the beach, bad memories, and drunk people, all singing and crying and telling me… telling me… telling me—"

"Telling you what, cabbage?" The effort to discern puckered up the girl's face.

"I don't know, I don't know, *I don't know!*" she cried. Then she grew very quiet and her chin began to pulse a "No," right, left, right, left, right, like a metronome. Then came the boom of her heels spurring at the soil. Someone else might have thought this was the onset of a seizure, but Anastasia could hear the music underneath. The Earth was asking the girl for a dance.

Poised, Attila looked on, stealing quick glances at the discarded breakfast. The crone began to snap her fingers to the tune of Carla-Earth. Snap, boom, head-shake, snap, boom, head-shake, snap, boom, snap… Crone, earth, girl, wolf, crone, wolf, girl, earth, wolf, girl, earth, crone.

Anastasia stood up. Snap, step, cha cha cha. Clover kneeled at her feet. Boom, "No," snap, boom, boom. Carla's heels thundering at the ground. The echo fierced its way through packed earth and up their legs, reaching the woman and the girl's hips at the same time. Snap, boom, head-shake, sway, snap, boom, "Huh." The song was melding the four of them—earth, crone, girl, wolf—into one writhing machine. Then the girl's face was in the sky and her frown ironed out into the shadow of a smile. She lifted her arm to reach for a cotton-ball cloud as her hips dug deeper into the clover. Anastasia clapped her hands and twirled an elaborate twirl between Carla's ankles. Step, clap, clap, step, boom, thud.

Attila took this as his cue to inch closer to the eggs. He cleaned Carla's plate in two laps and was moving on to the crumbs Anastasia had left in hers when Carla yelled, "I'm not! I'm not! I'm not! Leave me alone!"

Anastasia's feet stopped shuffling, but her torso was still swaying to the inner music. Standing over Carla, she placed the palms of her hands above the girl's face. This seemed to bring some relief.

What Carla could see was little Lou, curled up under a tattered blankie with her pink flamingo Sam. *What is this place?* Carla wondered. The respirator's tubes made small warrior scarifications at the bridge of Lou's nose and, with her hair in a tangled mop, she looked feral. It was dark and dank. *A good place to hide,* thought Carla. *Wolves, too, will look for a hollow in which to let themselves die. No one wants to journey to the underworld in the open. Dying wants intimacy.*

The hollow was small, but clearly delineated by adobe and stone walls. Although it was partly filled with debris, you could guess that the shape had originally been circular, like the kivas, those ritual spaces that focalized the religious and social life of the prehistoric Pueblo people. Carla recalled the kids telling bedtime stories of The Center sitting on top of a prehistoric *pueblo* built by the Tewa Indians several centuries ago. Broken bits of pottery could be found once in a while, but no one had been able to unearth actual ruins. Maybe Lou had uncovered an access point?

As loud as she could manage, Lou called, "Prune! Pedro! Alia!" The answer was only the echo of her own voice, the aimless names of her friends coming back mangled, "Pru… Pruu… Pe… Nnnn… Al… dro-dro-dro… lia-lia." The little girl recoiled and pressed Sam's taped-back-together head tighter against her cheek. "Mommy!" she hissed, bracing herself against the void.

Carla wanted to talk to her, tell her about—What? Maybe

191

the waterfall, and the warm rocks, and Attila's swimming. Maybe Anastasia's goulash. But Lou wasn't listening.

The little warrior stood up. She set her flamingo down, so she could secure her blanket around her neck. Equipped with her magic cape, she picked Sam back up, tucked him in the belt of her pants, and started into the uncharted. With each step, Lou twisted right and left, legs bent at the knee for spring, small hands feeling the black air.

It must have been coming from five o'clock, a tired mosquito at first. Lou leaned in toward the sound, trying to touch its vibrations with her fingers. The noise bounced off the tip of her index, traveling the length of her arm, up the side of the neck to the ear. Almost at the same time, the smell hit her. The buzzing got so busy, the stink so loud, that for a moment, even Carla was deaf. Lou buckled, but she draped her blanket about her face, latched her hand onto Sam's hard head, and started again. She turned a corner and daylight fell from a pinhole in the red-rock ceiling. Lou pulled the blanket down just enough to see.

Amid swarms of flies lay several corpses, each with small feet and a loose bump around the midriff. Each a pregnant mass of decomposing flesh. Carla counted seven. Seven girls and seven fetuses, in various states of development and decomposition. None of the girls could have been more than sixteen, although it was hard to tell.

Lou's face hardened. In a snap, Carla saw the indomitable Kali there, blue skin and tongue sticking out. With a roar, the demon-slaying goddess swung her sword, cutting down avatars of Dawn, Anthony, a battalion of soldiers anonymous inside dark helmets. Bloody arms, hands, calves erupted, and Kali crunched them in her teeth!

Then the little warrior collapsed to the ground, her cape pouring softly after her. Spine curved, head bowed, she crumpled around Sam, arms and legs drawn in like a fetus next to the other children, and died.

Was it minutes, or hours in shared stillness?

When Carla began to speak, eyelids fluttering at blinding clouds above, she was saying, "Sorry. Sorry Sorry Sorry Sorry Sorry Sorry Sorry Sorry Sorry. *Pardon. Pardon. Pardon Pardon Pardon Pardon.* I'm so sorry, Lou! Sorry. Sorry. Sorry, Lou. You were right. I think you will like it there. Yes, do crawl back in her womb: the Earth says she welcomes you. It will be fine now. It will be fine. Good-bye, Lou. *Adieu,* sweet one."

"She could have come stay with us," Anastasia offered limply.

Carla chuckled. It wasn't a morbid or a cynical chuckle. Just the sound of when sobs are out of reach. She said, "No, Lou isn't like us. That girl has no fear. She said there is no birth, no death. No more waiting."

Carla pushed herself up to standing. Twigs and grasses had caught in her hair. For a moment, crone and girl stood facing each other.

Then Anastasia said, "I saw what you saw. Everything. And I'm going to be right here with you. Personally, I think I want to wait a bit longer before I die. It is worth waiting. Look!" Attila was licking his chops guiltily, and both plates glistened clean. "Attila thinks so too." She leaned over to stroke the thick fur around his neck. "It isn't fear that keeps us here, squirt. It's commitment. The power of commitment is that it has the ability to make something—anything—sacred. You commit to life? You make life sacred—and I mean Life, not just survival. You commit to death? You make death sacred. And I mean Death, not just resignation."

"But this Dreamscape is neither life nor death. What is it you have committed to?"

"You're right. This is neither life nor death. This is more than either. This is the between. This is what I make sacred. The between, the invisible glue. My Karl used to call it love."

IX

Full of Grit and Grace

At Paris-Gare-de-Lyon, the seven A.M. crowd was all charcoal pants and sailor coats with satchels wheeling behind. In the three years Prune had been away at The Center, the bullet-train had been spiffed up to compete with Cheap-o-Jets from Britain. Her free first-class upgrade landed her in a car with primo leather seats suspended in quiet so pillowy, it could have been snowing all night in there. Stylized plexiglass signs reminded the passengers that cell phones were *interdits*.

The train started as soon as Prune tucked her pack in the overhead shelf, but there was no lurching, no stumbling, no vapor-burping doors: only the imaginary snow-flakes dampening everything—except it was a gorgeous autumn day with nothing but leaf-dust in the air.

Her assigned seat had her facing the back of the train. Her shoulder blades hurled at tomorrow at 320 km an hour didn't feel right, so she moved to the center seats with the folding tablets and no one across. She made sure she was facing the right way, and let herself sink into the crisp leather, toeing her sneakers off her heels to prop her feet on the seat across from hers.

Prune's heels remembered digging their own little trench in the brown August sand at *Les Saintes-Maries-de-la-Mer*. The Mediterranean sun held her body like a teen boy, all hunger and warmth. Sleep disputed her consciousness to the breathy romance of a red-haired Underground fighter with a Gestapo violinist, but the book was mostly for shade anyway.

194

There was a muted announcement, "Avignon, Marseille," then a lurch. They were only now leaving the station. Another train had departed before, creating the illusion that hers was moving. "*Tout est relatif*," she shrugged, remembering how Carla rolled her eyes every time their grandmother Alma said it. Everything is relative.

Ka-chunk, Ka-chunk, Ka-chunk. Prune sunk deeper, with the train sounding like the sea lapping at the shore. She rested her temple against the cool window and closed her eyes.

At the beach, Marc had asked about her book, but instead of answering Prune had crawled across her mother's empty towel, not caring that hot sand was sticking to her coconut-oiled legs. Prune laid her cheek on her father's sun-heated belly. Marc was ticklish and his stomach muscles tensed up, but she took care to tie her hair in a bun and breathe lightly. Eventually, his belly relaxed and, with her head bobbing on her father's twisting and creaking stomach, Prune watched Rosa teach Carla how to carve butterflies in the sand with her arms and legs. Predicated on the production of awe-inspiring beauty, their mother's method for teaching swimming was infallible.

In the dream, Prune was her mother, who was a Frida Kahlo self-portrait. Her enormous face filled the frame, with its downy upper lip and coal-miner's stare unperturbed by drips of water so cold, they burned a hole in the crown of her head. She felt herself shape-shifting. Political activist, mother, lover, daughter, sister, fervor… then the black hole of childhood memories, all the way back to infancy, before the skull seals itself off and the brain must learn detours, become dependent on human blood for air. Her spine, broken and screwed back together; the forced integrity of a *dolor* of geological proportions; the isolation of suffering, sedimented in her baby-girl glands. Torture, yes, and the torturers invisible. She, searching with her glassy, not-yet-seeing eyes, thinking "I must find them," but the face remained unbothered and the spider-monkey sitting on her shoulder yelped—not like a monkey's yelp but more like a doorbell—then a crackling,

"Prochain arrêt, Avignon. Assurez-vous de ne rien oublier."

Outside the train window, black and white cows zipped by. Also, a blue Ikea outlet, the familiar bulk of a pink stucco Provençal house, rows of cypress trees, gnarly and naked vineyards, a space-age bridge rushing over whitewater, a church steeple, more trees (the ones with the vitiligo patches on the trunk), more cattle of some kind—hard to tell what kind from the bullet train. *Hard to tell.* Hard to tell was making Prune dizzy, and she squeezed her eyes shut to reboot.

In the dream, a gray sloth with natty hair is crossing a road. It is a narrow, one-lane road, with no lines and scattered gravel on its flanks—a gray road, the kind that could work in a government office. A long road. And the sloth is crossing it, its Zorro eyes low on the tarmac, noodly arms a mockery of support. The sloth goes at his sloth pace, present to each knuckle's creak, each wheezing hair. Shu, shu, shu, like tired skis on new snow. And the road blazes in noon's furnace, suddenly so white as to make Prune squint and search the horizon for absent shade. Then, out of her long shadow thrown against the tarmac, like a Pollock squirt, rises her mother. Rosa, squat and with the garden-gnome cheeks of an *Altiplano* girl, black-pearl eyes pierced with the abyss of the blind. As if chasing chickens with the click of her tongue, Rosa takes off running after the sloth, *"Vamos, vamos, vamos.* Pot, pot, pot." Poised as a sloth, the sloth looks up at Prune, who stands by the side of the road munching on her cuticles and waiting for her mother to see her. But Rosa sees only the sloth. And Rosa sees a black van barreling down the mountain. Rosa clicks her tongue again, and pushes the sloth, trying to make it get across. Prune sees the van; she sees the blazing road in the shiny black paint; she tries to scream. The sloth yawns and Prune wakes up, her hair natty and damp like Carla's in the weeks after Rosa was taken from them, before Prune learned to brush it herself when Jérome started pulling on it, saying, "It is nasty, and probably there are bugs in it."

Out the train window, a small white horse jumped over an

196

electric fence and kept on grazing, as if insubordination was no big enchilada. This made Prune happy-sad, this nonchalant transgression by the indigenous Camargue horse. Happy because it was vertiginously free. Sad because it wasn't that simple.

By now, her mother had probably died from insubordination, with Carla not far behind, eager to give up on this life—unless Prune could find something here leading to their parents.

The woman at the bookstore had said that Michelle Briens, Marc's editor, was in Arles. If Marc had managed to complete his book after his disappearance, Prune reasoned, then it was likely that Michelle Briens was one of the last people to have seen him.

Arles was just like Prune remembered, blinding white light and knee-weakening beauty. You'd think you were having a near-death experience.

Songs popular thirty years ago wafted out of tall windows as Prune wandered down narrow lanes, crimson vines steering her gaze up toward the blue that brought Van Gogh here—a blue pure enough to go mad over, brawl with your friends, cut yourself.

Saturday, eleven A.M. Along the remains of the medieval ramparts that have kept generations of Moorish invaders out but succumbed to twelve hours of Nazi *Blitzkrieg*, the artichoke vendors were proudly bantering away their stuff in baroque poetry, *"Elle est pas belle, ma gigine? Ronde et féconde comme une blonde! Allez, Allez!*

"Oh Looord, won't you buy me, a color T.V." The gravelly English brought Prune right back to the pot-holed asphalt, the hard shadows that the plane trees were tossing across the oyster trucks, the small brass change in the can at the busker's feet. His cheeks were a blowfish, purple and puffed. His eyelids swallowed his eyes whole. He looked forty but could have been twenty, skinny limbs and orbed gut. Obviously a native speaker of Janis Joplin, he stomped the ground with one heavy boot and slapped his thigh. "I'll wait for de-li-very, each day until three."

You have to applaud the belting it out, thought Prune. With his face raised toward the maddening blue, the white of his eyes showed a little at the rim. He didn't care if anyone was listening. This was between him and his Lord.

Prune dug into her pocket and found a few coins. In the years she'd been gone, her memory of value had gotten amputated with lack of use, like toes. The coins jangled upon landing—one in the tin and the other rolling off the sidewalk to disappear in the gutter. The busker didn't notice, and Prune walked on through the old city gates.

As with all first snows, everything was muffled, the air itself on codeine. Dawn watched the window of her office fog up. With yet another kid dead—some little girl not even yet of breeding age—the General was all up in her hair. Sure, this wasn't good publicity, but if McMitt had actually done his job and unblocked the funds Dawn had been asking for, they'd have had a better chance at covering it up. He was the one with the pull on the Hill. She was the true creative genius. Wasting her energy buggering with damage control was never what Dawn had had in mind, so *let the paper-pushers and validation-famished handle this one,* she thought.

Actually, Anthony was proving to be an apt executive, if a reluctant fuck. The fact that the man she fancied found every excuse not to get naked with her didn't do much for Dawn's morale. But his consummate managing skills freed up more time to think than she'd had in twenty years. *Most people would kill for that,* she told herself. But the truth was, being alone with her thoughts was more medieval rack than the peace of mind touted by the mindfulness manuals she'd been ordering off the internet.

An unusual gathering on the far east corner of Hetherington

Square made Dawn look up from her desktop. A swift push against the mahogany desk, and she relished the smooth ride of her new executive chair on the Persian rug. She used the cashmere shawl she kept draped over the back of the chair to wipe the window. It left the glass annoyingly blurry.

A clump of children stood with their feet planted in the snow, arms open wide, faces turned up at the white sky like sunflowers. Immaculate but for the small trail of footprints leading to the open field, the ground glistened a blinding blue—*a Botticelli kind of blue*, thought Dawn, recalling a speedy run through the *Uffizzi* with her father, and in quick order: a frowny business lunch on the *Piazza della Signoria;* dapper men talking fast; she, making a parmesan dungeon on her fettuccine Vongole, and the waiter slapping his forehead operatically, calling her a Pasta Killer. The shame. Another life.

What the heck have they come up with now? Careful not to touch the scorching radiator, Dawn leaned into the bay window. More of them were coming. She counted twenty-two, all standing in an identical position, faces eaten by hats and scarves, mouths agape. Tiny cotton balls floated in the metallic air—so tiny that the droplets they left on the window were too small to glide down. They drifted, dissolving on contact with the children's warm eyelids and tongues. Occasionally, a drop would thread its way through a crack in the scarf and raise goose bumps all over. Dawn hated to think that such obscene sensations of aliveness were theirs—not hers, not ever. She reached out toward the vision but her fingertips recoiled from the frozen glass like snail antennas. With her luck, her digits might forever stay glued to the window. Then, how would anyone ever identify her when she'd get lost in an avalanche? Such things happened. Back at Saint Hilda's where she'd boarded, hadn't the matron told her so, told her so, told her so?

The Mexican janitor joined the kids. He stood just like them, face offered up, palms out, one tall Masai among Pygmies. It went on for a while, them standing like that. *Those cretins aren't just enjoying the snow kisses,* Dawn realized. *They're praying!* Then came that bitch whom Anthony got mushy-brained over and who'd birthed his baby. At least, she wasn't having any of the idolatry—*Too cool for ghouls.* Dawn bitterly watched Grenadine run her mouth and gesticulate like a conductor.

The snow was falling hard now, in diagonal packs like in old Noir movies. Dawn's window fogged up again. She looked around for something more absorbent than the bloody cashmere but found nothing. *Screw it.* She toed her seated self back to the desk, where she lit a fag and smacked the space bar to wake the computer back up.

Drrring! Drrring! *Golly!* She wondered what kind of a mood stabilizer she was on when she picked this ringtone. She squawked her annoyance when she saw the name on the caller ID, but picked up the phone anyway.

"Yes, General, what do you want?"

"Halloo?" Dawn winced. "Hetherington, I have a good one for you, you have got to hear this! Are you seated? Make sure you sit your ass down. 'It is a truth universally acknowledged that the body follows the mind and the mind follows the breath,'" McMitt read as if with effort.

She waited.

He said, "I just read that in some obscure Indian manual from the eleventh century."

Dawn wanted to know what the heck a four-star General, veteran of three wars, with an electrical engineering degree and the imagination of a hen, was doing reading eleventh century Indian manuals—but the thought of stretching the conversation to anything remotely personal was enough to stir up the gout in her toe. She lit another cigarette with the butt of the first and poured herself a glass of Porto.

"I have no fucking clue what it means," the General continued, nonplused by her silence. McMitt was the kind of man who cared not a wee bit what people's response to his behavior was. *What makes people like him such winners is total obliviousness to a world outside their ego*, Dawn reasoned. Her father had been blessed with this talent. She was mesmerized by these men's capacity for indifference. They find no more pleasure in approval than displeasure in disapproval; perfect emotional autarky; just don't give a fuck. *Imagine the freedom!*

"But I thought it might have something to bear on your—or should I say, our—little enterprise. What do you think?" McMitt asked.

Dawn thought, *What do I think? I think that this is not "our" little enterprise. The Center is mine. I think you're an impotent, knuckle-brained walrus who's lucky his country fought enough wars during his lifetime so he could acquire some status, and that if the Pentagon hadn't funded the Viagra research, your love life would have to be confined to a few braying mountain goats in the back roads of Afghanistan.*

She said, "Uh, the breath follows the body, and the body follows the mind?"

"No! The body follows the mind and the mind follows the breath!"

"What difference does it make?"

"Much more promising! Don't you see? You already have control over their breath. If that claim's true, then your little harvesting machines might open up possibilities for a lot more!"

"You snake. Mind control."

"There's my sharp little dove! It's no secret that we've been looking for inexpensive ways to do that forever. Too many questions arise whenever a cent is spent these days. But this, Hetherington, may be worth investigating!"

As much as she hated to admit that McMitt may have a point, and as much as she despised the thought of Pentagon snouts foraging in her business, if he was right it meant *lots* of potential— and all the additional resources that go with it. *With Prana proving to be such a cash crop, ancient yoga lore has not let me down so far,* thought Dawn. *So why not let General Hogwash here inject extra juice into the project for a little expansion?*

On Hetherington Plaza, Grenadine was clipping away at a scrawny box tree. Refusing to look at Anthony she said, "You think you gave her to them. Your own blood, the black soul you've pawned in exchange for white approval. But she was never yours to give!" She spat at the ground where his shoe had just been. "Shit," she continued, "I'm wasting my spit on your negro brain. Look at you. Fear. It's oozing out of you like pus. You call your fear Reason like others call theirs Patriotism, or Jesus. Yeah, right, Reason: fear's most efficient disguise! But you, Anthony, are just as full of it as any other neocolonialist vulture out there. Yeah, I know, your poor mama working three jobs so you could have a better life, yada-yada. We're all worried about lack, obedient scarcity-phobes that we are. I worry about lack. I worry about these kids' childhoods eviscerated; I worry that no one gives a fuck, and I worry that we've all gone insane enough to put up with it. I worry that I've let the likes of you and Dawn live long enough to do this to me, and to Gaia. I worry that I've no idea how to stop you now, or others like you later, elsewhere, everywhere. And I look at those three little initials wagging behind your name, Ph.D., and I can see that they haven't made you an expert in anything, except disguise and denial."

Anthony's eyes were nailed to the tips of Grenadine's fingers peeking through the holes in her work gloves. He said, "You're right."

This took her by surprise. It was the sadness in his tone, more than his approval, that was disconcerting. Grenadine felt at home with men's aggression. But their vulnerability? What the heck was she supposed to do with that?

"At least Gaia looks pretty healthy, I guess," she added by way of mitigation.

"I lied." The bench Anthony sat on was shaking with the nervous bounce of his knee. "I said I'd given her to them because I knew you wouldn't leave without her."

"When can we get her out?"

"Assuming I can, who'll change her diapers? Feed her every four hours? You?" Grenadine considered slashing the smirk off Anthony's face with her pruner. Pleadingly he said, "I would have never seen either of you again." With one hand, Grenadine grabbed his throat and squeezed. He could smell the coffee on her breath. "It worked," he choked. "Look. Here we are, you and me, together. We're in the same boat, Grenadine." At that, she let go and took a step back. Anthony massaged his throat and swallowed a couple of times to make sure everything still worked. "I know I'm a cliché," he said. "That makes me exist nowhere but in the minds of those who shy away from the Real and its complexities. I am nothing, Grenadine. I am less than your scorn makes of me, even. And that means I can be anything, anything you want me to be." Tentatively he added, "I could be a father." Grenadine chuckled. "It's not what it looks like, Gren. I did it for you."

"I should finish you off right now. No one will miss you."

"You're right, no one will." Anthony stood up. He had tried and failed. Fine. He started to walk away. "But I have made quite sure you'd never get to see your daughter again if anything unfortunate, er, you know… You don't want Gaia to end up like little Lou, do you?" He stopped, turned back around, and pointed at the temple behind Grenadine. "By the way, I think your *amigo* is waiting for you over there. Don't you guys have a revolution to start? *Bonne chance, mon chéri.*" Making infuriating kissing noises, he crunched down the fresh snow.

Inside Ana Maria's cell, the signal was too weak. She snapped her 'Droid shut and shoved it in the pouch she'd sown on the underside of her scapular. She sighed as she weighed what she was about to do.

Mother Carmen's orders were clear: Stay away from modern communications, they're spawned by the devil to lead sinners astray. But Ana Maria knew better than to obey shortsighted orders, and by Saint-Francis, this was one instance where Mother Carmen was misguided.

Ana Maria took care to lift the door and guide it open to keep the gigantic iron hinges from squeaking. When she stepped out under the arches, the desert winds howled, ruffling even the heavy serge of her skirt. *Thank you Lord. Your breathing will be my cover.* She trotted across the patio, took a moment to dip her fingertips into the fountain and, powered by the frozen arrows shooting up her wrists, she traced a quick cross sign between her brows. A migraine was coming on, but this wasn't the time for self-indulgence.

Is tweeting breaking my vow of silence? Ana Maria climbed over the parapet that edged the convent's penitent track. Before her stood the desert's colossal night, glowing like a saint's halo. *Of course it is.* She smiled, glancing above at the star-pinned sphere. The elation of transgression, a misdiagnosed childhood agoraphobia, and the biting wind all combined to sharpen Ana Maria's senses. Briefly, she imagined herself a coyote—all ears, night-vision, and noiseless pads underfoot.

Alia had coached Ana Maria on how to post on social media the latest updates. They hoped it would ignite an #OccupyTheCenter movement and force a public conversation. Of course, there was no guarantee it would put an end to the evisceration of the future. But many of the kids could be saved and a few consciousnesses raised in the process. *You plant a seed, knowing that the sun, our God, is in it,* thought Ana Maria.

Still, she wasn't going to risk logging in to Mother Carmen's computer. A talented leader, Mother Carmen never pointed out novices' faults, never showed impatience with the sisters' petty disputes. No matter which sin you were guilty of or which pious deed you'd done, the Mother Superior would lock her wrinkly eyes with yours, let the sparkle burn its imprint in your retina, and then beam out the calmest, most merciful smile. Ana Maria thought the effect vertiginous as, deprived of the relief of either reprimand or praise, she was left to fall right back in the dank pit of her own conscience.

When Bob the handyman agreed to sneak in the smart phone, he explained that the only good spot for reception was over by the old well, that hole in the ground that used to be a hot spring. The Pueblo Indians called it "The Eye of the Mother," after an ancient belief that hot springs were just that: Mother Earth's all seeing eyes—warm, moist, healing.

The well was only about eight-hundred meters away, but with the gales whipping against her it was a trek. Ana Maria had to stomp around a little, phone held up at the stars, before she could connect. A revolting smell rose from the well, but it was swept away by a virulent gust.

After Alia's PowerPoint exposé in front of the assembled sisters, Ana Maria had basically stopped sleeping. At Vespers, she was flooded with mental images of infants hooked to gibbet-like machines that sucked the life out of them, and barely pubescent girls being artificially inseminated in tungsten-lit labs. No amount of Hail Mary's or icy-creek-water-foot-spas could make the images go away.

Growing up in São Paolo, Ana Maria had become relatively unsentimental about the exploitation of children—sometimes the last barrier against an otherwise certain death. And at almost twenty-six, she was no little girl herself. Here she was, continents away from home, bringing the Good Word to the ancient people of the New World. Here she was, distributing tepid lentils nightly to bruised-up mothers of eight in the richest nation on earth—a place where she and her childhood friends had imagined they would one day drive up to the skate rink and park their limo with tags in their own name alongside all the other rainbow people there.

In short, Ana Maria had had enough of this *porra*. She knew that it is by being oppressed that we learn to oppress. She knew that the oppression of children is the wheel that keeps all other oppressions turning—that without it, misery would have to be imposed afresh on each new generation instead of being passed down like a bad gene. In fact, Ana Maria's decision to become a nun hadn't been motivated by the love of Jesus so much as by her staunch dedication to put an end to this cycle. Becoming a bride of God seemed as good a manner as any to get reacquainted with her own innocence, and monastic life—being subjected to ubiquitous rules and regulations—was an effective way to reconnect with childhood, the only disenfranchised category through which all people pass.

So, roused by Alia's exposé about The Center, Ana Maria had jumped to her feet and shouted, "All adults share in the privileges of adulthood! We share those memories of systematic subjugation, humiliation, control—even those of us who were not treated cruelly, who had loving parents with decent parenting skills. Still, we endured arbitrary decisions, disrespect, patronizing, ridicule, control over our eating, and involuntary confinement. In our bone marrow we have internalized the appropriateness of these 'small' cruelties. How often have we told ourselves that it was 'for our own good?'"

Impassible as an owl, Mother Carmen regarded her wards. Some of the sisters nodded. Ana Maria had had plenty of time to chew on this when, night after night for one whole year, she slept on the bench in the police station near São Paolo's *Favela do Moinho*, one of the city's poorest shanty-towns. Her self-assigned task had been to make sure the kids who were brought in didn't get too knocked around by the police supposed to protect them. Also, just last week she'd spent the night in the Saint-Francis hospital lobby waiting to hear if her seven year-old mentee was going to survive her father's home-made attempt to "cure" her bed-wetting habits. But beyond the gruesome reality of childhood's disenfranchisement, what Alia's presentation about The Center's practices had brought home for Ana Maria was that childhood is the standard for acceptable powerlessness. Aurora Levins Morales herself said it, We tolerate for children a level of disenfranchisement that we would protest for any other constituency. "And," Ana Maria added, "isn't it because women and blacks are said to be 'just like children' that patriarchal imperialism has had such global leverage? That Hetherington and Co. are willing to suck the life out of kids for profit is repugnant. But that the richest liberal democracies, the loudest and most heavily-armed human-rights advocates would not only warrant, but underwrite the project?"

The nuns started to voice their indignation. Mother Carmen frowned at the chatter, but she sensed that this needed to run its course.

"The truth," Ana Maria continued, "is that childhood has never been a protected time of sweetness. Children make up the majority of the world's poorest people. Children are the most vulnerable to sexual abuse and exploitation. Without any form of political representation, children remain in many senses the property of adults in their lives. It is illegal for them to run away, no matter what level of enslavement or humiliation they're subjected to. In the end, it's really only a matter of luck for the child whether or not she ends up with enough loving, benevolent, and consistent adults in a position of authority to shield her from all those who just cannot wait to siphon the life out of her!"

The sisters' chatter rose to a clamor. Chairs scraped the tile. The jumble sounded like a small aircraft. Mother Carmen stood up and officially lifted the ban on talking for the rest of the evening.

Clearly, this was an emergency situation, and one that prayer alone wouldn't solve.

The meeting lasted until dawn. Sister Margaret, from Buenos Aires, made several pots of coffee and when they ran out she served Yerba Maté from her own stash. By then, the most sensitive among the novices jumped in fright each time one of Mother Carmen's mighty snorts shook the adobe walls.

"You're right, 'tis the same old broken record," cried Sister Felicity, with long strands of hair feverishly escaping from her wimple. "The arguments against the enfranchisement of children are identical to those used to oppose suffrage for women and former slaves. 'They are innocent and cannot understand politics. They will be manipulated by those more sophisticated than they. They aren't ready for responsibility.'"

"But what readies people for responsibility is being allowed to take some!" Shouted sister Bernadette.

"Don't forget, though. In spite of the odds stacked against them, children do resist," Pedro pointed out. He recounted for everyone Little Lou's eruption against Anthony, her broken pet flamingo, how empowered they had all felt, over and beyond their fear, by the four-year-old's audacity.

"You bet you, kids resist!" cried Ana Maria. "Look at you two, not only resisting your own condition but, perhaps most importantly, resisting the cruelest effect of this abuse: the pressure to take on the perpetrator roles of the nasty adults you've been dealt! Bravo!"

"Bravo!" shouted several nuns.

"Children have far less tolerance for injustice than adults do," added a blushing sister from South Africa. "We have seen young people take to the streets and propel mass movements forward faster than adults could build organizations behind them."

A visual survey of the sisters revealed exhaustion. One was nervously picking at her brow with questions burning in her eyes. A couple had taken Mother Carmen's cue and their faces had melted in their arms. But the women also showed more fervor than Ana Maria had ever seen at Santa Clara. She was sure of it: they were now waiting for their battle orders. *Of course,* she thought, *no twenty-first century woman became a catholic nun out of docility or convenience. It took each of us staunch defiance of societal norms, ruthless commitment, fanaticism even. And maybe a pinch of unconsciousness.* She turned to face Pedro and Alia. "Tell us how we can serve you."

Several Amens and a few Hallelujah's were uttered. Then the bell rang and all forty-four sisters of the Santa Clara Convent in Rio Arriba County, New Mexico, came to their knees to intone the Angelus as the Mother Superior snorted herself awake, wiped the drool off her chin, rattled her throat, and intoned, "Hail Mary full of grace, the Lord is with thee. Blessed are thou amongst women and blessed is the fruit of thy womb."

The gravel thundered under Grenadine's feet as she rushed by Anthony's quarters, but making it on time for her first ever teaching gig mattered more than obsolete fears of displeasing men. An enormous Venus hung over the temple like a dot on an i and her nipples hardened against the chill. She was wide awake. *Ruben is right,* she thought. *Time to harness the fire of anger and turn it into inspiration.*

Rage had been a great friend. It had kept Grenadine alive all this time—unlike her sister Evangeline, who had died of not enough rage: too much shame instead. But rage hadn't kept little Lou alive, and rage wasn't going to raise Gaia. It wasn't going to play peekaboo, teach her numbers, cumulonimbus, Africa, periods, or how to recognize the people you can trust with your joy. *I might not have much to give,* thought Grenadine, *but maybe the old witch knows something I don't. That Kundalini yoga she showed me certainly knows something I don't.*

So when Ruben asked Grenadine if she'd help transmit yoga to the kids, she said, "Why not?"

Not minding the dragons that kept watch over the temple's gate, Grenadine pushed open the first set of doors. In the dim glow snaking out from under the second set of doors, she noted all manner of small shoes, scattered about like November leaves. She managed to cross the foyer without tripping, but she jumped when Swami John appeared in the doorframe of the Meditation Hall.

"What the fuck are you doing here?"

"Good morning, Grenadine." He waved her in. "I have listened deeply to my suffering over the discomfort caused to the children, and I have come to understand. I want to save our Mother-the-Earth, but I cannot save her by sacrificing these children's life force. They are Her future. Lou is a cloud that lives on in them, in you and—"

Grenadine flicked him off and walked on in.

Ruben was already sitting in front of the altar, legs crossed, hands folded in his lap, eyelids smooth as a lake. A few kids turned their heads and watched Grenadine walk up to sit next to him. They were all so small, and their faces so gnarly in the trembling light of the votive candles they held in prayerful hands. It was like stepping into an old-fashioned *anime* where gnomes hold court. Such earnestness was disturbing in ones so young, but also strangely inviting. Grenadine herself had never known levity. Why would they?

It was muggy in the temple. Had she not kept away from this purported House of God on principle, Grenadine might have found out that it was the perfect tropical greenhouse, hot and humid like a hungry vulva. Her Birds of Paradise would have relished it. She detected the filthy smell of decay underneath the Nag Champa. She found the culprit as she struggled to cross her legs without crushing her ankle bones into the wood floor next to Ruben. Someone had left on the altar an out-of-season bouquet—

wild flowers, brown zinnias, and arthritic sunflowers. The water in the mason jar had clouded over with tiny swaying hair. There was minuscule life swimming all up in there. *Decay, not death. The difference is major,* thought Grenadine.

The shuffling of clothes and limbs abated and soon, she could hear a stomach gargle in the temple. Ruben's eyes flipped open like a doll's. He said, "Good morning, dear friends."

A handful of children said, "Good morning."

"It is a very meritorious act to be gathered here at this time we call the ambrosial hour. Just before sunrise, the subconscious world of dreams is closer to the surface, so the veil between the world of actuality and the world of potentiality is at its thinnest. This is prime time for magic." One boy on the first row had his pillow's creases still imprinted on his cheek. His eyes crossed with sleepiness. "In the world of actuality," Ruben continued, "our dear friend Lou is dead, and we miss her very much." Here, Ruben paused. Sniffles cracked the silence. "She suffered so much in her body and in her heart that she preferred to leave this plane. Maybe there are others among you who suffer almost as much as she did. Maybe you feel lonely, and you think you don't have the strength to grow older. Maybe you feel like it doesn't matter much what happens. Maybe you feel like you don't matter."

Several heads nodded. Ruben took his time to make eye contact with as many children as were willing. "But in the world of potentiality, each of you is a promise of excellence, of change, of a saved world. No one is ever alone. Everyone you miss is right there inside your heart. Your father and mother are in your bones. Your ancestors and their ancestors are in the air you breathe. Going back to the beginning of time, think of all the love that had to be made in order that you exist today. You each have each other, and all the people whom you don't yet know, but who cannot wait to roller-skate with you one day, and build helicopters, and maybe even make children." A few kids turned their heads around to look at each other, quizzical. "In the world of dreams, you can become anyone you want to be," Ruben finally said.

"I want to be the Hulk!" one little girl cried from the back.

"I want to be a toad-tamer!" said another.

"I want to be a computer-game inventor!"

"Deal!" Ruben said, index finger pointed at the latter. Then he added, "My friend Grenadine here is a powerful magician. You've seen her around campus. She can put a tiny brown seed in the dirt, and in a few days or weeks there is a red, or pink, or yellow flower big as your buttocks instead!" A boy on the first row lit up at that thought. Shiny thumb suspended in the air before his mouth, he regarded Ruben.

Where the heck are you going with this, Ruben? thought Grenadine. "Get on with the yoga," she hissed. Ruben leaned into his audience, lowering his voice as if to tell them a secret.

"Grenadine wants to help you become magicians, too. She told me she wants to teach all of us how to transform one dull, dead-looking little thing like a seed into a bright beautiful vibrant sunshiny thing. Do you want to learn to be magicians? Do you want to bring the world of dreams into being?"

A few timid "Yes's." A few "Huh-huh's." Finger in nose, Ruben's first-row buddy nodded. With a glance at Grenadine, Ruben passed her the baton.

"Ok, Houdinis, let's bring our palms together in front of our chests in prayer pose." Grenadine's voice carried naturally to the back rows. "That's right. Close your eyes, roll them up and in toward the third eye, that point between the brows that lets you dive in the inner world, the world where your innermost dreams become reality. There we go. And take a deep, deep breath. Imagine that there's a big red balloon inside your lungs, and you must blow it up, up, up so that your chest grows big, your entire back swells, your wings are getting ready to flap open... Aaaand let all the air out, squeezing the balloon tight, tight, tight into a crumpled little ball. Breathe in again, blow up that balloon, feel those wings flap open, get ready to take off like a big white bird. Now let's tune in with each other, and all the great magicians that have ever been, all the David Copperfields and Houdinis and Merlins, to the song of *Ong Namo, Guru Dev Namo*—Aaaaand breathe all the way out so that your next in-breath is brand new, pure potential—it means, I call on the greatest within me to help me do my best. Here we go, Oooooooong Naaaaaa-moooo, Guru Deeeeev, Naaa-moooo."

The temple filled with all the little magicians' voices. There was croaking, and fumbling to land on an octave where they could all meet. But in it, everyone heard what was not quite yet there: the possibility of unison. They felt it in the trembling of their throats and in the fluttering of their lungs, this magic that they understood they would, somehow, have to bring about—because it was time someone did, and no one else would.

They hadn't spoken in thirteen days, since Prune had loaded up her French Foreign Legion backpack to walk right into the night.

"Where are you?" asked Grenadine.

Prune had a hard time matching the memory image of Grenadine's magnificent stance with the teeny voice inside the pay-phone. "Arles," she said.

"Arrrrghle?"

Prune missed her lover. She missed how the sunset bounced off the bruised plum of her eyelids. But, more achingly, she missed her friend, the indisputable presence with whom to share the silence that came when fear wouldn't stop flickering on the blank ceiling. So Prune started to talk. She told Grenadine about the bridges of Paris, with all the little locks glistening in the sun left by lovers; the *croque-monsieurs;* the pussy painting at Orsay; and Sisyphus. She told her that no one at their old apartment remembered seeing anything—that the old *concièrge* had retired in Knokke-le-Zoute with her geriatric pet rabbit, and the new one spoke only a rare Bosnian dialect. Of course, Prune told Grenadine about her father's book, and how it must mean that he was alive. How she'd come to Arles hoping to find his editor, who must know *something*. What Prune didn't tell Grenadine was how daunted she felt, now that hope was real. How much harsher it can feel to have something rather than nothing, because there is so much to lose, then.

Grenadine told Prune about her visit to the Dreamscape, and how Carla thrived there. She told her about Anastasia's teachings and Ruben's kindness; about the plan they'd made to teach the kids Kundalini yoga, so they would learn to master their breath to resist The Center's vampirizing and channel their life force into their own flourishing.

What Grenadine didn't tell Prune was that little Lou was thought to be dead, and that no one knew where Alia and Pedro had gone. She didn't tell her how elated and terrified she was to have met her Gaia, or how much she wished Prune would be by her side as she, Grenadine, was beginning to realize for the first time in her life that her hands were not tied. And when the awkward silence that enshrouds truncated truths came, Grenadine wanted to keep hearing her lover's voice.

"Tell me about Provence," she said.

Prune was happy to comply. "What I missed the most was the market. It's a world of its own, here, like the circus, or the fair. Roller-coasters of nougat and carnivals of ogre-faced tomatoes, bantering potato peelers, miracle panties by the kilo, seventeen species of lettuce, cheeses with names to make poets blush, and live quails." Grenadine chuckled. The sparkle in Prune's voice was contagious. "Years ago I got lost on this very market, and that's how I fell in love for the first time," Prune teased.

"Tell me all about it!"

"Mom had sent Dad and Carla and me on a mission to collect Earth's most tantalizing flavors for the feast that the last picnic of our summer vacation was to be. I leaned in to smell an artichoke-flower the size of my skull, and when I turned around, they had left me. I scanned the sea of midriffs all around but could spot neither Carla's yellow head, nor Dad's sprouting above the crowd. Mounds of olives glistened on either side of my face, their urine and garlic smell like gauze over my eyes and ears. All the banter went very quiet. I watched one vendor's lips move as he talked to the stern homosexual who was palpating his apricots. I must have kept walking because suddenly, I came face to face with a croissant the color of scorched earth. A boy about my age was holding it out, saying, "*Pourquoi tu pleures?*" I didn't know I was crying. "*Tiens, c'est mon père qui l'a fait.*" He waved the croissant in front of me. His hair was a tangle of black curls, his eyes a washed-out blue. I remember thinking I'd thought only old, old men had eyes that way.

"Tristan had a Southern accent that made every sound bob atop a sea of song. His striped sailor shirt bore the most extraordinary collection of stains. I decided right then and there that he would be my knight and I, his fellow knight. I took the croissant and its skin broke, scattering butter flakes on the asphalt. A purple pigeon lurched at the crumbs. Just as skilled at avoiding market goers' feet, a rat-terrier charged, but the pigeon stood strong with one claw on the largest flake, daring the dog to try for it. The dog yapped, snout to the ground, tail wagging dementedly as his mistress dragged him away.

"Come," Tristan said, disappearing between elbows and straw baskets. I popped half the croissant in my mouth before taking off after him.

"Nyum nyum," Grenadine offered.

"Tristan was swift, and keeping up with him was a hunt. I bird-dogged him right on through the donkey-sausage stand and the paella lady. He waived at each vendor, who bellowed some greeting in return. I heard one nectarine guy shout to a buxom granny who was selecting at a leisurely pace each item for her kilogram, 'Lean in, but don't drag your boobs through it!' This made me laugh and I bumped hard into Tristan, who'd frozen in front of a life-size Buddha head. Tristan was so transfixed, he didn't notice I'd almost thrown him to the ground. I stood next to him. The croissant had resorbed into a greasy ball inside my fist. I was debating popping it in when the rat-terrier hiked up and casually lifted its leg to splatter a few drops of lime-green piss directly on Gautama's neck. The mistress didn't notice a thing. Tristan looked at me and we busted out laughing, until the incense vendor came barking at us.

"The peach fuzz above Tristan's lip glistened in the slanted sun. I wondered if a kiss from him would be as smooth as the apricots that lay, bursting with sweet, just across the sidewalk." Prune hesitated. "I can barely remember what a kiss from you tastes like, Gren." She waited. "Gren, you still there?"

"Hmmmm."

"What is it?"

"We believe that Lou is dead. I'm sorry. I wish there was a better way to say it."

" … "

"Prune?"

"Shit! Shit! Shit!"

"Prune, I know you've got to do this. But we could use your help over here."

"Shit! My calling card is running out, Gren. *Merde*! It's going to cut. I—" Beep! Beep! Beep! Appalled, Prune clanked the receiver back on its hook. For a moment she stared blankly through the cracked plexiglass of the phone booth. Someone had drawn a large penis in black marker and, in a last attempt at decency, someone had placed right on top of the glans a sticker. It advertised the services of Madame Marabout, extraordinary fortune-teller—"Psoriasis! Infidelity! Hair loss!" There was no number but there was a street address and what could have been the hours of operation: 4:06 - 7:09, 18:41 - 22:04. Prune rummaged in her pack and found a pen. She scribbled address and numbers inside her wrist and started up the boulevard des Lices toward the Roman amphitheater. Last she remembered, right next to the amphitheater was the Pilgrim's House which, for only a "heart's donation," welcomed those on the Camino de Santiago. She wasn't hiking the camino, but she sure felt like a pilgrim. At least, the price was right, considering that she'd already spent most of her nest egg on transportation.

The sun set abruptly. On place de la République, children were riding their scooters in the pink light that bounced off the limestone Cathedral. Mothers and fathers chit-chatted inside a cloud of cigarette smoke while leash-free dogs sniffed each other. Prune thought she'd caught sight of Lou crying near a fallen bicycle, but a man broke out of the smoke circle to sweep the girl in his arms. She squealed as he plopped her up on his shoulders with one hand, swept up the bike with the other, and began to trot like a pony around the square, the other children hee-hawing in tow.

Prune started climbing up the steep *rue du Cloître*. All she could hear was her own footsteps. In her mind's eye, images of her sister inert on her bed mingled with little Lou's stiff, pale corpse. Prune shook her head to chase away the ghosts. *It's time I pay a little visit to Carla*, she thought. *It shouldn't be so hard. All I have to do is settle in and meditate, right? If the dorms are crowded, I'll try the bathroom.*

Footsteps echoed behind her. In spite of herself, Prune picked up the pace. The footsteps picked up too. They were getting closer. Prune wanted to look back, just to make sure, but she talked herself out of it. She wasn't really that scared.

The street-light buzzed, then went out. Two fourth-floor windows of one narrow building had their lights on, but other than that, the town had gone fast asleep. *A few more steps, then the ninety-degrees turn, then the rue de la Calade and the brightly lit Roman ruins.* Prune sped up. The steps behind her turned into a jog. She started to run and, when she finally glanced back over her shoulder she saw a skinny guy staring up at her, his face deformed by the effort. Prune switched to fourth gear. Sharp turn, then there was the *Théatre Antique,* with its two-thousand year-old marble columns shooting up at nothing. Prune stole another glance over her shoulder. *Holy shit!* The guy was on her heels as the blade flashed out of his fist like Jupiter's thunderbolt. *Oh putain! Oh putain! Oh putain!* She'd never make it around the amphitheater to the arenas, where cafés and restaurants would provide cover but... yeah, if she could just—

Ancient soccer drills kicked in and Prune suddenly switched direction to disappear down a set of stairs that plunged under the *Théatre Antique* towards the public park. The surprise effect earned her a few seconds. The guy huffed and cursed. She could tell by his accent that he was a Gypsy. What in the heck was a French Gypsy doing trying to slice her up?

Flying across a bed of pansies, Prune tripped on something. An old ankle injury screeched inside her leg, but she bounced right back, grabbed the fallen branch, and made for the children's playground where she and Tristan had exchanged their first kiss.

The Gypsy came close enough to take a swag at her. She felt a rip in her back-pack. This made Prune really mad and she swung around, flailing her branch about. The guy looked stunned when the branch grazed the side of his head. He growled, showing several golden teeth, and when he lunged at her, Prune was already standing in the center of the merry-go-round, branch brandished and with death in her eyes. He landed on the spinning wheel, and before he could grab onto a hand-hold, the centrifugal force tossed him off to the rubberized ground. Electro-pop beats announced a group of teenagers with their bluetooth speaker. The kids saw Prune standing in the center of the merry-go-round with her branch held up like Joan-of-Arc. They saw the limping Gypsy grab hold of the merry-go-round and block the wheel. The girl who was holding the speaker set it carefully down on the ground, and started to climb up the monkey bars. The others followed her.

"*Salut, ça va?*" the girl called out to Prune, who struggled to keep her balance as the guy jerked the merry-go-round to and fro. This was a familiar trick girls used on French streets—calling out to a girl whom they knew was being harassed as if she were an old friend. It usually took care of the situation and convinced predators to walk away. The guy let go of the wheel, and the blade disappeared. Prune squatted down in the center of the merry-go-round, hissing, "Does that make you feel like a man, slicing up little girls in parks? I bet your mother is real proud of you." He hawked and spat a large slimy glob at the ground, then he locked eyes with Prune and made a throat-cutting gesture with his hand.

"I wouldn't insult my mother if I were you. She might well be the only one who can save your skinny ass now." And he walked away.

"What do you mean? Who sent you after me?" Prune called after him as he disappeared behind the black fence.

Seated on her rock by the waterfall, Anastasia was meditating. Or rather, she was praying. The difference is moot for most, but a great sage once said that praying is asking, meditating is receiving. Presently, Anastasia was asking. She knew she'd messed up, and having Ruben be cross at her felt worse than sitting on Piotr-the-Armenian-barber's stool for tooth work.

Yesterday, Ruben came sauntering like a kid-goat wanting to know what spell she'd put in the Kundalini yoga. "It's a miracle!" He twitched with excitement. "It's only been eleven days since they've started the training, and most of the children have put on real flesh on those bones! I even saw them play, you know, like children do? There was a tickle-war going on in the quad last Thursday. On Friday, I happened upon an earnest debate over whether dogs can smile. They asked me to settle it for them."

"What was your verdict?"

"Of course, dogs smile. They grin, smirk, frown, and wonder. What's this stuff you gave us, Stasia? I knew it was making me feel good. But healing on that level is alchemy."

Cleaning her crystals with an old tooth brush in the shallows of the swimming hole, Anastasia gestured for Ruben to stretch out the front of his shirt so she could cradle her stones there. While she was at it, she snuck a peek at the corridor of hair that descended from his navel.

"It's just Kundalini yoga." She dropped the crystals in the improvised hammock. "No more, no less. It's the most ancient, sacred, powerful technology for healing and enlightenment known to woman. And man. I am glad it's helping." She grazed his belly hair with her wet knuckle. It jolted her but he didn't seem to notice.

"How does it work? How come the kids are so vitalized even as they're grieving the loss of yet another friend, their practice is cutting into their sleep time, and the harvesting has not abated a bit?"

Anastasia said it again, "Just yoga. The stuff works on all levels, all systems. Their glandular balance is probably wrecked by the harvesting, and it's being restored by the yoga; their electromagnetic field has been virtually annulled by the machines, and it's being revived." She ran her knuckle against the grain of his belly hair. "Also, I wouldn't underestimate the power of having an adult advocate. A parent by proxy, if you wish. For the first time since they've been in that hell-hole, they are no longer alone."

"Yes," Ruben granted, "that could be part of it."

"Not only an advocate, but also someone other than an incapacitated parent or a vampiric disciplinarian to emulate." Her hungry eyes were glued to his midriff. "In short, with decent, benevolent adults around, what these children are getting is the imagination of a future—their future. This is what you're giving them, my sweet."

Ruben was oblivious to her vamping. "Still, the transformation is nothing short of a miracle. Do hope and validation have that kind of power over physiology?" Of course they do. They both knew it.

"But the real key," Anastasia said, letting his shirt flop back over his belly, "is exactly what Dawn and her minions know so well. The key is breath control. Each emotion needs a certain breath pattern to sustain itself. When you're afraid, isn't your breath shallow and quick? But fear simply cannot maintain itself on deep, slow breath. So when you master your breath, you master your emotions. And when you master your emotions, you master your mind. The body becomes a participant in spiritual awakening, a conduit for energies of a high spiritual nature."

Ruben was connecting the dots. "So, making her afraid of her own body is the worst you can do to a child."

"That's true. Because then not only do you snatch away her anchor, her Earth. You take away her fulcrum. You forbid her from entering her heaven." Anastasia hesitated. Pensive, she added, "In this, almost always, harvesters succeed. Like rapists. That had to stop."

"So with this yoga, you basically gain the ability to control the flow of your Kundalini. You gain mastery over yourself as a connector between heaven and earth? You can, er"—Ruben was getting excited—"You can turn Fate into Destiny!"

"Exactly. When the gross physical energies and the subtle vibrations are attuned, what you get is Kundalini Rising. In one of her manifestations, Kundalini is Shakti, pure potential actualized. Stupendous creativity, supreme intuition, superior discernment. And Shakti is picky. She doesn't readily lend herself to thievery and exploitation."

There was silence as Ruben played with the crystals, making a spiral that sparkled against the granite. When Anastasia realized that her lover wouldn't look at her, the soothing sound of the waterfall morphed into an aggravating racket. She ached to ask what was wrong, but her mother's sullen nag—"Don't ask questions if you don't really want to know the answer"—kept her mum. Still, the answer that Anastasia didn't want came.

"In short, you've known the antidote to the harvesters' venom all this time. Why did you keep it to yourself for so long?" Ruben tucked in his shirt. Anastasia pretended to remain absorbed in polishing her crystals with desiccated moss.

"There was no guarantee—"

"But you knew. And you let them die."

"I didn't have a transmitter."

"You didn't look for one."

"Not my job."

"That's what the citizens of Dachau said in 1942. Upon every atrocity, there's thousands who could have stopped it, but 'It wasn't their job.'"

"Mind your hyperbole, my darling. The Nazis gassed my mother's entire family."

"But you could have stopped this earlier. And you didn't." There were ice pellets in Ruben's voice, a chill so new to her that she didn't know how to shield herself from it.

In a whiny voice that made her gag she said, "No one asked, Ruben. I cannot intervene in the gross plane unless I am being asked. I am not God."

"Then who are you?"

"I am Anastasia. I am in love with you and it tears me up to watch you turn to ice because I fail to fulfill your fantasy of me." She hesitated. *Shut up, mom!* "Can you love me, Ruben? Or can you only love an imaginary, flawless projection of your own confining mind?"

Ruben was genuinely confused. He struggled to keep his eyes from looking away. He worried he wouldn't want to look at her again if he looked away now. And he wondered if that meant he wouldn't want to look at himself, either.

"You know the weirdest things, and yet—"

"I know." Dawn silenced Anthony with a snap of the fingers and a curt, "*Garçon!*" Anthony shook his head. How had he not seen this sooner? Dawn's entire life was a B movie. Here she was, fancying herself some Hollywood Rita Hayworth in *Chinatown*, when this was Española's Viet Hoa seven-dollar all-you-can-eat, and the only garçon was an obese busboy with earbuds and a droopy chin.

Anthony prodded his chow mein with his fork. He had brought his boss here hoping to have a real talk. He had tried the only tablecloth restaurant in town, but they were closed for Hanukah. Clearly, he was wasting his time. Trying to make Dawn see the shit storm that was about to hit them and coordinate a response to the General's maneuvering to push them out of the way was like Santa Claus. *Heck, she can barely see the tip of her own tits these days,* Anthony thought as he watched her down half of her Tsingtao in one gulp.

Obviously, the goody-goody Swami wasn't going to be any help either. The French pest was out there freeloading across the pond, and Anthony couldn't even get ahold of the local mobsters he'd hired to track her down. If she had a smart phone, things would be so much easier. Maybe they should start giving them away to all The Center's wards—surely, some shareholder would agree to sponsor that?

Also, the search team The Center had dispatched to locate Pedro and Alia hadn't yielded anything but an albuterol inhaler and a training bra. *There might be two more kids' carcasses being pecked on by vultures out there, waiting to become front page material when some drunk fisherman happens upon the remains,* thought Anthony. The cherry on the cake, of course, was Grenadine pandering to that Mexicano cleaning guy and teaching the kids calisthenics! *What's up with Gren's sudden mommy complex anyway? Is that a case of the Bioclock, or what?* Sure, it made sense that she would be a little upset about Gaia having been kept away. But Anthony had assumed Grenadine might come around when she realized he had done a pretty good job of keeping the child healthy. Organic purées, organic diapers, bisphenol A-free toys, a play nurse. Shit, he'd even arranged for the baby not to be harvested.

The spring roll was rancid. Anthony searched the droplets of frying oil congealed on its shaft for inspiration. McMitt was coming at five "for Tea" (a recent Dawn attempt at sophistication), and it looked like, for now, Anthony would just have to improvise. He watched his boss light up when the busboy came to stand beside her.

"These chopsticks are plastic, aren't they?" Dawn tapped the bottom of them on the formica to prove her point.

The busboy snapped one earplug out. Very loudly he said, "*Que quieres?*" Dawn shot an outraged glance at Anthony.

"What do *I* want?" She said it like it was some major epiphany. "What *do* I want?" It must have sounded great to her because she said it a third time, bringing her plastic chopstick up to her mouth like a cigarette. "What do I want?" She waved the busboy off and with a grand gesture, she traced Anthony's silhouette. "I want a baby with you," she said, winking.

When Dawn showed up for tea, it wasn't just her eyes that had glazed over, it was all of her. Even her suit, usually perfectly pressed, looked waxy. The skirt sagged in the hips and her shinbone was catching the light from the pallid sky outside her office window.

"Have a seat." McMitt stood behind Dawn's desk like a President under the flag. He pointed at the sofa.

She blinked a puffy, slow blink, and dropped into the couch as if from great height. She pulled her skirt toward her bony knees and immediately started to nod off. She jumped when Anthony spoke.

"President Hetherington, the General and I were just

wondering, er... how do you think The Center is faring?" She clearly hadn't noticed Anthony there before. In the time it took to focus her eyes on him, her face twisted into an older Liz Taylor. "Dawn?" Anthony called from the other shore of the sofa.

The General was marble, arms crossed high on his bling-coated chest.

Dawn looked flustered. Her hands struggled for leverage on her thighs but kept slipping on the nylon. Finally she gave in, dived over her legs, and started palming the carpet as if looking for a family heirloom. Her neck craned one way, then the other.

"Ah, it's you my love!" She glared up at Anthony from below. She tried clawing the air but the effort to lift her arm and grasp his was insurmountable, and her wrist thumped on the rug. "Give me a fag," she slurred. "If you're not going to knock me up, at least you can get me a bloody fag. Will somebody give me a fucking cigarette, for fuck's sake!"

Planted like an oak, McMitt was reveling in their little daytime TV skit. Anthony tossed away mental images of charred black men just like himself lynched by righteous white men just like this one. The tension in his jaw was making his ear ache as he pushed away more images of flames in the night, of an accidental hoe slammed into that white man's smirk, and slicing his shiny skull in half like the knife that stayed in Maw-Maw's butter on the kitchen counter.

Dawn was holding her head in her hands, now, rocking back and forth. She chuckled a bit, then nothing. Right as Anthony was beginning to wonder if she'd stopped breathing, her shoulders started to shake, soundlessly. Then the sobs came. Sobs like a toddler's. Sobs that made his tailbone shake through the sofa cushions. He scooted closer. Soft as a mother, he set his hand on her forehead, pulled her up, and laid her down in his lap. Running his fingers through her hair he said, "There, there. Don't you worry, we'll find you a cigarette."

Arles sits on the road to Santiago and the Pilgrims' House was full of pilgrims. German pilgrims, Peruvian pilgrims, Italian—even New-Zealander pilgrims. Most wore their crosses sparkly around their necks, and some just wore them in the form of varicose calves and scratchy socks. It was a good fifteen-hundred kilometers to Santiago, and December freezes were to be expected near the Basque country, but salvation rarely comes with climate control.

The girl at the check-in glanced disapprovingly at Prune's flimsy high tops, but she found her a top bunk, waved at the donation box, and slipped a macaroon on the saucer that her herbal tea came in. She also handed her a flyer with a list of weekly church services and a map of the city-center which showed each church pink and enlarged, like delirium tremens.

After a quick shower, Prune decided that the Church of Saint-Trophime might indeed be a good place to access the Dreamscape. During their family vacations at the nearby camping in *Les Saintes*, she and Carla had shared lively memories of horror-fueled giggles before the impressive display of saints' knee bones and other relics exhibited behind murky glass.

Blessedly, the band of nurses from New-Zealand that shared Prune's dorm wanted to catch Vespers. Prune offered to show them the way, trusting that their gaggle would provide cover from the Gypsy cutter.

It was perfect. The church was even darker than Prune remembered, with only a few votive offerings, pillar candles on the altar, and a dusty candelabra hanging over the nave. On a Thursday night, the flock was scattered and bare like winter trees, with only a handful of old maids and a couple of grieving drunks attending. The priest's sermon droned down cavernous aisles, inviting just enough devotion without demanding full attention.

Prune scouted the perimeter of the church a few times before settling in under a dragon biting its tail on splendid stained-glass windows. The symbol struck her as good omen for her situation—Completion? Resolution? Absurdity? She wished she'd brought a scarf to insulate her bottom from the frigid bench. She closed her eyes and let the lull of halting psalms rock her to inner listening.

Ruben had said to begin with the breath, always. How had he put it? "The body follows the mind, and the mind follows the breath?" So, if you bring your attention to your breath, you reel in the body, the mind, the emotions.

Prune started to reel it in, reel it in, reel it in. It came in swirls. The shiny blade, the plush train, Grenadine's incredibly teeny voice on the phone, Carla cataleptic, Janis Joplin, little Lou's ashen face, the merry-go-round, the beach with their whole family, Rosa's warm hand swooshing around her bare back when she was ill, Tristan's peach fuzz, the Gypsy's gold teeth, Marc frowning over Lévinas, smoke rings rising from Dawn's lying lips…

Prune gobbled up another big breath and tried to conjure up Carla—Carla's tan flat chest on a warm rock by the waterfall; Carla paddling about the water hole with the crone's wolf; Carla glowing as she poked the bonfire's embers. But no. All Prune could muster was Carla, inert under the yellow blanket, hair too dark, in need of a wash, cigarette-paper-thin eyelids trembling.

Prune realized she'd forgotten to breathe out. Ruben had warned her against that. "Most people don't know how to breathe," he'd said. It had struck her because it was one of those things she'd never thought about. "Of course, I know how to breathe," she'd said. "Or else I'd be dead!"

"No, most people have no clue," Ruben explained. "They barely take in enough air to keep their basic vital functions going. They don't know how to invite the breath, welcome the breath, make the breath feel at home, let it be cosy, let it lend a hand, even, and take out the garbage on its way out."

Here we go again. Deep breath in, deep breath out, all the way out. Deep breath in, all the way to the bottom of the belly, and deep breath out, all the way out, navel to spine, squeeze it all out. Aaaaaand …

Carla, Carla, Carla, Carla, Carla, Carla, please, please, please I miss you hermana. You've got to tell me, you've got to let me know you're alright. I have super news, I'm pretty sure Dad is alive, I'm going to bring him over to see you. Carla? Shit, Carla!

"Ça va mademoiselle?" The old hunchback who had sat surreptitiously on the end of Prune's bench sounded genuinely concerned.

"*Oui oui, ça va.*" Prune tried to smile.

"So, why are you crying?" Shit, it had happened again. Prune didn't know she was. "Have you lost a loved one? My husband, sixty-two years we were together. Five children, nine grandchildren, and not one of them came down for the funeral, not one! He proposed right here in this church, right over there, you see, in front of *Sainte-Angèle*. He had on his torero suit, all gold and pink, perfect fit in the hips—"

Quietly, Prune stood up and walked out of the church. A few steps off the place de la République, the staccato of Flamenco guitar beckoned her into a cul-de-sac. Across from a façade crawling with crimson leaves, the door of an art gallery was propped open with a yellow chair. Wine glasses in hand, a handful of people had huddled in the bright center of the room to be gazed at by an old man and his horse caught inside bigger than life-size photographs on the walls. The silver processing had left cold, crisp traces that Prune could taste in her mouth.

"*Côtes du Gard ou bien Sauvignon aux airelles?*" Like many *Arlésiennes*, the waitress had the profile you see on ancient Roman coins. Her nose sloped directly from the point between her brows. The drop was vertiginous, like jumping off a cliff, and in the eternity it takes there is time to wonder how much longer before you crash. She had pinned her black curls up in a loose bun that seemed to weigh her head down to one side. She was magnificent.

Prune ran her tongue between her gums and the inside of her lip. The metallic taste was still there.

"*Merci.*" She took the Sauvignon.

On the server's platter, the wine glasses began to chatter as an old Gypsy man started to knock on his guitar. When he wailed, the cluster in the center of the gallery huddled closer together like Arctic penguins, looking alarmed.

Michelle Briens had dyed her hair. From champagne blond, she'd become tangerine. Her taut cheekbones had filled out some, and she'd traded her pinstripe suit for a red leather skirt. She trotted in from the street like one of those small white horses that dot the marshes of the area, head down not in defeat, but from the simple axiom that she is free. She looked up when the waitress knowingly handed her a glass of *Côtes du Gard*. The editor deposited a peck on the girl's cheek, nuzzling her ear in passing. Both women giggled.

Michelle Briens noticed Prune staring at her, but there was no flicker of recognition as she floated by to go drape her arm around the musician's neck and kissed his stubbly cheek. He kept on strumming, so hard that a string popped. He didn't skip a beat, though, and started hammering his heel on the wooden box he was seated on. On the stone walls, the movie-size pictures didn't budge, but the spotlights screwed to the archaic beams began to tremble. It set the scene inside the photographs in motion. The horse was shivering.

Prune felt like an idiot, standing there like a dog looking for a place to piss. The song ended and in the time-lapse this created, Prune grabbed another glass of Sauvignon, gulped it down, and walked over to ask Michelle Briens if she had any idea what might have become of her father.

The boisterous breakfast bells had muted to a ting when they reached inside the temple but all the same, the children stirred in unison, squaring their pillows like basic trainees before shuffling out the doors. Swami John picked up two chirping bassinets and he followed suit with one baby dangling from each arm. Ruben needed a little more time to think. He remained in corpse pose, brow buried under an eye-pillow, physical body dead to the known world, intuitive body all the more awake. Next to him, Grenadine was taking her time to stretch. This yoga routine was leaving her hamstrings and rotator cuffs sore, making this new awareness of her living flesh a torture she found scrumptious.

She made her way up to sitting. "Hey, *compadre*! How about a bouncy pair of sunny sides up?"

Ruben smiled but he didn't budge. Grenadine stood up, rubbed her eyes with her fists, and yawned as she took in the empty temple, then the dusty slant of sun falling on Ruben's extremely well-groomed toes. She stomped an exaggerated stomp around the altar, shuffled things around, decided against discarding the swampy vase water, wondering how much longer before tadpoles would grow in there.

"Oh, come on, man. I'd gut a puppy for a caramel latte!" She could hear Ruben's breath, long and light. "Alright," she finally said, "I'm off."

"Wait!" This was clearly an order, coming from a man who never gave them. Grenadine sighed but she waited. "Sit." Grenadine checked her watch. Twelve minutes before the kitchen closed, and all the latte she'd be able to get was twice-brewed sock juice with powdered hazelnut creamer. But she sat in the only straight-back chair the temple had to offer.

Ruben removed the eye-pillow but kept his eyes closed. "They need a leader."

"I thought we were it."

"No. They need a leader they can identify with. One of their own. It's the only way this will truly be their struggle, their freedom."

"Huh huh. I'm afraid all the other rats have deserted the ship, though."

Ruben said nothing.

"You worry they're gonna go Wretched of the Earth on us?" Still no response. His forearms were the same walnut finish as the wood floors, the sinewy flexors twitching in the pale morning. "You know," Grenadine added, "Frantz Fanon. The Dialectic of Liberation. The part where the revolutionaries can only bring out against their own ranks the aggression that has been deposited in their bones? From their shared sense of humiliation, they've gathered momentum. From the realization of the injustice, they've gathered the fire. They're ready—they feel ready. But they haven't gotten rid of the fear. Nor have they liquidated the self-hate that continuous, repeated, normalized abuse instills. So that it's each other that they beat up. Like we blacks continue to shoot-up, and shoot at our own in our ghettos, our prisons, our schools, instead of—"

As if on cue, a racket burst in the foyer. They heard the crumple of bodies shoving bodies, then a thud. "Ouch!"

Ruben propped himself up to sitting. Grenadine was already tromping toward the foyer, where the sound seemed to come from. Before she could reach the folding doors, a boy tumbled out, head first, and fell inert at her feet. Ruben squatted down by him while she lurched through the doors, crying, "Hey! hey! hey!" The kids had scampered off before she could recognize anyone.

There was blood trickling from Hakim's nose and he squirmed about the floor.

"Motherfuckers, I'll kill you!" he groaned.

Ruben gently lifted the boy's neck and torso, and wiped the blood off with his shirt tails. "We need to get Prune back here," he said to no one in particular.

Grenadine said, "Prune's in Provence, chasing memories. I don't know that she's got time for us."

The cherubic grin Ruben was dispensing for the hurt boy turned anthropophagous. He screwed his glare into her. "Don't *you* be the deserting rat. And quit feeling sorry for yourself. These kids need you *now*." He shook Hakim a little. The boy moaned. Ruben grabbed a pillow and slid it under his head. "What do you need, Hakim?" he asked almost in a whisper, patting the boy's forehead.

"Give me a blade. I want to feel their skin break when I cut it. I'll bleed them slow, like goats."

Grenadine whistled. "Jeeesus, kid! How about you start by telling us who they were?"

"I'm no snitch. And what are you gonna do? Wag your finger at them?"

"Well, I think I'll start by whipping your clever little ass. Then I'll whip theirs until—"

"That's enough, you two!" The tendons in Ruben's neck were ready to pop. "Can't you see you're playing right into their hand? They want us to tear at each other, keep us busy feuding with each other instead of confronting them." Hakim had stopped bleeding. Grenadine was picking at the thin scabs inside her forearm. Ruben sighed.

"Cruelty only perpetuates itself by making us hate our tormentors enough to want to act cruelly toward them—or toward *someone, anyone*. When we've been hurt, we think that hurting back will make us feel better." He glanced at the scars on Grenadine's wrists. "It doesn't." He wetted his finger with his tongue and rubbed off a faint blood trail off Hakim's cheek. "Revenge is the path of least resistance; it is *their* path. It won't bring liberation or lasting change. If we're only going to plug new puppets into old socks, I'm out."

Hakim and Grenadine peered at each other, sheepish. Ruben wrapped his big hand around Grenadine's forearm and added, "*Your* kid needs you *now*. Are you going to hide inside your rage and keep pointing the finger at those you love for not galloping in on a tall white horse to sweep you off into the sunset? Or are you going to make the only decent choice you've got available and figure out how to bring Prune back over here so she can get this *cabrón* uprising on track?"

"Fuck you, Ruben. You know you're the biggest, baddest pain in the ass? When this shit's over I'm going to have to hire you as my shrink. Also, I don't know how to get in touch with Prune. And they've got us wired now, so why don't you try directly dialing up her brain? Do that telepathy thing you do?"

"No. I don't have that power. She'd have to be tuned into me. But she isn't: she's tuned into you."

Grenadine shook her head no but she said, "Alright. I'll give it a shot. But it's a loooong shot. Even assuming I find her out there in Oz-land; assuming she agrees to come back; assuming they let her; assuming she makes it alive…" She glanced at Hakim, who'd settled into his pillows and was listening with his hands folded behind his head. "I bet it feels to those kids like it feels to me— like I can't help but feel, even though I know better… Like she *abandoned* us." Hakim nodded. "So yeah, I'll woman up and do my part. Meanwhile, I suggest you figure out how to bring Carla back over here. She's the martyr. She's the one the kids can agree to trust. What do you say, Hakim?"

In addition to its *férias* (meaning, copiously liquored bullfight festivals), the Camargue is known for its pink flamingoes, its wild horses, its annual Gypsy pilgrimage, its salt marshes, and its mosquitoes. Above the door to what Michelle Briens had speculated might still be Marc's studio, the salty winds had the iron sign rusted and wincing. To the right, a skinny tabby was splayed out behind window bars. He squinted at Prune and waved a lazy tail. Under one hundred coats of paint, the door revealed medieval coats-of-arms—sea monsters, possibly. There was no buzzer and the centuries-old wood, dense as concrete, hurt Prune's knuckles when she knocked.

There was no answer.

Michelle Briens had been reluctant when Prune first approached her at the art opening, but she lit up when Prune reminded her of Marc's historic couscous dinner in Paris. Prune had to gobble down another glass of wine when the editor told her that yes, Marc was alive, and in fact, the last she'd heard he was living here in Arles. Michelle began to frown when Prune kept pressing her with one feverish question after another. The gorgeous waitress hovered, watchful. Michelle's answers became increasingly evasive.

Finally, the waitress jumped in. "Look, *mademoiselle*. My girlfriend hasn't had anything to do with Michaux in a while for a good reason. The guy might have been a genius at some point, but he's gone *loco* in the head." She pretended to screw her index finger into the side of her head as she said this.

Prune searched Michelle Briens' face. She nodded. "PTSD. He hasn't recovered from your Mom's—" Michelle was grasping for the right word but she didn't find it.

"It's called post traumatic battiness," said the waitress. "One moment he's almost a regular guy, acting like he's known you since kindergarten. The next he looks at you like you're wearing an endangered species fur-coat... Not to mention his dubious personal hygiene."

"*Je suis désolée*, Prune," the editor concluded. "Let me know if there's anything I can do." And then she'd trotted over to chat with the evening's featured artist.

Prune knocked again on her father's door, harder this time. The door gave imperceptibility. She took it as an invitation and pushed it all the way in with both hands, calling out, "*Hé ho! Y'a quelqu'un? J'entre, hein!*"

Barely wider than her shoulders, the hallway smelled of chalk and cat piss. It took a moment for Prune's eyes to adjust. A few steps in, she attempted another, "*Y'a quelqu'un?*" A thud made her jump.

On the floor tile behind her, the tabby was grooming his inner thigh, not paying her any attention. Just above the cat, the breeze made the ancient casement windows knock against each other. A mechanical sound, like the click clack of her grandmother's clock, was rising from a dark opening in the wall.

The stone steps were damp, sweating centuries. The downward twirl made Prune thank whomever had been so thoughtful as to string through heavy rings a hefty rope, of the kind they use on ships at sea. A tea light in a small glass broke into a cakewalk as Prune stepped by. At the bottom of the steps, the dirt floor cellar was big enough for a fanatical monk to self-flagellate, but not big enough for a normal human to spread her arms.

Now, the ticking sounded more like an old engine. Again, Prune had to wait for her eyes to adjust before she noticed an arched opening that led to another cell. Across the doorway, shadows moved in petals. Prune had to bend over in order to enter.

It was a movie of sorts, projected against a white sheet. But the film was a meter-high band of lace, simultaneously coiling and uncoiling itself loosely on the rickety reels across which it was stretched out. Humming in the center was a slide projector on a milking stool. The sheet told the story of a silent shipwreck, complete with whales, mermaids, and a raft, cobbled from the superimposition of color photographs of the sea with the aggrandized shadows from the lace. It was mesmerizing. If you looked directly at the lace before it crossed paths with the projector's light, you could predict what was coming. An Ancient-Greek-looking man (or God?) riding a whale. A pensive mermaid sitting on a rock with her hand shading her brow. And then the shipwreck all over again. The lifeboat. The drowning. The man-god straddling the whale. The mermaid. There was no way to tell whether the mermaid was anticipating the wreck, causing it intentionally, grieving it after the fact, or just a neutral witness. Was she the man-god's friend, or his enemy? The reel moved slowly enough for a standing observer, like Prune, to consider all possibilities.

"She didn't mean for the ship to sink." The voice rose from the cell's darkest corner.

"*Papa?*" Not so much a question as a summoning: there was no question.

"I call it Ulysses but it should really be called Penelope. He's the hero, the actor, but she's the rationale, the essence—the sense. Do you like it?"

"*Papa, c'est toi?*" Prune stepped toward the heavy French accent, but her foot caught in the fishing net that was delimiting the artist's space from the viewer's. Struggling to untangle her legs, she clawed for a visual confirmation. A pale oval, small enough to be Marc's fair-skinned face, hovered against the mildewed stone.

Like a shipwreck she called, "*C'est moi, Prune!*"

The sound of a lighter being lit, twice. Marc's face flared up. The tip of a cigarette turned red, bright at first, then too quickly dimmed.

"*Enchanté, Mademoiselle.*"

Prune's whole body was abuzz. Elation. The impulse to run into home's arms held in check. Relief. Disbelief. The pit in the stomach, like bungee jumping. "Marc? Marc Michaux?"

"Oh, call me Marco." Only Rosa had ever called him that. He took the three steps that brought him within arm's reach of his daughter. "Cigarette?" He held a soft pack of Camels out to her.

Prune had never smoked but she said, "Sure. *Merci*," just so she could peer into her father's eyes as he leaned in to light her first cigarette.

X

You Are Not Alone

$\mathcal{T}$he sisters decided, unanimously minus two, that a public demonstration was called for, and Alia came as a natural choice for the leader of Santa Clara's #OccupyTheCenter campaign. For one thing, unlike the nuns, Alia wasn't under an oath of silence. And while she wasn't the only one there with freedom-fighting experience—many of the sisters hailed from Central America—Alia was the only one with four-thousand-and-three Facebook friends and a Twitter following of twice that at #girls4revolution.

In Cairo, Alia had kept up with the protests at Tahrir Square from the very first day. One hundred idealists, one guitar, and a couple of dumbeks.

"Arrest the drummers, sir," her father's driver Rachid had told the rearview mirror as their BMW glided by what looked like a Bohemian festival. "Drummers are the heart-beat. Everyone worries about their heart. Everyone wants a better one. They say they want jobs, but they want the same thing you and I do: a stronger, bigger, fuller heart. They want dignity. They think jobs and free elections will give them that. Who can resist? Mark my words, sir. These two drummers will cast this whole city into a dervish trance that your tear-gas will never manage to quell." Alia's father had stopped scrolling down on his tablet for soccer game scores, lifted his reading glasses, leaned into the tinted window, then placed his palm between Alia's shoulder blades.

In the following weeks, Rachid had agreed to drive Alia by the Square every day on the way from school in exchange for her old ipod and earbuds, which he wanted for his wife's at-home Zumba practice.

"I love watching her shimmy, but I love it best when I cannot hear the music. Makes me feel like she's doing it just for me. Men in love are silly, no?" He told the rearview mirror, laughing. Then, as they drove by the white tents flapping in the wind, listening to the loudspeaker, Rachid frowned. "But men not in love are dangerous."

Within a month, hundreds of thousands of protesters had converged on the square. Hundreds were arrested, tortured, and wounded by the Mubarak government forces. Still, Muslims, labor unions, poets, feminists, and students kept coming, and Mubarak was forced to step down, leaving the army in charge. Later, Rachid joined the protesters, after so-called elections left the Muslim Brotherhood in charge and his adult daughter was told by an official that she need not waste time in the line to apply for her master's degree at Cairo University when she should instead be at home making more little Muslims to redeem the country.

By the time Alia's father, High Secretary of Budgetary Affairs for Mubarak's Ministry of Economy, had left on a private jet to Dubai that had enough room for his twenty-two year old secretary, her son, and the boy's cricket bat collection—but not for Alia and her mother—Alia had already understood that the battle wasn't in the stones or the firebombs that hit the hospitals where bleeding protestors lay. The battle was in the images posted on YouTube and the memes on Twitter that prompted the authorities to kidnap the head of Google Egypt. It wasn't the water cannons and the batons that had tens of thousands converging on Tahrir Square. It was the other images, that CNN and BBC and al-Jazeera weren't showing—all the Facebook posts of people dancing, organizing, throwing rocks at tanks *together*. The handsome young man who'd just returned to Egypt from studying in England said it just right in the clip Alia loved to replay on Mother Carmen's laptop: "As long as there is a camera, the revolution will continue."

The Santa Clara sisters set up camp, and Mother Carmen had to cast many a stern glare at the novices, who had trouble containing their screeches upon returning from their rounds at the Salvation Army with a truck full of sleeping bags, fleece mittens, and igloo tents. But Carmen's real worry was latitude. Española, New Mexico winters present challenges that Cairo, Egypt doesn't. They're called frostbite and bobcats.

For Pedro, the hard part this morning wasn't the hard ground so much as the absence of feet. Zip. Gone. The tweet of whatever polar critter was out there telegraphing vaulted the black wall of night, and Pedro closed his eyes again. From within, he could visualize his own feet. Duck feet. His mother preferred to call them Roman. Alia said T. Rex, and wanted to paint his nails purple. Size thirteen on a five-foot-five frame. Flip flop, flip flop. *So huge, they must have dropped off like too ripe fruit,* thought Pedro. Plonk.

"Concentrate!" Pedro scolded himself. He tried to move. The soft lining of the sleeping bag tickled the hair on his thighs and the bonier parts of his knees. But still no feet. *Phantom limb*—the words, from a manual about war-amputees he'd found in the Santa Clara library—flashed before him. "The sensation that a missing limb is still attached to the body and moving appropriately with the other body parts," said the manual. Except there was no "appropriate moving" here. Only dread. Like when Pedro woke up thinking his mom was about to saunter in, open the blinds, kiss his eyelids, but then he remembered the impossible angle of her arm and the black stains on the ground after the *Federales'* dogs were finished with her.

Noticing how cold his nose and eyeballs were, Pedro pulled up the duvet to bury his face. As he did, something loosened up on the other end of the bag, a dam let up, like a wet dream, and there were his clunky feet again. It felt like fire ants crawling all up in them, but *Phew!*

Breath held, Pedro listened to the shuffling just outside the tent. Yawning noises. *Good, bobcats don't yawn. Whatever they do —yelp, growl, hiss?—they don't yawn. Alia yawns. Alia loves to yawn. Alia's yawns are insanely contagious. And she's the best stretcher too. Sometimes when she stretches, her blouse rises just enough to reveal dark down on pale belly skin.* Alia, lying just like him, swaddled in her sleeping bag under the tent next to his. *So, so near, she could just as well be right here.* Pedro waited for the pangs of wanting to crawl out and go snuggle up with her to subside. Soon it would be time to get up and go stand outside The Center's fence—stand strong, determined, heroic: hopeful that the world would notice it was feeding off of its children.

Meanwhile, Pedro waited, listening for the shush of Alia's hair against the nylon of her tent.

Dawn scrolled down the long list of unopened emails on her desktop without wanting to double-click on any. Squeezed between the ivory cigarette holder and her tired manicure, her knuckle was about to shatter when she remembered to take a drag—quick peck, long inhale, breath suspended to make sure that each alveoli inside the lungs got its share. Surprisingly, there was smoke left to exhale and it came out in a dry little cough; then another; a salvo; heaves upon heaves. Dawn needed both her hands to keep her entrails from spilling out, so she went to set the fag in the ashtray, but the coughing stopped and she changed her mind, stole another drag—hesitant this one, like one who's been bit pats a dog's head.

The lit tip crackled when it reached the rim of the tusk. Dawn held it out as if to ask, Why? Didn't wait for an answer, and the tip disappeared inside the mouth of the holder as she took one last, long drag. She tossed the whole thing at the ashtray, missed, watched it tumble on the mahogany and come to a stop against the sticky ring from an old gin and tonic.

With one hand on the desk, Dawn pushed herself to standing. With the other, she grasped the back of her executive chair, found her balance, opened the top drawer, rummaged for something, forgot what, tried to whack the drawer closed but the smooth rails slowed it down. She scanned the room, struggling to remember what it was she was after. She glossed over the scattered crumbs on the coffee table and the half-empty bag of Chex rustling in the air from the fan vent above. Ah! There it was, all shiny in the dull crease of the leather sofa: the platinum Cartier lighter her father had given her for her twenty-first birthday, saying, "When are you going to find a lad? You clearly need to get laid." Dawn stumbled over to the sofa, picked up the lighter, tucked it tight inside her fist, and with a snicker at her coat and scarf hanging by the door, she walked out into the snow.

In the glacial expanse between the blockish Welcome Center and the adobe Cafeteria, Dawn caught a glimpse of turmoil. *Bobcats*, she told herself, gathering her thin sweater into her chest to cover her bare neck.

Once she'd eye-scanned her way into the F Ward that housed the Daycare, the guard called her name a few times, but she didn't look back.

As she'd hoped, Gaia was asleep. Even in her sleep, the baby was kicking. It made the plump on her thigh uncoil like petals to reveal the seed of a leg, the evocation of a knee. Dawn held out a tense hand, the veins a blue bramble over the twigs of her tendons. Next to the supple clay of Gaia's flesh, this hand was steel, like something meant to cut or bruise —something like Dawn's mother's hand, that pinched to break the skin, then rubbed in the sting of alcohol, saying, "Quit gesticulating, it's nothing. Mommy will take care of it," and she did, Mommy did.

With her steel hand, Dawn pushed the memory aside. With

her soft hand, she grazed the baby's leg. Upon contact, Dawn's entire lifetime flashed past, like dying. But she found nothing, no frame of reference for the plushness of that baby leg, not even the fluffy kitten she'd hidden in the closet and fed with a drinking bottle, until her mother found it and flushed it down the toilet.

Gaia stirred. Dawn held her breath.

The guard's voice echoed down the hallway, "President Hetheringtooon?"

"Shut up and sod off," Dawn whispered through gritted teeth. Gaia stirred again.

"President, are you in here?" The guard's voice was getting closer. Dawn knew she could just pick up the baby and walk out of there. She could lie that Anthony had asked to see his daughter. She could say she'd offered to come get her because Anthony was busy lobbying the Joint Staff to convince them the nuns and hippies camped out there were bloodthirsty terrorists and traitors to the Flag. *Shit!* she thought. *I don't need an excuse. This is MY Center! Listen to this—*

"President Hetherington?" The guard's broad face filled the frame of the nursery door. "Is everything ok?"

Dawn nodded tightly. Gaia's eyelids fluttered open and Dawn froze. She'd never actually looked into a baby's *face,* never really thought of it as a face—a living, singular thing. Gaia grinned, uncovering a few tiny white teeth against bright pink gums.

"Ga!"

"Hi!"

"Gaga!" Gaia was moving her arms, reaching for Dawn.

"She's probably ready to get her diaper changed. I have four at home. You?" The guard was smiling at the baby over Dawn's shoulder.

"No," Dawn said. "No."

"Hey Gaia girl. What's shaking today? She's such a happy one! Easy peasy. Not like my second daughter. You should have heard that one. Sounded like a cat in heat. All night. Took us five months to figure out the poor thing was allergic to my wife's milk. Acid reflux. Hey baby girl!" The guard waved at Gaia, who let out little shrieks.

His babbling was a distant buzz. Dawn was mesmerized by the baby. Her baby. *My baby... my baby.* She was trying it out like a sweater, to see how it fit. *My baby?* Good. It felt good. She would hire a wet nurse, or whatever they were called—someone to teach her the specifics, help with the bathing, feeding, playing. Anthony wouldn't come after her. He'd made it clear he wanted Dawn out of the way, and probably the baby wasn't part of his plan for world dominion. The mother? The gardener had shown more interest in composting and raising hell with the Mexican janitor than getting the baby back. *Besides, if Grenadine manages to survive what the General has in store, soon enough all she'll be raising is bonsais in prison.* The thought of Anthony's bitch in jail made Dawn feel all fuzzy inside.

"Anything I can help you with, President?"

"No." Dawn tapped the guard's shoulder as if to say, Good dog. Glancing at his name tag she added, "Not now. Thank you, Pontiac."

"Just let me know." Gaia started to grumble. Pontiac cooed, "There, there, baby girl. The nurse is on her way. Who's gonna get a nice clean diaper on her fluffy bottom?"

"Oy!"

"Oy, Pereira!" The guard greeted the nurse, who was pushing in a cartful of supplies. Her squeaky shoes made Dawn wince.

"Oy, senhora Hetherington," the nurse called in her heavy Portuguese accent.

"President," Dawn corrected.

"Oy, senhora Presidente."

Gaia was whining, now. Imperious, Ms. Pereira parted Dawn and the guard aside, went to pick up the baby, and laid her down on the changing table. The nurse and the guard both whistled admiringly at the healthy heap she found in the baby's diaper.

Horrified, Dawn had to look away.

Usually shimmering with waxy leaves, the Dreamscape had stayed dull for too many days, now. Even Attila, an avid swimmer, was reluctant to splash about the swimming hole. No sunshine meant wet fur deep into the night and voracious midges stealing the moonlight. Wet fur meant no sacrum scratching from Carla, and it meant an agitated ten-year old clawing for sleep as she cussed her moss pad, cussed the midges, cussed the rotting-egg smell on him, cussed like a Bosnian sailor.

Attila didn't like cussing. At thirteen, he was an old wolf, hankering for Persian poetry and Zen koans: verses about the after-life, the tides, the orderliness of nature. Sure, having been taken in as a cub by a recently widowed Anastasia, Attila had never been insulated from angry words, broken pots spilling their spite, mantras of revenge hurled at the moon. But he'd never grown used to it. Wasn't going to.

They needed sunshine. But the Dreamscape had grown from soul stories passed down generation after generation of wild women and girls, like breasts. The place had to answer a few archetypal rules. One such rule was, The sun shall only come out when Anastasia smiles. Now, ever since that falling out with her human lover, the one who smelled like buttered corn, Anastasia hadn't smiled. She had smirked, sneered, chuckled even. But no real smile, the kind that enlists the eyes, the nose, the crow's feet. Not a one.

Looking bored with her hula-hooping, Carla declared, "I had to nuke Mom from my memory. Just had to. It was me or her."

"Did it hurt?" The crone looked up from her nut-cracking.

"No, not at first."

"Later, then?"

Carla grasped her hoop and began to twirl it around her wrist. "Later there were bubbles inside, like when helium balloons are unleashed and they bob up, ding, ding, ding. So pretty, so colorful, ding, ding, ding." She tossed the hoop up in the air to illustrate, and it landed, still perfectly twirling, around her other wrist. "Until they're gone." Carla snapped the hoop and it jerked to a stop. "It happens so fast—like some cancers, the lucky ones. You know it's there, you want it gone, you pray to see it fly away. Then it's gone, and you're left with an empty sky. Empty."

Anastasia nodded, intent on peeling her pecans. She knew empty. It called to mind her late husband Karl's protracted, slow death. She said, "Well, I'm not going to nuke Ruben. Instead, I'm going to love madly the part of me that's choking without him. I'm going to love her so snug that she'll quaver in my arms, and her tears will be my sap, and I'll remember to remember that I, too, am a wave, and have always been, and that I don't need to search for the sea. Then I'll be ready, and she and I will dance our vast shimmering dance with the tides."

With this, Anastasia seized Attila's front paws and shook them up and down like puppets. Wobbly on his hind paws, the wolf groaned with a desperate glance toward Carla. The girl chuckled, let go of her hoop, grasped Anastasia's hand in one hand and Attila's paw in the other. All three stood, cotillon-ready, the women sparkling, the wolf stupefied.

As they started to twirl, the tear-drops on Anastasia's cheeks were diamonds in the sudden sunlight that peeked under fat clouds. Attila was biting the air in front of him, and when the women finally let him go, he scampered off toward the edge of the clearing and disappeared inside a sprawling candle bush.

Crone and girl fought their urge to call out apologies. This wasn't a time to act delicate: it was a time to be vast and brilliant, to let their bodies weave their fears with their bliss, their aloneness with their oneness. They knew Attila could sense it too, and so they kept dancing. They danced until their tears dried, their breath panted, and gravity was no longer the problem but instead, became the solution.

Marc Michaux's desk had always been an arctic lake. Notepads and photocopies stayed stacked at right angles. The only visible color belonged to the small post-it tongues that stuck out of closed books. But here, in his Arles studio, global warming had claimed its merciless right and it took Prune some time to unearth enough flat surface to set down a teacup. So, teacup in hand, Prune stood in the doorway, watching her father stir the paint for his new art piece, a three-meter tall *papier maché* sea horse. The bits of newspaper it was made of showed the chubby French President, topless models, and garish TV programs.

"Come on in!" Marc waved in Prune with that heavily accented English he insisted on using with her and one enthused hand, while the other kept stirring the Afternoon Breeze. The gallon of house-paint skidded on the glass table. Prune lurched, a reflex, but Marc stabilized it with both hands. Rosa used to make fun of those hands—a city dweller's hands, the hands of a man who's never had to dig, scrub, split, or punch things. Fingertips narrow and pink, skin ghostly with pulsing blue veins showing through, nails cut short, unstained, naturally shiny. But now there were small purple scars, paint specks, one thumbnail bruised black.

Who is this man? Prune was all the way inside Marc's studio now. She stood on an iceberg, floating in a sea of blotches and half-chewed dog toys, wooden hangers, a doll's head with one eye closed, screws, bits of broken tile, scraps of fabric, plastic flowers, mint-wrappers, credit card receipts, an actual credit card, broken-spined books, a tuxedo jacket, a wig.

"Come meet Ovid," Marc called, jovial. Prune searched the floor for another island on which to set foot. She kept thinking of the cool citrus on her father's polished chin when he used to kiss her good morning. She had written a poem about that in her diary. In The Center's herb garden, she'd had Grenadine point out the verbena, the English thyme, the sage, hunting for a hint of her father's after shave, a sensory confirmation that there had indeed been comfort, once—and home.

This man hadn't shaved in days. Uncannily, his stubble showed a reddish tinge, even as his hair had remained black as a Friesian horse. Prune wanted to part the messy sea, walk over to her father, kiss him good day, feel the Spanish Spring on his cheek sticky like pine sap against hers. She wanted to know that it was time to put down the shield, the spear, the sword—all the sharp things she'd been carrying. But this Marc treated her like a long lost friend, showing no sign of awareness that they'd shared a lifetime (her lifetime), that she was his daughter. His smile kept sparkling. *A smile much too free, much too happy to be real*, she thought. It was infuriating. Disarming. Devastating.

Marc didn't take offense at Prune's paralysis. He quickly forgot she was there, and with his tongue sticking out the corner of his mouth like a third-grader, he began to slather paint onto the sea horse. Prune was still grasping for something to say or do, something that might bring her real father back.

"Carla is in a coma," she said. "*Elle a besoin de toi, Papa.*"

"Mmmmh?" Marc didn't look up.

"Carla. Your other daughter. My little sister."

"Mmmmh mmmh." Total bust.

Prune's brain was starting to defog, though. She began to discern something like patterns among the jumble; more distinct shapes. In a corner, she noticed several paintings leaning against the wall and each other. On the largest one, she thought she recognized the lush jungle of her mother's friend.

"Is that Rodrigo's?" They'd had several of his paintings hanging in their hallway in Paris—until Marc grew so jealous of the man that he demanded they'd be taken down, and they ended up in a closet in Prune's bedroom. Prune liked Rodrigo, and she liked to know that his leafy leopards and pensive iguanas were guarding her things.

"What?"

"There." Prune pointed at the stack of paintings. She started toward it.

"Leave that alone," Marc snapped.

Prune ignored him and pulled out the canvas. "It is!"

"*Merde!*" Marc cried. A half-gallon of Afternoon Breeze was dripping down the side of his pant legs onto the floor. The only time Prune remembered her father looking this deer-in-the-headlights was in the long, vague days after Rosa was abducted, after the police had rifled through everything the kidnappers had left spilling over rugs. There were no prints, no leads. The inspector, or whatever rank she was, had given the girls a desolate grimace, saying to Marc, "We'll call you. Please don't leave the Schengen zone."

Prune set down the canvas and a bulky craft envelope dropped onto a heap of rusted toy cars.

"*N'y touche pas!*" Marc cried.

Unmistakable, the handwriting stung. Prune picked up the package like it was a brand new kitten, all frail and clawy. In her wiry longhand, Rosa had addressed the parcel to *Mis Cariños.* My darlings. That included Prune.

For seconds, Marc stared right through his daughter's midriff, where the brown envelope rested, at some distant, terrifying thing.

"*Papa?*"

Marc adjusted his stare to lock in with his daughter's. Tears welled up. He wiped his brow with his sleeve, tossed his gooey paintbrush on top of the table, brusquely got up from his stool, and stormed out of the studio, shaking his head no. He mumbled, "*Morte, morte, morte, morte, morte, tout le monde est mort, tout le monde est mort, tout le monde, mort!*"

"*Papa!*" Prune heard the heavy front door whine open; a

humph as it closed. Heidegger meowed reproachfully. Then dead silence.

Once again, she scanned the room for a place to sit. Her father's barstool stood in a pool of Afternoon Breeze. Clutching her mother's envelope like a lifebuoy, she carefully worked her way out of the studio. The cat froze when she settled down next to him on the hallway rug, then he picked up his grooming where he'd left it.

Mexico City, one too many days away from you

Marco, mi amor,

The Museum of Modern Art has fallen in love with photography, here. Something about the illusion of immediacy, I think. Something for your wonder-mind to ponder.

There is a story told on the wall next to this photographer's "rectangles of the moment," as he calls his pictures. Each one could be a metaphor for us—not our love, no. Our love is too solid for poetry and figures of speech. But a metaphor for the work we do. Like this one, "Saving Nature," in which a white man in a suit stands in a row of wheatgrass as tall as him. The wind is sweeping the grasses to one side, but the man is hanging onto one strand, trying to keep it straight. Futility and resolve. Desperation and idealism.

Here I am, so close to home yet continents away from those I love most, and my old compañeros, terrified I'll get shot, or worse, must keep me in a cave. I escaped. Not to organize a march; not to foment another rebellion, although my opponents would like to say I did. I escaped to go see art. Is this luxury? Betrayal? Survival?

Keep my girls safe, Marc. Keep them snuggled and curious. Keep them soft and free and fearless. Save nature, my love, like nature saves us.

We cannot succeed, but we cannot fail. We cannot fail.

I love you the most,
Your Rose.

There was no postal stamp, no date, no address on the envelope: only *"Amor"* in Rosa's handwriting.

Next was a piece of thin white paper folded in four. Rosa's nervous cursives transpired from the other side. Prune unfolded it. No date, no place, only this:

Forgive me, daughter: I died. I died many times and still, la fuerza carried enough of my burdens, forcing me off of those knees callused from too much coffee picking, too much yielding.

My abuela needed me to carry her clean water, and keeping her alive mattered more than my safety. Many of our lives depended on hers. She waved us away, rotten-toothed swarms of relatives' and neighbors' kids, but she always kept the tortillas coming, the stove burning, and the stories.

I was her Rosa, the rose with enough thorns to keep her affection away, but not enough to hold back the paramilitaries' greasy hands.

There were eight of them. It must have been June, the maize was taller than me. I walked slowly to keep the water from spilling over the buckets. The three kilometers to the pueblo's only clean water well were endless on the slippery trail. Perhaps, if I had walked a little faster. If I had reached the compound before dusk. If I had screamed, they wouldn't have… or someone would have stopped them?

But I didn't. One after another, their sperm spilling out of me to lubricate the next one's cock. I think this turned them on more than my barely-there breasts, more than my "Please don'ts" and the limpness that took over me.

I do not know which one of them fathered you.

Forgive me, my Prune. I had died inside before I could forgive you.

Daylight was almost gone. A tungsten street-light suddenly came on, tossing green on the letter Prune was holding. Heidegger

stopped grooming and came to rub against her knee. She put down
the letter with the rest of the bundle. As she went to caress his back,
the cat slithered away from her hand to go sit a few inches away.
Reaching for him, Prune crawled down on all fours. Heidegger
conceded that she rest her hand on his head, but swatted at it with
a soft paw. Finally, he let her curl up on the rug next to him.

For a long time Prune scratched behind his ears. He purred.
The church bells rung. When her wrist fell limp by his side,
Heidegger scrubbed it raw with his tongue. She wondered if he'd
let her sneak him into her room at the Pilgrims's House. *Probably
not.* So she got herself up, slipped the bundle of her mother's
papers back into the brown envelope, carefully placed the envelope
inside her backpack, and walked out of Marc Michaux's house.

In the beginning, Carla hadn't been too thrilled with the
stupid side glares, the ill-camouflaged secrets, the palpable
longing between the lovers. Anastasia and Ruben acted as if she
needed to be shielded from love. It was insulting. And yes, she did
feel excluded—not because they were falling in love, or lust, or
whatever those clownish grins were, but because they felt the need
to hide it from her and thought her dumb enough not to notice.

Their first arguments were sinuous. Anastasia threw jabs with
a twinkle in her eye. Ruben let it slide. But over time, the distance
between his shoulders and ears got shorter. The children's training
kept him away more often. *Men must have invented work so they
could keep away from their wives,* Carla thought, remembering the
patina on her father's home-office door.

Back home, Carla had developed a sort of cargo cult around
the opening and closing of her father's office door after her
parents' fights. She'd grown convinced that her gaze held a certain
power in it. She even began to place bets with herself on how long

her father's office door would remain closed. Less than twelve minutes, and she could ask Prune to heat up a *crêpe* for her in the micro-wave. More than two hours, and she'd have to skip breakfast for two days in a row. Thanks to Carla's powerful intent, Marc's office brooding had never exceeded two hours and twenty-three minutes (one-hundred-and-forty-three minutes) before he'd pop out between the sliding doors to ask if the coast was clear, like she was his trusted scout and he on a dangerous mission.

This morning, Anastasia was so maddened by Ruben's refusal to fight that she chased him around with an iron skillet. Attila took off after her, his jaw slack and the arthritis in his hip forgotten. The crone could have outrun man and wolf, but she never caught up with either, not until all three ended in the swimming hole, roiling with splashes of laughter. The racket made it impossible to concentrate, so Carla put down her book and jumped in on their heels. It was so quiet underwater, the girl decided to stay there. No one noticed.

From the boulders on its rim, the water was an eternal dusk but from within, it was translucent, the granite bottom speckled like grass under a fruit tree. Their bodies were fizzy. Anastasia's phantom white legs did a moonwalk. With algae arms, the crone helped herself out of her shorts, and in two kicks she was a grapevine around Ruben. Headless, they struggled briefly, then became very still, one trunk. They let themselves drop under, their mouths wanting to swallow each other's faces. Carla kicked up for a breath, then dropped right back under. Anastasia' bust pressed against Ruben's. She slid under to bite one of his nipples, pinching the other between her fingers. Carla wanted to laugh, gag, swim away. Instead she stayed, picturing herself filtering in the O in $H2O$ through the pores of her skin.

The lovers were several feet away, but it was like looking through a microscope. Carla recalled the skinless frog from biology lab, its tiny leg throbbing when her lab partner applied the electrode. Then there was an elephant stepping on her chest.

Clearly mighty. *I surrender*, Carla thought. A volcano erupted in her throat, and when she opened her eyes, all three of her friends' faces were blocking the clouds. Attila's bad breath made her cough and water came out her nose. It was like drinking inside out, and it hurt.

With her forearm, Anastasia wiped the backwash from Carla's face. "I knew you'd come right back, squirt."

"I would miss you like salt, *muñeca*." Ruben sniffled, then offered a hand to lift her up. They all four sat in a circle in the grass and the evening chill descended on their meadow.

Anastasia said, "Maybe Grenadine has a point. This isn't quite working, is it?" That night, across the bonfire loomed the two-hump camel of Ruben and Anastasia's combined bodies. In the glow of the flames, their teeth were fireflies, their faces wax figures. Carla expected them to begin to melt hideously anytime. But for now, they glistened.

All of a sudden, the night's rhapsody kicked in. A certain crackling of the fire, perhaps the hot embers in the damp dusk, switched on the crickets. Then the frogs jumped in. One bold one calling out to the empty night, then two, five, twenty-two. It was ear-splitting on rainy nights but eventually it would rock Carla to sleep, exactly like the aerial metro in Paris used to.

As she drifted off to sleep Carla thought, *It isn't Ruben and Anastasia's geriatric romance that bothers me. I've lived long enough to know that nothing seems to matter to old people quite as much as love. What bothers me is that they have lost their brains in the process. Just tossed it right in the fire. If I squinted hard enough, I might even see that gray matter sizzle and spit like bacon, except mushy as American bread and flavorless, flavorless.* She propped herself up. "I'm not leaving without Attila!"

"I know." The creases in Anastasia's face seemed to fill with ash. "But it's going to be up to him."

"I know." Carla stared at the circle her toe was tracing in the moist black dirt. "I don't *have* to go." She sniffled.

"No, you don't." Anastasia sounded relieved. "She doesn't," she added defiantly for Ruben's benefit.

"No, *muñeca*, you don't have to do anything you don't want to do. And maybe your friends can make it without your help."

"Listen to yourself, trying to guilt trip the kid! Don't fall for it, Carla, it's a trap!" At that, the smaller camel hump moved away from the other.

Carla sighed. After a moment she added, "I'll go if Attila comes with."

In Arles, most street corners are looked after by small medieval statues of saints perched like birds' nests on the edge of stone buildings. Their faces, weathered by centuries spent watching over brawls, gossip, drunken pissing and late night kissing, bear the stoic affliction of martyrs. On the corner of rue de la Roquette and rue Baudadoni, Prune looked up to see a genderless figure staring back at her, inquisitive.

How am I supposed to know? Prune wanted to shout. She could feel the bundle of her mother's papers throbbing in her backpack, heavy like the cross. She knew it held more agony as it promised to replace the anguish of not knowing with the pangs of knowing too much. And yet. The more answers Prune found, the more questions she had.

Was Marc out of his mind, or was he pretending? Did it make a difference either way? Did he know that Rosa had been brutally raped, and that Prune's real father was a gang of animals? Did he know what had become of Rosa, and was *that* so horrible that he'd rather renounce all that he'd built with her, including their family? But Marc was a philosopher: a lover of the truth. Prune had always known him a relentless seeker, a scholar of the first order—which is to say, a detective, ruthless in his tracking down of delusion.

She decided that Marc's madness couldn't simply be the malady of denial. But then, what was he so damn afraid of? He must have known that she wasn't his biological daughter, and clearly it had never mattered to him. It didn't matter to her—did it? *Does it?* If not this, then what was Marc trying to protect her from?

"*Bonsoir!*" A couple walked by, hands in each other's back pockets.

"*Bonsoir,*" Prune replied in a coarse voice. Their footsteps echoed in the empty street as they walked on.

At her rear, the backpack was like a bulging disk. In spite of the December chill, heat had pooled about her kidneys, where her mother's papers sat. Prune wanted to believe it was a sign that they were holding her answers. Some answers, at least. Was there a connection between Rosa's disappearance and The Center? How could their own grandmother Alma have dumped Prune and her sister Carla at The Center? There were millions of unclaimed minors out there. Why them?

The breeze was blowing harder. Probably the *mistral* was coming up. Prune shuddered, thinking, *Bed, blanket, now.* A wooden shutter banged above. She raised her hand to shade her eyes from the streetlight. Between ochre buildings, a slice of night sky scintillated like the sea. Prune yawned, noticing the faded address and numbers she'd scribbled inside her palm: Marabout, *3, rue Balzac 4:06 - 7:09, 18:41 - 22:04.* The "Extraordinary Fortune Teller" from the telephone booth. *The one who can cure psoriasis,* Prune remembered. She started down the rue de la Roquette toward the Pilgrim's House and felt a small surge of Maybe. Answers? *Demain.* Tomorrow.

Grenadine had been staring at her bedroom ceiling too long, and the shadows were taking on a life of their own. She knew that no good ever came out of an incest survivor's imagination—what with the eternal presence of her father's skin pores looming over her crumpled Winnie-the-Pooh gown. She contemplated trying to snap out of it. Ruben and the kids were expecting her at the temple. But her bones were fastened to the cot.

On the nightstand, between the pillar candle and the bottle of *Patrón*, the lean blade of her pocket knife—a present from her father—caught the first stirrings of daylight.

"You're not fooling anyone," Grenadine whispered. "Fucking sham of a friend." Louder, loud enough to convince herself, she spat, "Don't you just sit there with your shit-eating grin pasted on. I've got a life now. I've got work to do. I've got a girl. I've got friends. Animate friends. Friends who breathe, eat, want to help. Friends who stick around even when I feel decent. But you? You only show up when I'm down in the dumps. It's perverse, this fascination you've got, like the fags at the Curl Up and Dye hair salon back in Yazoo City, who hung around getting off on the world's misery. I want my friends to be there for me when I'm well. Not like this, weak, fucking insane, blabbering on to a knife who wants me to think it's my friend."

The spring was sprouting green things everywhere. When Grenadine reached for a Kleenex to blow her nose, her finger grazed the soft wax that rimmed the candle. It felt strikingly like skin—like Prune's skin after she'd slathered on every bit of her that entrancing Tahitian oil.

"Prune," Grenadine whined. "Prune." She said it again, to taste the shape of the word against the roof of her mouth. The candle flame quivered, painfully bright if you tried to look at it. From the blade's steel, one thousand dancing flames beckoned. Grenadine reached past the candle and the knife for the *Patrón*, took a swig. "Shit, Prune." Grenadine's finger was now toying with the wax. When it burned, the tip of her nail let off a baking chicken smell.

The blade traced a soft L on the skin of Grenadine's forearm. The O raised her eyebrows like a question mark—the blunt cold always so surprising, even when she ached for it. Her lip tickled as she uttered the V and the small ravine from the delightful pressure garnered depth. Infinitesimally more pressure, and the skin finally broke. The red came with a sigh and a settling of the ribs inside the body they caged. "Eeeeeeeeee." Grenadine let that E out like a child's wail, unrepentant. "LOVE. All is well." She cocked her head to the side and held her arm out to better observe the slow drip from her work of art. "All as it should be."

When Ruben came looking for Grenadine, the thin wounds had already started to clot. He dragged her by her arms to the bathroom, turned on the shower, made sure it was neither too hot nor too cold, then went back to sit on the end of the bed, leaving her naked as a snake on the cold tile. After he hadn't heard her stir for a while, he called, "Take your time; don't you skip the mouth rinse!"

When Grenadine came out of the shower, Ruben was standing by the bed with one heavy blanket thrown over each shoulder.

"Here," he said, "Pick one and wrap yourself in it. Which do you like best?" Grenadine sighed, pointing at a canary-yellow blanket with green diamond shapes. Ruben handed it to her. She took a moment to caress the uneven fabric, tracing with her finger the edge of a diamond. Ruben nodded. "Good, you must encounter the blanket." Grenadine lifted the heavy fabric to her face and tentatively rubbed her cheek against it. Then she buried her nose in it, taking in the muttony smell and the vagueness of urine.

"Now, wrap yourself in it."

Grenadine sat directly on the cold tile and struggled to get the stiff blanket to bend around her back and all the way around to cover her knees. Ruben sat down, legs crossed, a mirror image of her.

"You must cover everything." He was earnest as an accountant. "Even the pink toe." He pointed at the round dot still peaking through.

While she was finishing her adjustments, he closed his eyes and began to sing—sounds neither human nor animal, but more like bones and raindrops. Grenadine closed her eyes. She was sinking in quickly. The warmth of the blanket spread from the outer edge of her skin into her muscles, her spleen and ligaments. Ruben's chant grew dimmer, more distant, although she knew he was sitting right there.

"Now, press your fingers into your pulse at the wrist. Feel your heart-beat." Grenadine did.

After a long time, Ruben added, "There is nothing wrong with you, Grenadine. It was rage, what your father called love. It was impotence and power-hunger, not love."

Quickly, Grenadine found herself cascading down a torrent of crushed berries. Inside her mouth, a raspberry explosion, and there was red, red everywhere. It was like walking inside her mother's home photo lab, with the black and white prints pinned on the clothesline next to the bras and panties.

"Stay with your heartbeat, feel the pulse of your life." Ruben was a murmur inside her head now. The torrent carried her deeper within, to memories of other lives, other times. A cave, the sound of a drip—ploc, ploc, ploc, ta toum, ta toum—*Is this drums? I have never been in a cave...*

"This is your pulse, Grenadine. This is your life. It's happening right now." The voice flickered across the cave walls like anger across her father's face, to reveal a large cauldron over a bonfire. *It's getting hot.* Sweat tickled as it trickled between her breasts. Inside the cauldron was a thick magma. "This is your blood."—*Whose voice?* Neither male nor female: a voice without a body.

Grenadine couldn't resist dipping a finger into the substance. She thought of chocolate fondue, wishing for the birthday clown her mother had hired once. Wishing for the farting sounds and the toy trumpet. Instead there were shackles on the dirt floor. The magma wasn't as hot as she'd expected, perhaps one hundred degrees, body temperature. She brought her finger to her mouth and licked. Iron, dirt, summer grass. *No doubt, this is blood.*

"Your blood." The voice. "Listen."

At the Pilgrim's House, one of the Maori nurses suffered from severe sleep apnea. You could hear her honking like a seal all the way from the bathroom down the hallway. Prune felt too drained to brush her teeth but she did anyway, a quick affair. Feeling her way in the dark of the dorm, she stumbled on someone's shoe and stubbed her toe on the metal foot of her bed. It knocked the air out of her and she considered screaming, pulling her hair out, briefly fantasized about having a gaggle of stout nurses pour over her misery. She decided against making a scene, skipped taking off her clothes, and simply kicked off her sneakers, unbuttoned her jeans, and crawled under the coarse sheets. The seal from New-Zealand was making the five-hundred-year-old walls shake, but Prune was ready to zonk out.

In the dream, Grenadine was all legs, leaning into a massive cauldron. When Prune called her name, Grenadine swiveled around guiltily, like a child caught cleaning out the chocolate bowl. All the same, she looked regal in her gold and emerald poncho.

"You," Grenadine said. Not a question, but rather the answer to a prayer. Prune nodded, trying to assess where she was. She noticed the hard shackles lying between them. "I've never been in a cave. You know me, not a fan of enclosed spaces." Grenadine waved her arm as if to say, "Like this." Just then, one black wall gave way to a wide open space where the grass shimmered by a bubbling brook. This made Grenadine chuckle. "Wow! Talk about, 'Ask, and you shall receive!'"

Prune knew about lucid dreaming, that state where you're asleep, aware of it, and able to consciously intervene in your own dreams to direct their outcome. She was pretty sure she was asleep, but as much as she'd been pining for her friend, she knew she hadn't consciously brought this about.

"Come on!" Grenadine's sudden change of tone, so sincere it could be mistaken for scolding, pried Prune out of her reverie. It felt real. So did the heat of Grenadine's hand on Prune's arm, pulling them both toward the brook, the big sky.

They lay down in the grass, Prune's head deliciously heavy on Grenadine's belly. Grenadine's fingers ran channels along Prune's scalp, whole new canals for the irrigation of her tears. Neither of them wanted words to steal the moment. For once, Grenadine did as she'd been told and she listened. She heard Prune's sobs and the nucleus of loneliness they slowly released. She heard the small wails and all the screams —impotence, rage, fuck you's— contained there. She heard all the Why's that no one would ever answer—that only humiliations, and chances, and unfathomable amounts of faith could. Through all this, and their silence, and the trembling and shifting of weight, Grenadine also heard love pounding through Prune's ribs, banging at her own temples like Javanese gongs.

What does this have to do with blood, my blood? Grenadine wondered. She'd assumed that Ruben had meant Negro blood. The cauldron, icon of Western cannibal mythology; the shackles— weren't images like these precisely what Grenadine was trying to peel away with the slivers she cut from her wrists?

Fully clothed, Prune let herself roll off of Grenadine's lap and into the stream. She yelped as she sunk into the shallow water. Soon, clothes were the memory of an itch.

Later, Prune's fingertips, wrinkled like soft apples, fluttered from the water's skin to the angles of her lover's feet. Grenadine's ankles dangled just above the surface. She let out merry hiccups each time cold droplets landed on her as Prune snatched at the traces of moonlight in the wake of leaping trouts. And all the while, Grenadine kept listening. What she heard was elation, relief. Then it hit her. It hit Grenadine that perhaps this is what blood means: you are not alone. Ancestry, memory, oxygen and carbon dioxide, life and death. In the end, it all boils down to the simple fact that You (I, She, We, They) Are Not Alone.

Through the adobe walls of John's bedroom, the slogans of the protesters merged with his own morning practice and lent a rebellious groove to his Sutra recitation.

March nineteen. Spring throbbed with vigor, and the equinox was sure to bring blossoms that the Swami envisioned with a quiver he labeled hope and angst by turn. He made himself surround trepidation with stillness and the cold of the earth seeped through the concrete, the mat, the pillow, the long-johns, and the folds of his robe to crawl up his *Shushumna*, the subtle energy pathway that hugs the spinal cord.

One of the things he loved about this practice was that the instructions were so practical and could be summed up in a few words: breathe, you are alive! The teachings worked if you worked them—if you woke before the sun, ate mindfully, approached all with compassion, and accepted that life is suffering only if you think that it ought not to be. Over the years, his spiritual practice had held John through the trials of failed relationships and the worse trial of academic triumph. As a novice, he had breathed himself through wet dreams and angry sexting, through the hall of mirrors of ego grasping, through his teachers' disdain, his mother's ambivalence, his best friend's suicide, his dog's cancer. But here, in this unheated bedroom, in a place he'd helped build where the oldest children were losing permanent teeth and an army general was lobbying the Free World to drop tiny smart bombs on passionate nuns, John had to accept that equanimity had become, simply, out of his reach.

Breathing in, I see myself as a flower. Breathing out, I feel fresh...
Breathing in, I see myself as a mountain. Breathing out, I feel solid...
Sitting became unbearable. It was time John took his meditation
out for a walk.

The campus was mostly deserted, now that the children
weren't allowed to step outside. The General called it a matter
of Homeland Security. The kids' identities were classified
information, and McMitt meant for it to remain so.

Breathing in, I see myself as space. Breathing out, I feel free. John
waved at an armed recruit who stood on the edge of Hetherington
Plaza. The boy couldn't be more than eighteen and his puckered
lips belied braces underneath. McMitt had called in elite troops to
track down the spy drones from the Liberal News Conspiracy that
he *knew* were hiding inside creosote bushes and flower pots. John
tried to discern the "elite" in the young soldier's red-rimmed eyes.
He saw only boredom.

*Breathing in, I see myself as still water. Breathing out, I reflect
all that is.* Another round of mantras, and John found himself
squinting in front of a fence. Shiny new barbs had been added to
the chain-link fence. A few hundred feet into the other side, he
spied a smattering of dusty igloo tents, a little red wagon full of
mushy Bud Light cartons, and a ratty sleeping bag airing out on
a clothes line.

A shih tzu appeared from between two tents and trotted toward
John. His heart skipped a beat when the dog scampered right
under the fence, as if it wasn't there. When the monk crouched
down to pet it, the dog lapped at his hand, bouncily trying to
climb up in his lap. A young man in pajama pants crawled out of
his tent to holler after the dog, "Lao Tzu! Come back over here!"

John giggled. "Lao Tzu, really?"

"Dude, you're the Buddhist monk!"

"What makes you think that?" John pinched his saffron robe
like a curtsy.

"Dude!" The man was staring at John, an apparition. "Hey,

Marge! Come check this out!" The man called out toward the campsite.

"STEP BACK!" The loudspeaker startled them both. The pajama man stumbled back several steps. John stood in place, looking around for the provenance of the voice while Lao Tzu yipped at his ankles. There was no one to be seen on his side of the fence, only a few cacti with yellow flowers blooming so bright that they seemed fake. On the Occupy side, Marge was gathering a small cluster of colorful youngsters.

"THIS IS NOT A FREE SPEECH ZONE. PLEASE STEP BACK OR WE WILL HAVE TO INTERVENE."

John thought he could pick up on the General's screechy whine. *Breathing in, I see myself as a mountain. Breathing out, I feel solid.* The Swami rooted his feet in the dust. The dog kept yapping, darting back and forth between the monk and the Pajama man like he wanted to knit them together.

"Go on, Lao Tzu," John said under his breath. The cluster was fast turning into a small crowd. Several people were holding out their phones, taking in the scene through their touch screen.

"I REPEAT, THIS IS NOT A FREE SPEECH ZONE, PLEASE STEP BACK IMMEDIATELY." The small crowd backed off a few more steps and huddled closer together.

"Lao Tzu, come back over here, for fuck's sake!" The pajama man whistled. Panting, the dog came to a stop and his head ping-ponged between his master and John.

"Go on," John said again.

"LAO!" The dog finally opted for the pajama man, who snatched him up and whisked over to join the other protesters.

A young soldier appeared behind John and the protesters started to boo. Someone threw a rock, but it landed a few feet short of the fence. A timid voice rose from their midst, chanting the Movement's familiar slogan, "Free the Ch'i, Free the Ch'i, Free the cheeeeee-ldren!" Several voices joined in. "Free the Ch'i, Free the Ch'i, Free the cheeeeee-ldren!" More soldiers lined up behind

John. This seemed to egg on the protesters, who began to march forward in a clump.

"BY THE AUTHORITY OF THE FEDERAL GOVERNMENT OF THE UNITED STATES OF AMERICA, STEP BACK, OR—"

"FUCK OFF!" The shriek rose from the crowd. "Where are the kids? Free the Ch'i, Free the Ch'i, Free the cheeeeee-ldren!" Their singing was carrying them forth like a wave now. On the crest of it, John noticed heavy camera gear. The soldiers surrounded him. He counted twelve rifles pointed right at him. For the first time in his life, his mind wasn't racing. He felt calm as the proverbial lake. The boy with the braces had half of his face twisted up into his visor. John smiled at him but he didn't smile back.

"Come on man, don't be a jerk." This from a woman with medals who seemed in charge and kept her rifle pointed at the sky. "Jesus, you're not going to make us shoot the hippies, are you? Isn't that against your religion?"

John glanced at the thin silver cross dangling from her neck, and back at her eyes. "Why so much fear of little children?" He asked.

The protesters had stopped. In silence, they began to fan out and, holding hands, they lined up into a human rope about thirty feet away from John and the soldiers. The Swami could hear the shuffle of the protesters' clothes and the heavy breathing of the boy with the braces. He found that soothing, beautiful. Human.

The Christian soldier held her rifle pointed right at John's face now. "Whose fear?" She spat.

Beyond her, John took another look at the crowd. He noted at least two TV cameras. Lao Tzu was yapping hysterically, each ear-splitting bark rippling out along the prairie. John was thankful for the irony. He reached inside his robe for the jerry-can he had tied to his waist and quickly doused himself. The smell reminded him of his mother's Zippo lighter, how much he loved lighting her cigarettes for her, how grown up and necessary it made him feel.

"Holy crap!" Stunned, several soldiers looked up from their visors at each other. Through the vapors, the Swami saw the woman in charge trying to grab his hands, but he had rehearsed well and the flames were already shielding him. The soldiers tumbled away like dust balls as a blue blaze flared up from the hem of John's robe, where the gasoline had pooled. Lao Tzu's barks pierced through the cries of the protesters—Jesus's name invoked in vain.

Against the clouds, amidst the fumes, Avalokitesvara Bodhisattva was smiling a radiant smile, not because he relished the agony or the smell of death, but because he could sense the inexhaustible courage that was being ignited by it.

The mouthpiece didn't quite fit. Carla's lips bulged like a boxer's as she struggled to seal her mouth shut over the tuba and tiny bubbles rose out the corners. She chewed on the plastic for a moment, her jaw slipping sideways like an old man's. Her twig legs, translucent as a jellyfish, poured behind. Finally, she gave Ruben the thumbs up and clasped her hands around the wolf's tail. Ruben made an O with his thumb and forefinger, winked inside his goggles, and gathered his attention back into his chest.

Truth was, Ruben had no idea whether this would work. They specualted that if they could get Carla across this Rubicon, Kundalini would pull her back into the flow of time—where she needed to be for the children's movement to acquire the momentum it needed.

The goggled girl clutched the wolf's tail and batted her flippers; together they'd become one of those grotesque sea creatures that only exist deep where the light never reaches. Ruben paddled after them, thinking, *Archetypal monsters live in such depths—things with fangs and pinchers—the stuff of bad dreams and bad films.* But this, before Ruben's fogged-up goggles, wasn't a bad dream, although together they had dreamt it up.

The *Opus Mercuriam* that Anastasia had dug out of Karl's antediluvian boxes said something about becoming-water as a means of bridging the different planes of existence. *Of course, it makes sense*, Ruben thought. *Our body, brittle anchor into the world of matter, is after all 70% water.* Abanal, author of the *Opus*, claimed that dreams themselves are but condensed vapors of God's out-breath. In fact, Abanal dedicated the better part of his *Opus* to a close examination of the mechanisms by which the pure exhalations from the Divine devolve into the minutiae of human imaginings. One thesis built its proof on an analogy between clouds and dreams.

Abanal surmised that just as the clouds' infinitely variegated forms come from the pressure of heavy pockets of void—the exhalations of sinners—against God's breath, nightly human dreams result from the pressure differential between God's pure out-breath and the sinner's aspirations—what Dr. Freud would several centuries later call 'drives.' Sadly, Abanal wasn't able to pursue adequate empirical verification of his insight, as he disappeared under mysterious conditions at the tender age of twenty-seven while performing his Vesperal ablutions in the lake near Padua, Italy. This did not stop the Inquisition from putting him on trial *in absentia*, condemning to the rack an unfortunate bale of straw dressed up in the only shirt Abanal was known to own, which one of the monastery's neighbors' dachshunds found tied to a reed.

Interestingly, the charges of magic and heresy that the Spanish Inquisition raised against Abanal in the year fourteen-seventy-eight were *in fine* not much different from those that have been consistently leveled against Carl Jung since the nineteen-forties. In fact, Karl (Anastasia's late husband Karl) had noted in the margins of the *Opus* that Abanal's speculations about the nature and function of dreams were more in tune with Jung's than they were with Freud's. While both scholars agreed that dreams provide a window on the unconscious (that is, other planes of consciousness, including, why not, God consciousness), Freud posited that dreams and fantasies always function like repressed wishes. Dreams, then, would necessarily show themselves as a displacement of the real, since said wishes are usually perceived by the conscious ego as morally reprehensible (sinful) in one way or another. In short, for Freud the inner mechanism of dreams is always one of revealing while aiming to hide.

"So you're telling me the old Prussian fool thought dreams were hypocrites and traitors," Anastasia said when they were studying the old parchment on sun-warmed rocks.

"Something like that. But Jung sees it differently." Ruben held his fingertip at the beginning of a new paragraph. He squinted to decode Karl's scribbled notes. "Jung thinks that dreams are so creative, not because they're trying to hide anything, but because they're trying to *do* something. Something really important."

"Like, what?" Carla's eyes looked twice as big behind the goggles she insisted on keeping on at all times lately.

"Yeah, like what?" Anastasia echoed.

"Like trying on solutions to a problem you are facing in your waking life. Like guiding the waking self toward wholeness."

"You mean healing," Carla puffed, releasing the breath hold she'd been practicing.

"Ah, I knew it!" Anastasia triumphed. "Considering I'm a bit of the stuff dreams are made of myself, I don't mind being called a sinner and all that. But there's no way I'm some goddamn traitor!"

Ruben didn't quite buy all this esoteric fluff, but objectively, their situation had already eclipsed most of the Newtonian certainties he'd been served back in middle-school. Like his grandmother's Orishas, Anastasia may not have existed, strictly speaking, on the actual plane. But he knew from first-hand observation (the hungry curl in her lip when she saw him, the pockets of heat that formed between their bodies when they touched) that she was real. Besides, hadn't knowing her inspired them all to bring indisputable changes to the children's world? The Dreamscape was an efficient cause. That fact alone granted Anastasia incontestable existence. And Anastasia's testing of Abanal's becoming-water hypothesis by means of protracted and repeated fluid exchange with Ruben over the long, slow course of a starlit night had left no doubt that the bridging of planes, climactic and blissful, was more than speculation.

But Carla? Attila seemed to have no trouble breathing under water. He swam conscientiously, his chops curled away from his fangs by the pull of the water. Those weeks of intensive Pranayama, holding their breath and pumping their bellies in the swimming hole, were bearing fruit. Anastasia called it faith. Ruben called it *cojones*. Bottom line, it was a fucking miracle. That Carla managed to remain so calm was perhaps the greater miracle, although Ruben had counted on her connection to the wolf's tail as to an umbilical cord to keep her tuned in. Their plan relied entirely on the girl's unfailing trust in the wolf.

Presently, the wolf-girl *criatura* was approaching a strange river-bank where fat algae blossomed like hibiscus and a golden cloud of bugs haloed a crumbling shack. *Could it be that crossing over was that easy?* Ruben wondered. Shamanic wisdom was clear on one thing—and here, all sources agreed, from the steppes of Siberia to the craters of Haiti. Once you cross the river, real initiation can begin. Few survive. All bear the scars, in life or death. Some go mad. Some stay mad. On the Hopi Indians' vision quest, initiation shoves you in the face of your worst fears and fantasies, all the projections of that from which you've been running away all your life. For many, these fears take the monstrous shape of demons, slimy, tall, ruthless, indifferent, and sometimes as cruel, even, as we each are to ourselves. For others, they remain formless and all the more terrifying. In Karl's crumbling parchment volumes, Ruben had read several accounts comparing the experience to having one's skin slowly peeled off of one's entire body while being buried alive, with the dirt clinging to raw flesh like glass shards to a wound.

At the Occupy headquarters, there was no way of knowing what was going on inside. Ever since Pedro and Alia's escape, there had been no real news from The Center other than CNN's bird's-eye view of The Movement's meagre encampment, and the exalted blog of a middle-aged Trotskyist who had joined their ranks after quitting his job at Goldman-Sachs.

Alia was overwhelmed with her tasks, but she successfully orchestrated peaceful dialogue between the Hula-Hoopers and the Survivalists. She testified before Oprah, the United Brooklyn Zionists, and the U.N. Commission on the Rights of the Child. There was the protracted wait on the proper authorities to take action. The Vatican reprimanded Santa Clara for its daringness, then reprimanded the United Nations for its complacency. The U.N. swore that their hands were tied as long as no armed conflict or sexual slavery could be proven. Alia had to fend off charges of Muslim Invasion of Public Discourse, in response to which it was decided she could no longer appear on camera without Ana Maria by her side, or at least one of the sisters duly sheathed in a holy Christian tunic.

Alia was well-practiced at recalling, in a systematic and orderly way for the benefit of leery interviewers: the banality of evil coated in plush bathrobes; the humiliation of the harvesting machines invading her flesh against the background of elevating lectures on Mindful Citizenship and Sustainability; the impotent witnessing of her friends' waning vitality; the sense of isolation and shame that comes with chronic exhaustion.

"But what is it like inside, *now*?" Pedro wanted to know.

It angered her that he'd interrupted her meal. She wished him away and bit into her bologna sandwich. Pedro ignored her intimidation tactic. "What is Lou feeling when she has to pick soap scum from her scalp because no one is there to help her rinse off the shampoo? What is Hakim thinking when he wakes up to empty beds next to his?"

Alia tossed the remains of her sandwich onto the paper plate and picked up the pickle that Sister Bernadette had thoughtfully set there. She gazed at it while Pedro's remarks burrowed past her executive sheath and she found herself thinking, *The helicopters' roars; the distant cries for Justice; finding out that for some people, somewhere, what is being done to you is unacceptable; daring again to imagine something else, but having not the strength, the means, the resolve, the unity, the leadership, the conviction—whatever it is that it takes—to fight for it. Isn't all of this, in some vile way, more oppressive than the dull ache of normalized terror? The ancestral drive to avoid this torment is what keeps so many in the bondage of denial. It's what kept my own mother tethered to my father, even as she could smell the other women's Shalimar on his collar. Even after he'd forsaken us in the crater of a revolution.*

"Maybe the kids are fomenting their own rebellion." Alia tossed the pickle back onto the soggy plate. A mental image of the children pulsing with hope and hatred, their lips bulging with growing fangs, delineated itself.

"Maybe Prune is coming back?" Pedro could see Alia needed a reprieve, and he consented to play along. "Maybe Ruben has cast a voodoo spell on the whole thing?" After all, Hetherington had made no public appearance, leaving Anthony and the General to stand side-by-side like penguins as they took turns making cautious but confident statements about scientific progress, economic necessity, and Jesus' guarantee that Chinergy would save them, us, the planet, from the nearing apocalypse.

"Maybe the kids have shredded Dawn to pieces with their teeth?" Alia retorted. She was enjoying this. But more somberly, she craned her neck to see what Pedro was hiding behind his back. Suddenly, urgently, Alia did want to know. "What else do you know?"

Pedro hesitated. "Nothing's for sure. The Belgian journalist said he found a well, and underground trails."

"And?" Alia was upon him and he produced what he'd been holding.

"He found this next to a corpse." It was Sam, Little Lou's pink flamingo. Or rather, it was the bean-shaped hard plastic that was left of Sam after Anthony snapped its neck in half. "He mentioned a grave, Alia. A mass grave. Girls. With child."

They stared at each other. The wind from an ABC News helicopter lifted Alia's heavy, untrimmed hair.

"We have to go in," she shouted over the noise.

Pedro nodded.

"Find Ana Maria," she said.

The girl-wolf combo was gaining momentum. They looked hazy, like myopia, and the water was getting murkier, with all sorts of micro-algae floating about. A colossal koi startled Ruben when it gaped its gargantuan mouth in his face. After the fish drifted away, Ruben could only distinguish a silhouette— *Attila's tail?* Ruben kicked his flippers harder, but he couldn't seem to gain speed. The view was closing in. He called out, wanting to ask them to slow down, but he only managed to swallow swampy water. *Something's wrong*, he thought. *The river cannot be that wide.* He looked at his oxygen tank. They'd factored in spacelessness and its attendant time differential as best they could. He quickly calculated that he most likely had about fifteen minutes left. More if he slowed down his heart-beat. That meant *not* panicking. *The mind follows the breath and the body follows the mind.* To reel back in the frantic tentacles of his thoughts, Ruben settled his mind on his breath. *In, out, deep, slow.* He kicked harder. *Focus, focus, focus.* He mustered a mental image of Carla and willed his mind to contact her. He saw himself inviting her to a game of chess. She responded by offering an arm-wrestling contest. He saw himself accepting the challenge and holding her small, cold hand in his. They had to place books under her elbow to prop it up. Ruben looked deep into the girl's eyes. "Wait for me. We don't know the way." Sweat dripped from her forehead as she shook her head no, leaning all of her ten-year old muscles into his grown man biceps.

"Me and Attila won't wait for you. Anastasia needs you more." The top of his hand thudded onto the table.

Anastasia cracked open one eye and intoned the familiar blessing, "May the long-time sun shine upon you…" It had been at least twenty-two minutes since she'd actually touched Ruben, and his absence hurt already. "All love surround you…" Beams of light were shooting out of his seated body every which way, like the headpiece of a Mardi Gras Indian. His eyelids rested, still, over trembling eyeballs—the Rapid Eye Movement proof that he was enthralled in a trance of his own. Anastasia delighted in her power to induce this in him, but contained a burst of anger at his being gone too far away now. *If* Ruben did make it back to The Center; *if* Carla survived; *if* the children's rebellion did triumph—*then* what need would Ruben have to come back to her? And if the if's didn't turn out? What then?

Anastasia made herself continue the recitation. "And the pure light within you…"—What kind of teacher was she, to wish her pupil hers so totally? To bend sacred technologies for her own juvenile lust? In her mind's eye, she saw him struggle to catch up with Carla and Attila. She felt him choke on swampy water, lose his breath, try and fail to control his fear. "Guide your way on." The words balled up like a sock inside her throat. Their vibrations rose anyway, and a second vision replaced the first. Ruben, walking down a tunnel of gold, his back to her, the coils of hair at the base of his neck almost indiscernible now. *Ruben is sitting right here,* Anastasia tried to calm herself, eyes wide open now. She dropped the tenuous thread of her attention down into her solar plexus. Her nostrils bellowed like fish gills. Ruben's bare chest glinted in the canopy-filtered flutter. The purple of his lips drew a moon crescent across his face—the smile of the ravished. Anastasia envied this smile, wanted it hers badly enough to crave biting into it. Perhaps her palms joined in front of her heart had been more separation than she wanted. Perhaps this posturing of her Goddessness was the wall demanding to be hammered down, ground into crumbs. Or maybe this prayer *mudra* was precisely the degree of separation she needed? Maybe this reminder of her divinity was the cornerstone upon which to erect, out of the shattered crumbs of herself, a shelter for their sweaty, fleshy love? "... *Saaaaaaaaaaaat Naaam,*" she concluded. Truth is my name.

Draped in the halo of his truth, Ruben's body fluttered his eyes open. In the batting of his eyelids flashed every face he had ever had, and in that kaleidoscopic instant, Anastasia *learned* him. She learned the revolutionary martyr as she learned the blond boy who sighed at his mother's breast. She learned the scab-kneed boy who stood iron stiff while the teacher's ruler came wheezing down on his fingertips. She learned the white-haired man who would lead thousands to freedom.

Anastasia's wrists poured down to settle on her knees, palms up, index and thumb touching, and her invisible shield shattered to pieces in her lap as she conceded, "Go if you must, my love."

Finding his breath again, Ruben realized that he believed. He believed that with the wolf by her side, Carla was indeed invincible, for Attila was loyalty, and the power that forgiveness holds over past and present. He was wild, his instincts exquisite, but he knew how to play tame. He had chosen Carla, and she had put her unrestricted faith in him.

Ruben checked the oxygen tank. *Eight minutes or less.* His legs were beginning to feel heavy. The flippers were too broad, the pressure on his ankles painful. *I could go back*, he thought. The Dreamscape was only a few breaths away. *And then what?* It occurred to him that he hadn't thought about the future—Nothing beyond freeing the children, annihilating The Center. *Is Anastasia right? Am I a dreadfully normal man, ready to sacrifice anything in order to cast myself as a hero? Just another Odysseus, who wouldn't think twice before breaking a woman's heart in the name of Greater Pursuits?* He'd thought Anastasia had just said that because she was afraid he would leave her—and again, what if she was right? What if he were more afraid of intimacy than death?

They had no real way of knowing what would happen to the Dreamscape once Carla left and no further heroic feat demanded that Ruben cross over. *If the portal does shut down, on which side do I want to end up?*

The oxygen tank beeped. The levels were getting dangerously low.

Like a fly on the wall, Ruben saw himself walking down a blindingly bright tunnel. He tried to avert his eyes, but couldn't seem to close them or turn away. Yet he could sense the stabs of Anastasia's silent crying behind him. The loneliness grabbed him by the throat—Anastasia's absolute loneliness, but also his own— that of the boy he had been, still was. That boy who had noticed one morning that his mother's lipstick was gone from her shelf along with her tattered suitcase.

Veering back in the direction he came from, Ruben took off his flippers and began to kick. The beep of the oxygen tank was driving him mad, so he tore the mask off of his face, unlatched the harness, and glided away from the sinking tank. The relief was immediate. He felt his lungs fill up, as if committing to this choice was enough to make him able to breathe underwater. The water was clearing up and Ruben was glad to see the rocky bottom with the tiny algae dancing in the current. The surface still seemed far away, but ribbons of light were swaying up there, just out of reach. With a decisive pull, Ruben dove in a little deeper, parting the waters in front of him with strong arms. When both of his feet found firm grounding on the bottom, he squatted all the way down, then gave the most vigorous push. With his arms extended, his body perfectly aligned, his muscles hugging the bones tight, the water's resistance was annulled and Ruben sprung out like a great white bird into the Dreamscape's midday sun.

On the warm rocks, Anastasia sat up, all bare skin, silver locks, and fervor.

XI

They Wouldn't Say That in Hell

After the nurses from New Zealand left at dawn in a flurry of hugs and promises of Facebook friending, Prune lifted her backpack onto her bed and began to peal off of her mother's parcel the bits of scrap paper—pages torn off of notebooks, credit card receipts, heavy bits of watercolor paper where the ink had smeared. All bore Rosa's nervous scrawl—sometimes just a few enigmatic words ("Genocide never happened??")—other times, what looked like drafts for press releases. And then there were the diary entries, like this one.

Montreal, August 19

"I thought I would drown my sorrows, but I can't. Sorrows can swim." Tranquilino Ramirez is about sixty-years old but he looks antediluvian, his face like a Utah Canyon, and there is sweet liquor on his breath as he says this. Romero and our Argentinian compañeros have flown him here from Las Cruces so he could meet with his son Oscar tomorrow. The last time they saw each other was thirty years ago, when their entire village of Dos Erres was slaughtered in medieval conditions by the Guatemalan army. Tranquilino was out working the fields that day, and he came back to babies' corpses spilling out of the village well where the soldiers had hurled them. No one was left. Tranquilino lost his nine children, his wife, and everyone he bore any heart-tie to.

What he didn't know was that one small boy had survived. The Commando officer who abducted the highly prized, light-skinned, green-eyed, three-year-old boy from the scene of the massacre raised him as his own.

276

It has taken Romero and me seven years to find Oscar. He lives in Michigan now, and remembers little. But the Argentinian anthropologists who have analyzed the remains of the two-hundred women and children the commandos tossed down the Dos Erres well have been able to identify Oscar's brothers' and sisters' DNA. They have matched it with old Tranquilino's.

I swear, I won't ever say I hate fucking science again. This is what Romero needed to make her case and finally bring to trial Lt. Carias, who planned the Dos Erres massacre and is still the area commander today. I will not rest until every single one of these dogs has night terrors about bending over in the shower of their 40-year sentence. I want them to wake up drenched in sweat, only to realize that their reality is scarier than their dreams.

Before I left the aseptic Hilton room, Tranquilino lifted his rundown face and asked if he could say the names of his children. He didn't wait for my answer and recited the list. "Esther, Etelvina, Enma, Maribel, Luz Antonio, César, Odilia, Rosalba. Y Octavio, el màs joven." The youngest, now known as Oscar. "I believe it is my duty to mention them by name because they were my children," he said. "Out of the nine, one is still living."

Marc says I must stop running after the dead, open my eyes to the living. But how can I, when so many of the dead's names are still unknown, and the living go on repeating the history that this forgetting keeps hidden, even from them?

Prune got up to switch on the electric kettle. There was one lone tea-bag lying on the bottom of the basket and one stained tea-cup sitting next to it on the narrow shelf. When she poured the boiling water, flakes of kettle fur came with. Her head hurt from trying to connect all the dots, but some things were beginning to make sense. Did her mother's involvement with human-rights activists to bring to trial those responsible for the genocide of her people, the *Quiché* Indians, during Guatemala's civil war hold the key to her disappearance? Prune knew that Rosa often traveled to Mexico, Canada, New York. She knew that she was no longer welcome in Guatemala due to her past involvement with the

Leftists. Prune remembered the late-night Marxist gatherings in their cramped Paris apartment full of song, smoke, arguments, and reconciliation. But Prune hadn't known that Rosa was still dedicated to tracking down witnesses in trials against the current Guatemalan military and other Right-wing leaders.

Could this be what Marc was so afraid of?

The rusted sign above Marc's front door hung like a guillotine. Prune knocked, even though her knuckles didn't stand a chance against the black-hole density of the ancient wood. She tried the door knob—limp, toothless. She tried pushing the door in, but it didn't budge. The cat in the window stretched and smacked his lips, full of reproach.

"*Salut*, Heidegger." Prune was searching the sidewalk for a rock, a brick, something harder than her own knuckles to knock on her father's door. Heidegger waved his tail, or what was left of it—about two thirds. Splayed out on his side, head lifted at an impossible angle, he meowed.

"I know, Heidegger. I'm bothering you." Prune wasn't looking at him. She was busy searching the curb with the gray tip of her hi-tops. "The French keep their streets way too clean, Heidegger. Don't you think? Where's trash when you need it?"

Suddenly, Heidegger was on high alert, and out the corner of her eye Prune saw him as a Sphinx, glaring, like he wanted her answer to the riddle of existence. She ignored him. There was a plastic sac a few meters away. Prune toed it about and a bottle-cap clinked out, wobbled down the curb, then landed flat on its top.

"There we go!" Prune picked up the bottle-cap to tap a *clavé* rhythm on the door. It sounded teeny, but at least it didn't bruise her knuckle. "While we're waiting, tell me this, Heidegger. What do you think? Should I keep running after a man who isn't who I thought he was, doesn't seem to remember he raised me as his own daughter, and probably doesn't have a clue as to how to find my Mom—What?"

The cat was hissing like a snake and Prune barely registered a swift shadow before someone jammed a bag over her head and twisted her arm behind her, breathing into her ear a garlicky, "*Un mot et j'te coupe*" ("One word and I cut you") before shoving her onto a scooter. She winced when her shoulder was torqued and her breasts jammed between two stiff bodies. They made a couple of hard turns. She heard a gun shot but since she was still alive, it must have been the scooter backfiring. She started kicking her heels into shins, ankles, knees, whatever they could reach. The torque turned into a vise, and she felt something snap. The scooter stopped. There was the sound of a screechy gate. The scooter started again, the pull almost throwing her and her tormentor off, then it stopped again. She was snatched and shoved, heard the sound of a door slamming, and was kicked hard in the ass. The bag flew off of her head as she tumbled to the ground. She spun around to see two identical scrawny guys—her Gypsy cutter from the playground, and his clone.

"I was wondering when you were going to try to slice me up again," Prune told the space between them, not sure which one to address. "But I wasn't expecting that God was so perturbed as to make two of you." She rubbed her shoulder, glancing back and forth between them.

They chortled, with no trace of geniality. Her shoulder was killing her and the throbbing in her right heel didn't bode too well.

"Introverts, I take it?" The men glanced at each other, looking confused. The room was cramped with a primitive TV box set, a rusted bike, and an uncomputable mess of small electronics. Prune crawled toward a wall against which she could lean her sore body. "I guess I'm just going to take a little nap over here. You guys let me know when you remember why you kidnapped me and fractured half of my bones." She could hear voices on the other side of the door, children clamoring at each other over the ruckus of the television. She went to yell for help, but the twins saw it coming and one grabbed the bag on the floor, tossed it to the other, who stuffed it inside her mouth, nipping her scream in the bud. The motherfuckers were swift, you had to hand them that. Fighting them with her limited physical abilities was not the way to go. Without a word, one handed his scarf to the other, who tied it too tight around her mouth, covering her nostrils. Suffocating, she panicked, and jabbed her fingers into his eyes, missed, ended up with her index up his nose.

The last thing Prune remembered was the jolt of him punching her in the throat.

⚜

Against Dawn's neck, Gaia's breath was a condensed version of everything the chairwoman abhorred: warm, slobbery, unfathomably sweet. Yet Dawn took great care to lighten her step so as not to wake the baby. Her hand on Gaia's back seemed larger than it had ever felt as she took in the immediacy of its power to crush, or to sustain.

In the parking lot, Dawn's silver Hummer gleamed next to the battle-gray trucks and the General's black limo. She could picture her yacht, wading in the harbor in Monaco under the watchful gaze of the Albanian crew that would take them to the small Sardinian island she'd purchased at an exorbitant price from a retired Corsican judge. All she had to do was climb in her car; hand a couple thousand bucks to the guard on duty; simulate a health emergency for Gaia that would certainly buy her a pass through the cordon of concerned Occupiers; get to the Española heliport, then on to the Albuquerque airport, where her father's private jet and three highly qualified nannies were waiting.

During their latest Skype conversation, Sir Hetherington had snorted over her bringing back a girl rather than a boy. But the recent media hoopla got him concerned enough about his daughter's fate—and the possible repercussions on his reputation—for him

280

to send his favorite pilot, along with the required good-as-real passports for Dawn and her ward. All the same, Dawn couldn't hold back a smirk as she pictured her father's reaction when he'd find out that the baby—his soon to be granddaughter and only heir—was black.

With one hand, the Chairwoman rummaged for her car key inside her purse. Gaia was suckling softly on her neck now. It tickled and gave Dawn goose bumps. There, wedged between a pack of cigarettes and her phone, was the elusive electronic key card. Through the car window, she caught a glimpse on the passenger seat of the blond wig she planned to wear. She pressed the button and the satisfying beep signaled imminent shelter.

"Where do you think you're taking my daughter?" The voice raised the hairs on the back of Dawn's head. In the tinted window, Grenadine's reflection towered like a Titan over Dawn's five-foot-three.

The President turned around to face the Gardener. Nine or ten children were outlining a ring around them. Dawn noticed an expression she was sure she'd never seen on any of them, but before she could find a name for it, Grenadine had her throat in a grip. The jolt woke up Gaia, who launched a shrill, trembling scream into Dawn's ear. Instinctively, the President pulled the baby away, and Grenadine snatched her right up with her free hand. Gaia's screams redoubled, and the grip on Dawn's throat tightened. Grenadine nodded and a blond boy stepped in to take the baby. He cradled her in his arms and began to rock her, uncomfortably fast it seemed, but the baby fell silent and took a sudden interest in his curly bangs. Gaia and Hakim were both cooing as he stepped back onto the rim next to the other children.

Dawn's face turned very red. She couldn't think of anything to say. Contempt was distorting Grenadine's features, making her look uncannily like Dawn's Welsh mother. It occurred to Dawn that she should be scared, but the Xanax and gin were doing a great job of keeping her relatively cottoned away. She could feel

281

herself growing redder in the face, and wished she'd worn her foundation. Grenadine's hold loosened a bit as the ring of children tightened. Grenadine must have been saying things: her mouth was moving. Dawn knew she should try to focus... she heard "Lou"... she regretted having upgraded her old-fashioned car key to an electronic card... she heard "symbolic act"... or she could have jabbed Grenadine in the eye with it.

When Grenadine let go, Dawn bounced against the door of the Hummer. The sun-heated metal felt warm against her back, although it was almost completely dark now. She could make out only the pink contour of the blue mountain and the dancing shadows of the protesters' bonfire over on the other side of the Main Hall.

All of a sudden, rabid roars came out of a small girl who lurched at Dawn, punching her in the ribs with all her might. The President held up her hands to fight back, and her purse dropped to the ground. She heard the contents spill in the dust. That made her mad and she grabbed the girl's pigtail, yanked as hard as she could to sling her out of the way, but there were four or five of them on Dawn now, punching her gut, kicking her shins, just wouldn't stop fucking yelling. The little motherfuckers were much stronger than she'd have thought.

Dawn did put up a fight. She punched, and jabbed, and kicked, even though her Giuseppe Zanotti boots were quickly peeled off of her feet. Sharp little nails began to claw at her face and she yelled, "Not my face, for fuck's sake!" but that didn't stop them.

Her head was tucked against the Hummer's gigantic tire now, and she tried to crawl under the car for shelter, but several poky hands took hold of her ankles, immobilizing her. Someone started to use her belly like a trampoline. Dawn felt her ribs crack. The pain began to crawl in through the cracks. The breath! Dawn wished she could breathe, but each bounce knocked all the air out of her, again and again—and there were too many, too fast, too many, too fast, too many, too many, too many.

She curled up to protect her vital organs, and caught a glimpse of Grenadine's lanky silhouette against the night sky. The Gardener looked on with her arms crossed. Seeming brittle next to her, the blond boy was still cooing at the baby.

Inside the bay window of the President's office, General McMitt stood next to the dimmed floor-lamp, a pair of night-vision binoculars glued to his eyes. When it was over and the kids began to file away behind Grenadine, leaving Dawn looking like a pile of laundry fallen out of the car, McMitt took out his walkie-talkie and in his best battle-field voice—the one he'd swiped from a Steven Spielberg movie—he said, "Phase 3, operative." Then he picked up his knapsack, neatly folded his jacket to hang over it, and walked out.

When he got to the Hummer, he had to toe Dawn's body away so as not to drive over it. He could have sworn she moaned a little. He searched the ground for her purse, found it gutted in the dust, gathered the credit cards and the envelope that lied scattered next to it, tossed the whole affair on the passenger's seat, and drove off. The guard leaned out of his cabin with his hand already out for his envelope, since he was expecting Dawn at the wheel. He started a little when he saw McMitt, but quickly caught himself, stood up, jutted his chest out, chin in, and gave the General his best military salute as the gate rose smoothly. McMitt chuckled when he noticed two moonlit bottoms peeking out of the bushes. The Occupiers on watch were too busy making love to notice him.

Had the guard been curious about this change of circumstance, he might have walked over to the parking lot and found that once the dust had settled behind the Hummer, a boy was sneaking out from under the Army truck's tarpaulin. Careful but determined, Hakim slinked over to the crumpled pile of Dawn. He straddled her, raised one arm and, with barely audible groans, he began to punch with relentless, methodical jabs into the President's face, throat, chest.

283

Unlike the rest of Lou's pink flamingo, Sam's beak proved to be indestructible.

Hakim stopped when Sam's head, hot and sticky with blood, slipped out of his hand and tumbled to the ground. Then the boy stood up, wiped his face with his sleeve, and walked down the gravel path toward Ward Q, where the other children were sound asleep, unplugged.

In The Center's parking lot, all that was left of Dawn's life-breath was the ashtray smell of cold cigarettes, hovering like crows over her corpse.

Prune awoke to markedly sore bones and the big brown eyes of a snotty boy. When she fluttered her eyes open, he squeaked like a dog toy and screeched out of the room so fast, he left his stuffed walrus behind. Prune was still assessing the damage to her physical integrity when a great big Gypsy woman filled the doorframe. She cursed at the boy, who was crawling between her legs to come snatch his ratty walrus from the floor. Prune managed to stand up with the help of the wall, and the woman said something in a language Prune didn't recognize.

"*Hein?*"

"*Sors de chez moi avant que mes imbéciles de fils reviennent, pétasse!*" meaning, "Out of my house before my idiot sons get back, whore!"

Prune wanted to snap back, but this wasn't the kind of woman you talk back to. She tucked her head down and dashed through the small opening that materialized when the woman stepped aside.

The narrow hallway was lined with children of various sizes who glared imperviously. Prune heard someone spit at the ground behind her. Anger billowed up, but the front door was right there, and beyond that the street, people, normalcy. Prune had learned from her parents to despise conformity, but she felt a sudden craving for politeness, middle-class security. She all but lunged at the door-knob and banged her forehead against the locked, immovable thing. Fear, soreness and anger transmuted into rage. Swiveling around, she found herself face to face with the woman. Her body spread across the width of the hallway, and all the children, as if scraped from the walls like pealing paint, had huddled in a small alcove tucked between their mighty mother and Prune. One girl in a day-glo pink mini-skirt and halter-top had one hand on her little sisters' shoulder, and was teasingly dangling a key from the forefinger of the other.

"*T'es perdue*," the old woman said flatly. Prune struggled to sustain her gaze. She may not be so old after all, but her face was hollowed out from missing teeth.

"Give me your hand." She grabbed Prune's hand. Prune tried to pull away, but the woman gripped her with strong, rough fingers. As she dropped her chin to read Prune's palm, a bare lightbulb came on overhead—one of the kids must have been on cue with the light switch. With their mismatched outfits, the family looked much friendlier than in the semi-darkness. The matriarch was ugly, but there were cheery crow's feet at the corners of her eyes. Prune relaxed her hand a bit. The chapped thumb pressed inside Prune's palm like a spell, sending warm waves throughout her body. Prune was thawing out.

Deeply absorbed in Prune's hand, the woman frowned.

"What?" The kids were getting antsy, and two of them got down on all fours to scamper away.

"Give me money!" The woman snapped.

Prune hesitated.

"Come on, I'm no thief! I'll give it back."

Prune reached around for her backpack pocket, took out her wallet, found only very small change, rummaged about for more, and pulled one of her last two twenty-Euros bills half-way out.

The woman snatched one and, like magic, a laurel leaf appeared in Prune's palm.

"You have many children," said the Gypsy. She beamed like sunrise.

No, thought Prune—realizing that Yes, she sort of did.

"You are needing help, but you are too proud to ask. Ask." Prune stared at the hair sticking out of the women's mole. "More money!" She barked. Prune knee-jerkedly pulled away again, without success.

"I'll pray for you to Saint Sara. We're taking the bus to the crypt tomorrow. Give me more money." As if hypnotized, Prune pulled out her last twenty.

"You must convince the philosopher. Move him is not enough. Sentiments are no help."

"How?"

"Your answer is in the cave."

Great, thought Prune. *So I just go back to sleep and hope I dream of Grenadine?*

As if Prune had spoken her thoughts out loud, the woman said, "No. Dream is for incubate and heal. Now is time to act."

"I'm trying."

"Don't try. Act."

One of the smallest kids, whose diaper looked very heavy, pulled on his mother's skirt, pleading, "Momma! Momma! Momma!" His sister plonked him on the head with a beach bucket and the matriarch slapped him up the side of the head. Prune was incensed, but she did nothing.

"Convince the philosopher with the cave," concluded the woman with a definitive nod at the door. The girl with the key took the cue to squeeze by Prune and quietly unlock the front door.

Prune's money was nowhere to be seen, but she walked out into the blindingly bright street with her laurel leaf.

Anthony took to Dawn's whirlpool like a tick to its dog. The plush carpet, the home cinema with surround sound, and the mini-bar that he kept stocked with diet Dr. Pepper all provided estimable consolations for his thorny situation.

With the soldiers' assistance, he had managed to dispose of Dawn's remains, but the Swami's sensational self-immolation continued to steal prime screen time on every damn channel. *You have to hand it to John, the brother was a wizard communicator.* Mesmerized, Anthony watched blurry reruns of the spectacle— the tall blue flames eating at the saffron robe, the Shock and Awe on the soldiers' faces, the oohs and aahs of the crowd mixed in with the mad barking. Of course, commentators ran the gamut, from charging John with mortal sin and vile cowardice, to hailing him as America's very own Second Coming, martyr for children's rights, human rights, religious rights, Liberty! Some French anchorwoman made a patronizing connection between #OccupyTheCenter and Vietnam War protests, wanting to know when the uprising might lead to either another impeachment, a civil war—or, at the very least, a small bout of financial anarchy?

Anthony poured in another batch of Dead Sea salts, turned down the volume, added a little hot water, reached for the loofah, and began to scrub himself vigorously. He wondered whether John's act would have had as much impact if his name had been NGuyen, or Abdul.

With Dawn dead and the General gone—evaporated, actually—Anthony was officially in charge, but of what, it wasn't quite clear. Ch'i production had been suspended and, while a couple of troops were still assigned to securing The Center, Anthony knew that what was being protected were industrial secrets and expensive machinery, not his person—unless, of course, you counted him as part of the secrets, or the machinery.

He reached for the mini-bar and sighed at the sight of his neat rows of frosty sodas. He grabbed a can, applied it to his jugular. The contrast with the steamy bath made his veins surge agreeably. He popped the can open and cursed himself for having left the straws on the marble counter. The first sip hurt his teeth. It stirred a mild headache, but he went for seconds anyway.

No major media had responded to his repeated offers of tell-alls. He had managed to leak a few pictures of Dawn in her corset and chastity belt, but somehow his name never quite made the news. At random times, Grenadine haunted the grounds with her pride of enraged children in tow. She made no secret of how Dawn had found her fate, and made it clear that, were Anthony to stumble upon their lot while unaccompanied, she wouldn't answer for what might become of him. So he took to sneaking over to the kitchen in the middle of the night to gather nuts, saltines, eggs, and the last cases of Dr. Pepper. He stocked up on enough oatmeal to last a while. He'd never been too keen on gastronomy anyway, never understood why folks made such a racket over what was destined to be defecated.

He went to switch on the super jets, the ones that dig into the tightest bits of your sciatic nerve almost as expertly as a Thai teen. He clapped his hands twice, slowly, when the pretty nun and that Arab girl who was always pestering him for books appeared on the screen. The volume went up, and the commentator yelled something about desertion. The Occupiers were shown standing just on the other side of The Center's fence, holding up large mirrors to the armed guards. Two soldiers had gone awol already— *how come I wasn't even told?* thought Anthony. Apparently, some of the boys and girls of the U.S. Army weren't thrilled to see themselves brandishing automatic weapons and locked jaws at their own image. A larger polemic over the dehumanizing training of the Free World defenders was being stirred, and a new bill had been submitted to Congress.

"Of course it's dehumanizing!" Anthony blurted at the screen.

"How else are you going to shoot terrorists, the fuckers don't even look any different than any old civilian. Shit, they even have *little girls* strap bombs to themselves. What are you gonna do? Let little girls blow you up? For fuck's sake!" Anthony slapped the water, and foam splattered all the way over to the bay window. He watched it slide down along the window pane and pool on top of the sheepskin. "Fuck!" For good measure he slapped the water once more, and the half-full can of Dr. Pepper fell off the ledge into the whirlpool. At that, Anthony flew out of the tub. Dripping foamy water, he stomped toward the telephone and dialed the White House.

In front of a bakery that could have popped right out of nineteen-thirty-one, Prune realized she was starving. She dug into her wallet and hurray, there were enough coins for a *pain au chocolat*. She chose not the fattest one, which stood on tippy-top of a mouth-watering pile of its analogs, but a narrow, amber-colored one that looked the crispiest. The *boulangère* wrapped it in protective paper and counted the change. With a smile sad as a dead bird, she handed Prune back five Euro-cents, saying, "*Y'en a trop, là, ma p'tite dame!*"

Further down the street, Prune found a stone bench in which centuries of bottoms had made a soft dent. She sat down and ate. It made her cry a little.

Marc wasn't at the house, and neither was Heidegger, so she started toward the river. She'd heard that rivers carry warrior energy and she figured she could use a little infusion of that. Around the corner of rue des Douaniers, she ran into a mountain of bougainvillea. A slant of sun had burrowed its way between narrow buildings, and the blossoms were glowing with that phosphorescence that only uncut flowers and happy people put out. Behind the bougainvillea, there hung a bamboo-curtain and between the slats, Prune was sure she'd caught sight of McMitt on the TV. The nausea was immediate. She took a step forward to watch through the beads.

The General's medals, patches, and ribbons filled the lower-right half of the screen, and these seemed to be the main theme of tonight's news. The upper-left corner swayed with stars and stripes dancing in the ocean breeze, and beyond the tooth-white guardrail of a yacht, Prune spotted a tidy ultramarine horizon. Unmistakably Mediterranean. The close-captioning marching through the bottom of the screen explained that on his way to Belgrade for a celebration of the anniversary of Franz Ferdinand's assassination, McMitt was visiting on his yacht his old friend of international finance fame—Her Majesty's very own Sir Hetherington.

"Ça vous intéresse ces cochonneries, mademoiselle?" Shirtless and all smiles, the man waved Prune into his kitchen. "*Venez, venez, on va mettre le son.*"

Ali was from Marrakech but French at heart, he said, because he'd fallen in love with Margueritte at twelve and had courted her until he was seventeen, old enough to marry and follow her to Arles where she had been transferred to teach elementary school in nineteen-sixty-one. In between dispatches from Ali's life and the most amazing sweet-almond pastries, Prune gathered that the General was deploring the devious management that The Center, flagship of the most forward-thinking resource-management to date, had lately been subjected to. A blurry photograph of Anthony in a hoodie in front of the gym appeared on the screen. Prune held her forefinger before her mouth to shush Ali.

Over the roars of the helicopter, the anchorwoman shouted, "There is good reason to suspect that this man has murdered his boss, Chinergy CEO Dawn Hetherington (black and white photo of Dawn in her best Armani) in cold blood, and managed to usurp her authority in order to commit abuses on an as-yet unknown scale on the troubled orphans and debilitated children that The Center had made it its mission to rehabilitate" (Bird's eye views of the desert, the mountains, the compound, and the meagre camp scattered around it). The anchorwomen kept shouting, "Elite troops have been sent in to protect the children and assess the situation, McMitt reports, but we have received intelligence that Anthony Jones and his ex-girlfriend (old photo of a frowning Grenadine in cut-off shorts and silver handgun earrings) have brainwashed the children into believing that Army personnel present a threat. The two have been charged with kidnapping, and highly trained negotiators are working around-the-clock to insure that the remaining children come out unscathed" (photo-montage of sturdy white children playing in a wheat field; none of them Prune recognizes).

Prune thanked Ali profusely, kissed him good-bye on the cheek (three times, right, left, right), and headed down the rest of the way to the river.

Merde, she thought. *They're going to blame it on Grenadine.* Staring into the reflections of sunset in the Rhone's murky waters, Prune pictured some crazy shootout, Tarantino-style, with Carla running around bleary-eyed in her flimsy gown and Grenadine spouting blood from too many gunshots. *Talking to the press clearly won't help. I have to get the hell back there!* Prune could feel the magnetic pull of that return plane ticket in her backpack. *Marc can wait. All I need is fifty bucks to make the train back to the airport.*

Along the Rhone river, fluffy clouds were pinned to mauve skies and street lamps curled like ferns. The turrets of the ancient city-wall took wanderers back to the year one-thousand. A church that was once a cattle exchange bureau advertised a Baroque music recital tonight. Next door, the cinema/bookstore/restaurant/ Turkish bath presented À Bout de Souffle. Prune regretted she never could stand Godard's movies—suspected she could learn to love them given enough time or abandon. The lamb roast from the restaurant smelled like Sunday. Prune understood why Marc had chosen this place to quell his torment. Arles makes you want to have faith in humanity.

In front of the bookstore, clusters of people were milling about with glasses of *rosé* and their dresses, scarves, and hair blowing in the just-risen wind. From across the street, their babble reached Prune in waves.

One voice rose above the others. "Prune!" Goose bumps, the good kind. "Prune! *Par ici!*" Marc was waving at her over a parked Fiat 500. "*Viens ma chérie, que je te présente.*" He sounded as if they'd had breakfast together this morning, and every morning of the last seventeen years. A regular father and his real daughter.

Prune stepped down the irregular stone steps that separated the Riverwalk from the road, the restaurant patio, the book launching, the gathering of hipsters and thinkers. The man laughing next to Marc was tall, almost as tall as Marc, and handsome in a Bela Lugosi kind of way. She thought she recognized the famous American writer whose *The Invention of Solitude* she had devoured. She wove herself through to them. Marc clasped her arm and greeted her with a quick pucker on each cheek.

"Paul, I want you to meet my daughter, Prune. She worships you. Prune, this is Paul Auster." Paul Auster's smile was shy—new moon rather than sunshine.

Prune nodded. "*Papa*," she began. "Er, Marc."

Paul Auster said, "So glad to meet you. Your father can't stop talking about you and your sister, Marla, is it? Is she here with you?"

"Carla. No, she isn't," said Prune, staring at Marc. Auster got it—he was, after all, a great writer, better versed in human emotions than any depth psychologist.

"Ah, there's Michelle!" he cried as he deployed long legs toward Michelle Briens. "Delighted to meet you, Prune." He winked and was gone.

Marc had not taken his hand off of Prune's shoulder, and it perched there like a big cuckoo. His eyes darted left and right. He was either probing for an exit, or just wanting to take in everything about her—the last three years, the next five, ten, fifty.

"Prune." He said her name the French way, rolling fields of blooming fruit trees. Rosa, climbing up a rickety ladder to straddle a branch with Carla, who makes petals snow down on them. Prune and Marc standing, arm in arm, too afraid of heights to follow. A bird's nest falling and a tiny, ugly baby bird tumbling while another takes flight, and the parent bird rockets in, screeching. It is melodramatic because sometimes living is like that, big and screechy.

Prune set her cheek against her father's chest. The shirt was crumpled, but it smelled like soap and English thyme. His chest-bones were close to the skin, the effect corrugated. His chin was sharp and trembling on top of her head, but his arms around her shoulders were frank, unwavering. In one sigh, Prune dropped one hundred pounds of sobs she didn't even know she'd been carrying—just dropped them. Felt them dripping like golden honey through the sandy joints between the cobblestones.

"*Ma fille*," Marc whispered into her hair. Prune clutched tighter at the back of his jacket.

"Marc, I need your help," a rotund youth with a handlebar mustache cut in. Prune jerked her head up and glared at the intruder. He could have been thirty, or he could have been sixteen. His seersucker pants and navy-blue blazer looked sweetly out of place and time. "Am I interrupting?"

"Yes," Prune said amiably.

"*Oui*," echoed Marc.

As if he hadn't heard them at all, the young man grabbed Marc by the sleeve and pulled him toward an ebullient group. Marc laughed, shaking his head as he glanced back at Prune. "*Je reviens*," he mouthed.

For minutes, Prune stood there, thumbs tucked into the straps of her backpack, taking in the chatter, the waning light, the smell of sweet wine and cigarettes. Marc looked even thinner than the father she remembered. His hair was stringier, his stubble like ash, but he laughed a lot, seemed at ease. People knew him, women and men kissed his cheeks, glad to see him.

Suddenly, she felt furious. *Look at him, the peacock, the courtesan!* She remembered her mother cursing him after the University functions he dragged her to—"Here, meet my wife, Nobel Peace Prize nominee last year, those Swedes are so indecisive, neutrality is overrated, don't you think?"

The last train for Paris was leaving in twenty minutes and the train station was another fifteen-minute walk away. Tomorrow: Carla, Grenadine, Pedro, Revolution—or else breakfast with Dad, the first in three years. The weighing was making Prune dizzy. She pictured Rosa, dangling on the edge of hatred like a spider looking for his landing. Prune had seen it elsewhere—those marriages where infinite tenderness peaks into sparks of revulsion at random times.

She found a chair, plopped down in it. Paul Auster waved at her from behind a lady in red who flailed about as she spoke. He looked concerned, seemed to be searching the crowd. Prune's eyes fell on a clump of discolored cigarette butts at her feet.

"Daddy, I need your help," she whispered. Saying it felt OK, the ground didn't burst open to swallow her. She stood up. Maybe she didn't need to say it to him. Maybe saying it to flat cigarette butts was enough? *Train. I need to catch the train,* she thought.

"*Pizza, ça te dit?* They make the best one this side of Naples down the street. Let's go." Marc grabbed her by the hand, tugging her after him through the bramble of ancient alleyways.

"Attila, halitosis alert!" were the first words that came out of conscious Carla's mouth. The wolf stopped licking her face to take up panting. She pinched her nose and tumbled onto the hard ground. Attila hopped off of the stone slab after her and tried to lick her face again, but she fought him off with her fists. "I'm fine!"

Attila sat down while she took in their surroundings. Dark, dank, low-ceilinged cavern. The smell of metal and rain. The silence was quick to enfold the faint echo from her voice and the plop-plop of a water drip somewhere. It was hard to tell where what little light there was came from.

"So this is what real life is like. Welcome to the Realscape, Mister Wolf!" Carla tried to stand up. Her knees felt wobbly, her feet heavy. She grabbed onto Attila's fur to steady herself. It was rough, warm, humming with life, almost electric—the sensation ancient and singular. Touch. Carla felt buoyed by it and carefully, like an old person on a walker, they began their tread.

She assumed that finding the source of the luminescence would lead them out of the cave. She vaguely remembered an old Greek myth that her father liked to read to them at night. Socrates, was it? or Plato? Something about prisoners spending their lives watching distorted projections against their cave walls and growing up to believe that the shadows are the real things.

Her eyes were getting used to the dimness, and she was able to follow a tenuously brightening trail into a much vaster cave.

Attila noticed it first. Carla felt his neck grow long as his snout searched the air above him.

"What is it, bunny boy?" Carla sniffed too. She couldn't quite identify the smell, but it was no longer the clean iron and rain reminiscent of her parents' tiny Parisian wine cellar. This was more like something forgotten in a plastic bag for a long time. Something corrupt, foul. Attila was speeding up in spite of his effort to wait for her. He began to whine like bad brakes. She dug her fingers deeper into his fur, bracing herself for the ride.

They made a beeline across a chamber and ducked into a narrow tunnel to emerge into the tallest and brightest cave formation yet. In the dead center, a dusty pillar of light twinkled. It was elating. The sun falling through a hole in the ceiling turned the cave into a cathedral. Carla half-expected a choir to bust out some Hallelujahs.

Attila couldn't hold it anymore, and snout to the ground, he bird-dogged toward the light.

The carcasses were all smooth, like driftwood. Except the one. On it, the eyes had made way for vortices and the exposed skin on the face, neck, and chest had caved in. Carla couldn't take her eyes off of it. Lou's yellow blanket made a patch of lemon custard next to the deep purples, the white ooze, and what must have been the pink neck of Sam.

Carla searched for Attila's fur and, failing to find it, she faltered. How had she not seen this coming? She'd watched it *happen*, for God's sake! The cave, the tunnel, the smell. The light. How could she have not remembered? Some kind of evolutionary amnesia, like women who give birth forget the abhorrent pain of it all—or else, who would ever do it more than once?

The continuous, sterile beep on Dawn's direct line to the White House infuriated Anthony. The phone-receiver, obsoletely tethered by its coil, bounced right back at him when he slung it against the wall. Anthony cursed the phone, the President of the United-States, the Founding Fathers, his own mother, and marched over to the mini-bar. Above the blue curaçao, Dawn had set up the surveillance cameras monitors. She especially liked to stand in front of the Nursery video, watching grainy black-and-white images of Gaia. Gaia sleeping, Gaia piling up cubes, Gaia grabbing her toes. Anthony found it creepy.

Presently, screen number four was displaying something he didn't expect. There was a sure enough *wolf* trotting about "The Crypt"—as they'd dubbed the median cave, to evoke a semblance of dignity for the corpses of the girls who'd failed at the Multiply section of the Prospero program. The beast looked rather scraggly, but *aren't all wolves supposed to be scraggly? It must be old, maybe blind. Must have fallen into one of the wells that converge on the underground maze. Are there even supposed to be wolves in New Mexico?*

As if to answer Anthony's question, Attila looked up straight into the camera, locking eyes with him. The yellow eyes got bigger as the wolf continued to pace, poised, until it was practically on Anthony, its monstrous snout filling the monitor with dankness. Anthony felt a chill, realized he was still naked, went to wrap himself in a silk robe from the walk-in closet, and came back. Only the wolf's tail was on the screen now. Clutching it was a small human hand. Attila circled around, and Anthony saw that the hand belonged to a girl in her frumpy gown, nine or ten, skinny as a black man's hope.

What now? Thought Anthony. *Is that the French pest's comatose sister?* On the ground in front of the counter he found the walkie-talkie that McMitt had given him when they were still conspiring against Dawn.

"Allo? Allo?" Anthony cried in the doohicky. Only crackling answered.

There must be a code word, some damn military abracadabra that would make someone say, "Yes, I'm here, I'm listening, help is on its way, we're taking care of it." Anthony searched his mind, wishing he didn't hate war movies—he might have gathered useful information. Feebly, he tried, "Roger?" More crackling. Where the fuck was the U.S. Army when devoted citizens needed them?

Anthony tried pep-talking himself. *For fuck's sake, Jones, get yourself together! It's just a little girl, a little sickly girl.* He managed to talk himself into transcending his loathing for firearms and went to find the loaded Luger that Dawn liked to masturbate with. He'd have to trust her morbid perversion on this "loaded" business, because he had no clue how to check if it was indeed loaded, or how to load it in case it wasn't. He slunk to the door, peeped through the panoramic peephole, remembered he was butt-naked under his robe. He looked around for his boxers, found a decently clean pair crumpled by the hot tub, and also grabbed the leather belt from his pants. He slipped on his boots without socks, tied the belt around his waist, and stuck the Luger down in it, making sure to point it away from his testicles. He peered through the peephole once again, decided the way was clear, and undid all five of Dawn's deadbolts.

On the terrace of *La Régalade,* the blue, red, and green party lights coiled about the pergola. The voices of chattering customers bounced against the old ochre façades that framed the small square. Italian opera wafted out of a third floor window. It was like sitting right in the midst of the décor for *Rigoletto.* Across the table from Marc, Prune felt like a little girl, but also strangely dignified.

They did what families do when they finally get to see each other after a long absence: play up the wrinkle-free, leave out the awkward questions, avoid the kind of truths that might spoil the moment.

Marc smoked a lot, and reordered some wine. He barely touched his truffle and prosciutto pizza, boring grave eyes into Prune's as she tried to explain about Carla. He was horrified and mesmerized. He wanted to know everything about Anastasia, asked if Prune would know how to guide him to the Dreamscape. She said she could try. He didn't linger on where he'd been when his own mother, Alma, had signed the papers to have his girls board a plane to The Center. He said that the French authorities had never closed the Rosa Tum-Michaux file, although their enquiry hadn't yielded much. As the husband, he was still under investigation and he would have loved to come with her to New

Mexico, but he was not allowed to leave the E.U. He said he was sure Rosa was still alive. He could feel it in his bones. Playing with the crumbs on his plate, he asked Prune if she'd read everything she'd found inside the envelope. She said she had. He pretended to have to go to the bathroom and had the waiter plant a candle in the tiramisu. He'd remembered her eighteenth birthday, which she'd forgotten. They ate their tiramisu in silence. The opera lover on the third floor put on some Cuban piano. Ruben Gonzales, Rosa's favorite.

Then Prune asked Michaux-the-philosopher about Plato's cave. He said, "The main ally of oppression is the oppressed spirit. As long as the oppressed believe that their oppression is justified, be it on the basis of their natural inferiority—as African slaves were made to believe—or because of their so-called need for protection—as all women, children, and citizens of the Free World have been told—they will not find the means to free themselves."

Seamlessly, Marc's voice had shifted to his Professor voice, commanding the attention of the women at the table next to theirs. His hands became animated, marking his words like a conductor. "Therefore, before force or negotiation, solidarity or revolution, what liberation requires is a radical shift in perspective—a miracle, if you will. Usually that miracle won't happen without tremendous suffering. Why bother questioning the status quo unless it has become insufferable?" The women nodded. Marc noticed but pretended not to. "For Plato, Socrates represents that questioning. The man was, after all, put to death for 'corrupting the youth,' which is always the conservatives' code word for questioning their status quo." The women nodded energetically. "And Plato concludes that it is the philosopher's responsibility to facilitate the shift in perception that will grant his or her freedom. For this she must, number one (counting on his fingers), break the shackles that keep her tied down inside the cave. Number two, she must make the journey outside the cave in order to see the actual objects whose shadows have come to form her tribe's reality. This is bound to be a lonely and arduous journey."

"And then, she must look directly at the Sun," Prune interjected.

"The source of all light, hence of truth (light) and illusion (shadow) alike." Marc was tracing air parenthesis in front of him.

"But Plato wouldn't recognize that ambivalence, would he? The inter-being of light and dark, the fact that there cannot be one without the other and that in fact, they are made of each other?"

"Correct, mademoiselle Michaux. For Plato, the Sun stands for the very Idea of Truth: pure, unadulterated, uncompromissible essence in which all things and thoughts that are true participate more of less perfectly."

"Then what?"

"What, what?"

"What is the philosopher supposed to do with that truth?" There was an urgency in Prune's question that told Marc this wasn't just intellectual curiosity. He felt a surge of pride for his daughter, remembered that this was precisely what he and Rosa dreamt of passing down to their children, their students, their companions—anyone who would listen, really. Not just discernment and contemplation, but commitment. Not just "This is wrong" but, "What am I going to do about it?"

Tenderly, Marc said, "I think you remember that."

"Well, I know she's supposed to go back down in the cave. Teach everyone. Show them the light. Help free them too." Marc nodded his approval. The ladies at the next table were getting antsy. They asked the waiter for their check. Marc took the opportunity to order two cognacs.

Conspiratorial, he leaned across the table, lit another cigarette, and said, "I'd be pushing dear old Plato a bit further, but I'm sure he won't mind, and I'll say that what he really means is that for true liberation, it is not enough to destroy the actual forms, those concrete incarnations that oppression takes. You also have to give the oppressed, and all of us complacent accomplices, the means to overcome the illusion that keeps them (us) in the dark."

"Are you saying it's not enough to see to the destruction of The Center. We must rid ourselves of the illusion that—that what?"

"The illusion that we need this energy The Center claims to be providing."

"Don't we, though?"

"Look at you, Prune. In you, it's spilling out of every pore! It's not just your youth, or your education, or your curiosity, or even some damn genetic disposition. That Sun is burning inside of you, ferocious as August in Provence, simply because you have the audacity to embrace your humanity. You, Prune, are not dependent on fuel stolen from others because you are, unrepentantly, a child of the Gods. You love, you grieve, you fight, you forgive. *That* gives you direct access to infinite energy. Teach them that."

Prune slapped at an invisible mosquito on her calf. "But what if the philosopher gets killed? Socrates was killed."

Marc reached across the table and took Prune's hand in his. The ladies scraped their chairs against the cobblestones to get up. "Socrates was given a choice: death or exile. He chose death because to him, it meant dignity—or no, better: it meant integrity." Marc's voice broke imperceptibly at this. The ladies' heels rung like an ax down the darkened street.

"Dad, I have to go back. Carla—you've seen the news. And there's someone else, too."

"I know you do." Marc let go of her hand. "And I don't watch TV. In any case, you'll be a much better philosopher-king than I could ever be."

"You could come with me. Carla needs—"

"Children are like the years: you never see them again," Marc snapped, quoting Alma's favorite writer Céline, whom Rosa despised because of his known association with the anti-semites.

Anthony's cell phone buzzed ticklishly inside his robe's pocket but he couldn't answer it because he needed both his hands on the slim ladder leading down into the *Ojos de la Madre* maze. *Don't look down, don't look down, don't look down,* was all he could do not to blast out of the rat hole. *Also, remember the smirk on the guard's face, just back of the gaping mouth of his rifle, when you tried to walk out the gate.* And the tight cordon of outraged protesters eager to believe Anthony had single-handedly planned and profited from The Center's activities. *They have the whole campus fish-netted.*

Once both of Anthony's feet were firmly on the cave's ground, he glanced at his phone. The bars indicated no network, but the text message glowed blindingly in the semi-darkness. It was from a +33 number: France. Anthony was pretty sure the Gypsy boys were the only French people who had his number. The message read, "Momma lose the girl, we think her is returned in America."

Great, we've got the whole Michaux family reunion now! This hardened Anthony's resolve to find the little sister before anyone else did. She was pretty much the last thing standing between him and a round-the-clock, thousand megawatt-lit cell filled with horny men and hungry roaches (Anthony's vision of prison was a compound of images from Guantanamo, countless Law and Order reruns, and Kafka's *Metamorphosis*). He was already charged with kidnapping, so he might as well get some negotiating power out of it.

With one hand on the Luger at his waist and the other clutching his cell-phone—now only good as a flashlight—Anthony started his halting exploration. The CCTV cameras were set up only in the central nave cave upon which all others converged, and that was of course where Carla (*and a fucking wolf!*) had last showed up. Technically, all Anthony had to do was follow the tunnel, be quiet as a goldfish, and swallow his irrational fear of spiders, bats, pigeons, wolves, naked mole-rats, and free-range children.

In transit at the Detroit airport, Prune was nodding off over acrid dark-roast when Grenadine came onscreen. Despite the handcuffs, Gren kept her head high, her stride down the tunnel of armed U.S. soldiers undisturbed by the constant lightning of the photographers' flashes. Her hair had grown into a gorgeous Afro, which she wore like a halo and a clamor. "Flight 2096 for Albuquerque is now boarding at gate B7. Passengers for Albuquerque, please go to gate B7." Feeling intolerably docile, Prune gathered her notebook and pen, threw away the nasty coffee, kept the mushy muffin it came with, picked up her backpack, and encased herself in the orderly line in front of gate B7.

After his cell-phone ran out of battery, Anthony had to feel his way through a pitch-black shaft most likely crawling with spiders, bats, pigeons, wolves, naked mole-rats, free-range children, and god knows what else. The initial mania made way for intense depression, and was on its way to morphing into some sort of low-caliber resignation. Anthony wished he'd brought some Diet Dr. Pepper.

Other than the loud bangs of his heartbeat and the occasional mouse squeak he gave off when his hand landed on something too soft to be dead, the silence was a tomb. Anthony thought he did a fairly good job of not letting his mind wander too far in the direction of the consequences this adumbrated for his own vulnerable person.

Suddenly, a growl and a shuffle. The Earth stopped. He could have sworn he'd caught a flash of white, although the total absence of light seemed to make that impossible. There was an odd smell too. Unhygienic. Foul. Corrupt. Anthony pulled the Luger out of his belt and placed his finger on the trigger.

"Who's there?" he asked meekly. A scuffle.

"Wait, Attila!" The voice was squawky, but too echoey to judge how far away. Then there was a sure enough flash, an electric shock in Anthony's forearm. The gun made sparkles when it hit the ground, and the squalid smell was all over him, heavy, biting.

"Attila!" The voice was mangled by the inhuman growl, the humming of torn silk at Anthony's elbow—and that smell!

Anthony screamed. He screamed until all the air in his body had transmuted into terror, frustration, regret, grief, hatred, defeat, defeat, defeat, defeat.

When he was done, the pain in his arm was notable and he was on his back, belly exposed like a dying beetle, but the attack had relented. Too close to his face, Anthony could make out a ghostly silhouette he assumed to be the girl's. It gave off a faint buzz. There was panting as well, as if the wolf wanted his foul insides made tangible—as if to say, "You will rot, my man. In my own gut, or somewhere in the gut of this Earth. You. Will. Rot."

Carla ran sticky, roach-like fingers all over his face. Anthony could feel the pulse at the tip of her fingers, his own temples, nostrils, eyelids—threatened life throwing itself against the skin like it was a prison wall it wanted to break down.

"You made Lou do it," she said after a while—the while it took for her to identify him. Or to decide.

It was not a question, so he didn't answer. But Anthony wanted to say, "No, I didn't. The Center did, inept parents did. Engineers, and financiers, and the media, and the WTO did."

Regardless. The girl stood up and the beast was on top of Anthony, claws tearing at his groin, fangs clicking by his ears. Anthony saw his mother crossing herself and kissing her prayer beads over his faceless remains. He saw that no one else would be there to watch his mangled mummy pulleyed down into the ground. He saw his mother's lone handful of dirt drop pitifully over his coffin.

Terrorists, I tell you. Little girls strapping bombs to themselves.

Then there were flashlights, and human voices, and faces. A pretty woman in a disorganized headdress, like that nun who spearheaded the uprising. Anthony wondered if he was dead; considered the possibility not so unpleasant after all; rather enjoyed the opportunity to feel sorry for himself.

Ana Maria said, "We'll get you out of here," so he figured he wasn't dead—they wouldn't say that in hell.

Outside, it was way too bright. Splayed out on a stretcher under the aluminum sky, Anthony was dragged across a battleground of cameras, police and ambulance flashers, children's faces, soldiers' rifles and butts, more nuns. Then he saw her.

Grenadine, profiled like a mountain peak, arms stretched behind her back, chest out, cops on either side. She glanced down and he tried to smile, but he didn't know if he still had a face to smile with. The doors of the ambulance slapped shut on him and there was no more sky, only the tight woven chain-link covering the windows and a man in a white blouse who stabbed a needle inside of him, saying, "This will make you feel better."

Made in the USA
Middletown, DE
07 August 2017